MURDER LIVE AT FIVE

By the same author:

Nice Guys Finish Dead
The Big O

MURDER LIVE AT FIVE

David Debin

Carroll & Graf Publishers, Inc.
New York

CP
M
FIC
DEB
c.1

First Carroll & Graf edition April 1995

Carroll & Graf Publishers, Inc.
260 Fifth Avenue
New York, NY 10001

Library of Congress Cataloging-in-Publication Data

Text design by Terry McCabe

Manufactured in the United States of America

For Bernajean, my steady light.

"The media *is* the message, so have fun with it."
—Robert Shapiro, *My Dinner With O. J.*

MURDER LIVE AT FIVE

PROLOGUE

"Whatever joy there is in this world,
All comes from desiring others to be happy
And whatever suffering there is in this world
All comes from desiring myself to be happy."
—The Buddhist Sage, Shantideva

Y ou know about the guy from Beverly Hills who went looking for the meaning of life? Sought out rabbis, priests, scholars, gurus—nobody satisfied him. Finally finds a high Tibetan monk who tells him, "If you truly desire to learn the meaning of life you must leave all your worldly goods behind and go to the peak of Mount Phurbi Chyachu in Tibet. There you will meet the only living master who can give you the answer you seek." Guy's all excited, quits his job, sells everything, goes to Tibet, gets to the mountain ... takes him a month to climb it, his feet are bleeding, hair's in knots, he's got lice, dehydration, malnutrition, guy's a total wreck. Gets to the top, finds this little old barefoot guy in a diaper sitting on a rock. Falls down in front of him, cries, "Father, I have found you! Please, tell me, what is the meaning of life?" Old guy smiles, answers, "Life, my son, is like a pickle." That's all. Just, "Life is like a pickle." Guy's dumbfounded, can't believe his ears. Screams at the old guy, "That's it? 'Life is like a pickle?' I give up everything, sell my Lexus, travel halfway around the world, kill myself climbing this mountain, and you tell me, 'Life is like a pickle'?"

1

Old guy looks at him, blinks a couple of times and says, "Life is *not* like a pickle?"

I think of this story a lot lately, for a number of reasons, not the least of which is that I seem to be caught in a spiritual crisis of my own.

Everything was so clear back in the sixties, when I was young and blessed with the incurable conviction that everything I did had a higher purpose, was inspired by a Divine Will spreading its message of Peace and Love throughout the universe. Driving in beat-up cars and shitting in freezing bathrooms while fighting for the good of others, for something larger than ourselves, didn't make me doubt my mission, it made me certain of it.

Now, with the world writhing in tribal hatreds and Milkenesque economics, John Lennon's anthem, "All You Need Is Love," is laughable. All you need today is financial security and self-esteem. Today, people treat the pursuit of happiness like a blitzkrieg instead of a blessing, rushing into battle with the self-forgiving cry, "If I don't look out for Number One, no one will!"

And I find myself peering, horrified, into this spiritual quagmire, clutching at my sixties roots while the treacherous nineties sucks all but the most relentless idealists into the irresistible pit, the final descent—the cult of Personal Happiness At Any Cost.

DAY ONE
SUNDAY, MARCH 12

    "That's an astonishing story you just told, Marx. You have as good a chance of me buying it as you have being Grand Marshal of the Rose Bowl."

I'm sitting across the desk from Lieutenant Joseph Danno, Homicide Division, LAPD. Danno and I go back a long way, to the late sixties, when I was a high-profile yippie rabble-rouser and he was a hippie-bashing pig cop on narcotics detail. It was hate at first sight and the years have done little to mellow our passion.

"What part don't you buy?"

"To begin with, that whole routine about five hundred people—we're talking intelligent, successful people—swaying to Gregorian chants."

"They were mesmerized by Ozzie Baba."

"Mesmerized? You think he could mesmerize *me*?" He drags on a nonfiltered cigarette, inhales it all the way down to his toes and blows the smoke in my face. Then he angles the top of his hairless head, polished to looking-glass perfection, and bounces a beam of flourescent light into my already irritated, secondary-smoke-filled eyes. "You say you saw the man drop out of a tree?"

"I did say that."

3

"But you also say your vision is unreliable without glasses."

"I said my eyesight is 'in decline,' not 'unreliable.' "

"Then you say a girl named Carol, wearing a chauffeur's uniform, was standing beside you when you saw him."

"That's right. Carol, my limo driver. She pointed him out to me."

"But there is no Carol. No Carol and no limo."

"You can't find the limo? Call Bert Holman's office, they sent it."

"You bet I'll call Bert Holman's office. First thing in the morning."

"Are you going to book me or not?"

"Why didn't you do something to stop the killer?"

"I did. I screamed 'Don't shoot!' "

"That's all?"

"I was fifty feet away."

"Nobody heard you."

"Carol heard me."

"Carol, the disappearing chauffeur . . ."

I suddenly flash on Carol, on the wedding, on the chain of events that led to my arrest . . .

At the insistence of my boss, John Shrike, the world's leading cynic and publisher of *UP YOURS* magazine, I was writing a piercing profile of Jack Schwarzberg, the mystic from New York who first came to prominence as a channel for the spirit of an old Sioux Indian, Chief Ozuma Blackfoot.

Then, about five years ago, Schwarzberg (aka Ozuma Blackfoot) "evolved" into the highly visible spiritual teacher and guide known today as Ozzie Baba, the Beverly Hills Guru.

Airing the dirty diapers of a guru to the stars isn't my idea of being useful to society, but Shrike always reminds me he has to put out a magazine every week—and we know that some stories are more commercially pungent than others.

Ozzie Baba and the teachings of his Happiness Foundation are now known and revered by thousands of spiritual cognoscenti, particularly in the upper stratas of the Los Angeles and New York show business colonies.

As all Hollywood knew, Ozzie was scheduled to appear at a private Beverly Hills ceremony and reception for Bert Holman and Sheila Petersen: the game show king, his young bride, and five hundred of their most intimate friends. Ozzie was slated to perform the wedding rites, to plaster the opulent gathering with a jumbo hit off his spiritual bong, as it were.

Physically, Ozzie's a tiny fellow, a shade over five feet tall, of indeterminate age. Aside from intense, gleaming black eyes, he has no memorable features except for a saucer-size bald spot which gives way to a shoulder-length fall of fine flaxen hair.

What propelled this unprepossessing little man into the hearts of the LA elite?

The answer is, his no-nonsense approach to achieving spiritual salvation with the least amount of time and effort. No hours pissed away in non-income-producing meditation. No hand-me-down mantras cooked up by destitute sages from third-world countries. Ozzie Baba gives it to you straight out—*God wants you to be happy.* Moods, anxiety, depression, regret—forget 'em. God doesn't hold your soul responsible for the happiness of others. When you can't make yourself happy, how can you make someone else happy? If you have time on your hands and it makes *you* happy to pray for others, be Ozzie's guest, but your soul is responsible only for itself. Ozzie's followers all use the same affirmation, which they repeat silently through the course of their day: *"It Is Not My Job To Make You Happy."*

This new and inspiring take on the boring old question of man's relationship to God has given this particular Beverly Hills crowd a passel of fresh and exciting, spiritually evolved reasons to continue their work on earth: doing unto others *before* others do unto them—plus ten percent.

The fact that Bert Holman chose Ozzie Baba to perform his ceremony is enough to convince any doubter that, if they gave an Oscar for Best-Connected Guru In A High-Concept Role, Ozzie would win affirmations down. Bert Holman is one of the highest rollers in the entertainment industry. It's said he recently met Sheila Petersen at one of Ozzie Baba's exclusive Happiness Hour lectures and was so moved by his own happiness that he proposed to her on the spot.

Sheila, for her part, characterized by an aggressive press as an actress of little note and shorter memory, is an intimate friend and fervent supporter of Ozzie, the sage of self-satisfaction. Though she's a good thirty years younger than Bert, she must have thought it a sin to turn down all the happiness one could purchase with a man worth a billion dollars. As they say around here, money makes the heart grow fonder. And even if it doesn't buy happiness, it sure as hell buys off unhappiness.

Holman's wedding was one of the hottest tickets in town. Everyone who's anyone wanted to rub wallets with the legendary mogul who created a media giant with the stupendous profits from his megahit TV game show, *The Shame Game.*

He's currently a principal player in the biggest media takeover yet, the merger of Holman Entertainment with Southwest Telephone and their attempt to purchase Sovereign Communications, composed of a movie studio, soundstages, movie theaters, TV stations, cable networks, a book publisher and theme parks.

The only obstacle in Holman's way is his longtime rival, Mitchell P. Gluck, Chairman and CEO of Gluck International, a conglomerate of record labels, cable companies, TV syndicators, video game makers and advanced cable software companies.

Gluck and Holman started their careers together, in the William Morris mailroom, and they've been fierce competitors ever since. Mitch Gluck hungers for Sovereign as rapaciously as Bert Holman does, and the two behemoths are currently going at each other in the most vicious dick-measuring contest in public memory.

Originally, I wasn't invited to the wedding. I had made several requests to Ozzie Baba's attorney, Walter Armstrong, who also happens to be Bert Holman's attorney, for an interview with Ozzie for my piece in *UP YOURS.* The Happy One, knowing the revelatory nature of the magazine, had declined.

Probably because Shrike had been promo-ing my profile of Ozzie in the last two issues of *UP YOURS,* I received a phone call from an anonymous tipster urging me to look into an incident in Ozzie's past involving a young girl named Jeannie Locke. I called Ozzie's attorney again and said I wanted to ask his client about the girl in question.

That's when Bert Holman himself called back and invited me to the affair. He felt that his wedding would be a relaxed and casual setting in which I could break the ice with Ozzie. I'd see for myself the depth of Ozzie's inspiration and the uplifting effect he has, not only on his followers, but on "people of every stripe," as Holman put it.

Holman went on to tell me he had refused all media, even his own, admission to the wedding. But he was making an exception for me because of his devotion to Ozzie.

I agreed to meet Ozzie with an open mind.

A few days before the wedding, Bert Holman's assistant, a woman named Adele Smith, called from Holman Entertainment to ask if I would be one or two people. I told her I'd be one, that my current girlfriend had gone to Hawaii for a one-week vacation three months ago. Adele laughed sympathetically and said Bert was sending a limo for me, adding the cryptic message that I be *especially nice* to the chauffeur.

Which finally made sense when the limo showed up on wedding Sunday. The driver turned out to be an awesome young lady named Carol, who added a whole new dimension to the concept of *chauffeur*. She was wearing a classic chauffeur's cap, pristine white gloves and a blue uniform that fit like she'd painted it on. You wouldn't want to see a man wearing it that snug. Unless your version of Carol is Carl.

Some people have criticized me for thinking with my cock (and we all know only crude, shallow men do that), so I won't enrage anyone by describing the thoughts that went through my think tank as Carol smiled sweetly and introduced herself.

She asked if she could use my phone for a moment, the cellular in the limo was on the fritz. I tried not to stare as I escorted her into my house. The mere proximity was making my temples pound.

She said was calling in to report that she'd picked me up. When she was finished, she hung up and cheerfully apologized for starting off on the wrong foot. I assured her she could have started off on any foot and it wouldn't have mattered to me.

Once on our way, we established immediate eye contact in the rearview mirror. I never looked out the window and I don't remember her ever looking at the road. Who cared?

"Bert Holman sent instructions to be especially nice to you," I informed her.

"Do you like instructions?" she asked.

"Sometimes. Do you?"

"From the right person. At the right time."

"That's honest."

" 'Honesty is the only policy.' That's what my dad says."

"Are you a chauffeur full time?"

"I'm an actress full time."

"Don't tell me. This is research. You're playing a chauffeur in a movie."

"Close. I'm playing someone who plays a chauffeur in a movie."

"Not a bad guess. What happens to her?"

"She's supposed to kill the guy she's driving, but she falls in love with him instead."

"Why was she supposed to kill him?"

"She was blackmailed into it. Someone threatened to kill her brother if she didn't do what she was told. It's based on a true story."

"What makes her fall in love with him?"

"Something he does when they're making love. You'll have to see the movie to find out what it is."

"I won't miss it, believe me. I envy the actor who plays your lover."

"He sort of looks like you."

"He does?" I wondered if this was really happening. Or did I accidentally wander into one of her dreams? Either way, I was enjoying my part.

"What do you do?" she asked.

"I'm a writer."

"For movies?"

Did I detect a note of wishfulness? "No," I answered, hoping I hadn't let her down.

"Good," she said to my relief. "My ex-boyfriend was a screenwriter. A total maniac. What do you write?"

"I'm a journalist. With *UP YOURS* magazine. You know it?"

"I *love* that magazine. You're not the Albie Marx from *UP YOURS*?"

It was getting too good to be true. "That's me," I crowed humbly.

By the time we got to Beverly Hills, Carol and I were married, had two kids and lived in Colorado. I decided to share that with her on the way home.

The entrance to Bert Holman's estate was choked with a lineup of limousines, Rolls-Royces, Mercedes, Jaguars, Porsches, Ferraris . . . Red-coated parking valets ran frenetically back and forth to accommodate the powerful VIPs forced to wait powerlessly in line.

Hemming it all in was a chain of media vehicles, huge vans with multiple aerials and satellite dishes, supporting a circus of reporters and camera operators madly scrambling for quips and quotes from the Beautiful People.

While we waited, Carol reached back and took a cold bottle of champagne from the bar well, popped the cork and poured two glasses. We toasted to the future.

When we finally got up to the front gate, I was ready to forget the wedding and take a drive anywhere. She got out and opened the door, insisting I go in, if only to show my face, so that she could tell Holman's people she'd successfully delivered me. I gave in, but said I'd be back in about six minutes. She laughed and told me to take my time, we had the car all day.

I took a minibus up the quarter-mile driveway, and at the massive carved doors to Holman's thirty-five-thousand-square-foot Spanish castle I met up with Shrike, who had managed to wangle an invitation through his current flame, a rowdy redhead named Bonnie Basset.

Bonnie's a good-time girl, a drinker and carouser, and she has her own local access cable show where she chats endlessly with people nobody else will talk to, the rock bottom of the gene pool. I think she herself has a gene or two out of control, but she's my boss's girlfriend and you know how that goes. Like Bert's bride, Sheila Petersen, Bonnie is tight with Ozzie Baba, whom she considers the guiding light in the barely navigable waters of her life.

"Talk about conspicuous consumption," Shrike croaked as we ogled our way through the colossal portal and gallery. "You could open a mall in here."

Shrike isn't your typical publisher. He likes to think of himself as a two-fisted barroom hardnose. He's tall, lean, and black-eyed, with jet-black hair pulled tight in a pony tail and a black beard and mustache framing his corrugated kisser. He dresses all in black, the silver tips on his motorcycle boots, which he wears even to weddings, his only concession to light. Even his ancient cigarette lighter, which sets fire to fifty Kools a day, is made of black onyx.

"Will you cool it, John," Bonnie complained. "I promised Ozzie you'd behave."

"*Ozzie,*" Shrike grunted. "He's got himself one hell of a business. Wedging these bloated camels through the eye of a needle."

"And what do *you* do?" she challenged. "Go through people's garbage and dig up their dirt?"

"We tell the truth," he barked back. "We're society's watchdogs."

Bonnie threw me a look. "You'd better not write something bad about Ozzie."

"I'm writing this at the direction of my employer."

She looked at Shrike. "If you do something to hurt Ozzie, I'll never forgive you."

"Those are the chances a journalist takes," he replied, more bluster than conviction.

She narrowed her eyes and was about to take it to the next level when I broke in. "Have you met the groom?"

She gave him a final warning look, then turned back to me. "Not yet. But Sheila says he's really sweet. A regular down-to-earth guy."

"A man of the people," Shrike jeered. "Or so he describes himself in this week's *Fortune.*"

"Well, he is," she insisted. "Look at *The Shame Game.* That's a people show if ever there was one."

The Shame Game, in case by some infinitessimal chance you haven't seen it, is a show where real people compete for refrigerators, washing machines, luggage and compact cars by confessing, in the most lurid detail, the most secret and horrible things that ever happened to them. Picking up on the incredible success of the daytime talk shows, *The Shame Game* runs the gamut of human misery. Each contestant bares his soul, going all out to tell the most affecting story. The winner has to convince a huge interactive voting home audience that they are the most abused victim.

It's a pathetic display: people who were sexually abused by priests, parents, camp counselors . . . old folks fleeced of their life savings . . . women ripped off by garage mechanics, men hustled by diseased hookers . . . casualties of stabbings, muggings, pistol whippings . . . victims of pride, anger, lust, envy, gluttony, sloth, to name just a few. Graduates of the show have even started their own offshoot, the socially oriented *Victims International.* The viewing audience is addicted to the show and tens of millions of people vote each day for the winner (or *loser,* depending on how you look at it).

Until last year, *The Shame Game,* the crown jewel in Bert Holman's empire, was second only to *Wheel Of Fortune* as the most profitable game show of all time. It had been sold into multiple domestic syndication and the usual foreign markets, garnering profits upward of three hundred million.

Then Bert ripped through the Jade Curtain and sold it to China, the world's most rapidly expanding economy, locking up access to its half billion TVs and the dominant position in worldwide television syndication.

I was watching the wedding guests milling through the cavernous rooms of the grandiose Spanish palace and gawking at the astounding assortment of paintings on the walls. Had they been in the Prado itself, I doubt they'd have been more impressed.

Holman's art collection is an outlandish fusion of timeless genius and show-business kitsch. Next to a Picasso he'd hung a Leroy Neiman, beside a Renoir, a Sylvester Stallone. An early Tony Curtis vied with a Hans Holbein for dining room-glory and the gardens outside fairly bloomed with sculptures by Moore and Rodin and Mickey Rooney.

Shrike and Bonnie were busy pointing out celebrities to each other. "... Look, over there. It's Gregory Peck. Looks incredible for his age, how old is he, ninety? Is that Geena Davis? She looks like a duck. There's Dustin Hoffman. Where? Standing under that statue. God, he's short ..."

Outside, a billowy white tent the size of a small western town had been set up for eating, dancing, and commercial schmoozing. The house band was the Benedictine Monks of The Order of Angels, whose two-CD set of ancient Gregorian chants could be purchased in special designer cases at Georgio's Boutique on Rodeo Drive, where they were selling faster than low-fat croissants.

I was lifting my fourth glass of imported champagne from a waiter's tray when someone brushed against me.

"Hello, Albie." A throaty voice, sexy.

I turned to look. She was wearing a slouchy hat with the brim pulled low over dark shades. She wasn't giving anything away with her eyes.

"Do I know you?" I asked, hoping I wasn't boorishly forgetting some long-ago romp in the hay.

"I'm Bambi Friedman." She extended a fine-boned hand with gleaming navy-blue fingernails. Her near-perfect nose was a little too bobbed at the end, a sure sign she'd bought it from some plastic surgeon. The nose wasn't all she'd bought from him. I guessed she was a very well-sculpted forty-something.

I took her hand. "Great manicure" was all I could think to say.

"Don't worry, you're not embarrassing yourself. We never slept together."

"That's a relief. Or should I say, a regret."

"Don't bullshit a bullshitter," she said. "I want to talk."

"Okay."

"I have a story for you."

"I hope it's a long one."

"It's a big one." She was still holding my hand. "Are you interested?"

"I like your hat," I said.

She pulled her hand away. "Try to contain your excitement."

"What's the arena?" I asked.

"Media giant. A major player."

"More."

"How about tipping the scales on the Sovereign deal?"

It was getting more than interesting. "In whose favor?"

"Bert Holman's."

"Talk to me."

"Not here." She handed me a card. There was nothing but a phone number on it. "Tomorrow. Call me."

"Tell me more," I prompted. "Light my fire."

"One at a time or both together?" she asked, smiling coquettishly, then slid off into the crowd before I could answer. What a set of teeth. I estimated thirty grand in dental work.

The crowd was herding imperceptibly toward the great salon where Ozzie Baba was slated to join Bert and Sheila in blissful matrimony. I tried to see where Bambi Friedman went but the room was too packed. If she had something on Bert Holman it could be a major story.

The Sovereign takeover is the last and biggest merger to precede the establishment of the great Information Highway, that all-pervasive, interconnective cable and software linking of home to business and consumer to product which the highest hopes for twenty-first-century prosperity are currently pinned on.

The winner of the battle for the media powerhouse, Bert Holman or Mitchell P. Gluck, will wield more power than any President, king, or dictator. He'll set the parameters for the way the world works, shops, informs and entertains themselves.

That's a lot of responsibility for one man. And riches. Just as software magnate Bill Gates III became, in a stupefyingly short period of time, the richest man in America, so will Bert Holman or Mitchell P. Gluck. It all hinges on who wins the war for Sovereign Communications.

That makes any information possessed by Bambi Friedman extremely valuable. Like high political office, such a position of power and social responsibility asks that a man be, at the very least, not morally reprehensible. If Bambi's story were to expose a gaping moral hole in Mitchell P. Gluck's life, Bert Holman would be the de facto winner of the Sovereign sweepstakes.

As all this was going through my mind, I recognized my gastroenterologist, Dr. Al Rissman, trim and tanned as always, chatting with one of the five hundred guests I didn't know. The sight of the physician who only last week had me on the receiving end of a barium enema brought on the stabbing gas of anxiety in my stomach.

In the place where I work, a meager cubicle in the *UP YOURS* offices in the middle of Hollywood in the dying dream called Los Angeles, I sometimes stand and look out my window at the medical complex across the street. All these third world doctors in hospital blues, wearing turbans and prayer caps, are coming and going in five-year-old Subarus. If I were the invincible Albie Marx of old, I tell myself, I'd take my poor stomach right down to these bearded exotics, in rabid defiance of the American medical establishment.

But being the Albie I am now, steaming toward fifty, with more miles on my body than Route 66, the only doctors I trust are in Beverly Hills, where I pay outlandish fees to spend hours in waiting rooms to get examined by guys with perpetual tans and Porsches, who write me prescriptions for state-of-the-art antiflatulents at out-of-the-world prices. Some revolutionary I turned out to be.

I reached into my pocket, popped a couple of Zantac gas eaters and waved to Dr. Al Rissman who pretended not to see me. Too bad he's not that snobbish about cashing my checks.

A restless rustle in the salon told me it was getting to be time for the service. Immediately I had one of those high anxiety moments where you suddenly remember something incredibly important you forgot to do. I realized I was too sober to make it through the wedding. Acting out of instinct, I collared a passing waiter carrying a tray of used champagne glasses. I was draining the dregs from the last glass when I felt a hand on my shoulder.

"You never change, do you, Dad?" It was my son, Freedom, aka Jonathan Grant.

I looked at the glass in my hand—it had a red lipstick stain. "Magenta Madness," I said appraisingly. "What do you think? Should I stick with it?"

He made the kind of face reserved for hopeless parents. "You're the last person I thought I'd see here."

I didn't tell him I figured he'd be there, too. He's a rising young movie executive at Disney and wouldn't pass up a shot at schmoozing with the heavyweights.

"I'm on Ozzie Baba patrol," I explained. "Nothing social." I looked questioningly at the huge, round brunette taking up two spaces beside him. She was oblivious to me, scanning the crowd for familiar faces.

"This is Melinda Mason," he said to me. To her, he half muttered, "This is my father, Albie Marx." She glanced at me perfunctorily, smiled condescendingly, and went back to scanning.

"Pleased to meet you," I said to Her Obliviousness.

"Melinda's a VP at Disney Cable," he explained, as if that excused her horrendous manners.

"Way to go, Melinda."

"I hope you're not doing a hatchet job on Ozzie Baba," Freedom said. I still call him Freedom, even though he changed his name to Jonathan—not Jonathan Marx, mind you, but Jonathan *Grant*—as if he hadn't driven the point home enough. "Ozzie does a hell of a lot of good in this community," he informed me.

"If he's a saint I'll enshrine him. If not, his flock deserves to know. How are you? You look tired."

"I'm fine. I'm incredibly busy."

"Oh, well, that explains why you couldn't sneak in a minute to call me." God help me, I'm becoming my mother.

"I'm *sorry*, Dad, I do the best I can."

"Don't mind me. I'll be out of your way before you know it." He grimaced. I've spent the last year trying to nail him down to a lunch date, but every time I do, his secretary cancels at the last minute.

"Actually, there *is* something I wanted to talk to you about . . ." he began tenuously. "Do you remember Stevie McDonald?"

"Jim McDonald's son?"

"Uh huh."

"Sure I remember him. Little Stevie. God, I haven't seen Jim McDonald since . . . must be '71 or so. The big Kill Nixon rally—"

"There's Michael Whitehead!" Melinda interrupted, pointing. Patronizingly, for my benefit, she said, "He's the head of BMA—Business, Management, Artistry. Only the biggest agency in the world."

"Where is he?" Freedom asked, following her gaze.

"Leaning against the statue of Kenny Rogers."

"Wow. That thing must be eight feet high . . ."

"What about Stevie?" I asked.

"Stevie who?" Melinda mumbled, eyes still glued to Michael Whitehead, holding court under the marbleized stare of Kenny The Gambler.

"He came to my office last week," Freedom went on.

"He must be the same age as you, isn't he?"

"I guess so. He lived with me and Mom for a year. When his father went underground. You were probably too drugged out to remember."

"I remember. I remember very well. I was the last person to see Jim McDonald before he dropped out of sight. I went over to Jim's place and picked Stevie up and brought him to your mom's house. I remember perfectly. He cried all the way. How's he doing? Jim never came up for air, did he?"

"No. But Stevie's taken after him. He's a radical, too."

"There are no radicals anymore, except for the rappers. And their solutions are worse than the problems."

"Really? What kind of solution was Kill Nixon?"

"That was a metaphor."

"For what?"

"There's Ted Turner!" Melinda interrupted again.

"Where?" Freedom asked, straining to follow her gaze.

"Talking to Dustin Hoffman . . ."

"I didn't know he was so short . . ."

"So what about Stevie?" I demanded of Freedom.

"He gave me some spiel . . . about the power of the media . . . the information highway being Big Brother, controlling people's lives . . . making everybody believe the same lies. Crazy stuff about fighting 'homogenization of the culture' . . . to tell the truth, I don't remember all the rhetoric. He said, there was going to be a *blitz*, I remember that. 'The blitz is about to begin.' "

The word had a horribly familiar ring. It's what Jim McDonald and I used to say on our more fanatical days, when we told each other the only way to wake up the Establishment was to bomb it. Terrorists for freedom, we thought ourselves. Hippie fundamentalists.

"Why did Stevie come to *you*?" I asked. "You don't take after *your* father."

"He said Disney was high on the list . . . that he'd feel bad if I got hurt."

"He's going to bomb Disney?"

"There's Barry Diller!"

"Shut up!" I snapped. Melinda glared at me. "Stevie threatened to bomb Disney?" I asked again.

"Stevie *who*?" Melinda demanded.

"He didn't come out and say he was going to bomb Disney ..."

"But is that what he meant?"

"Stevie *WHO*?" she almost yelled.

"Stevie *McDonald*," Freedom answered.

"Don't know him," she said with a dismissive toss of her big pug nose.

"Did he leave a number? An address? Is there a way to reach him?" I asked. If Stevie McDonald was thinking of bombing Disney or anyone else, I wanted to stop him. At the least I owed it to his father, Jim, a stand-up guy and loyal friend, who marched with me in Selma, sat in with me at Berkeley, challenged the police with me in Chicago. Wherever Jim McDonald was now, whatever identity he's hiding behind, whatever life he's living, it's because of what we both believed.

"There's Ozzie Baba!" Melinda croaked.

We looked around. The beloved little guru had stepped into a heavenly keylight at the top of Bert Holman's grand stairway.

From the foot of the stairs to the distant arches of the great salon, like a wave of rapture rolls across the celestial sea, all heads began turning, eyes uplifted, to the beaming face of the radiant avatar. A hush fell over the crowd.

"I didn't know he was so short," Melinda unwittingly blurted out.

A battalion of censoring eyes swung menacingly in her direction. My heart raced with delight as she glowed a deep purple with embarrassment. A deep silence enveloped the room.

Ozzie Baba waited for the last pin to drop, then suddenly whirled in our direction, pointed straight at Melinda and exclaimed, in a commanding voice magnified by a floor-shaking system of theater-quality speakers, "IT IS NOT MY JOB TO MAKE YOU HAPPY!"

Five hundred throats roared as one with approval. Melinda's face went from purple to blue. Even I felt sorry for her. Then, as the thunder subsided, the Baba man struck again, hurling a lightningbolt of compassion into the hearts of the rapt assemblage. Eyes still fas-

tened on Melinda, he turned his palms to the sky, smiled beatifically
and intoned: "But I forgive you because it makes *me* happy."

Five hundred throats gulped as one. His mercy was boundless.
There wasn't a dry contact lens in the house. Even Powers Boothe,
who won an Emmy playing Jim Jones, couldn't hold back the tears.

Ozzie waited patiently until most of the handkerchiefs were put
away, then began conversationally, "The other night I went out to
dinner with my good friends Bert and Sheila and we were talking
about their life together and what each of them could do for themselves to ensure their individual happiness.

"Bert, whom I've come to love like a brother, generously opened
his heart and shared his deepest feelings. He told us that closing the
deal for Sovereign Communications and becoming the most powerful
man in the world would make him happier than he's ever been. It
took guts to admit that. Why? Was it about money? No. We all
know that money doesn't *always* buy happiness.

"It was about power.

"And that's what happiness is. Power. The happier you are the
more powerful you become. The more powerful you become, the
happier you are.

"I wish you could have seen Bert's face when he talked about
the deal and how much it means to him. He was all lit up like a
little boy. And you know what? His happiness was so vast and all
encompassing that, merely by existing in his radiance, Sheila and I
reached a state of bliss.

"My beloved teacher, Baba Bill, once told me, 'Happiness equals
happiness squared.' What did he mean? Laugh and the world laughs
with you. Cry and you cry alone. Is there anybody here who wants
to cry alone?"

Surprise. No takers.

"Well, Bert doesn't want to and neither does Sheila. That's why
we're all here today, isn't it? To see that these two beautiful people
never cry alone."

A swell of kinship with the bride and groom rolled through the
crowd.

There wasn't enough champagne in me to take any more of this,
so I looked around to see if some waiter with a tray was within

reaching distance. What I really wanted was a shot of Cuervo Gold and a Corona beer, but considering the spot I was in, I figured, what the hell, any bottle in a storm. Then I spotted something better.

Standing beside the massive French doors opening out to the gardens, signaling me to join her, was my new fiancée, Carol the acting chauffeur. Her chauffeur's cap was off; and with her long, rich hair spilling down in ringlets, she blended in seamlessly with the tony show folk, looking like just another movie star wearing an expensive, high-chic ensemble.

Up on the landing at the top of the stairway, the Benedictine Monks of The Order of Angels had joined Ozzie Baba and eased into their hit Gregorian chant, which sent the crowd on the floor into a blissful swaying motion.

I took the moment to begin swaying myself—in Carol's direction.

As Ozzie Baba and the Forty Monks continued to mesmerize the gathering, I reached the side of my thespian driver.

"I've been waiting more than six minutes for you," she said, with a put-on pout.

"But I came as soon as I saw you."

"Was it good?"

"I'll try to make it last longer next time," I whispered in her ear. Her hand found its way into mine. It was warm and supple, unlike the bony fingers of Bambi Friedman. I had no idea what we were leading up to, but I couldn't wait to get there.

We watched together as Bert Holman made his entrance, accompanied by his best man, whom I immediately recognized as the venerable show-business attorney and dirty lying bastard, Harold Armstrong. Holman walked slowly onto the landing, swaying ever so slightly to the chant, and positioned himself where his guests could clearly see him, between Ozzie and the monks.

I was surprised at how old he looked. Bonnie Basset had told me that Bert was in his late fifties. This guy looked more like late sixties. Maybe she'd made a mistake. But then again, Shrike hadn't corrected her and he'd just read Bert's profile in *Fortune*.

Ozzie Baba, who "loved Bert like a brother," spread his arms wide, brought his hands together, fingertips to chin, and bowed ever so slightly at the groom. Bert Holman, who probably couldn't love his own brother like a brother, returned the gesture. Harold Armstrong looked embarrassed to be there.

A gasp arose from the throng at the appearance of the bride, Sheila Petersen. In her mid-twenties and a classic beauty to begin with, she looked every bit the billion-dollar property she was about to become. The girl may not have been able to act her way out of a paper bag, but she could sure make you not give a shit.

As Ozzie Baba gazed fondly upon his two pet devotees and segued into his personal happiness pitch, Carol nudged me and pointed to a huge oak tree out in the gardens, next to the party tent.

"Look at that . . . in the tree," she directed.

From the lowest limb, a man dropped a long, narrow object to the ground, let himself down, picked up the object and moved quickly behind the tent, out of our line of sight.

Because of the precipitous decline of my eyesight in the past few years, I couldn't tell what the object was. I refuse to wear glasses. Here in the land of beautiful people, we spare no inconvenience putting off till tomorrow looking old today.

"What could he be up to?" I wondered out loud. "Beating the crowd to the punch bowl?"

She shrugged, searching the grounds with her eyes for another glimpse of the man. I sort of looked around for a security guy, one of the beefy walkie-talkie toters I'd noticed lurking around the edges. I thought maybe someone should check it out. But it was the old story, they're never there when you want them.

I tried to turn my attention back to the ceremony. Ozzie was holding hands with Bert and Sheila and babbling, ". . . and do you pledge to each other that, though the path you travel may twist and turn, through fields and forests, sunshine and clouds, good fortune and adversity, affliction and health, yea, even though calamity itself may break down your door, neither you, Bert, nor you, Sheila, will place the happiness of the other before that of your own, will not encumber your union by denying yourself what you cannot give to the other . . ."

Christ. Was he serious or what? There wasn't enough champagne in the world to make me listen to that.

Carol was preoccupied with the man from the tree. "Let's see what he's up to," she prompted, squeezing my hand with the excitement of adventure and leading me out through the huge French doors.

Out on the range, our curiosity had room to roam. All around, people in catering clothes scurried about, frantically preparing for the impending onslaught of the hungry crowd. Here and there were little huddles of servers, peering into the windows, intent on witnessing— *live*—the high-power nuptials that for the last month had been trumpeted with Trump-like fever on the tabloid front pages and voyeur TV shows.

Following Carol, I ambled toward the side of the tent where the man first disappeared. I didn't know what I expected to do if we found him, but Carol had stirred my journalist's juices. I was committed to the encounter.

We hadn't reached the tent when Carol breathed, "Albie!" with a burning urgency. She was pointing to our left.

Behind us and closer to the house stood a huge Henry Moore sculpture of a gumby-shaped woman reclining. Beside it, leaning forward but still in its protective shadow, was an unshaven, painfully thin, cadaverous man, hunched over a high-caliber rifle with a telescopic sight. He was aiming his weapon through the French doors and into the house.

At the moment I opened my mouth and yelled, a roar exploded from within, a tumultuous crescendo of cheers, whistles, and applause that smothered my cry of alarm.

And then he fired.

And the crowd fell silent.

Then there was screaming and panic and hysteria.

And I was running toward him, with no earthly idea why.

And he turned to face me, rifle in hand.

He could have killed me if he'd wanted to.

Instead, he held out the rifle with both hands and said, "I give up."

I took the weapon and I was instructing him to get down on the ground with his hands behind his back when the burly security guards swooped in full force from all sides. Not knowing if one or both of us was the bad guy, they slammed us both to the ground with equal fury.

My first thought was, shit, I'm holding the gun. And I'm the only guest at this wedding wearing jeans and boots. These motherfuckers might think I'm the shooter. Then I realized that, however ragged I looked, the other guy looked worse. And besides, Carol was standing right there, she would tell them what happened. I looked around quickly but I didn't see her.

Then, before I could plead my case, my head was forced into the ground, my arms were yanked roughly backward and my hands cuffed behind my back.

I looked up again. The barrel of a .45 automatic was vibrating inches from my face, with a wild-eyed security guard at the controls. All around us was chaos.

I later was told that the wedding guests never heard the rifle shot. They were raucously cheering the long-awaited moment when, having been legally pronounced man and wife, Bert Holman took his beautiful young bride in his arms and, kissing her tenderly on the lips, his head exploded in her face.

"There is no Carol . . ." Lieutenant Danno was saying.

There is no Carol. How do you explain that, Albie? It was all so perfect, too perfect. We hit it off so good you had us married. Schmuck. You think with your cock, you pay the price.

"There is a Carol. And she heard me yell."

"The yell nobody heard."

"I'm telling you I yelled. Nobody heard it because they were cheering the bride and groom. What are you busting *my* balls for? What, is the war on drugs over? You have nothing to do? I didn't shoot Holman. I'm the hero. I caught the guy."

"I have only your word for that."

"Come on. I didn't kill him. Stop wasting my time. Talk to the guy who did it."

"Your *accomplice?*"

"Get a life, Danno."

"He's not talking."

"*Make* him talk."

"You can only slap a guy so many times without abusing his rights."

"So, he's not talking. You have the rifle. You have his prints. Put them together. Don't make a fool of yourself."

"Your prints are on the rifle, too."

"Because I took it away from him. Maybe I should have let him shoot more moguls."

"Why is it, every time I run into you there's a corpse in the picture?" That remark goes back to 1970, when I was going with Janis Joplin and she OD'd on heroin. Danno and his narc pals tried to frame me as an accessory.

"I didn't tell you to go into this line of work," I snap. "You don't like corpses, get into Mail Fraud."

He squashes his cigarette in a government-issue ashtray, then looks down and flexes his meaty, hairless fists and mutters, "Good thing for you these don't have a mind of their own."

I have about thirty comebacks for that, but why antagonize him more than I already have? "What do you want from me, Danno? I told you everything."

"I could hold you on suspicion."

"Why would you want to?"

He serves me a big, nasty smile, full of stained, horsey teeth. "Because I don't like you."

I volley back with a wounded, coquettish look. "Not even a little bit?"

That's it. He jumps up, flings his chair backward and hovers menacingly over me, his wolflike gray eyes flowing down into mine. The silence throbs with his venom. I'm trying to remember the name of a bail bondsman when he finally growls, "Get the fuck out of here."

As I slowly get out of my chair, Son of Kojak leans over the desk and snarls, "If I have to make more than two calls to find you, you better get yourself one motherfucker of a criminal lawyer."

Downstairs I phone for a cab. I'm preoccupied with chewing myself out for pointlessly provoking Danno. The man almost sent me up once. I could be making license plates for two bucks an hour and going steady with who-knows-what right now. That experience cost me. Scared me so bad I dropped out. For years I lived anonymously, paying my rent and bar bills with the dwindling royalties from *Roger Wellington Rat*, my sixties best seller. Luckily, five or six years ago,

Shrike lured me out of retreat to write a column for *UP YOURS*. And now that I'm out, I want to stay out. So why would I fuck with the guy whose whole mission in life is to put me away?

Think back to the beginning of the day. Carol shows up with the limo . . . uses my phone . . . drives me to the wedding. She was there when I saw the guy jump out of the tree—or did she see him first? We went outside to see if we could find him—that was her idea, wasn't it? Then I saw the guy with the rifle. No, *she* saw him with the rifle and told me where to look.

Genius. They were working together. I was led through the course, step by step. Even when he held out the rifle and gave up, it was prearranged. What was I supposed to do? Refuse to take it? For all I knew he could have changed his mind and blown me away. Anybody would have taken it.

I was set up. But why me? I didn't know Bert Holman. The only reason I went was to meet Ozzie Baba . . .

Ozzie Baba. Can he be so afraid of what I might find out about the incident in his past involving the girl named Jeannie Locke that he had Holman killed just to frame me? That's one hell of a stretch.

Tracking down Carol is the first thing to do. Tomorrow morning I'll call Holman Entertainment and get the name of the limo company from Holman's assistant, Adele Smith. That's the first step.

By the time I leave the building, the sun's given way to one of those silky Los Angeles nights, where twinkling lights mask the city's dark core and you can't see the shit you're breathing.

Walking down the front steps, I'm suddenly caught off guard by an invading onslaught of lights, cameras and feverish faces, mouths working, tongues wagging, thrusting microphones in front of me and shouting questions so loud I can't hear them.

They have me just about surrounded when the cavalry comes to my rescue in the form of my cab, pulling up next to one of the news vans. The driver is looking around in confusion for his fare.

Lowering my head, I rush the wall of jabbering weasels, knocking over a particularly fat, unkempt reporter who tries his best to block my way. I narrowly make it into the cab before they close in.

"Santa Monica and Sweetzer!" I yell to the driver.

He guns the motor, nearly running over the fat reporter who idioti-cally tries to block our way.

"Shit! Missed!" I complain.

The driver grunts.

In a few seconds the screaming swarm is left in the dust and I'm on my way to the safety of my second home, The Rock, a bar in Hollywood that never emerged from the sixties. There I've pursued happiness, God, and an occasional female, inspired by the mystical spirits of Cuervo Gold and Corona.

The cabdriver is a Russian immigrant who listens to Mexican radio, drinks cappucino from a styrofoam cup and wears a Disney-land sweat shirt and Raiders baseball cap, with the bill turned back-ward. That's Los Angeles culture for you. Like the plague, it devours everyone, leaving no brain alive.

The cab speeds along, the two big fluffy dice hanging from the rearview mirror dangling in time to a Mexican polka. If only Carol were driving, this would all be worth it. Tomorrow, I tell myself, I'll find her tomorrow. Now it's time to sort out today.

I figure the shooter sneaked onto the grounds, probably with the caterers, and hid in the tree to avoid attracting suspicion. None of Bert Holman's friends or associates at the wedding could identify him, so if he did know Bert, it was a private acquaintance. The question is, why did he do it?

God knows, a potentate like Bert Holman, who ruled a veritable empire, who gave us shows like *The Shame Game, It's Not My Fault* and *Me First,* who touched so many lives in a spiritual quest to put his own happiness above all others, must have had enough enemies to start a religion based on his crucifixion. That gives the killer any one of a thousand reasons for nailing him.

On the other hand, if he's a hired gun, the question becomes, who stands to gain the most from Holman's death? Certainly, no one will be happier than his public enemy, Mitchell P. Gluck, who now seems assured of acquiring Sovereign Communications and pogoing straight to the top.

Then there's Sheila Peterson Holman. She got the gold ring, and just in time. Barring some medieval prenuptial agreement, she stands to add ten figures to her already impressive numbers.

Then, too, Sheila's under the spell of Ozzie Baba and his cult of happiness. I'm sure she'll be making a sizable donation to the Happiness Foundation now that Bert's off in heaven. That gives the balding guru even more of a motive to have rooted for Bert's departure, beyond putting a stop to me. At five feet tall he doesn't look dangerous, but Stalin was only five two and how many millions did he kill?

Then there was that woman at the wedding . . . what was her name, the plastic surgery queen? Bambi Friedman. Claimed to have something on Bert Holman. She could be a key.

It's all guess work, but since the killer isn't talking (if Danno is to be believed), the story is up for grabs. That's why every network, tabloid TV and local news show in town sent people to cover my exit from the Hollywood precinct. These people know what they're doing.

The fact is, this story's got it all—money, power, sex, violence, not to mention a cult for the rich and famous. I should write it myself, I'm the closest to it. Maybe *too* close. Shrike would love it. A guaranteed bandwagon.

Going west, the cab rattles down Santa Monica to Sweetzer and pulls to a stop in front of The Rock. I give the Russian a generous tip, a reward for not joining the Russian mafia.

He barely drives off when a white Chevy Blazer with blacked-out windows and a cellular phone antenna zooms out of nowhere and screeches up to the curb. The driver's door flies open and a determined young woman wearing jeans and an expensive leather jacket jumps out and marches up to me.

I'm immediately struck by the intense laser blue of her eyes. I've seen those eyes before. Where? She's almost my height in her lizardskin cowboy boots, and her hair is the kind of rich, dark chestnut that makes you want to see the rest of it . . .

"I'm Samantha Shelton," she declares in a tone that packs major reserves of self-esteem. Hey, if I looked like that, I'd love myself, too.

"You're Albie Marx, aren't you?" I nod. "You caught Bert Holman's killer today."

"It was an accident."

"Don't be modest."

Where have I seen her before? "Pardon the oldest line in the world, but where do I know you from?"

She laughs lightly, flashing a very slight, very appealing, Lauren Hutton space between her two front teeth. "Don't worry, people ask me that all the time. I'm the host of *Real Life*. That's probably where you've seen me."

Real Life. The tabloid TV show.

"Excuse me for not recognizing you. I avoid TV like typhus."

"We give people what they want and we tell the truth, which is more than I can say for the so-called straight press. But that's a subject we can discuss later if you like. Right now, I'd like to talk to you about what happened today. If you don't mind."

"When was the last time a man minded talking to you?" I ask.

"This morning when I fired an assistant," she answers easily. "He minded it plenty."

Feisty and beautiful—lethal. "Well, you can't fire me, so I'm safe. You feel like a drink? We'll need something to loosen my tongue."

"Then I'm buying," she declares. She looks up at the sign over the entrance to the bar. "The Rock . . ." she says thoughtfully. "Didn't Jimi Hendrix play here?"

"Way back. When they had live music. Before your time. You like Jimi Hendrix?"

"He's my morning CD. Gets me jump-started."

Well, at least we're off to a good jump-start, I think as we walk into the joint and we're greeted by the friendly smell of old smoke and stale whiskey.

Seeing Samantha, my friend Leon the bartender slips me an imperceptible nod of approval. It's Sunday night and the place is relatively quiet except for Jefferson Airplane's "White Rabbit" hopping out of the high fidelity speakers in the classic old jukebox.

Samantha prefers a table to the bar so we slide into a booth and Leon comes over to take our order. It's clear he recognizes her, but he's cool and doesn't say anything. He's been around a long time and seen his share of celebrities, major and minor. In The Rock, a celebrity is just another customer.

I don't have to tell him what I want. Samantha orders a Perrier with lime. Straight arrow.

Looking at her, I remind myself the reality is she's one of the leading faces on tabloid TV, she's used to getting what she wants whether you want to give it or not, and the only thing she wants is a story. Which she'll get one way or the other. This woman will not only lead you to water, she'll make you guzzle it like you jogged through Death Valley in a camel's hair coat.

"You don't drink?" I ask.

"Not during business hours." It's after eight o'clock. I guess they're all business hours with her. "What a great place," she says, taking in the funky decor with its genuine sixties concert posters. "I can't believe I've never been here."

"It's been my haven for more years than I'd like to admit," I admit. "My 'rock,' you might say."

"I was a *kid* in the sixties."

"We all were. Relatively speaking."

Leon brings our drinks and leans in to Sam. "I like you on *Real Life*."

There goes his famous celebrity cool. I guess she overwhelmed him.

"Thanks," she says, experienced at graciousness. She has the look of a one-time Miss America. Pretty, midwestern, healthy, determined—probably wells up inside when they play the "Star Spangled Banner."

Leon nods approvingly at me again, this time openly, and splits.

We clink glasses and tell each other, "Cheers."

"Let's talk about you," she begins, shifting fluently into her business mode. "What do you know about James T. Gardner?"

"Who is James T. Gardner?"

"Did you know Bert Holman?"

"Who's James T. Gardner?"

"Do you know Mitchell P. Gluck?"

"About as well as I know James T. Gardner."

"Then you *do* know James T. Gardner."

"Samantha . . ."

"Sam."

"Sam. I don't know nothin'. I grabbed the guy who shot Bert Holman. Period. End of story."

"You're minimizing your accomplishment, Albie. I don't think you realize the magnitude of what's happening here. Do you know what Bert Holman's death means? Holman Entertainment has a ten-billion-dollar offer on the table for Sovereign Communications. *Ten billion dollars.* For fifty-one percent of the stock. This could wind up being one of the biggest media deals in Wall Street history." She pauses to let that sink in. "And the principal player in the deal is murdered at his own wedding. You're a journalist. How big is this story? Big time? Major big time?"

"It's big, we both know that. I might get into it myself."

"Pardon me for being blunt, but this is out of your league. Why? Two reasons: you write for a weekly and this story is breaking by the minute; and, more importantly, you don't have the resources to cover it."

"Resources? As in . . . ?"

"Money. Lots of money. I'm offering you twenty thousand dollars to come on the show tomorrow night and tell your version of what happened."

"Twenty thousand dollars?"

"Twenty thousand."

"That's journalism?"

"That's journalism today."

"Why does it sound like show biz hype?"

"Because it's not *your* idea of journalism. What's the circulation of your magazine? Fifty thousand? A hundred? A hundred and fifty? You're in a different universe. Competition in our world boils down to one thing: who pays the most for the best information."

"People competing to sell their stories . . . a little ticklish, isn't it? What happens to the truth? It doesn't get bent in the direction of an extra ten thousand?"

"We don't pay people to lie. Let's say you know something substantial about a crime. Take your information to the police and you get zip. Bring it to us and you can get a good five figures. It's the same information and it reaches more people."

"It's not the same information. People will tell you whatever brings the best price."

"Have I asked you to alter the facts?"

"No."

"If I paid you more than twenty thousand would you tell it differently?"

"Is twenty thousand top dollar for my story?"

"We're top dollar and we're top of the line."

"What's top of the line?"

"We have the best staff, the best reputation, and the highest ratings. What else is there?"

"What would you want me to say?"

"Tell your story. The *whole* story."

"You know the whole story."

"I don't think so."

"What do you mean, 'you don't think so'?"

"I know people," she says. "I'm a personologist. I see it in your eyes. I'll raise it to twenty-*five* thousand. But it better be good."

"Who's James T. Gardner?" I ask, hoping to get more out of her than she's getting out of me.

"You don't know?"

"No."

"Will you agree to an interview if I tell you?"

"No."

"Well," she says with finality. "I think we should keep in touch." She takes out a twenty, puts it on the table. "Tell Leon to keep the change." Then she stands and hands me her business card. "I have your number, now you have mine. Call me tomorrow."

She's gone before I can kiss her good-bye.

I'm in a cab going home to Los Feliz, a one-time wealthy section of LA high in the Hollywood Hills where movie stars and oil barons once freely roamed. Now, the rich and famous have long since fled west and any free roaming is done at your own risk. We don't have the constant flow of natural disasters that plague high-end enclaves like Malibu and the Palisades, but we're exposed to human elements equally fierce and determined. Not that we're in the middle of Riot country—but we're on the broadening flank of those to the east who seek ever-expanding felonious horizons.

The cabdriver's keeping an eye out for roving carjackers, *high-*

waymen they used to be called, and I'm building my mental profile of Samantha Shelton. Sam.

I'd say she's around twenty-seven or -eight, obsessive about weight and exercise. She's total whitebread, Miss America to a T. I haven't known many women like her; you don't meet them at radical demonstrations and sit-ins. You never see them raging against the Establishment or sermonizing about the way things ought to be. I always had the impression they like things the way they are because the system works fine for beautiful women. If it works lousy for the rest of us, well, like Ozzie says, it's not their job to make us happy.

It would be interesting getting to know her, though, if only to see how the other side ticks. But it's not likely. I'm too old and funky for a woman that mainstream. I can imagine picking her up for the Golden Globes in my boots and jeans and my '67 Jag sedan that looks its age more than I do. Right. She probably goes for guys who wear Versace, have personal trainers and drive cars that are younger than she is.

When the cab finally turns into my driveway, its headlights illuminate a tableau that makes me tell the driver to stop while I marvel at the grandeur of life.

My cat Tank, one-eyed wonder and terrorizer of the neighborhood Lizard, Rodent and Bird Association, is sitting on the front step, chowing down on some creature whose cute little back legs and tail dangle chipperly from his mouth.

Beside the preoccupied cat lies Jed, a dirigible-shaped golden retriever, happily chomping away on an avocado. Jed was left in my reluctant care by the girlfriend who went to Hawaii and didn't come back. I don't mind, he's easy maintenance. He discovered an avocado grove in the hills nearby and eats about thirty a day. The dog can hear an avocado drop at a hundred yards. He's gotten so fat it takes two and a half minutes just to get to his feet.

Me, Tank and Jed. Three wild and crazy Hollywood bachelors. Life in the furry lane.

My little house, where I've lived since diving into obscurity after the Joplin/Danno affair, is actually the caretaker's quarters of what was once a great estate, built by the Steinberg piano fortune. That grand old mansion, in a sorry state of disrepair, is the victim of never-ending litigation between the various and far-flung Steinberg heirs. It's been sporadically rented out over the years by a real-estate management firm, in order to produce enough income to cover the taxes. I haven't been up there in a while. Last time I was inside the place, there was still a smattering of timeworn furniture and two or three dirt-encrusted, dormant old grand pianos, which hadn't been moved from their spots in seventy years. Like, *eerie*, dude.

For the past month it's been rented to a screenwriter named Norman Devore, whom I've seen zooming up and down the long, potholed driveway on his vintage blue Electra-Glide. We haven't talked, but I've been told he's well known in the movie business for writing hits and engaging in psychotic behavior. They say that every so often, when he gets too far out there, his shrink sends him back to the funny farm for observation and treatment. Whatever that means.

The flashing light on my telephone answering machine tells my stomach it's time for more gas eaters. I wash down a couple of Zantacs with a swig of Mylanta and wash down the Mylanta with a shot of Cuervo. No callbacks tonight, folks. It's been a long day, I'm closed for business.

But then again, there's always the chance Carol called to explain this whole nightmare . . . and maybe to ask me to come over and soothe her jangled nerves . . .

Albie. You dirty old man. Thinking about sex with a woman you hardly know. Purely for physical gratification. How shallow! How sexist!

Hey, I'm a shallow sexist. That's part of my spiritual crisis. I'll play back the messages.

First up is my son: "It's me, Dad." (Sarcastically) *"Nice going today.* I can't believe you're still fighting with the police. Anyway, forget what I said about Stevie McDonald. He called me tonight. They switched focus, they're going to bomb some other studio, not Disney, so there's nothing to worry about. Ciao."

Nothing to worry about. Stevie's blowing up somebody else. Is my kid so busy he can't even hear himself? Is studio competition that fierce? Is he taking Ozzie Baba too seriously?

Shrike: "Great work, Marx, grabbing that bastard. Son-of-a-bitch ruined a beautiful moment. Listen . . . About the Ozzie Baba story

. . . Let's put it on the back burner. Ozzie told Bonnie she'll have to stop seeing me if I publish something that detracts from his happiness. Just what I need. Blow my sex life 'cause she thinks he's God. Since when is it my job to make that joker happy? Whatever. You're off the hook. I'll talk to you in the morning.''

Great. And I just held myself up to Sam Shelton as a righteous journalist. Now my boss wants me to give up a story so he can keep getting laid. I'd like to see me explain that to Sam.

But, I ask myself, what *is* the point of digging up Ozzie's past? Twenty years ago something happened with a girl—how bad could it have been? According to my research, he never spent any time in jail, so what was it? A pregnancy? Drugs? Ozzie isn't the criminal type. He's a quack with a limited following, he's not whipping up masses like Sun Myung Moon or Jimmy Swaggart. He's a duffer compared to those shit-stirrers.

On the other hand, David Koresh had a smaller flock than Ozzie and look at the damage he caused. Not that I think Ozzie's as dangerous as Koresh, but the concept of making yourself happy above all else can spread pretty easily in a place like LA, where people are threatened more by other people's success than by their own failure.

What's dangerous about that? People who resent other people's success make themselves happy by taking out their resentment on the people they resent. Hence: robbery and murder.

But we're taught to make ourselves happy first, aren't we? Making ourselves happy is the American way. America is the "leader of the free world." Therefore, the world needs a strong and prosperous (subst. *happy*) America to maintain world order. Without a strong and prosperous America there can't be a strong and prosperous world. Therefore, it is America's duty to the world to make itself happy at any cost. Hence: robbery and murder.

I know. It's a stretch to blame Ozzie Baba for our national perversions. It's just as well to give up the story.

The last message is: "Albie, it's Sam Shelton."

Obviously calling from her car, knowing she'd get my machine.

"For your information, James T. Gardner is the man you caught today. I enjoyed our chat, even though I did most of the talking. That sounds egotistical, doesn't it? It's not meant to be. Anyway, my offer is good until noon tomorrow. My beeper number is 213-462-2608 and it's right next to my bed. Call anytime if you change your mind.''

Careful there, Beautiful—all business all the time makes Sam a dull girl. Guess you're not used to being turned down, especially when you're waving twenty-five thousand bucks around.

Twenty-five thousand bucks. For doing what?

What a town. A jackpot around every corner. A jackal in every closet. A Jack-loves-the-script on the lips of every self-styled movie producer.

But she did find out the name of the killer. She's a bulldog.

I open a Corona, take a deep breath and gaze out my picture window. I love my little house at night, hovering over the star-crossed city, the endless carpet of lights below, above the traffic, above the smog, above the murder, the ruthless craving for fame and fortune. A black widow town that lures you with rumors of glamour, promises of riches, smiles from beautiful people ... then bites you with fire, flood, earthquake, and mangled dreams.

From up here on the hill, *down there* is the netherworld, an inferno of unfulfilled promises. Up here you can imagine you're not in hell, you can pander to the illusion that you're safely above it all ...

DAY TWO
MONDAY, MARCH 13

I wouldn't say running is my life, but I can't imagine life without it.

How could I live without taunting myself every morning with doomsday threats of potbellied flaccidity? Without dragging myself out of bed in spite of every conceivable variety of ache, pain, and hangover. Without a mouth that feels like I ate a sand sandwich. Without fumbling my way into running gear with my eyes stuck together and my hair like Don King. Not a pretty picture.

But every day I get out there in the oxygen-starved hills of Los Feliz, braving bandidos who take even your sweats and your running shoes, and wheeze through the full eight mile course. Up and down and around I run, an institution among garbage collectors, dog walkers, and late-working second-story men. I can't imagine the neighborhood without me.

The inescapable truth is, if you want to convince yourself you're not getting old as fast as everyone else, if you want to drink like I do and stay trim like I do, you gotta work at it like I do. Running is the secret of being a fit, healthy drunk. Not that I'm perfectly fit and healthy right now, but this stomach ailment is just a passing thing.

This morning is an LA rarity—bright, crisp, and clear as a bell. From my house you can see from the streets of Hollywood all the way to the shimmering ocean and from the buildings in downtown LA to their mirror image fifteen miles west in Century City. And for once you can see the snowcapped ridges and peaks of the graceful mountains that embrace the city. It's the kind of day that makes you understand what all the fuss was about way back in the twenties and thirties, in those old home movies and newsreels of famous people frolicking like gods at star-studded parties and, always, palm trees and sun, sun and palm trees.

It's just turning seven o'clock. I'm halfway through my eight miles, clutching my palm-size canister of Mace and thinking about Bert Holman—how one moment with James T. Gardner ended thirty years of building an empire.

Last night, before falling asleep, I carefully read Holman's profile in the copy of *Fortune* Shrike lent me. It was particularly interesting because, like me, Holman had migrated from New York to Los Angeles in the late sixties.

LA, '66. When Bert and I came here, this place still had the magic to steal your heart. Coming from a lifetime of apartments, concrete, and cold, for a minimal amount of money you could rent an actual country house in an actual rustic setting in year-round sunshine. And you could drive to wherever you had to be in a matter of minutes. What a change from cloudy, cramped, and crowded New York. The smog hadn't yet overwhelmed the atmosphere, the cars hadn't throttled the freeways, the architecture hadn't been torn down and replaced by sterile, cookie-cutter mock-Spanish malls on every corner.

The place still had beauty then and yes, even character. There was the funky old Ranch Market on Fountain and Vine—now a mock-Spanish corner mall. And the classic Tiny Naylor's Drive-in with its rosy-cheeked roller-skating carhops—now a mock-Spanish corner mall. The famous Schwab's drugstore, where Lana Turner was supposedly discovered in her form-fitting sweater—mock-Spanish corner mall. The Unicorn night club where Lenny Bruce paved the way for everyone from Richard Pryor and Kim Bassinger, from *Saturday Night Live* to Ice-T—you guessed it.

Like it or not, LA in the sixties had displaced New York as the cradle of popular culture. Movies were already here. Rock and roll, born of the Chicago blues and reared by the disc jockeys of New York, came of age with the freewheeling youth on Malibu beach and the Sunset Strip. Fashions, however garish, appeared first in LA, then swept the country.

And given that every body of culture (like any other body) needs an anus to spew out its waste, the three TV networks, which still monopolized the airwaves, moved west at the end of the fifties and from Burbank and Hollywood provided America with its national asshole. Which in 1971 sucked a foresighted young agent, Bert Holman, out of the William Morris Agency and into a minor executive job at ABC.

One of his clients at William Morris, a game show host, told Holman about a network position that had just opened up. He grabbed it.

He was assigned to cover the network's game shows, a liaison between the daytime programming department and the producers of shows like *Name That Tune* and *Supermarket Sweep*. In his first TV job he learned the television business from both perspectives, buying and selling, and quickly saw that the producers were reaping profits while the network executives were drawing salaries.

Bert's mentor at ABC was the director of daytime programming, Harvey Grant. When Grant moved up to prime time programming, Holman moved into Grant's old job. In those days, according to Holman, the director of daytime programming had the power to pay a producer to develop an idea, authorize a pilot and, ultimately, make a network commitment to put the show on the air. That was a lot of power, the kind only network presidents wield these days.

Producers came to him all day, every day, producers of soap operas, cartoons, and particularly game shows, trying to sell him ideas. In most cases the game show ideas were so unoriginal and stupid that eventually Holman figured he could do better himself.

He knew that game shows, when they hit, were and still are, along with talk shows, the most profitable of all TV programming. They cost the least to produce and generate enormous revenues from first run on networks and from syndicators, who, for a percentage, sell a show locally, market by market, to the highest bidders. Holman de-

cided he would not only produce game shows, but become a syndica-
tor as well, thereby saving the thirty-five percent commission he'd
pay on his own shows and collecting commissions from others as
well.

He told Harvey Grant he was striking out on his own and that
he'd picked a hard-working young man three steps down the ladder,
Robert Edwards, to replace him as director of daytime programming.

Holman bragged to the *Fortune* writer that, since success in the
TV business, like any other business, is based on contacts, favors
and inside information, his hand-picked successor provided him with
all three when it came to the network. In the space of two years he
had two shows on the air, *Face the Music* and *It's Not My Fault,*
both handily winning their time slots in the ratings.

Holman Productions spawned Holman Syndications. The money
poured in and Holman branched out, forming Holman Entertainment,
which produced sitcoms, one-hour series, TV movies, and, more recently, reality based and tabloid shows. I wasn't surprised to learn
that *Real Life*, Sam Shelton's show, is in fact owned by Holman
Entertainment.

By the late eighties, Holman Entertainment was a TV power. But
Holman was just another big player until he came up with his greatest
brainstorm, the show that transformed his company into the mega-
multi-media giant it is today—*The Shame Game.*

That "highly entertaining yet heartbreakingly poignant" show (*TV
Guide*), which showcased the spectrum of human debasement in a
contest for prizes with the contestants being judged by a massive
interactive voting audience, swept the country and, soon after, the
rest of the world. After six years on the air *The Shame Game* is
still bringing hundreds of millions of dollars each year to Holman
Entertainment.

With the supercharged boost from *The Shame Game*, Holman took
the company public and its stock tripled and split in its first year.
With an excess of cash, solid backing for its stock and a golden goose
called *The Shame Game,* Holman Entertainment began to acquire film
libraries, news organizations, shopping networks ... it gobbled up
properties like a wolf in a petting zoo.

Last year, Holman pulled off a stock switch and merger with

Southwest Telephone, one of the huge and highly profitable deregulated baby bell companies. The reason? Each baby bell owns lines wired into tens of millions of homes. With the development of something called digital optics, the phone lines can conduct video signals as well. Transmitting TV through existing telephone lines could put the cable companies out of business.

For their part, the baby bells want to own the entertainment companies so they'll be able to transmit their own product. Sounds like a monopoly, doesn't it?

At any rate, Holman Entertainment and Southwest Telephone made a bid to the stockholders of Sovereign Communications, the last of the big movie studios, which owns TV stations, a cable network, a book publisher, and theme parks. The merger would make the combined companies the biggest media giant on earth.

Immediately after Holman made his offer, his sworn enemy from the old William Morris days, Mitchell P. Gluck, whose financial strength and power base lies in cable companies, made a competing offer for Sovereign. Holman had some choice descriptions for Gluck in the *Fortune* article. Words like "megalomaniac," "sociopath," "evil," and "parasite" peppered the paragraphs pertaining to the rival tycoon.

Being that it was *Fortune* magazine, they pretty much glossed over the personal aspects of Holman's life: two marriages, estranged children, bouts with poor health—the kind of stuff I really wanted to know about.

After reading the piece from beginning to end, I came out with the feeling that if I were Mitchell P. Gluck, I'd be shedding no tears over Bert Holman's murder.

At the six-mile mark I tell myself I can't run anymore, my legs are too weary, my stomach too turbulent, my lungs too desperate for air. But the fear of not being able to finish, which I equate with a portent of imminent doom, drives me on.

A quarter mile from the end of this torture I'm thinking that maybe this morning I'll start teaching Jed, the golden retriever, to bring my *Los Angeles Times* in from the driveway. But when I get back to the house he's sprawled out on the lawn, unconscious in a pile of pits, the aftermath of another unbridled avocado binge.

Forget the lesson. If he starts getting up now I'll be showered and shaved before he's upright. Besides, I remember, last month, in a fit of political pique, I discontinued my subscription.

I do the shower and shave drill in a quick fifteen, throw on my jeans and find a clean, folded shirt under a stack of laundry. I'm just pulling my boots on when the phone rings.

"Dad. You're on TV."

"What . . ."

"Channel 2 News. Quick, check it out. I gotta run."

What a kid. Couldn't say, "gotta run, *love you, Dad*?"

I flick on the TV. Sure enough, there's Bert Holman's house . . . police cars, stricken faces, a lot of movement . . . James T. Gardner— and me, looking mad as hell—being hustled through the crowd by grim-faced cops . . . a quick sound byte with Danno, answering questions with nonanswers . . . a reporter on the spot, building the drama . . . then me again, coming down the stairs of the Hollywood precinct . . . running into the crowd of newspeople . . . a camera swinging around as I bull my way through . . . knocking over the fat guy with the microphone . . . jumping into the cab and speeding off . . . That's enough. I snap off the TV.

Why is this happening? I'd better get ahold of Carol, pronto.

I dial Holman Entertainment and ask for Holman's assistant, Adele Smith, the woman who called me about the limo. The switchboard operator puts me on hold, forcing me to listen to 1,000 Strings, doing their elevator version of "Jumping Jack Flash." If I knew this was going to happen back in the sixties I wouldn't have bothered.

The operator comes back on and informs me that no one by the name of Adele Smith works at Holman Entertainment. I tell her she's wrong, check again. She informs me she's doing the best she can, the company just suffered a major loss. I give her my condolences and remind her that in her business they say "the show must go on." I tell her Adele Smith is on Holman's personal staff, to please check with them. Hold again, more castrated sixties rock, then she's back—no Adele Smith at Holman Entertainment.

What's going on here? How am I supposed to find Carol if I can't trace the limo she came in? And wasn't I given a message straight from Bert Holman, *"Be especially nice to the driver?"* That implies he knew it was a woman. Unfortunately, it's too late to ask Bert. But someone in his office must know about the limo and, if I'm lucky, maybe even about Carol. I'll go there myself. Even though it's the last thing I want to do, show up at Bert Holman's office with Danno's threats and suspicions hanging in the air, I don't have much choice.

As I'm backing the Jag out of the driveway I hear the muscular roar of Norman Devore's Harley Davidson coming around the far curve. I stop and watch as he comes into view, slows slightly, then guns the big machine up the long, potholed driveway to the broken-down Steinberg mansion. He's wearing a World War II helmet, high-top sneakers, a pair of boxer shorts, white with red hearts—and nothing else.

Shuddering to think what goes on with the crazy screenwriter in his spooky old house, I ease the Jag into the street and head down the hill. At the corner of Bronson and Franklin I run into Victor's Deli to pick up a few packs of Carefree sugarless gum. I chew a lot of gum when I'm stressed out.

Victor is one of my heroes. He's had this corner store for close to fifty years and they've come to him countless times with ever-increasing offers to sell, so they can build one of those you-know-what-kind of corner malls here. Still he refuses. He hates the malls, says they've defaced and dehumanized the city. Victor Jr., hates them, too. So the Victor family preserves this little piece of the real Hollywood for me. I also love that they don't cover the place with tacky eight-by-ten glossies autographed "To Victor," from obscure show business types whose only brush with fame is to hang on the walls of Hollywood cleaners and delis.

Victor himself, a spry seventy plus, is behind the counter this morning. "Hey, Albie! I thought I told you to stay outta trouble! What the hell's this?" He's waving the *Los Angeles Times* at me.

I take the paper and Victor watches with bushy, creased eyebrows as I read it.

Holman's name tops a page-one column heading. Some sketchy background on the big deal ... Sunday night ruminations by Wall Streeters that Holman Entertainment stock will suffer a steep drop when the market opens in the morning ... further speculation that the Sovereign board of directors will vote to accept the offer of Mitchell P. Gluck ...

In the third paragraph, Holman's killer is identified as James T. Gardner, who, "along with his apparent accomplice, the journalist, Albie Marx ..."

"This is bullshit."

"Which part?"

"Implication by intimation, the new journalism."

"What ... ?"

"Guilt by suggestion. The new craze. 'Did he do it? Says so in the paper. Then he must have done it.' No restraint, no confirmation, no giving a person the benefit of the doubt ..."

"You mean, *innocent until proven guilty?*" Victor says rhetorically. "That don't sell papers. It's your modern world for you, kid. Anything for a buck. People calling 7-Eleven's *delis* ... they don't have a clue about good, lean pastrami ..."

"But you believed *this* ..."

"Excuse me. I would never believe that. You're one of my favorites and you know it."

"I know they have to compete, but does the *Los Angeles Times* really need to sink to the level of *The Enquirer?* I hate it. No more truth. Tell the fools what they want to hear. The world is ending, Victor. Sinking into a pit of celebrity worship and empty gossip. Twenty minutes of fame, your life is fucked forever, and everyone blithely goes on to the next twenty-minute wonder."

"Well, you better get on the stick, son. Judging from this paper, your twenty minutes are almost up."

Back at the wheel of the Jag, I feel the pressure of a gas bubble the size of the Hindenberg floating down my esophagus and docking in my stomach. Which reminds me, I have an appointment with Rissman today, to get the results of my barium test. All I need on top of this Holman mess is a little stomach cancer. Make my life complete.

I pop a Zantac, wash it down with a swig of Cuervo from the pint in the glove compartment and load up with a couple of sticks of wild cherry bubblegum. Am I delightful or what?

It's maddening to be a victim of this insane system. The media has everyone trained to be satisfied with nothing less than a blood bath. Is it that people need someone to hate, to whom they can feel morally superior at the same time they rationalize away their own sins? What became of the higher qualities in human nature, the poetry, the understanding, the compassion? Is the demand for dirt dragging us so deep that only the tabloids emerge from the slime better off? And the lawyers. No matter who gets destroyed, the lawyers always come out ahead. Which accounts for Shrike's newest pet saying which goes, "It's never over till the fat lawyer sings."

I'd love to go down to the county jail right now, tell James T. Gardner to cut the mystery act and clear my name. But that would not be a brilliant move. If I go down there, everyone will know. Then, if the son-of-a-bitch still refuses to talk, I'll look more like a conspirator than before. I have to stick to the program—find Carol, take her to Danno, sneer at his limp apology.

The studio guard manning the entrance to the Holman Entertainment Center in Century City leans out of his booth as I drive up. He's sporting a black crepe paper mourning band on the sleeve of his uniform. I wonder if he took it upon himself or it was mandated by higher ups.

"Name, please?" he asks.

"Albie Marx." He scans the list of the names he's been given for passes. Knowing I won't get one unless I know somebody, I tell him. "I'm here to see Samantha Shelton."

"What's the name . . . Marx? You're not on the list. Is she expecting you?"

"Yes."

"Hold on." He moves back into the booth, dials a number and talks to somebody on the phone. He's apparently on hold for a few seconds, then he says something and hangs up. He writes out a pass, leans out and hands it to me, along with a black armband.

"Visitors have to wear these." He waits while I put the cheesy black crepe paper over the sleeve of my jean jacket. "Okay. Take this road to the second crossing, turn left and go down two more crossings . . . the *Real Life* stage is in the second studio on the left. Park anywhere that's not assigned."

As I drive past his booth I notice the flagpole on the little round lawn across from the executive building. The flag is drooping at half-mast in the bright, still air. I can just see the black-bordered cards clipped next to the lunch specials on the menus in the company commissary. "We mourn the passing of Bert Holman, citizen, entre-preneur and friend, who gave us the priceless gift of happiness through the despair of others." Signed by the staff and crew of *The Shame Game.*

I park in the executive parking lot, which is full except for two spots marked *Reserved For Mr. Holman.* I pull into one of them and go through a door marked *Executive Offices.* As I approach the sign-in desk, I hope Sam isn't waiting for me on her set, figuring I've come to take her up on her offer.

Everyone in the lobby is wearing the same cheap black armband, including the guard at the desk, who looks up from the sports section when I approach. The nameplate on his uniform says he's Stu White.

"I'm here to see Adele Smith," I tell him.

"Adele Smith? Hmmnnn. Don't know that one." He pages through his office directory. "You might have the wrong building."

"I assume she's in this building. She works—*worked*—for Mr. Holman."

"Everyone worked for Mr. Holman. Don't mean they're all in this building."

"Well, how can I find her? Does anyone have a complete list of people who work for Holman Entertainment?"

"Countin' all the shows and crews and what not?"

"I doubt if I'll have to go that far ..." But I'm beginning to wonder.

"Who you lookin' for again?"

"Adele Smith."

"Adele Smith ..." He looks through the directory again, shaking his head. "Not in this building."

"How about Accounting? They might know. They must have a record of everybody."

"They're in this building. Who you wanna see in Accounting?"

"Anybody."

"Need a name."

"Who works in Accounting?"

"Let's see ..." Checking the directory again. "Abbott, Bonnie ... Acker, Morton ... Alvarez, Marie ..."

"Bonnie Abbott."

"She know you?"

"No."

"Then she ain't expectin you."

"Look, *Stu* ... Why stand here and fuck with each other's heads on a terribly sad day like this? I need to find Adele Smith. You need to find someone who can tell me where to find her. Those are the assignments. Let's get busy."

He looks at me like I have a screw loose, then picks up the phone. "Got someone here wants to talk to Bonnie Abbott. I'll hold." He looks at his watch, adjusts his armband, then says into the phone, "Hold on." He hands the receiver over the desk to me.

"This is Bonnie Abbott," a pleasant, non-mourning voice chirps from inside the phone.

"Hi, Bonnie. This is sort of an emergency. I'm looking for a Holman employee named Adele Smith. Where do I find her?"

"Adele Smith? Hold on." Back on hold. I look at Stu. He's back into the sports section. "How 'bout them Lakers, Stu?" He doesn't look up.

Bonnie Abbott comes back on the line. "The only two Smiths we have are Jeremiah, in maintenance, and Ruth. She works here in Accounting."

"No Adele?"

"No Adele."

"Thanks, Bonnie." I pass the phone back across the desk. "Thanks, Stu." He nods without looking at me and goes back to the paper.

I walk out of the building, into the parking lot. I'm in a Kafka story. Adele Smith from Bert Holman's office calls me. No such person. A beauty masquerading as a chauffeur sets me up for a frame. Vanished. Did Bert Holman really send the limo? Did he send the message, "Be nice to the driver?" It looks like the whole routine was a set-up, from beginning to end. One thing's for sure—I'll never be able to ask Holman about it.

Adele Smith doesn't exist, but there is a girl out there who called herself Carol. Unless I'm about to wake up in my bed, gasping for air and covered with sweat, she was real. Why did she set me up? And who is James T. Gardner?

As long as I'm here on the Holman lot, I decide to go see Sam Shelton. She knew the killer's name right off the bat, maybe she knows more. Although she thinks I know more than she does. If she had any idea how much I *don't* know she wouldn't throw twenty-five grand at me. Maybe, though, in terms of ratings, it's a cheap price to pay to get me on the show. If she thought I was Gardner's accomplice. That would be a scoop. A first interview with one of the killers.

Stop it. Don't think like that. Gloomy thoughts lead to gloomy outcomes.

I get back in the Jag and follow the gate guard's instructions to the *Real Life* sound stage. I park across from a door marked STAGE with a red light over the words TAPING IN PROGRESS. The red light isn't lit, so I let myself in. No one is on set, but people are bustling about with critically busy looks on their faces.

A natty young man with a self-important air and a black armband of gathered silk asks if I'm looking for someone.

"Samantha Shelton," I tell him.

"Your name is . . . ?"

"Albie Marx."

His eyebrows jerk up like they're on puppet strings. "Follow me," he says gravely, and leads me past the set and down a long hall lined with production offices, which opens onto a large conference room and branches off into two more corridors.

I follow Mr. Important as he steps briskly to a corner office just past the conference room. The door to the office is closed, but a harried-looking male secretary is at his station, directly across from it.

"This is Albie Marx," Mr. Important announces somberly.

Judging from his eyebrow work, the secretary must have the same puppeteer as Mr. Important. They exchange privileged glances and the secretary gets Sam on the line.

"Albie Marx is here." He looks up at me. "She says to come on in."

As I open the door to the office, I hear the secretary whispering to Mr. Important, "... you think he did it?" and Mr. Important whispering back smartly, "Did Michael Jackson bugger the little kid?"

Jesus. That glorified gopher is convicting me.

"Hello, Albie," Samantha says simply. She's sitting in a large leather chair, behind a desk scattered with memos, magazines, newspapers, photographs ... what I take to be the woof and warp of tabloid titillation. The natural colors of her layered outfit, the shirt, vest, and jacket of muted browns, oranges, blues, and vermillion complement her soft chestnut hair and fresh, wholesome features, making her look like an advertisement for fall in Vermont.

Across from her on a small couch, is a disheveled-looking character, about fifty in a white shirt with tie askew who scowls openly when I come into the office. I don't like him, either.

"This is Harry Carruthers, our producer," she says.

"Can we talk?" I ask her, ignoring his pointed display of attitude. "Alone."

She looks at Carruthers, who stands, goes to the door, then turns to me with an expression of total loathing. "You couldn't shine Bert Holman's shoes."

"He had you for that," I retort. "Maybe your next boss will let you wipe his ass."

He starts to respond but Sam stops him. "Is tonight's script finished, Harry?"

He glances at her sullenly, throws me a dirty look and leaves.

"You're not wearing your armband," I observe. "Is that a statement?"

"I'm a reporter, I don't make statements."

"I'm sorry I was crude with your friend. But that was a low hit. What's with these people? They really think I'm involved in this?"

"Harry's worked for Bert a long, long time."

"How does he like working for Sheila?"

"None of us likes it."

"Is she capable of running the company?"

"Although I shudder to think of the things she *might* be capable of, running this company is not one of them."

"Do you think she had something to do with Bert's murder?"

"Time will tell."

"Does Carruthers?"

"Harry's a conspiracist. He suspects everybody."

"Then why did it feel like he put it all on me?"

"Don't be so sensitive. Until this is behind you you'll have to put up with a lot more of that."

"Until it's behind me? I have to *prove* something? What do you think? Do you think I had something to do with killing Holman?"

"No. That's why I want you to come on the show. To tell your side of the story."

"I don't have a side of the story. To me it's a bad dream—and it's not even mine."

"I want you to be on tonight's show."

"To prove a negative? It's impossible. The minute I answer one question, I'm convicted. That's the way you guys have it set up. That's what you've done to the truth. Sensationalized it out of existence."

She's patiently watching me rant and I suddenly feel bad for laying it all on her. "I'm sorry. It's not you. It's the media's frenzy to fill the void. To satisfy two hundred million flea-size attention spans. I know—it's squalid, but it's the way things are."

Her eyes project understanding. "You feel that you can't state your innocence publicly."

"Not even for free."

"Too bad. You could have been on with Gardner."

I'm stunned, not sure if I heard what I heard. "Come again?"

"We're taping Gardner in prison. He's going to bare his soul on *Real Life* tonight."

"James T. Gardner, the man who splattered Bert Holman's brains all over his bride's face? That James T. Gardner? That piece-of-shit, dirty, cold-blooded murderer? He's going to *bare his soul*? The last person they said that about was Jeff Gillooly."

"Gardner was going to tell somebody. He committed to us. Personally, I think you should be thrilled. Since you had nothing to do with it, he should exonerate you completely."

"Oh? I'm trusting my fate to a murderer? What if he doesn't? What if he decides to take me with him?"

"Then you'll come on the show and tell your side of it."

"How much are you paying this scum-of-the-earth?"

Levelling her eyes at mine, she answers, "Three hundred thousand."

I let myself slowly down onto the couch.

"He picked us over *Hard Copy* and *Inside Edition*," she says, unable to camouflage a gleam of pride. "I think we'll score a record rating for our time slot."

She doesn't see the moral crisis here. She's focused on her little world and it's all she knows.

"Isn't there a law against criminals profiting from exploiting their crimes?" I ask.

"There was the 'Son-Of-Sam' law," she states with assurance, obviously well versed on the subject. "When the New York serial killer David Berkowitz sold his story to a book publisher, New York State passed a law to take his profits away. It was challenged. Went to the Supreme Court. They ruled it unconstitutional. Said it trampled the First Amendment, his right to free speech. So, your answer is, James T. Gardner can take his murder to the bank."

"Un-fucking-believable. Three hundred thousand?" She nods. "And you only offered me twenty-five?"

"I think he's going to confess."

"What makes you think that?"

"I told you. I'm a personologist."

"Do you know what he's going to say?"

"Don't have a clue. Nobody does. But at three o'clock this afternoon we'll get it all on tape."

"I assume the police will be there."

"The only way he'll talk is on tape—they agreed to the deal. Everybody's happy."

Everybody's happy. It's a regular Ozzie-fest. All the sordid murderer's thoughts you ever wanted to hear. A banquet for ghouls.

And I wonder who gets to be the dessert.

Driving off the Holman lot, I pass a cluster of people standing around a stage door, two studios down from *Real Life*. They're sobbing, wailing, and pounding their chests in unbearable sorrow. I'm amazed at the depth of feeling Bert Holman engendered in these grief-stricken sufferers. Maybe there was more to the man than I've given him credit for.

Then I see the sign over the stage door, *The Shame Game*. These people aren't mourning Bert Holman. They're *Shame Game confestants*, as they're called, warming up their misery, getting ready to bare their souls for tacky prizes on America's favorite pain show.

How ironic. Here we have true victims with real souls to bare, and what do they get for it? Toaster ovens. Dishwashers. Samsonite carry-ons. Hair dryers. And if they've gotten *royally* screwed—like a lifetime emotional scar from parents who chained them in basements or an incurable disease deliberately passed to them by some human scumball—they'll score a sporty new compact car. While James T. Gardner, who murdered a man in cold blood, gets three hundred grand for a confession. Another bounteous gift from the asshole of culture.

As I flick on the radio for musical relief, I pass a block-long stretch limousine, white with black windows and solid gold trim, pulling up in front of the executive building. Emerging from the depths of the great white chariot, with a look of lament plastered onto his holy kisser, is the Pope of Self-Pandering, Ozzie Baba. He reaches a helping hand back into the car, providing support for the black-veiled beauty who steps out onto the sidewalk beside him—Sheila Petersen Holman.

At the front entrance, Stu the security guard, his folded-up sports page sticking ludicrously out of his back pocket, holds the door open for his new boss and bows obsequiously, nearly bending in half. The grieving widow doesn't notice he's there as she marches past him into the building, escorted by Ozzie Baba.

On the Jag's radio, *my* old guru, Baba Bob, is singing, *"Once upon a time you dressed so fine. Threw the bums a dime in your prime, didn't you . . ."*

Beautiful people doing beautiful things.

As soon as I find Carol, I promise myself, I'll look into the story of Ozzie Baba and Jeannie Locke.

Driving past the guard's booth and out the front gate of Holman Entertainment, I notice the sky, so blue and clear this morning, has attracted some somber gray clouds. Even the weather bows to Bert Holman's departure.

Gardner will be on *Real Life* at seven-thirty tonight. He's taping at three, down at LA County jail. Which means that Danno will be there, sucking up every syllable. Five hours from now Gardner will implicate me and Danno will have a warrant out. Based on what? The testimony of a murderer. And my fingerprints on the rifle.

But my prints are not in a position that would have allowed me to shoot the rifle, so Gardner can't claim I did the shooting. There's an up side. No gas chamber. I'm a lucky guy.

Danno was right. I need a lawyer.

From Holman Entertainment in Century City I have to go through Beverly Hills to get to *UP YOURS* in Hollywood. The timing can't be worse, but I have to run in and see Dr. Rissman. He was seriously concerned about my test results on the phone Friday.

But I don't have time to waste.

Hey, I tell myself, if there's something critically wrong with you, you won't have to worry about Danno and murder charges. Death solves a lot of niggling problems.

I find a meter and run into Rissman's medical building. In his waiting room I make a scene with Wendy, one of his nurses, insisting I have to see him immediately. Finally, she takes me into his private office, just to shut me up.

The good doctor pulls my file and tells me to have a seat. I'm thankful he makes no mention of the fiasco at Holman's wedding yesterday. Probably forgot the whole thing over tennis this morning. Instead, he gives me his traditional greeting, a joke.

"What are the two words you never want to hear in a men's room?" he asks, grinning in anticipation of his latest punchline.

"I don't know," I answer, without caring. "What are they?"

" 'Nice penis.' " He grins so wide I can see the cracks in his tan. I smile hollowly. "Have a seat," he says, turning his attention to my file. "Your X-ray results came in Friday morning."

"How'd I do?"

"You came in seventh." Another joke, another well-tanned grin.

"We need to talk," he adds on a serious note. He flips on his illuminator, clips up two X rays and using his pencil for a pointer explains, "This is your large intestine . . . this is your small intestine . . . here is the ileocecal valve, this connects the two. You see this white spot . . . right here . . . ?"

I see a small patch of white where he's pointing. "That's what's causing the pain?"

"Let's hope not."

"Why?"

"In the best of all possible worlds, your pain is being caused by gas—which is not my department. For the gas you go to a colon man. Personally—I'm a little out of my area here—I think your gas is being caused by taking in too much air with your food."

Too much air with my food? Should I eat with a nose clip?

"As far as this spot goes," he continues, "we can't tell exactly what it is. It could be a shadow on the X ray . . . it could be a natural obstruction . . . it could be some small growth, partially blocking the valve . . ."

"Small growth? What kind of growth?" I hear my voice getting higher. This guy's going to tell me it's over, call the crematorium.

"There's nothing to worry about at this point . . ."

"This point?"

"But I want to do an upper endoscopy right away."

Oy. "What's an upper endoscopy?"

"A simple procedure . . . done at Cedars Hospital on an outpatient basis. A scope is inserted orally . . . the upper intestinal tract is viewed. If this is a growth, a scraping is done . . . we do a biopsy . . ."

Biopsy. Now, there's a word I never wanted to hear in a men's room. Or anywhere else. "Who does this procedure?"

"An upper GI man. I'm sending you to Paul Pierson. He's a funny guy, you'll love him."

Just what I need, another funny doctor. *Don't make me laugh, Doc, there's a scope down my throat.*

"I'll tell Paul you'll call him today."

"Today? Actually, I'm booked up today."

"Well, we need to do this quickly. Wendy will give you his number."

"Great."

I get to my feet as he begins writing in my file. Popping a fresh stick of Carefree into my mouth, I'm halfway out the door when he looks up and asks, "Do you chew a lot of gum?"

"Gum is my life. Why?"

"Chewing gum can cause gas. Try to cut back."

"Cut back on gum? One of my few remaining pleasures?"

"Substitute something else. Take up smoking." He grins again. It's another joke. The guy is a riot. Mr. Saturday Night of the cancer circuit.

Wendy gives me the upper GI man's phone number then asks me for a check. Three hundred and fifty dollars. Here they make you pay at the door, like getting your car out of the shop. In a way it's fitting, since what I really need is a new muffler. I should skip Cedars and go straight to Midas.

From a phone booth on Roxbury Drive I dialed the number Bambi Friedman gave me at the wedding and reached her voice mail. Is there no escape from answering machines and voice mail? It was getting depressing beyond words. I left my home and office numbers.

Now I'm fighting my way through traffic to Hollywood, listening to 1070 FM All-News radio:

... Holman Entertainment stock fell from 62½ to 51⅞ on the New York Stock Exchange this morning, making the Holman bid for Sovereign Communications almost a billion dollars less than it was before Holman's murder ...

... Bert Holman's widow is currently meeting with the board of directors to assure those who might panic that the ship is not rudderless ...

... Mitchell P. Gluck of Gluck International filed suit in federal court to force Sovereign's stockholders to make a decision in the next forty-eight hours, claiming that prolonging the process jeopardizes Sovereign's position against third-party takeovers and stock profiteers ...

... Gluck offered condolences to Holman's widow and the

stockholders of Holman Entertainment but commented that he
felt destined all along to win the battle for Sovereign ...

... Police authorities confirmed the identity of Holman's murderer as James T. Gardner, as unemployed firefighter from Pasadena, California, but, pending government agency checks, were
unable to provide additional information ...

... Suspected participant in the plot to kill Holman, Albie
Marx, journalist and political columnist for *UP YOURS* magazine, was not held by police due to lack of evidence ...

... In other news, a crude bomb destroyed a building at Sovereign Communications in Hollywood. The building housed a computer complex controlling the Cross Star Satellite, a major
communications satellite owned and operated by Sovereign. The
explosion took place at 3 A.M. this morning, causing no deaths or
injuries. Loss is estimated at seven million dollars. Following the
blast police received a call from a man claiming to be with a
group called the AHA, the Anti-Homogenization Army ...

Anti-Homogenization Army? Why does that ring a bell? A radical
wing of the American Dairy Council? No. Wait, I know—at Holman's wedding ... what did Freedom say Stevie McDonald told
him? The rhetoric about Big Brother ... "the blitz is on" ... waging
war against the media, attacking the Information Highway, saving
the individual, *a crusade against homogenization* ...

Stevie McDonald. He bombed Sovereign. Hit a communications
satellite, a symbol of world-wide uniformity. He's crazy. Does he
know what he's doing? Fighting for some obscure principle—the
rescue of the individual mind. Assailing the media's tightening noose
around the cortex of humanity. Didn't Jim McDonald tell him the
age of protest is over? Challenging the Vietnam War was one thing,
we had body bags to make the killing real. How do you protest the
killing of brain cells to a world of TV junkies, people who don't
read and don't think? Protest? Rebellion? Revolution? Forget it,
Stevie. You missed the sixties by thirty years.

But they're still alive in some people's hearts, aren't they, Albie?

I just wish there was something I could do to stop Stevie. Before he kills someone and ruins his own life as well. I owe it to his father, for old times' sake.

At the *UP YOURS* building on Santa Monica Boulevard in Hollywood, I leave the Jag in underground parking and take the elevator to my office.

"Shrike wants to see you," Rachel Receptionist announces the moment she sees my face.

I walk down the hall to his office and knock on the door.

"Name, rank and serial number," he calls from inside.

"Albie Marx, murder suspect," letting myself in.

He gestures to close the door behind me. He's standing at the open window, smoking a joint and exhaling it out into Hollywood, whose inhabitants hardly need to get any more stoned.

"Trying some new conditioner," he explains. "I just bought a dozen bottles."

The guy who cuts his hair recently expanded into the conditioner business. He sells "bottles of conditioner," a euphemism for individual joints of the world's finest grass. In those small quantities, he says, at ten dollars a joint, if he gets busted it's only a misdemeanor. His shit is so good that everyone from street hookers to rock stars now regularly appear at the door of his obscure salon. He had to hire a bouncer to stand outside and separate the groomies from the doobies, the hair people who come to get spruced up, from the joint people who come to get fucked up.

"How's the latest batch?" I ask. "As good as the last conditioner?"

"Better. I'm completely silky and manageable, no annoying knots and tangles. Want a hit?"

"No, thanks, I'm already too manageable. I'm about to manage my way right into jail."

"Over a case of mistaken identity?"

"Without Carol, I can't prove I'm innocent."

"That is a drawback," he chuckles.

"I don't need humor, Shrike, I need a lawyer."

"All right then. Let's look at the practical side. You get picked

up, spend a couple of days in LA County. You can do an inside
story on the unspeakable conditions . . .''

"Don't joke about this."

"Hey," he grins, "just pulling your ball and chain."

"Are you going to help me or not?"

"Of course we'll get you a lawyer. Isn't that what I'm here for?
To dig you out of trouble every time you blunder into some act of
superfluous heroism?"

"You're talking to me about heroism? You, the courageous publisher who drops a story because it threatens his sex life? Who lets
a small-time guru come between him and his principles?"

"If he came between me and my principles that would be one
thing—but nobody comes between me and my testicles."

"You're spineless."

"And proud of it. You weren't crazy about writing the Ozzie Baba
piece anyway."

"But I feel like we sidestepped some code of journalistic responsibility. Which, sad to say, is the least of my problems right now. I
have reason to believe I'll be charged in Bert Holman's murder."

"How do you know that?"

"I know it."

"You're paranoid."

"I was set up."

"Why?"

"I don't know."

"By who?"

"Carol and the man who shot Holman."

"For what purpose?"

"I have no idea."

"You're paranoid."

"Not as paranoid as I'll be, surrounded by suitors with facial hair.
Sometime after three o'clock this afternoon Lieutenant Danno could
be at my door with a warrant."

"Why?"

"*Real Life* is taping Gardner in jail at three. He's baring his soul.
And taking my ass with him."

Shrike takes a last deep hit off the conditioner, then pinches it out with his thumb and forefinger. He exhales thoughtfully out the window, watching the smoke waft its way toward somebody else's lungs.

"Okay," he muses. "Let's run the scenario your way. Gardner says you were in on Holman's murder. You're picked up and charged on the basis of his word. You're arraigned, you plead not guilty, your lawyer negotiates with the judge, and I put up the cash for some insanely exorbitant bail. You get out, poke around, try to prove you were framed. You can't find the temptress, can't get Gardner to tell the truth, can't find out if anyone else was involved. Eventually the case comes to trial, Gardner's convicted and he takes you down with him. *What happens to my bail money?*"

"See you around, Shrike." I head for the door.

"I'm just asking! What's wrong with that? I'm not saying I won't do it. Come on, we'll get you a lawyer. We'll do what it takes. Would I let you down?"

"Ask me something else."

"You're my star writer, Marx. I need you. We'll fight this together. Back to back. We'll take 'em all on."

"That's what I want to hear. That's what *UP YOURS* is about."

"We'll take 'em on and we'll sell magazines, too." He's winding himself up. "This is a hell of a story, Marx. And you'll be on the inside—*figuratively*, I mean."

"As long as you're really behind me . . ."

"Was Lincoln behind Grant? Was Laurel behind Hardy?"

Before he conjures up Hitler and Goering or Sonny and Cher, I ask him to call Arthur Gruntman, a well-known criminal attorney he's used in the past.

"Forget Gruntman. He's booked to the hilt and priced through the roof. We need someone who can jump right in at the right price."

"I don't want a cut-rate lawyer . . ."

"You think charging five hundred an hour makes one attorney better than another?"

"Yes."

"Christ, whatever happened to the revolutionary who stood up in court and demanded a public defender instead of an Establishment lawyer?"

"He got a month in jail instead of a slap on the wrist."

Shrike picks up the phone and punches an intercom number. "Rachel. Would you come in here for a minute?"

"What are you doing?"

"Do you want a great attorney or not?" he says, taking a can of room deodorizer from a desk drawer and routing the sweet smell of pot. I don't know who he has in mind to defend me, but the insistent image of lying in a bunk on death row is making me queasy as a bungi jumper with diarrhea.

The door opens and Rachel follows her breasts into Shrike's office. Not a raving beauty, but she sure has the goods.

I wonder if women think of me that way? And if I knew they did, would I be insulted?.

Rachel is in her late twenties and, despite an invisible degree of motivation, manages to keep the phones answered and visitors to *UP YOURS* under control. I think she and Shrike are having at it in private, although he won't admit it.

Coming through the door she has the look most people at *UP YOURS* get when Shrike asks them into his office: a skittish expression of uneasy anticipation.

"What's the name of that attorney who got your brother off on the manslaughter charge?" Shrike inquires.

"You mean Boopsie?"

"That's the one. Give me Boopsie's number. Albie needs a lawyer . . ."

"Hold it. I don't want a lawyer named Boopsie."

"That's just what they call her," Rachel tells me. "Her name is Betty McDougal."

"I don't care what her name is. Forget it."

"She's a great lawyer," Shrike swears. "Never lost a case."

"That she remembers," Rachel mutters.

"That she *remembers*?" My spirits sag like a grizzled old scrotum in a Turkish bath.

"She's one of the best criminal attorneys in the business," Shrike reassures me. "And the price is right."

"What's the price?"

Shrike looks at Rachel for an answer. "Thirty-five an hour," she tells him.

"See?" he beams at me.

"You have to be kidding. That's what a plumber gets."

"In a court of law, she'll run circles around any plumber you name," Shrike argues. "And it's on me. I'll pay the bills."

That's his strongest point—and his only point. At five hundred an hour, a lawyer like Gruntman is way out of my reach. Even at thirty-five an hour, Boopsie could wind up costing three or four thousand, an amount I can't afford at the moment.

Shrike reads my expression. "Stop worrying, Marx, you'll love her."

Right. That makes two people I'm going to love. Paul Pierson, the hysterically funny endoscopy doctor, and Boopsie, the hysterically cheap lawyer.

By the time we found Boopsie, I was more than just flirting with panic. James T. Gardner's *Real Life* prison interview with Sam was only two hours from taping and I could feel Danno closing in on me.

The number we got from Rachel's brother turned out to be one of those personal injury law firms, Bledsoe & Wernick, who advertise on TV in English with Spanish subtitles.

I got ahold of Bledsoe, who told me that Boopsie McDougal had departed his employ several months ago. He sounded pissed off. When I requested her home number he gave it to me and asked sardonically if I knew what I was getting myself into. It was not an encouraging sign.

Nobody answered Boopsie's phone. I called Bledsoe back and wheedled her address out of him. Boopsie lived off Laurel Canyon Boulevard, in Studio City.

The Valley. Even though Boopsie's location was only a twenty-five minute drive from *UP YOURS*, I hated the idea of going to the Valley. It was always ten degrees hotter, twenty IQ points lower, and thirty times uglier than any stretch of land between San Diego and San Francisco. In desperation, I took another whack at convincing Shrike to call Arthur Gruntman—or any lawyer over fifty bucks an hour—but he was positive Boopsie was the counselor for me.

I left Hollywood hoping I could find her before the rains came. The sky, which had started so clear and blue this morning, was becoming engorged with corpulent, pewter clouds. The temperature had risen, too, enough for a warm, tactile humidity to drape itself over everything.

They say it never rains in Southern California—but it *pours*. And it looked like we were in for a pounding. When the deluge starts, it brings up the oil permeating the streets and freeways, accumulated from months of sun-scorched drought. Everywhere you look, people are sliding into each other like bumper cars. It's like nobody in Los Angeles ever drove in the rain before.

A half hour after leaving Hollywood, I was searching for the name Betty McDougal on a decimated building directory outside the locked gate of a tacky apartment complex (or *multiple dwelling*, as Californians so quaintly call them) in Studio City. From where I stood I could see the plain, three-tiered horseshoe-shaped structure with its pea-size, paint-cracked blue swimming pool studded with flea-bitten palm trees. Most of the names on the directory were either illegible or missing completely. There wasn't even a listing for the building manager.

As I was calculating my next move, a huge white convertible, battered, boat-sized, a Buick circa 1965, came flying out of the underground parking garage as if hurled by a medieval catapult. It left the ground as it hit the top of the ramp, came down on all fours, screeched into a left turn on two and blasted away down the street. My fleeting glimpse of the driver told me it was a woman with wild, flaming-red hair and bright, wacky makeup. A sadistic voice that whispered in my ear, *it's her,* made me shudder. That and the Buick's license plate, which read B-O-O-P-S-I-E. I knew beyond all hope that the lunatic in the Buick was my bargain basement barrister.

I ran for the Jag, which I'd parked in front of the building, cranked it up and swung into a full-tilt U-ie, taking off after Boopsie's Buick.

I managed to hit Laurel Canyon Boulevard just in time to see her hang an acute left into the parking lot of a Safeway market. By the time I pulled up beside the big white boat, Boopsie had gone through the doors and into the Safeway.

I got out of the Jag and inspected the car. It was a convertible, all right—irrevocably. No top. I wondered a lot of things, not the least of which was what she planned to do when the rains hit. Everything about the car had seen better days about thirty years ago, and I suspected its owner wasn't much different.

But she was a *lawyer*. Who ever heard of a lawyer driving a beat-up jalopy? Times may be tough for the rest of us, but since when are they tough for lawyers? You lose all your money, you need a bankruptcy lawyer. You can't pay your income tax, you need a tax attorney. You lose your dick in a penis enlargement, you need a malpractice attorney. There's an attorney for everything you lose. Your wife, your kids, your home, your business, your freedom . . . It's never over till the fat lawyer sings.

And speaking of attorneys, Boopsie was heading my way, cradling a shopping bag like it held the infant Jesus. She looked middle-aged and was wearing bright plaid pedal pushers, an oversize shirt, white with a tropical fruit pattern, its tails hanging out, and a pair of red sandals. Her bright red hair was barely tied together with a plaid ribbon which was sadly askew. Her face looked like she'd made it up for a stage show.

"Betty McDougal?" I asked, praying this was all a mistake.

"Yeah . . ." she said, smiling crookedly and exhaling a whiskey breath that made my eyes water. "And who the hell are you?" She was dead drunk.

"You're an attorney?" I just couldn't believe it.

"Who wantsa know . . . ?"

"A *criminal* attorney?"

"If you got a subpoena, drop it on the seat," she slurred. "I'll have my girl call your girl."

"No. I don't have a subpoena. I need an attorney. You were recommended by my friend's brother. Ron Larsen . . . you represented him in a manslaughter case."

"Guilty as a monk in a men's room," she wheezed, punctuating the verdict with a feminine belch and fanning it away before it knocked us both over.

"But you got him off."

"State couldn't prove *malice*. We contended Mr. Larsen did not have intention to cause bodily injury when he mistakenly hit his employer with the lead pipe."

"How do you mistakenly hit someone with a lead pipe?"

"How the fuck do I know? Lucky for Mr. Larsen, justice is blind."

She leaned over and placed her bag on the passenger seat with the utmost care and a musical clinking of whiskey bottles. "You're playing our song," she said to the bag, patted it lovingly, then went around to the driver's side.

"Boopsie ..." I blurted, visions of prison bars dancing in my head, "I need a lawyer."

"Thirty-five an hour," she said, climbing behind the wheel. "Hundred and fifteen up front."

"A hundred and fifteen ... ?"

"First hour, last hour and an hour's security."

"Security?"

"In case you bore me to death," she muttered, making an attempt to get the key in the ignition.

"It's a deal."

"Let's see your money."

I reached into my pocket, pulled out my cash and counted it out. "Eighty-nine bucks," I told her. "Will you take a check for the rest?"

She looked me over and came to a conclusion. "What else you got? How 'bout that watch? That real gold?"

"This was my father's."

"Good. He can't complain if you give it to me."

What could I do? I gave her the watch.

She looked it over, then said "Follow me." But she still couldn't jam her key into the Buick's ignition.

"Let me help ..."

"Don't need any help."

"Okay. Whatever makes you happy."

"Beefeater martinis make me happy. Shit!" She was incapable of getting the key in. "Fuck!" she shouted, loud enough to make everyone in the parking lot turn and look. "Who's been fucking with my goddamn car!"

I reached in, slid the key into the ignition and started the car. "There."

"That don't entitle you to a discount," she warned, threw the car into screeching reverse, then hit the brakes with a lead foot and lurched to a stop.

I was standing there, looking at her with what I'm sure was an expression of profound dismay.

"Well? You comin' or not?" she demanded, unhappily checking her makeup in the rearview mirror.

Boopsie's little one-bedroom apartment was dark and cluttered. It felt like she hadn't opened the blinds in years. No wonder her clothes and makeup were all wrong; it was too dark to see anything. The humidity had built up inside like an unvented bathroom during a long, hot shower. Even the TV screen was fogged up.

I dug a chair out from under a pile of old newspapers and unopened mail while Boopsie bumped and cursed around in the kitchen, looking for some ice and a couple of glasses that didn't need sterilization.

"Clock's running, buster," she said while she rummaged around. "Might as well spill your guts."

I was so hot and sticky I felt like taking off my shirt and boots— but I didn't want to give her any ideas. "I'm being framed by people I don't know for the murder of someone I never met for reasons I can't imagine . . ." I began.

She held up a glass the size of a small pitcher. "One cube or two?" she asked.

Talk about a drop in the ocean. "As many as you can get in there," I answered.

"I like mine dry," she said, filling her glass to the brim with Beefeater's. "You?"

"A touch of vermouth."

"Don't have any vermouth."

"Make mine dry then."

"Hmmnn," she mused, filling my glass as well. "Looks like we have the same taste in martinis."

She handed me the giant glass of gin and drained a third of her own like water. "Hits the spot, don't it?" she sighed, and sunk into an old brown felt sofa. From where I sat I could see the sofa's bottom brushing against the hideous orange shag carpeting.

As Boopsie sunk lower and lower into the cushions, I proceeded to tell her everything I knew about my predicament, from Holman's personal call inviting me to the wedding to James T. Gardner's imminent appearance on *Real Life*.

"How do you know what he'll say?" she finally piped up.

"It's obvious he and Carol—or whatever her name is—set me up."

"If the cops have no evidence except your prints on the rifle, they'll have a fuck of a time getting a grand jury indictment ..."

"What if Gardner implicates me?"

"The press will find you guilty."

"Great."

"But they do that to everyone."

"The press I'm part of doesn't."

"It's Gardner's word against yours. Think a murderer's got an impeccable record of citizenship?"

"You don't think they'll prosecute?"

"Unless they have more than you're telling me."

"Like what?"

"Like a motive ... Like further proof of a conspiracy ... Like ... Excuse me." She climbed out of the sofa. "The thunder mug calls ..." She stumbled off toward the kitchen, stopped, looked a little befuddled.

"I think the bathroom's the other way," I suggested.

"I know that," she huffed, then turned and lurched off.

That was the last I saw of her. She never came out of the bathroom. I wrote a note on an old cocktail napkin saying I'd call if I needed her. I took my father's watch off the counter, then stuck the napkin and a check for twenty-six bucks to her bottle of Beefeater's with a stick of wild cherry bubblegum.

I don't know if Boopsie was too drunk to know what she was talking about or if she'll even remember me if I call her again. I just hope she's right and the whole thing goes away. If it doesn't, I have Shrike's parting words reverberating over and over again in my mind: "Remember, Marx, it's never over till the fat lawyer sings."

On the radio coming back from the Valley the weatherman predicts

the imminent rainstorm may last as long as a week. Bad news when
you consider that rain in this town turns the streets to torrents and
the freeways to lakes. And, because fires have consumed all the
ground cover, the hillsides wash away in lavalike rivers of mud,
taking homes, cars, animals and humans in their beds, waving and
calling "Have a nice day" as they go. The perks of living in Southern California.

Just as I'm pulling into *UP YOURS*, the thick rain clouds burst
with a series of deafening explosions, like giant water balloons
blasted by howitzers. The Deluge begins.

Shrike is out of the office but he's left a message with Rachel—
he's saving the lead in the next edition for the Bert Holman murder
story, as told from the inside by the innocent victim of a vicious
conspiracy. The man is a tower of empathy.

Rachel also tells me I received an urgent call from Samantha
Shelton, who left her beeper number. Within minutes I'm on the
phone with her.

"How well do you know Mitchell P. Gluck?"

"We did that routine."

"Do it again."

"Why?"

"It's crucial."

"I told you, Sam—I don't know the man."

"Can you prove you don't know him?"

"How do you prove you don't know somebody? What's going
on?"

"I just wrapped my interview with James T. Gardner."

"What did he say?"

"He confessed to killing Bert Holman."

"That's appropriate."

"He also said he was hired by Mitchell P. Gluck."

"*Gluck?* Paid him to kill Holman? Jesus, these guys will do anything to win."

"You believe him?"

"Why shouldn't I? People were saying Gluck would kill his own
mother to get Sovereign. Turns out he only had to kill Bert Holman."
What a relief. It's over.

"You really believe Gluck hired Gardner to kill Holman?" she asks again.

"He confessed, didn't he? Why would he lie?"

"Why does anybody lie?"

"Does Gluck know Gardner blew the whistle on him?"

"By now, probably."

"What a bunch."

"Gardner blew the whistle on you, too."

"*What?* What do you mean?"

"He said you were both hired by Gluck."

"*Me?*"

"You were paid fifty thousand dollars apiece. To kill Holman before the Sovereign board voted on the two offers."

"Gardner said *me*?" I still can't compute it.

"You."

"I was paid by Gluck?"

"That's what he said. You just told me you believed him."

"I believed what he said about Gluck."

"Why would he lie about you?"

"Why would he lie? He's a murderer, that's why he'd lie!"

"But why would he implicate *you*?"

"I don't know . . ."

"You've never met Gardner?"

"This is unbelievable."

" 'Unbelievable' isn't good enough."

"What about the cops?"

"You haven't made many friends in the LAPD. They're on your case. You and Gluck."

"Jesus. What else did he say? Who the fuck *is* James T. Gardner?"

"You'll see the interview. One thing comes across pretty clear, though. He's a very ill man. Doesn't look like he's long for this world." In the background I hear someone calling her name. She tells them she'll be right with them, then back to me. "You didn't do it, did you, Albie?"

"Are you crazy? Why would I . . . Look, I've got to get to Gardner and make him tell the truth."

"He's not giving any more interviews."

"I don't want to *interview* him. I want to beat the truth out of him."

"He'd fall apart if you touched him. My guess is they'll get a warrant for your arrest ..."

"Just on Gardner's word? My lawyer doesn't think that's enough."

"Who's your lawyer?"

"You don't know her. She's, uh ... prominent in the Valley."

"Well, I hope she's right." Again, someone calls her name in the background. "Look, I have to get back to the studio and put the show together. I want you to keep in touch with me, okay?"

And she's gone. What does she want from me, I wonder as I agree to stay in touch. She already has her story.

Gluck paid me fifty thousand dollars? Where in the world did Gardner come up with that? I haven't seen fifty thousand in one piece since my first royalty check in 1969.

Given the size and breadth of his ambition, it's not an impossible stretch to believe Mitchell P. Gluck would hire someone to get rid of his rival. God knows it's been done before, by jealous cheerleaders, rising Wiseguys, greedy ice skaters. It isn't the most original way to beat the competition, but it's one of the surest—assuming you don't get caught. But why drag me into it?

The only answer is that whoever is behind this—Gluck, Gardner, "Carol," Ozzie, or someone totally out of the blue—has a serious score to settle with me, something worth going to hell and back for.

It's clear the one thing I absolutely *must* do is confront James T. Gardner face to face. Reluctantly, I look out my office window at the worsening storm. The savage rain, driven by Divine rage, brings an ominous, premature night as it scourges the City of Hubris with the ferocity of a full-on forty day/forty nighter.

And me without an umbrella.

On the drive downtown, pelted by golfball-size raindrops, the Jag was one of a million vertebrae in two endless serpentine spines of red-and-white lights undulating homeward in rush hour madness. The news helicopters were reporting "sig-alerts" (Los Angelese for traffic-snarling accidents) on all the major freeways and thoroughfares. My windshield wipers couldn't move fast enough to keep the glass from turning into a blur. It was like trying to see through Victoria Falls wearing somebody else's eyeglasses. But it didn't matter because nobody else could see, either.

After ninety minutes of commuter water torture I made it downtown. Even then I had to park four blocks away and run through the flooding streets to LA County Jail. Soaked to the bone, water swishing around in my boots, I held a newspaper in front of my face to avoid being recognized by the ubiquitous TV newspack and sloshed to the front reception desk.

The duty sergeant who, fortunately, was distracted enough that he didn't recognize my name responded to my press card with the information that Gardner had been fatigued by his interview and collapsed after the TV crew left. He had been taken to the prison infirmary where his condition was termed "guarded."

So there I was, sodden, foiled and befuddled, hiding from a pack of ravenous reporters and looking for a way to sneak into the infirmary, when I bumped into Lieutenant Joseph Danno, steaming full speed ahead toward the elevator. I guessed he was rushing to the side of his star murderer before the poor man could answer the final roll call.

"What are *you* doing here?" the human billiard ball jibed through a tight little smirk. "Checking out your new digs?"

"Give me ten minutes with Gardner and I'll straighten everything out, Danno."

"Sorry. Your friend may not have ten minutes."

"You can't take this anywhere on an accusation . . ."

" 'Accusation?' Give me some credit, pal. When I come for you, I'll have enough evidence to fry you twice over."

"There is no evidence . . ."

"Carelessness is not a virtue in the murder business."

"Wait a minute, Danno—"

"Lawyer, Marx. The word is lawyer."

And he's into the elevator.

What "evidence"? What had he found to pull me deeper into the web? I was starting to feel like a fly with its wings pulled off, buzzing around in feverish, helpless circles. Now there was *evidence.*

Or was he gaslighting me? Setting me up for a sucker punch? I couldn't stand around and wait till I got hit to find out. Since this nightmare started I've been the last link in the information chain. It's time I unearthed something, anything, before everyone else.

I was at the pay phone by the front entrance, trying to get Boopsie on the phone, when I spotted him. The fat TV reporter, the idiot who nearly got run over when he jumped on my cab last night as I fled the press at the Hollywood police precinct. He was about five feet away from me, hiding behind a newspaper, trying to eavesdrop on my telephone conversation.

Since Boopsie wouldn't or couldn't answer, I decided to give fatso something to think about, other than me.

"That's unbelievable!" I exclaimed into the phone. Then, in a confidential voice loud enough for him to hear, "Does anybody else know about it? No? You're absolutely sure? This is sensational. Mr. Rogers? Wow. The nice guy from the neighborhood? Who talks to the kids on TV? Man, that is sick. How many? Maybe a hundred? He sexually abused a hundred kids who came to see him backstage? Sworn affidavits? I'm devastated . . ."

I glanced over to where the fat man was standing. He wasn't there anymore. He was on the move. He had dropped his newspaper and was flogging his fat ass at top speed across the lobby to spread the wonderful news about Mr. Rogers. Paul Revere from hell.

Before anyone else in the media herd could become alerted to my presence, I slipped out the front door and made a run for it.

And what a run it was. LA is basically a desert, coaxed to life with water from other people's rivers. The sewer and drainage systems are unequipped to handle large volumes of water, so when it rains prolifically like this, everything backs up and normal streets become torrents before you can say *Yes, We Have No Flood Insurance.*

By the time I squished my way into the Jag I looked like a poodle wet down with a fire hose, a pathetic if not downright humiliating sight. But I was thankful to be out of the rain.

My gratitude lasted until I turned the key in the ignition. Nothing. Dead. My next set of options were: get out and run around in the monsoon, looking for a gas station or pay phone to call the AAA; try taking a peek under the hood to see if there was something simple, and I mean *simple*, I could do to get the thing started; or, sit in the car and wait for the rain to stop, even if it lasted a week.

I was halfway under the hood, peering incomprehensibly into the oil and grime, when a black limousine cruised up beside me. The front passenger window rolled down and the driver peered over at me.

"Need a hand?"

"How about a lift to a gas station?" I asked, shouting over the din of the deluge.

"Get in the back," he replied.

I smashed the Jag's bonnet down and dove into the rear of the limousine. Out of the rain.

But not alone.

The man sitting beside me in the backseat didn't change expression as I jumped in, soaking wet. His polished indifference made me feel like a slimy fish flopping around on the rich teak deck of some millionaire's yacht.

I had no idea who he was but he had the look of a man who was incapable of hearing the word "no" for an answer. Somewhere between forty and fifty, he was conservatively dressed in a double-breasted blue suit with white pin stripes. He wore round, wire-framed spectacles, had close-cropped salt-and-pepper hair and flat brown eyes that bragged they'd seen more than their share of brutality.

"Go," he commanded the driver impatiently, then looked at me as if inspecting a piece of potentially rotten fruit and said, "You're a piece of work."

"The first garage you come to will be fine," I told the driver, ignoring the genteel goon.

"Richard Sampson," he said by way of introduction. The rain was doing a Gene Krupa on the roof. "We need to have a chat."

"I hope you didn't fuck with my car," I warned.

"Very tough."

"Tough enough."

"I'm afraid you'll have to listen to me," Sampson said matter-of-factly, as if I were his kid or something.

"If you guys pulled the wires on my starter I'm gonna be very pissed off."

The driver smiled sardonically and shook his head as beside me, in one swift, veteran sweep, Sampson reached under his jacket, took out a .357 magnum, cocked the hammer and shoved it in my face. "If I weren't representing someone who abhors violence, I'd make a bloody mess in here," he said, too calm to be bluffing. Then, to the driver, "Run the tape."

The man hit a button on the dashboard and the screen of a TV monitor facing us from a built-in walnut cabinet lit up with test pattern color bars. "We're about to see your friend, James T. Gardner," Sampson told me, releasing the hammer and resting the gun in his lap.

Knowing it had just been taped and wouldn't be shown on the air till an hour from now, I asked, "How did you get this?"

"Connections."

The superimposed label on the uncut editor's version of the tape read: *REAL LIFE: CAMERA ONE: JAMES T. GARDNER INTERVIEW.*

Gardner was gray-faced, emaciated, losing his hair. The few wisps that hadn't fallen out were sticking up at odd angles, as if held in position by some field of static with a macabre sense of humor. His dull brown eyes were ringed by dark circles of tired flesh. He was seated at a table in a small holding room, wearing prison clothes, his thin hands clasped loosely in front of him. His condition had deteriorated dramatically in the thirty or so hours since I'd seen him, when he handed me the rifle after blowing Bert Holman's brains out.

Two burly prison guards stood behind him—as if the cadaverous bag of bones looking into the camera were in any condition to hurt anyone. Apparently, Camera One was focused on Gardner while Samantha Shelton's disembodied voice conducted the interview.

The first thing she said was, "We're going to try to do this without editing, James. Since this is the first time we're talking to you, some of the questions will be basic. We may not need them later. Are you ready?"

Gardner looked at the camera and nodded solemnly.

"Don't look into the camera," she instructed. "Look at me."

He adjusted his gaze and nodded again.

"Ready?" Sam said, apparently addressing the camera crew.

Someone answered, "Anytime you are."

Camera One held a medium shot of Gardner.

SAM: What is your full name?

GARDNER: James T. Gardner.

SAM: Where do you currently live?

GARDNER: 2343 Buena Vista Road. That's in Pasadena.

SAM: Have you ever been in prison before?

GARDNER: Yes.

SAM: For what?

GARDNER: Assault.

SAM: Who did you assault?

GARDNER: Which time?

SAM: How many times were there?

GARDNER: First time was my mother.

SAM: Your mother. When was that?

GARDNER: Maybe . . . around eighteen.

SAM: And you're . . . how old now?

GARDNER: Thirty-nine.

SAM: What did you do to your mother?

GARDNER: Slapped her. Couple times.

SAM: Did you hurt her? Did you hurt your mother?

GARDNER: Not too bad.

SAM: Who else did you assault?

GARDNER: My ex-wife. Wasn't ex at the time, though.

SAM: Your mother pressed charges against you?

GARDNER: We never got along.

SAM: Apparently not. We'll get back to this in a moment. You have confessed to murdering Bert Holman, the television producer, is that correct?

GARDNER: Yes.

SAM: How did you kill him?

GARDNER: Shot him with a thirty-aught-six game rifle.

SAM: Where did you shoot him?

GARDNER: What part of the body?

SAM: What part of the body and in what location?

GARDNER: The head. In the right temple.

SAM: I mean, where? Where were you when the shooting occurred?

GARDNER: Oh. He was in his house, I was out in the garden.

SAM: You're a marksman?

GARDNER: Been shooting since I was a kid.

SAM: What was Bert Holman doing when you fired the gun?

GARDNER: He just got married. I had a spot picked out on the lawn where I could see the ceremony inside. When the little guy pronounced them man and wife, I fired a round. I think it blew his head open.

SAM: Did you know Bert Holman?

GARDNER: No.

SAM: Why did you kill him?

GARDNER: For money.

SAM: You had nothing personal against him?

GARDNER: Nope.

SAM: No one close to you—family, friends—knew Bert Holman or had something against him?

GARDNER: No.

SAM: What do you mean, you killed him for money?

GARDNER: It was a job. I got hired to do it.

SAM: You're not a hit man, are you?

GARDNER: Not until now. I was hurting for money. I put out word I would do anything.

SAM: I'm anxious to know, along with everyone else, who hired you to kill Bert Holman.

GARDNER: A man named Mitchell P. Gluck.

There is a collective gasp off-camera. This is the first time anyone has heard this. A muffled ruckus ensues, people moving about, in and out of the room, doors opening and closing. After at least a minute of this, a voice off-camera says, "Sam, can we pick it up from the last question?"

SAM: Okay ... James. Tell me again—who hired you to kill Bert Holman?

GARDNER: Mitchell P. Gluck.

SAM: The Mitchell P. Gluck who owns Gluck International, the worldwide media company?

GARDNER: Yes.

SAM: Why?

GARDNER: Why what? Why did he want me to kill Holman? I didn't ask and he didn't tell me.

SAM: You have no idea why Mitchell P. Gluck hired you—if you're telling the truth—and I want to make it clear to our audience that we have no way of knowing if you're telling the truth—

GARDNER: Why should it matter? Gluck wanted Holman dead and paid me to do it. You want to know why, ask Gluck.

SAM: How much did he pay you?

GARDNER: Fifty grand.

SAM: Fifty thousand dollars? Cash? Check? Money order?

GARDNER: Cash.

SAM: Did Gluck personally engage you?

GARDNER: I talked to him a couple of times on the phone.

SAM: How did you know it was Mitchell P. Gluck?

GARDNER: I wouldn't do it 'les I knew who I was working for.

SAM: But how did you know it was Mitchell P. Gluck on the phone?

GARDNER: We met once. His bodyguard handed me twenty-five thousand in hundred dollar bills. Gluck said the other half would come when I finished the job. He's a big shot. Got a lot to lose if I crossed him. I believed he would pay.

SAM: Why *are* you crossing him?

GARDNER: Because I got caught, so it don't matter no more. I just want to tell the truth.

SAM: Who caught you? Albie Marx?

GARDNER: No. He supplied the gun.

There's a long silence on the tape as Gardner looks steadfastly in Sam's direction.

Even though she told me he said this, it's staggering to see and hear it straight from the murderer's mouth.

After a few seconds, Sam clears her throat and picks up again.

SAM: Albie Marx, the sixties activist, supplied the gun?

GARDNER: Is he sixty?

SAM: He's a writer and activist *from* the sixties.

GARDNER: Right.

SAM: Why did he supply the gun?

GARDNER: I guess he needed the money, too.

SAM: But why Albie Marx?

GARDNER: I don't know. I was told he'd be a wedding guest and deliver the gun.

SAM: How much was he paid?

GARDNER: Same as me. I was told.

SAM: Fifty thousand?

GARDNER: Correct.

SAM: Mitchell P. Gluck hired Albie Marx, too?

GARDNER: That's what I was given to believe.

"Okay, stop it," Sampson ordered the limousine driver. The tape stopped. My body was shaking. It may have been a chill from my wet clothes but I doubt it.

Sampson casually pointed his gun at me. "Explain this confession to me."

"What is this? Who are you?"

"I'm a friend of Mr. Gluck. What do you and Gardner want? This some kind of weird blackmail number?"

"I don't know Gardner. Whatever he's doing to Gluck, he's doing to me."

"Mitchell P. Gluck did not pay Gardner—or you—to kill Bert Holman. Mitchell P. Gluck is one of America's most successful businessman. He doesn't whack the competition. This story you guys cooked up has damaged Mr. Gluck's reputation, even though he's completely innocent. That's got to be remedied."

"I don't give a shit about Gluck's reputation. Gardner's screwing up *my* life. And I don't know why."

"I don't accept that."

"You don't accept what?"

"I'm telling you to clear Mr. Gluck and do it fast, before this gets legs and people start to believe it. Admit you and Gardner killed Holman."

"Who the hell are you to give me an ultimatum?"

"This show's gonna hit the airwaves in less than an hour. The shit *will* hit the fan. Do yourself a favor and confess. You and your friend never saw Mr. Gluck, never met him, never talked to him, never got hired by him to do anything for any amount of money.''

"You're asking me to confess to a murder? If I would do that, why would I be afraid of you?''

"Because in the justice system you always have a chance. With me, it's final.'' He adjusted his glasses with a thick forefinger, then glared at me through the lenses. "Is that a good enough reason for you?''

I didn't say so, but to myself I had to admit he made sense. Sick, twisted, unwelcome sense but, at this point, with a gun in my kisser, it was the only sense there was.

When we got back to the Jag, the driver reconnected my starter wires, then they drove off in the rain with a final warning, giving me twenty-four hours to exonerate Gluck and take the rap myself, or prove to the cops that someone else hired Gardner.

Sampson left me a number to call if I had any questions. I had questions, all right, but I knew there was only one answer: play ball or die.

Twenty-four hours to solve the puzzle, after which I could choose between a bullet in the head or a pellet in the gas chamber. And if I missed out on both of those, there was always the possibility of stomach cancer.

My options were starting to kill me.

I'm at The Rock, where I came straight from downtown, to meditate on my problems under the merciful eye of the God of Tequila, who makes me forget the forgettable and remember the memorable. Escape and nostalgia, don't fail me now.

I've tried Boopsie three times in the last hour from the pay phone. No answer, no machine. I guess she's out. Or out cold. I tried Shrike's number, to tell him the Boopsie thing isn't working. He's out, too.

I sat and watched *Real Life* with Leon, on the bar TV. The full interview with Sam and Gardner was more official, more damning than the unedited tape I saw in the limo. It made me sick to see it again. My stomach tied itself up in the kind of old-fashioned knot that used to inspire my mother to come charging out of the bathroom, waving her failure-proof red enema bag.

Even Leon said Gardner looked and sounded believable. Which led to another round of drinks but no easing up of the psychic noose. I'm sure I've been this low before—but at least I was able to get myself into an alcoholic stupor.

Leon, ever the optimist, has a fresh round of Cuervo and Corona waiting for me when I come back from trying to reach Shrike and Boopsie one more time.

"I might have to rent a kayak to get home tonight," I speculate, looking out at the rain which hasn't stopped pounding the city.

"Doesn't your kid live in Benedict Canyon?" Leon asks.

"Yeah. Why?"

"Supposedly having mudslides up there. Some people being evacuated."

"Has it been raining that long?" Am I losing track of time, too?

"You know how the canyons are. All those houses on stilts."

"My son's in a house on stilts."

"I wouldn't live in one of those."

"Who knows? Maybe this whole hopeless city will slide into the ocean. Solve some of my problems . . ."

"That's negative," Leon admonishes as the phone behind the bar rings. "You say things like that, you give power to negative thoughts."

Negative thoughts? What's to be negative about? I should be throwing a party, not worrying. A California bash for positivity purists, celebrating the Oneness of the universe, or the Harmonic Convergence . . .

I like Leon, but he's been here too long. Spewing the mush-brained psychobabble that makes this place a paradise for Ozzie Baba and legions of new-age con artists. Which reminds me, I have to grab the little guru and ask him point blank about Jeannie Locke . . .

Leon hands the phone over the bar. "For you."

I'm almost afraid to answer it. Ooops—more negative thinking. Gotta be positive. Maybe it's not bad. My house washed down onto Sunset Boulevard—but I wasn't in it. Leon would find a way to turn that into good news. And he'd be right, wouldn't he?

"Albie? It's Sam. I thought you might be there. How are you?"

"I'd be suicidal if I thought it would help." *Now there's a positive thought.*

"You saw the show."

"Twice."

"I want you to know I don't believe him."

"That'll impress a judge."

"I feel terrible about what's happening to you. I hope you don't think I'm responsible . . ."

"As long as you get your ratings."

"That's not fair."

"Fair? What's fair?"

"I want to help you, Albie. What are you doing now? Besides getting drunk."

"Besides getting drunk?" I ask, unable to think of anything else a sane person would do in my place. "Let's see . . . I was about to make a list of all the times I've been framed, persecuted, beaten, clubbed, shot at, or dumped, then rank them on a pain scale of one to ten . . ."

"Why don't you come over here and we can talk."

"Over there? Where's there? Is there a there there?"

"I'm in Malibu."

"Malibu?"

"Can you drive?"

"No, but I can paddle . . ."

"If you've had too much to drink I don't want you to try it."

"There's no such thing as too much to drink. If I had too little to drink, I'd be afraid to try it. What's the address? Where are you?"

She gives me her address. She's on the Pacific Coast Highway, on the beach overlooking the ocean. Usually, the Pacific Coast Highway is the first to go when it rains like this. The mudslides come down, wipe out the highway, then cross over and plow on through the homes lining the road on the beach side. People are so used to invading mud they just leave their doors open and let it come through. It wrecks the house and takes their expensive antiques and carpets out to the ocean. A friend of mine said, "You have to be rich to tolerate that kind of abuse. Thank God they can afford it."

Actually, they just call Allstate when the rain starts and a couple of weeks later a check comes through for the damage. A quaint California ritual. But don't feel sorry for the insurance companies. With premiums for flood, fire, theft, mud, and earthquakes, they find a way to keep making a profit. As long as they beat us three out of five, they're ahead of the game.

I guess I should celebrate. I made it to Sam's without getting washed off the road or crushed under some skidding truck hauling nuclear waste to Mexico.

The hot, humid day that gave birth to this storm has by now given way to a cold, rainy night, an atmosphere that gets under your clothes, your skin, your emotions. I'm feeling like Mother Nature's battered child.

I park in front of Sam's house, pull my jean jacket up over my head and run for her front gate, which opens into a little courtyard. Floodlights mounted on the corner eaves of the house light up the driving rain, giving it the quality of long, twisting needles, stabbing the earth with brutal wrath.

Tramping through the rising waters I make it to the vestibule and ring the front bell. When she opens the door I have to hold myself back from fainting into her arms. Good thing for her real men don't faint.

"God, you're soaked . . ."

"Been working on it since this afternoon," I tell her, shivering from head to toe.

"Take off your shoes and come with me."

I gratefully obey, like a stray dog finally allowed into someone's warm house. She's wearing baggy work-out clothes that advertise a state of mellow remove yet hint at exciting curves beneath. Unfortunately, I'm too depressed and not drunk enough to grab her right here and pull her into my arms.

I follow her through a comfy, spacious living room done in muted afghans and kilims, warm candlelight, large, plush sofas and chairs, tasteful antiques, pre-Columbian pottery.

One entire wall of the room is a huge, river rock fireplace where tree-size logs are fiercely burning away. The wall opposite the fireplace is all glass and faces out to the sand and beyond, to the ocean. Out there, in the elemental chaos, the frenzied surf pounds the beach, and even in the darkness I see white breakers snapping off, one after the other, first crashing with a full, heavy roar, then hissing their way onto shore.

"You can take off those clothes in here," she says, leading me into a guest room done in simple but tasteful patterns. "I'll get you some dry things."

"Can you help with these boots?"

I flop down on the bed and she grabs hold of the heel and toe of first one boot, then the other, tugging them off with erotic little grunts of exertion.

"Need help with the rest?" she asks.

Some character flaw, maybe the same one that tells a man he isn't supposed to cry, makes me say no. A last-gasp effort at maintaining the appearance of macho strength and independence in the face of crushing misfortune. She shrugs and leaves the room, returning to bring me a clean, dry set of work-out gear like the stuff she's wearing.

I gratefully change out of my wet, constricting clothing and, a few minutes later, we're sitting among large, soft pillows in front of the fire, sipping rich amber brandy from crystal snifters.

The brandy floods my insides with liberating tentacles of warmth. Combines with the deep relief of being safe, here, in the company of this beautiful woman . . . could she be one of Leonard Cohen's "Sisters of Mercy"?

I feel suddenly vulnerable, as if my guard has been disengaged. And, with each passing moment, I feel less inclined to fight against it. So I'm a man and I'm vulnerable, what is that, against the law? Who's going to arrest me, the Virility Police? The Macho Squad?

"Whose clothes are these?" I ask, surprised at how well they fit.

"My ex-husband's. He keeps meaning to come and collect them . . ."

"Ex-husband. Who in his right mind would be your ex-husband?"

"I never went for men in their right mind."

"Did he split? Did you kick him out? Am I getting too personal?"

"You've been married before, haven't you?"

"Who hasn't?"

"More brandy?"

"Always more brandy. The quickest way to a man's heart is through his liver."

"I'll keep that in mind."

She refills our snifters. "I asked him to leave. It wasn't working ..."

"Sorry ..."

"Nothing to be sorry about. If he were here, *you* wouldn't be."

She smiles. Or should I say, she shines. Even without the candlelight she would shine. I can see her gleaming inside, lighting up. I want to touch that light, to tell her I know it's there and to share it ...

Shit. I must be getting really drunk, thinking like an old romantic.

"I thought you didn't drink ..."

"Not during business hours."

"This isn't business?"

"No. Not that I don't want to hear your story ..."

"Why are you so interested?"

"You interest me."

"Me? Why me?"

"Do you want to tell me about it or not?"

Mobilized by the brandy, I relate the saga, from beginning to end ... The piece for *UP YOURS* about Ozzie Baba ... the invitation from Holman to meet Ozzie at the wedding ... Adele Smith and the limo ... Carol ... Bambi Friedman ... spotting Gardner ... the shooting ... Danno, his so-called evidence ... the confrontation with Gluck's man ... I even called up the looming specter of my biopsy ...

I'm so ripped by the time the whole rotten mess is out on the table, I just want to get my arms around her and not let her go till they come for me ... Sister of mercy ...

She's saying something ... What is she saying ... ?

"... find out what kind of evidence the police have ..."

The light dancing in her eyes, the deep luster of her skin ... Her words are reeling through my mind, brushing against meanings, barely connecting ...

"... want to talk to Gardner again, privately, see if I can get him to tell me why ..."

She's so concerned ... why does she care so much ... why did she pick me ...?

"... why he would finger you if he was hired by Gluck ..."

Sam ... so soft ... She wants me to believe it's all going to be all right ... She has a deep place for me, something that existed before we met ... I don't know why I interest her now ... Maybe the old me, the dashing darling of the Revolution ... but now ... so much older and poorer in spirit ...

I lean forward and kiss her. She kisses me back. Only our lips are touching. Her scent is sweet, electrifying, essence of spontaneous sex ...

The ocean crashes. High tide. Senses on the verge. The ebb, the flow, the everlasting givingness, giving us knowledge that there's more, that the world is bigger, wilder, more wondrous ...

She lies back on the pillows ... I press against her ... she holds me ... our mouths come together again, strong, hard ...

Does she know what she's doing? She thinks she knows me. But does she want to know my unknown ... face my unfaced ...?

This is where I've always stopped, isn't it, at the pain of the truth—because to admit I wanted more than I got is to admit that all my bravado and defiance was an act, that in my heart I secreted away passion for life ...

Now, faced with terrible possibilities, I don't want to give up, I want to keep on ... I want to know this woman, to be part of the air around her ... But what can I offer? The worship of an exhausted man? She needs more. More than a man who knows there's so much he should have found out but didn't, that there was nothing he could learn anymore ...

And then, he saw the Light again. Her Light. The Light of a Woman. The Light that says, live ...

Her body is long, taut yet fulsome ... her skin firm, smooth, filled with senses ... her breasts full, nipples straight, the curve of her hip, the ever so slight round of her stomach ... wonder of wonders ...

Naked, we two, before the fire, before each other ... my hand gripping hers, tightly as she moves on top of me, taking me inside her ... my heart rushing to hers, rising with passion ...

And I feel this can't be, that this hunger is something you satisfied on the spur of the moment when you were young, before the Age of Responsibility, when there were no ramifications to anything because all of time was stretched out in front of you and there were no wrong turns, only turns, because direction was not as important as movement itself . . .

Only now with the clarity of hindsight, near the top of the climb, can you see how you took the scenic route . . . And you wonder if it's better that way because what does it mean, after all, to make it all the way to the top? What's at the top? A pat on the back from God?

With her, tonight, my hand, traveling down her spine, from her neck to the small of her back, feels no age, only vitality, immortality . . . I move inside her, the rhythm becomes fury, we see it all in each other's eyes as we reach up together, circle the world as one . . .

A woman teaches a man to integrate into the natural rhythms of life . . . to avoid the long summer followed by hard, short winter and painful death . . . a time for all things, an equality to all seasons . . . A man will burn out his flame without a woman . . . He needs her to feed the fire . . . Not women, but a woman . . .

All these things I try not to think about because they seem so distant, so unattainable, but they are there always, reminding me, in every love song, every romantic movie, every glimpse of unsuspecting lovers holding hands, feeling the same wind, hearing the same ocean, seeing the same stars . . .

Everyone who has realized that this is it . . . not more, not again, not somewhere else, some other time . . . this is it . . . and that's why it hurts so bad because we can never get it to be what we really want it to be and we know there won't be another chance.

DAY THREE
TUESDAY, MARCH 14

⟨~⟩

The gray light insinuates itself into my consciousness. My eyes open me. Where am I?

In her bed. Alone.

Oh, my head. Everything hurts. Have to stop drinking. Body can't take the abuse it used to. This body isn't my partner anymore, it's my competetion. Challenging to see how much I can dish out, how much I can take. It's getting to be less and less.

She must have slipped out of bed. It's so soft and warm and fluffy ... I could stay in this bed for a decade or two.

Outside, the rain, showing no evidence of relenting, is filling the ocean to overflow, pushing the tide to within feet of the glass bedroom wall. Maybe Sam and I will be swept away in this house together, get housewrecked on some island with no supermarkets, no condos, no people, foraging for wild berries and living on lust. And maybe today won't be as ugly as yesterday—but don't bet on it.

A jarring blast of Jimi Hendrix snaps me to attention—the "Star Spangled Banner," Woodstock style.

"I told you, Hendrix jump-starts my day," she says brightly, ap-

pearing in the bedroom doorway, fresh and clean in a white terry-
cloth robe. "How do you feel?"

"Like twenty-five," I answer, as the sight of her suddenly rallies
the old bones. I could start all over again.

"You felt like twenty-five last night, let me tell you. Do you
remember last night?"

"I remember exactly . . . exactly how you feel under that robe."

"You said such beautiful things . . ."

"I did?"

"Are you surprised?"

"I guess I was saying what was on my mind."

"You were soulful . . ."

"I was?"

"You were drunk." She comes to the side of the bed.

"Come here." I grab her by the lapels of the robe and pull her
down beside me. "God, you smell like . . . wildflowers on a wind-
whipped ocean day."

She checks into my eyes with her twin blue lasers. "Are you
really looking for one woman?"

"Did I say that?"

"Does drinking bring out the truth in you?"

"Usually." Her eyes move off mine, look beyond me. "What?"
I ask.

"Nothing."

"Not nothing. Something. Tell me."

"I really like you, Albie . . ."

"But . . . ?"

"No but."

"I like you, too. I like your strength and intelligence. I feel like
I'm with a real person."

"But you hate what I do. You hate that I call myself a journalist."

"It's not you, it's your medium I have problems with. The interac-
tion between the audience and the vehicle that brings out the lowest
common denominator. But that's becoming true of all journalism.
From what I've seen, you do what you do as consciously and morally
as you can. What else is there? That's all I can do. All any of us
can do."

"But you think I'm the type who will do anything for my career. Anything to beat the competition."

"No, I don't. I think you'll go as far as your conscience will allow and no farther. I believe that."

"How far do you think my conscience will let me go?"

"To the edge. Wherever that is."

"The edge is where we are now. The police believe you're involved in Bert's murder. Depending on what it hears and sees next, the rest of the world will decide what it thinks. The next twenty-four to forty-eight hours are critical ..."

"What do you suggest I do?"

"Come on the show and defend yourself."

"How? Say what? I was framed? Who will believe me?"

"You have no choice."

"God. To be judged in public ... no defense, no protection ..."

"I agree. We—the media—have gotten too powerful. But I can't turn the tide, no one can. I have to go with it and try to bring out the best in a flawed system. What really scares me is the desperate power struggle going on now. The fight for Sovereign is just the first wave. More and more of the media is coming under the control of fewer and fewer people. Most of them don't have a conscience. They do whatever it takes to win. They take no prisoners."

"I guess you've known a few of them ..."

"I was married to one. Michael Whitehead."

"You were married to Michael Whitehead?"

"We all make mistakes. Do you know him?"

"I know who he is. Who doesn't? The most powerful agent in the business. The head of BMA."

"Business, Management, Artistry. In that order, unfortunately. People who know call them BM for short."

"Funny, but I can picture you a lot easier with Michael Whitehead than I can with me."

"Don't. Michael was a learning experience for me. A potent one."

"Married to Michael Whitehead ... worked for Bert Holman ... How did you manage to stay so sweet and unaffected?"

"You think I'm sweet and unaffected?'"

"Don't tell me you're not."

"Okay, I won't."

"You asked if I'm looking for one woman. What are you looking for?"

"One man. One very good man."

"How good?"

"Not too good . . ."

I kiss her and she winds herself around me.

"Don't take this the wrong way, Albie, but I see a . . . a ragged nobility in you. Like a banner still waving after the bloodiest battle. I like it. It's got character."

"I'm not insulted. I'd wave for you any day, baby."

We kiss again and roll around on the bed . . . then she's on her stomach and I'm on top of her. I'm so hard it hurts, pressing myself against her bottom.

"Make love to me . . ."

"Where?"

"Anywhere you want."

"How about everywhere?"

"Make love to me everywhere."

"Are you sure?"

"Yes. Don't leave anything out."

It's an amazing thing, isn't it, when a fantasy becomes a reality. There are times when it's happened in the past where I've had the feeling, *this isn't as great as I thought it would be* or, *I should have wanted more.*

One good thing about getting older—you have a greater appreciation for moments like this. And boy, did I appreciate it. I appreciated it better than I've ever appreciated it before.

We made love everywhere.

Right there in the bed.

"I'll make some coffee," she says, switching on the TV.

"TV? Now?"

"You can't hide from TV, Albie. It's our on-ramp to the information highway."

"I'd rather live in the Dark Ages."

One of the local news shows is running up-to-the-minute footage of floods, mudslides and road washouts. "How would we know what doesn't exist anymore?" she asks, disappearing down the hall to the kitchen.

My attention is suddenly mugged by pictures from Benedict Canyon, where my son lives in his recently purchased (against my advice) hillside home on stilts. A number of houses have collapsed and slid down their hills. Others are being evacuated. I can't tell if Freedom's is among them. More anxiety for my current overload ...

It's time to spring into action, Marx. Time to get up and go save your life ...

The news scene shifts to the front lawn of Mitchell P. Gluck's Bel-Air estate, where the besieged mogul, standing under an umbrella between two bodyguards, is making a statement to a rain-soaked press corps.

"... an outrageous lie by some person I have never seen or spoken to in my life. This is a bold attempt to destroy me and my reputation without the slightest shred of evidence or proof."

"Go, Mitch! Attaway, Mitch!" I shout, bringing a wide-eyed Sam bouncing back into the room.

Gluck is a short, meticulous, sinewy person. He appears to be in perfect physical condition, as if he's planning to live forever. He wears the modern mogul uniform of perfectly pressed jeans, Ralph Lauren Polo shirt, Versace windbreaker and multiple face-lifts. At the moment he's radiating torrid indignation, the tendons standing out on his neck.

"Before you convict me in the eyes of the public, I suggest you consider the source of this accusation—a lifetime petty crook. A coward who beat his own mother. Do you seriously believe I would personally engage this man? To commit murder? I wouldn't engage him as a janitor. This whole affair is totally ludicrous ..."

Like they were cued, the newspeople suddenly begin shouting incriminating questions at Gluck, like *"Where did you first meet Gardner?"* and *"Who had the idea to bring in Albie Marx?"* Poking sharp verbal sticks through the slicing rain into his I'm-so-perfect veneer.

Gluck gestures he's not taking questions. One of the reporters suddenly bursts out of the pack and thrusts his microphone into Gluck's face.

"How much did you pay Albie Marx to supply the gun?" he screams.

One of Gluck's bodyguards, playing it safe, tackles the man, the camera skews crazy and the press suddenly attacks, triggering a melee. The press and the bodyguards go at it with abandon, sliding and wrestling around in the mud, while a terminally agitated Mitchell P. Gluck makes a considerably less dignified exit than he'd planned.

"No way he hired Gardner," I tell Sam. "Not him."

"You don't think so?" she asks. "Who did?"

"Maybe nobody. Maybe Gardner killed Holman on his own, knowing someone like you would come along and pay him a fortune to confess to the world."

"I doubt it. Where would he spend the money? In the gas chamber? And why go to all the trouble of involving you? And why the girl?"

"I don't know, I don't know . . ." My pounding head suddenly reminds me I have a killer hangover. "The only people who seem to be making out from all this are Bert's widow and her portable guru. Who, incidentally, never liked me to begin with."

"You don't think Ozzie Baba . . ."

"I think Ozzie Baba would consign his own mother to hell if she fucked with his godliness."

"Did you fuck with his godliness?"

"No, but he's worried I might."

"Really? Does he have something to hide?"

"What do you think?"

"I think if people had nothing to hide, I'd be out of a job."

"I rest my case."

The TV news switches from the fight at Gluck's to a new location. Standing in front of KCET, the Los Angeles public television studios, is the fat reporter who was eavesdropping on my imaginary phone conversation at LA County Jail yesterday.

". . . Officials at KCET have refused to comment, but according to reliable sources, hundreds of children have testified to sexual intimacies performed on them by Mr. Rogers . . ."

"Mr. Rogers?" Sam says, astonished. "That sweet little man from the neighborhood?"

". . . Stay tuned to Eyewitness News for all the fast-breaking developments in this major story of sexual abuse."

I can't take it. I snap off the television.

"That's insane," I mutter. I'm about to explain how the fat reporter got the story when Sam's beeper goes off.

She quickly checks the number readout. "My office."

She grabs the phone, dials, gets her irascible producer, Harry Carruthers, on the line. She listens a few moments, then tells him she'll be there soon and hangs up.

"The good news is," she says, unable to contain her delight, "we just got the overnight ratings. We not only killed in our time slot, we set a record. A fifty-four share. Seventy million viewers."

"That ought to make your new boss happy."

"Sheila? I doubt if it takes more than a pony to make her happy."

"A pony?"

"As in, the intellect of a ten-year-old."

She's obviously not very fond of Bert's widow. "Are you going to tell me the bad news?" I ask.

"Oh, yes. James T. Gardner is in intensive care. He went into a coma last night."

"No . . . What is it? What's wrong with him?"

"You won't believe it . . ."

"Tell me."

"He's got colon cancer. An advanced stage. He's on his way out, Albie."

What could be more ironic? My accuser dying from the same horror that's threatening me. Less than forty-eight hours after Bert Holman's murder and the quicksand gets quicker.

Besides putting a serious damper on any hope of Gardner clearing me, the morbid revelation spurred me to call Dr. Paul Pierson to arrange for my upper endoscopy. His nurse told me to come to room 1575 at Cedars Hospital at ten o'clock Thursday morning. To fast for six to twelve hours before the test. That the doctor would pass a flexible instrument through my mouth and that it would take about thirty minutes. She also told me a local anesthetic would be sprayed into my mouth and throat to calm the gag reflex—*gag!*—and that I would receive a sedative before the endoscope was inserted to help me relax, although I would remain conscious. Then a biopsy forceps would be passed through the endoscope to obtain a tissue specimen. Since I'm going to be an outpatient, she said, I should arrange for transportation home because I'll be drowsy from the sedative.

Just what I needed in the middle of everything else—a cancer party. I thought to myself, if these turn out to be my last moments on earth, thank you God for letting me share them with Sam.

Sam . . . The rain was still waxing biblically when we walked out of the house. I hated to leave her. I kept thinking, what if one of us has an accident in this storm? What if I never see her again? She had an umbrella and we stood under it and kissed as long as we could without running back inside and tearing each other's clothes off . . .

Two mature adults, with a sense of purpose and responsibility. Why do we have to grow up?

And how did this woman, a two-day-old acquaintance, suddenly become a focal point in my life? Am I that desperate for love?

Honestly now—isn't everybody?

Sam said she would have her mole in the LAPD get us every bit of information the police have on Gardner. What else was there to do?

Now I'm in my office at *UP YOURS*, having called the Happiness Foundation and Ozzie Baba's lawyer, Herbert Armstrong, and left messages . . . Bambi Friedman, left a message . . . My son, left a message . . .

In a clear state of pure anxiety (or a pure state of clear anxiety), I'm leafing through Volume 3 of *The Academy Players Guide*, a directory of actors and actresses, published annually by the Screen Actors Guild.

The Player's Guide is divided into five volumes: *Leading Men, Young Leading Men, Leading Women, Ingenues,* and *Juveniles.* There's a black-and-white photograph of each actor and actress listed, accompanied by their talent agency and their agent's name and phone number. Carol claimed to be an actress. Not that I believe it, but she played her role so perfectly . . . It's worth a try, anyway. Better than *hondling* with the cops to let me go through their mug shots.

Shrike pops in to remind me he's saving next week's lead for my first installment of the Bert Holman murder story—and to see if I've made contact with Boopsie yet. Which prompts a frenzied clamoring from my stomach for more Zantac. Once again I proclaim my lack of faith in Boopsie but it still doesn't alter Shrike's attitude—he swears she'll produce in the clutch.

Just what I need—a clutch for Boopsie to produce in.

Back to the *Player's Guide*. Faces staring up at me as I turn the pages. Famous faces: Goldie Hawn . . . Holly Hunter . . . Angelica Huston. Obscure faces: Pat Heaber . . . Joan Hunternick . . . Jennifer Hurt . . .

The rain, in a tantrum, banging its fists against my window, an infuriated, amorphous Rumpelstiltskin.

Stop!

There!

I can hardly believe it—it's her.

The photograph is black and white, so I can't swear to the color of the eyes and the hair of the girl in the picture—but it's her face. And that sly little twinkle in the eyes, the eyes I locked into in the rearview mirror of the limousine . . .

The name beside the picture is Virginia Hurley.

Virginia Hurley. Is Virginia Hurley my Carol?

Virginia Hurley's agent is listed as Marty Wilde of The Marty Wilde Agency, on Sunset Boulevard in Hollywood. Probably one of the hundreds of small talent agencies toiling in the trenches to get parts for no-name clients who leave them for bigger agencies the minute they get a decent role.

I dial the number and ask for Marty Wilde. When the girl asks, "And who may I tell Mr. Wilde is calling?" I tell her I'm Frank Levy, an independent producer casting a medium budget feature and I'd like to meet with Marty and go through his client list.

In Hollywood, nobody questions an individual who calls himself an "independent producer." Out here, everyone is an "independent producer," everyone's trying to get a movie made. There are so many hustlers ("independent producers") that any one of them at any given time stands a chance to hornswoggle some oddball group of investors or even a studio into putting up money for an idea, a script, or a movie, no matter how stupid or badly conceived. In Hollywood, being an "independent producer" requires only a fast mouth and a low handicap in golf.

In the case of Marty Wilde, the rain finally works for me. The girl says that Marty's meeting at Warner's this morning was cancelled "due to Burbank Boulevard being under two feet of water." (You'd think a guy like Marty would swim to Warner's in scuba gear to sell one of his *furshtunkener* clients).

If I can get to Marty's office in half an hour, his girl informs me in her most onerous show biz lingo, "Marty has a window he can fit you into."

Marty also has a hairstyle like Napoleon, I notice as I walk into his office, on the first floor of a tacky but well-kept three-story fifties-style office building on Sunset near Tower Records.

The Marty Wilde Agency consists of Marty Wilde and his secretary, a perfectly formed creature named Melissa. The office is composed of three rooms: a little reception area where you can sit and listen to Melissa's body moving around in her short, tight outfit; a file and work room; and Marty's office, which you get to follow Melissa to as a reward for waiting.

The walls are covered with photos of beautiful young actresses, the type of fresh, young, *Playboy*-quality girls who flock to Hollywood each year to take their shot at becoming Sharon Stone. And for whatever reason, they seem to be flocking to the office of Marty Wilde.

On second look, Marty's Napoleon hairstyle is permanent—probably hasn't seen a comb since Marty first glued it to his head. I judge him to be about forty years old, a hair too young to go totally bald without losing some sense of humor about himself. Or all of it.

"Marty? Frank Levy," I say, shaking hands as he rises from his desk to greet me. Marty's about six feet three inches tall ... wide-shoulders and a gut. He's wearing dark trousers with a silver-buckled belt, navy-blue Italian silk shirt with a small tomato sauce stain over the left pocket ... and tasseled loafers. This is a guy who's really got to be pissed about losing his hair.

"Pleasure to meet you, Frank," he says warmly in a deep, resonant voice, as if I were Darryl Zanuck himself. "Have a seat."

"Thanks." I sit opposite and hand him my business card:

CHALLENGE PRODUCTIONS
Challenge Studios, Hollywood
FRANKLIN I. LEVY, PRES.

It works every time.

"You know my company?" I ask.

"Of course. You'll forgive me if I don't remember the names of your films. I try to stay on top of everything, but you know how it is, there's so much going on . . ."

"We do about five medium-budget pictures a year, three or four million each . . ."

"Uh-huh . . ."

"Action/adventure/sex/suspense stuff for the domestic cassette market and foreign theatrical release . . ."

"Uh-huh . . ."

"Pictures where a name on the cassette box guarantees a return on our basic investment . . ."

"Uh-huh . . ."

"We buy a name, mid-level semi-stars like David Carradine, Beau Bridges, Shannon Tweed, Jennifer Beals. We presell the markets based on the star, then we fund the pictures . . ."

"Uh-huh . . ."

"The star takes about half the above-the-line budget and we go from there. Which is to say, we can't pay too much for supporting players, but we're a legit company with good distribution. We get the movies out there and people see them . . ."

"Uh-huh . . ."

"And we always need beautiful girls."

"You came to the right place, Frank."

"Beautiful girls who can act."

"I never take clients based solely on looks."

"But we also need beautiful girls who can stand around in night club scenes . . ."

"I have girls for that, too . . ."

"Little parts make future starlets."

"I have girls who are starlets already, in their own minds."

"Our investors are wealthy people. They like the glamour of movies. They like to come to the set and watch the filming. Sometimes they fall in love with the actresses. A girl can get lucky."

"I have girls who know how to get lucky."

"Some of our investors are women."

"I have girls who prefer female investors."

"But they have to know how to act."

"My girls give a thousand percent. What's the movie you're casting? You got action, adventure, sex, nightclubs. Any parts? Something a girl can sink her teeth into?"

"You got girls with teeth, right?"

"I got girls who will take their teeth *out* for a part. What are you looking for?"

"It's the role of an undercover agent . . ."

"Uh-huh . . ."

". . . assigned to dispose of a foreign spy, she's disguised as his driver . . ."

"Uh-huh . . ."

"She makes him think she's in love with him . . ."

"Uh-huh . . ."

"Then she kills him during the act of sex . . . at the exact moment he climaxes."

"I have girls who do that for a hobby."

"I was looking through the *Player's Guide* with my casting director. There's a girl who looks perfect for the part . . ."

"What's her name?"

"I hope she's still your client . . ."

"If she's not she will be. Who is she?"

"Her name is Virginia Hurley."

"Not available."

"Excuse me?"

"You wouldn't want her. She's not available. Let me show you some other girls."

"What's wrong with her?"

"Bad attitude. I don't represent her anymore."

"This is a leading role . . ."

"No offense, but I don't care if it's starring opposite Tom Cruise. She's a cunt. I wouldn't let her wash my underwear. I wouldn't fuck her unless she was tied up and caned first. I didn't say that."

"Did you two have a falling out?"

"A falling out? You don't fall out with Virginia. You get pushed out. With both hands. While she's telling you she loves you."

"That's perfect for the part . . ."

"She wouldn't know the truth if it came in her mouth. I didn't say that."

"I have twenty-five grand in the budget for the role. Your commission would be twenty-five hundred . . ."

"I wouldn't say hello to that bitch for less than a hundred grand, Jack."

"Frank."

"Whatever."

"Look, Marty . . . if it's an emotional thing between you two . . ."

"What makes you think it's emotional? I'd like to chain the cunt down and fuck her in the ass till she screams for mercy. I didn't say that."

"Maybe you could just give me her number and I'll call her myself . . ."

"You want her number? 1-800-WHORE, that's her number. How about a blonde for the secret agent? I have a new girl, your investors will love her. Twenty years old, tight as a drum, nipples so hard you could chip a tooth on 'em—and can she act. I mean, this girl is Meryl Streep, without the physical flaws . . ."

"We don't want a blonde . . ."

"She'll dye her hair. What do you want? A redhead? A brunette? A bald spy? She'll shave her hair off. What the hell, she shaves her pussy. I didn't say that."

"I don't know, maybe she'll work. I'll think about it. In the meantime, I'd like to see Virginia Hurley . . ."

"I like you, Frank. I know your company, I love your films even though I can't remember the names. But here's the one thing I have to say about Virginia Hurley: if you're looking to get stroked, fucked and castrated, she's your girl. Leave me out of it.''

"Will you give me her number?''

"I don't know it. Last I saw the bitch she was riding on the back of a Harley-Davidson with some maniac screenwriter, a refugee from the looney bin . . .''

"Norman Devore?''

"You got it, Ace. Now that's a toilet someone forgot to flush. Would you believe he has Michael Whitehead for an agent? I can't figure it out. But he's perfect for Virginia. Jump right in and swim around with the shit.''

"Well, thanks, Marty,'' I say, getting up from my chair. "If I see Virginia I'll give her your regards . . .''

"The only acting that bitch ever did was to cry when her mother died . . .''

"And I'll keep in touch with you on the other roles.''

"She'd have to pay me to shit on her face. I didn't say that.''

I left Marty Wilde simmering in his juices. Disgusting pig that he is, I didn't tell him that I, too, had dealt with Virginia, and could sort of see where he was coming from. I didn't say that.

Virginia Hurley and Norman Devore. Suddenly it clicks. Thinking back to the limo on the way to Holman's wedding, I remember her telling me her ex-boyfriend was a crazy screenwriter. The girl cooked with equal parts fantasy and reality—and I wolfed it all down.

I know I should get some comfort out of knowing I'm a step closer to finding her, but when your only lead is Norman Devore, comfort is the last thing you're likely to get. If Marty Wilde was right and Devore does have Michael Whitehead for an agent, that could make things a lot more uncomfortable. It would bring up a number of questions about Sam, the kind of questions that won't have answers I'll like.

Leaving Marty Wilde's building, I open the umbrella I borrowed from Rachel Receptionist and peek out in both directions. I'm half expecting to see a police car waiting for me, with Lieutenant Joseph Danno and a warrant for my arrest. It's going to happen. It's a matter of time. I want to avoid it as long as I can. I want to get to Virginia before Danno gets to me.

The next leg of my odyssey has to be Norman Devore's place, the haunted mansion above my house. I'll stop home first before tackling Devore, to regroup, check on the animals, the rain damage, my messages, Sam . . .

When I get to the house, Jed and Tank have divided the carport, their shelter from the rain. On one side is Jed with his pile of avocado pits and on the other, Tank with his maimed rodent and lizard collection. He's even left a love offering for me on the front step, a slight piece of gray fur, some whiskers, and two front teeth. As a tableau it's haiku, simple yet eloquent.

Totally out of cat and dog food, I fill up two bowls with Ritz crackers and granola, making a show out of how delicious it looks. When I present the bowls to the animals they look at me with cocked eyes, like: "What? You expect us to *kwell* over crackers and granola?"

Screw them. They'll eat what I have.

And so will I. I scrape the mold off a block of jack cheese and make a sandwich with some roasted red peppers from a jar I didn't know I had and some white bread that isn't all white anymore. Not the best thing for my ailing digestive tract, but, hey, I'm a man, I can take it. God knows it won't get any better in jail.

There are a couple of messages on the machine. Bambi Friedman says she's suffering from root canal, she can't see me until tomorrow. She leaves an address in Franklin Canyon and tells me to come at three o'clock. I shout at the machine that I can't wait until three o'clock tomorrow.

The other message is from Sam. "I'm trying not to worry about you, but I'm losing the battle. I hope you're all right. Call me when you get in. My contact told me Gardner's prints match his story. James T. Gardner is his real name, he's got two convictions for assault. He moved out of his Pasadena address a month ago. Oh, and he's married. The wife hasn't turned up yet. Call me when you get this. I need to hear your voice." Then, in a semi-whisper, "I'm still shaking from this morning. What did you do to me?"

I try calling back, to tell her what I did to her and what I'm going to do to her again. And about my meeting with Marty Wilde, and about Virginia and Norman Devore . . . I feel like I have to make contact with her, to be connected to her, even by a telephone line. But Mr. Important informs me she's out of the office.

My heart sinks.

Don't tell me I'm caught already, that I need to hear her voice, like she says she needs to hear mine. The thought of becoming emotionally dependent makes me want to throw up. It's been so long and it always ends in stomach lining damage. It's like being a trapeze artist, with the incomparable high of flying through the air—without a net. Why do I need a net? Since when do I play it safe? I don't. I'm the guy who never puts on a seat belt. Shit. I'm falling in love without a seat belt. Sounds like a country western tune.

When I get outside, the newest element in the storm, a raging wind, unceremoniously yanks the umbrella out of my hand and takes it off, like a kite, turning sommersaults and rising into the sky, then shooting off in the shifting current, in the direction of the HOLLY-WOOD SIGN two hills to the west. This is some serious shit. Could the world be coming to an end? LA would be the perfect place to start.

I tuck my head down and head up to the old Steinberg mansion, trying to keep my footing on the long driveway, which the rain has transformed to a sluice of flowing mud.

Reaching the front door, I stamp my feet to shake off the mud and suddenly become aware of Elvis Presley singing "Are You Lonesome Tonight" at an ear-shattering decibel inside the house.

"ARE YOU LONESOME TONIGHT, DO YOU MISS ME TO-NIGHT, ARE YOU SORRY WE DRIFTED APART ..."

I knock loudly on the door, hoping Devore can hear me over the piercing volume of the King's anguished strains.

"... DOES YOUR MEMORY STRAY TO A BRIGHT SUMMER'S DAY, WHEN I KISSED YOU AND CALLED YOU SWEETHEART ..."

I knock again—I *pound*. This is a guy whose help I desperately need. I'm running for my life here and he's blowing his mind with Elvis ...

BOOM!

A blast overhead. Thunder? I step back from the front door and look up at the second floor. Leaning out, brandishing a smoking .12-gauge shotgun, is Norman Devore.

"I'm Albie Marx! I live down there!" I yell up to him through the pelting rain, pointing down at my house, the tiny roof of which is barely visible through the oak trees below. "I want to talk to you!"

"*Vamoose, hombre!*"

I jump out of sight, into the alcove of the front door, just as he fires off another blast. It occurs to me that if this guy was too crazy for Virginia—a girl who was an accomplice to murder—he's way too far gone for me.

"I'm your neighbor!" I call from my safe position.

"You're a lawman!" he screams.

"No, I live right down there . . . I need to talk to you!"

"Let's see your warrant!"

"I'm not a cop!"

"What are you? A shrink?"

"I'm your neighbor!"

"I'm not going back!"

"Back where?"

"Go to hell, headshrinker!"

"I'm not a shrink!"

"What do you want?"

"To talk . . ."

"Where are you from? County Psychiatric?"

"I swear, I'm your neighbor . . ."

"Okay . . . Okay . . neighbor. Stand forward. Show yourself."

This could be the dumbest thing I've ever done, but I'm desperate enough to move into his line of fire, out in the teeming rain.

Leaning out the window with his shotgun, he's sopping wet, rivulets of water running down the wind-tossed, twisted strands of his hair like miniature rain gutters. He's a big guy, and younger than I thought, maybe late twenties. He's wearing a dirty flannel shirt with red suspenders and hasn't shaved in a country while. Disheveled and slovenly as he is, there's no denying he's a good-looking son-of-a-bitch, handsome in a virile, old-time movie star way, even though all I can see of his eyes as I squint up through the downpour is two raw, red rings.

"You solemnly swear you have no ties whatsoever to any peacekeeping or mental agency of any kind?"

"Yes! I swear!"

"Don't move."

I step back under the alcove. After a minute, the heavy wooden door swings open and an ocean of sound, Elvis's torment, breaks over me in a giant wave.

"... *DO THE CHAIRS IN YOUR PARLOR SEEM EMPTY AND BARE* ..."

I step inside cautiously, passing within inches of Devore as he closes the door. He's at least six four and broad-chested as a bull.

"*DO YOU GAZE AT YOUR DOORWAY AND PICTURE ME THERE* ..."

Locking the door, he whirls, leveling the shotgun straight at me. "Merry fucking christmas and happy fucking new year!" he screams. "Who are you?"

"Albie Marx!" I shout back. "I'm your neighbor!" I can barely hear myself. "Can you turn the music down?"

"What?"

"I can't hear myself!"

"What?"

"What?"

"I said, *what?*"

The old mansion with its cracked walls, chipped plaster, crooked sconces, leaking windows is not dealing well with the punishing sound. It gives the feeling it wants to collapse on itself and be left in peace.

"I can't hear myself!" I shout again, stepping closer to Devore. "Turn the music down!"

He looks me over carefully, like Tank would inspect a rat he's considering eating. Finally, deciding I'm not a mental ward bureaucrat or government agent, he takes a remote from his pocket, aims it into the living room, and severs the King's vocal. Like a dentist turned off the drill.

He focuses back on me. He's a mess—food-stained clothes, spaced-out eyes ... "Oh, man, this weather ... it's making me crazy ..."

"Maybe you should drink some coffee ..."

"Who are you?"

"Albie Marx. I live in the cottage below."

"Was the music too loud?"

Is he kidding? "Only if you're trying to talk or listen. Look I've got a little problem I'm hoping you can help me out with . . ."

His eyes, set deeply into the two red rings, give the appearance of spinning crazily in their sockets. He's ripped out of his ever-loving mind.

"Ever hear the saying, 'It's easier to love humanity as a whole than to love one's neighbor'?" he asks, head forward, eyes wide, waiting unblinkingly for my response.

"Loving everyone is easy. Loving someone is hard."

"Well said," he commends, scratching his stubble thoughtfully. Could I be winning his heart?

"Norman, I'm trying to get in touch with a girl . . . I think you know her."

"What's your name, neighbor?"

"My name? Albie."

"What time is it?"

"I don't know. I think it's around one o'clock . . ."

"Is your heart filled with pain, should I come back again . . ." he croons unmusically.

"Norman?"

"You want some toad? You do toad?"

"Uh, no, thanks . . ."

"You tried it?"

"No . . . not that I know of . . ."

"I have some. Hans and Franz. Check 'em out." Without waiting for a response, he leads me through the massive living room, with its mangled wood floors, cobwebbed furniture, and the wreckage of an ancient Steinberg grand piano. "I've never been into psychedelics, but I know great frog when I do it."

It suddenly occurs to me what he's talking about. I just read about it in *MOTHER JONES*. The newest drug craze sweeping the country—psychedelic toads. It's true. A sacred rite of primitive Indians, recently revived in a biology lab at Yale. One lick and you're high as a pterodactyl.

Devore leads me into what was once a grand, wood-paneled library. Anything of value that was once here has obviously been taken or ripped out, from books to hardware to expensive wood cabinetry.

The only thing in the room, sitting squarely in the center, is a metal chair and metal table with a lit-up computer sitting on top of it. The bareness, the gray light, the stark shadows, the incessant rain beating against the windowpanes, gives it all the quality of an insane asylum in a gothic movie. Which is enhanced even more by the stark wire cage sitting beside the computer. Upon close inspection, the cage contains two fat, bug-eyed frogs, staring at each other in a comatose squat.

"Hello, gentlemen . . ." Devore greets the impassive amphibians.

"Hans and Franz, I take it." I inspect the stoic brown leather creatures.

"Colorado River toads, neighbor. Primo quality. Try one."

"I think I'll pass . . ."

Leaning the shotgun against the table, he grabs one of the toads around the middle (I can't tell if it's Hans or Franz) and gently lifts the immobile creature out of the cage.

"You just squeeze these guys . . ." Devore squeezes the frog, making its legs start kicking wildly and its body blow up like he shoved an air pump up its ass.

"Don't worry," he reassures me, "I'm into animal rights, I'm not hurting him. Look. See this gooey stuff? Coming out of his skin? Behind his ears?"

"I didn't know frogs had ears . . ."

"Maybe it's his eyes . . . Anyway, this here's bufotenine, his natural defense system. It's venom. It'll kill anything trying to eat him, anything but a human. To humans, this stuff is the elixir of the gods." He proffers the toad to me. Yuk. "The ultimate psychedelic," he promises. "Take a lick."

"No. No, thanks."

"He won't mind."

"I might."

"It'll blow you sky-high." To Devore, I suppose that's a ringing endorsement.

"My stomach's a little empty."

"Okay. I see. I understand your reticence. We'll smoke him."

"I don't think so."

"Are you a cop?"

"No."

"Is this entrapment?"

"I'm not a cop."

"You'd better not be."

He takes a small, thin seashell from the table and begins to scrape the venom onto its lip. "We hit this stuff with a hair blower, dry it out ... stick it in the hash pipe. Whammo ... fifteen minutes on Planet X."

I realize I'd better get what I came for before he climbs aboard Mr. Toad's Wild Ride.

"I'm looking for Virginia Hurley." That gets his attention. "You know where I can find her?"

"Are you lonesome tonight ... ?" he sings off-key. Way off.

"Do you know where she is, Norman?"

"Do you miss her tonight ... ?"

"She put me in a bad position."

"Virginia doesn't have a bad position."

"Do you know where she is?"

"Is your heart filled with pain ..."

"Norman ..."

"What do you want with her?"

"She got me into a serious jam ... she's the only one who can get me out."

"I don't know where she is. I don't know who or what she's doing. I know nothing except she broke my heart. Broke it, neighbor, ground it up, ate it for breakfast. Most incredible woman I ever met. Beautiful, inside and out. Bright. How bright? Brilliant. Knows what you're thinking before you think it. Knows what you need before you need it. The ultimate lover. The ultimate female. I love that woman, God, I love that woman ..."

"What happened?"

"She loves me ... she lies ... she loves me ... she lies ... she loves me ... "

"Where is she?"

"Wish I knew. She left."

"She dumped you?"

"Dumped me? That's reducing her to less than the sum of her complications. Virginia doesn't dump you, she allows the world to share more of her . . ."

"Well, I got to share more than I wanted."

"That's why us Virginia veterans need guys like Hans and Franz . . ." He opens a drawer in the table and takes out a battery-powered blow dryer.

"What I need is to find her. It's urgent."

"It's always urgent. Everyone wants her yesterday."

"She's dangerous, Norman. You know that, don't you?"

"You know what motivates Virginia?" he asks, blowing hot air on the frog venom. "Fear of abandonment. She leaves you before you can leave her. That's her pattern. That's what she thinks life's about."

"Is that what she did to Marty Wilde?"

"The Tin Man? You can't break a heart that's not there. You can't leave someone you were never with. That was all in his rusted-out mind."

"What makes Virginia run? Why does she think people will turn on her?"

"A little psychological background? Her mother was a famous model. An A-list courtesan to the rich and famous. Left her first husband, Virginia's father, when she was a baby . . . married Roy Sellers, the English movie director."

"Her mother's in England?"

"France. She brought Virginia to London when she married Sellers, then left them both and went to Paris to marry a French count. Sellers married Tina Dorsey, the actress, moved in with her . . . left Virginia alone with the domestic couple . . ."

"How old was she?"

"Fourteen, I think. She met one of the Rolling Stones, came here with him, on tour. He went back, she stayed."

"Who did she stay with?"

"People she met . . . guys who made promises, Tin Men . . ."

"Did she know Bert Holman?"

"Anything's possible . . ."

"How about Mitchell P. Gluck?"

"I'm not her biographer, neighbor ..."

"You seem to know all about her."

"Just enough to love her beyond any reasonable state of mental health."

"How did you two meet?"

"Through my agent."

"Michael Whitehead?"

"That's the culprit."

"How did you get him for an agent?"

"He thinks I'm cute. And the last three pictures I wrote all did over a hundred million."

"Is he Virginia's agent, too?"

Having dried the venom, he takes it between his thumb and forefinger, rolls it into a little ball, then snares a short wooden hash pipe from his table and drops the ball into the bowl.

"A match and we're on our way ..."

"Is Whitehead Virginia's agent, too?" I repeat.

"I honestly don't know, neighbor ..."

"Are you in touch with her, Norman? I need to know that."

"Are you smoking with me?"

"Next time ..."

"Then we'll talk next time. Hard to trust a man who won't do toad with you."

We seem to have arrived at an impasse. He may have an idea where to find Virginia, but I'm not about to smoke toad to get it out of him. And he's too big to threaten.

He's looking around for a match as I take a step to the table and pick up the shotgun.

"Norman," I tell him, pointing the gun at him, "this is life and death."

"What else is there, neighbor?"

"If you love her like you say you do, there may be a way to get her off the hook. Otherwise, she's in serious trouble."

"What kind of trouble?"

"She's involved in a murder. Deeply involved."

"Virginia ... no way."

I nod somberly to let him know it's for real.

"Okay . . . you want to find her? You want to save her beautiful ass? I'm up for it. Let's go."

"Where?"

"We'll track her down."

I'm reluctant to put the gun down. "Can I trust you, Norman?"

"Can I trust you, neighbor?"

As an answer, his question settles the issue. We have to trust each other because, as desperately as I need to find Virginia, it's obvious that he does, too. We're joined at the hip by this common need, to seize and confront the woman who wounded us both, possibly fatally, for reasons we can't accept. And so, strangers bound together, we embark on our mission and head out into the deluge, to get the Jag and start hunting Virginia down. Halfway along the mud driveway, we become aware of flashing red lights below, reverberating up the hill through the heavy, swarming raindrops.

Devore stops in his tracks and sniffs like a pointer. "Cop cars."

"They're for me."

"They're all over the street."

He's right. From where we stand it looks like Danno brought along a battalion. Like I'm John fucking Dillinger.

"We can't go down there," I point out unnecessarily.

"You up for a flight from custody?"

"At this point I'm up for whatever's going to get me to Virginia."

"Then we go."

We plod back up the driveway, to the falling-down old four-car garage which once housed Dusenbergs and Bugattis and Rolls-Royces . . . Now its sole occupant is Devore's Harley-Davidson.

"Are you crazy? Take this in the rain and muck?"

In answer, he jams on his helmet, jumps on the machine and starts her up in that deep, unmistakeable roar of a Harley. "Let's ride, neighbor," he says, tossing me the other helmet.

Let's ride, neighbor. Now I get to be John Wayne. Well, here we go. Ready to bust out. What do I have to lose? Better off making a run for it than banking that Boopsie will "produce in the clutch," as Shrike puts it.

I mount up behind Devore, he lets out the clutch and launches the big blue monster into the vicious arms of the storm. In a moment we're churning down the driveway, sliding and swerving with the flowing mud, the rain pinging my helmet like a tin can in a shooting gallery.

Hitting the bottom of the road, as Devore focuses on keeping the Harley upright, I spot Danno, standing on my front doorstep, his pink head bone dry under an umbrella, craning his neck to scan up and down the street, a bald eagle cruising for prey. Unfortunately, the bald eagle spots his prey the moment his prey spots him—and lets out a squawk, flying off with a bound for one of the squad cars nesting with lights flashing red in front of my house.

"They got us!" I shout into Devore's helmet.

"We got them!" he shouts back, into the driving rain.

He twists the throttle. The heavy bike fishtails, straightens and zooms off down the hill. I look behind us—the patrol cars screech into sliding U-turns and come on in pursuit.

Racing through the Hollywood Hills on a motorcycle is hairy enough, but in a typhoon, chased by three police cars with lights and sirens—it's downright hirsute. At least it is for me. Devore, on the other hand, is having the time of his life, whooping and shifting gears, screaming and swerving . . . where does he think this will end?

Cresting Valley Oak Drive I peer through the rain, beyond Devore's helmet, at the next hill over. There stands the white-domed Griffith Observatory, where James Dean, Natalie Wood, and Sal Mineo stood off the police in *Rebel Without A Cause*.

It's been a long time since I really believed in being a rebel. So long. When being a rebel was the only thing worth being. Then, I didn't give a shit about the consequences. There was infinite time ahead to straighten things out.

Now, with time running out, with forevermore being closer than before, defying authority doesn't have the appeal it used to. Now, at any second, the two wheels under me, barely skimming the twisting road, can spin out, lose hold and send the big Harley out over the side of the hill and crashing down into oblivion. Defying authority doesn't seem worth it somehow . . .

I hear singing . . . it's Devore. He's wailing gospel at the top of his lungs . . .

"Just a closer walk with Thee, Grant it Jesus, if you please . . ."

Though I'm of Judaic persuasion, it happens to be a tune I remember from civil rights marches in the sixties and, strangely enough, seems appropriate here and now . . . so I join Devore in singing . . .

"Just a closer walk with thee, Grant it Jesus, if you please, I'll be satisfied as long, as I walk, dear Lord, close to Thee . . ."

Stop signs flash by like billboards as we eat up the twisting roads of Los Feliz with Danno and the squad cars behind us . . .

"I am weak but Thou art strong, Jesus keep me from all wrong . . ."

As we descend the hill, the pools and puddles get deeper, with less gravity to run them off, and the Harley plows through like a cigarette boat, spraying twin fountains at the bow, leaving a deep furrowed wake behind.

We're getting to the bottom of the hill and any second I'm expecting to see police cars appear in front of us, blocking our way. Suddenly, the street we're on ends, letting out at the western border of Griffith Park. The three patrol cars are bearing down on us.

Devore screams, "Hold on, neighbor!," and I tighten my grip around his waist as the Harley hits a low curb, lurches into the air, skids over the sidewalk, comes down on a small rise, churns into the mud and to the top, slides in three different directions and lands high throttle on a narrow bicycle path twisting through the park.

I look behind us, where the motorcycle jumped the curb. In a wild spray of water, the police cars are forced into a sliding, screeching stop.

"We got 'em!" I shout, slapping Devore's shoulder.

He whoops and bleeps a victory blast on the Harley's horn.

And we speed ahead under the trees, along the deserted, rain-washed bike path howling . . . *"Jesus wants me for a sunbeam . . ."*

The Steven Segall Repertory Theatre, financed by the movie star, is a small stage company, established for serious actors and actresses to "practice their craft in the framework of meaningful expression." The group is based in an intimate, two-hundred-seat playhouse on Beverly Boulevard, just west of La Brea.

By the time Devore and I splash our way through the flooded

streets, I'm ready to check into the Laundromat next door to the theater and take a personal spin in a super-size dryer. Instead, I drape my jean jacket over a space heater in the darkened lobby and follow Devore into the cozy little auditorium.

The comforting smell of cigarettes and coffee mixes with the moody plink of rain on the ceiling and the poetic southern inflection of actors rehearsing *Cat On A Hot Tin Roof*, to create an aura of serious, fifties New York theater.

The intense young director is wearing a black turtleneck sweater and chain-smoking a pack of Chesterfields. I'm encouraged. If the fifties are coming back, can the sixties be far behind?

Devore addresses him by the name of Frederick. It's clear by the look on his face that he's not an admirer of my crazy companion.

"This is a private rehearsal, Norman," he snaps.

"It's serious business, amigo."

"I'm not your amigo. We're trying to work here."

"Virginia's gone and gotten herself into a fix. My friend is trying to get her out."

"Who are you?" he asks.

When I tell him, he recognizes my name and condescendingly informs me his parents, ancient hippies, are followers of mine from the sixties and, for some unfathomable reason, still read my columns today.

Still alive for one generation, even as I become irrelevant to the next.

"I need to find Virginia," I tell him.

"I have no idea where she is."

"Were you working with her?"

"She was the heart of this show. I cast her as Maggie ..." For my benefit: "The part Elizabeth Taylor played in the movie."

"I saw the play on Broadway before you were born," I inform the little snot.

"Virginia's a giant talent. She'll be a movie star. That's what she wants, that's her destiny."

"From your mouth to God's ears. I hope she hasn't blown it."

"What do you know about our business? About what it takes to make it? About courage and conviction—"

"I've been around, son."

"Son? What's that supposed to mean? You know more than I do because you were a hippie five hundred years ago?"

"I know more than you because I've seen more than you."

"You've had more time to misinterpret everything. We see the same things—my take is fresh, yours is stale."

He sounds like I used to sound. Was I this arrogant, too?

"Why isn't Virginia in the show? What happened?" I ask, trying out a more conciliatory tone.

"What happened? She fell in love with this lunatic," he says, with a nasty look at Devore.

"And . . . ?"

"Threw herself into his life like she throws herself into everything . . ."

"And?"

"Called me a couple of weeks ago . . . very upset . . . under a lot of pressure . . . couldn't do the show. What's the matter? What's the problem? Wouldn't tell me. Couldn't talk about it. Was it something I could help with? Nobody could help, it was something she had to do . . . for Norman . . ."

"Hold it there, partner. She didn't say anything to me about that."

"What do you know? You're so involved with your own sickness you don't know what the hell's going on. The truth is, she asked me not to tell anyone—but since you asked, *Norman,* I thought you should know, you're screwing up her life . . ."

"I'm gonna screw up your face."

"Come on, lunatic, try it . . ."

"Hey, boys. Hold it. This isn't about you, okay? It's about me and Virginia. We're in trouble. She's in trouble. We've got to find her."

"I've got to rehearse. I have a show to put on. When Virginia wants something, she'll call me."

"Was that the last time you spoke to her? Two weeks ago?"

"I really don't have time for this . . ."

I grab the little shit and pin his neck to the wall with my forearm. "You're gonna get me to your leading lady or direct this show from a hospital bed."

"You can't threaten me . . ."

"*I* can," Devore says, pushing his wild-eyed face into Frederick's. "I can do horrible things and get off on insanity. Want to try me?"

"I don't know where she is. Safe from assholes like you . . ."

To my dismay and, I'm sure, Frederick's, a gleaming pearl-handled straight razor appears, poised for business, in Devore's hand.

"Freddie, me lad," Devore growls in a Long John Silver brogue, wiping the flat side of the blade on the director's nose, "I'll be slicin' yer up like a Christmas turkey if yer be not watchin' yer tongue . . . Now, where did yer say we could find the lass?"

"She left town, all right? I don't know where she went. She said she'd be gone for a while. Maybe a year. That's all I know. Now, would you mind getting the hell out of here?"

"How do you know all this?" I ask.

"I told you, she called me."

"You have no idea where 'out of town' is?"

"She could have been in China, for all I know. She was upset, she sounded scared . . . she wasn't talking."

A mutual look of agreement passes between Devore and me— Frederick's spilled all he knows. Devore pockets the razor and we leave the sullen director in the theater with a forceful admonishment, for Virginia's sake, to call one of us if he hears from her.

Out in the lobby, I ask Devore, "Frederick said she did what she did for you. Is there something I'm missing here?"

"You got me . . ."

"You never had anything to do with Holman or Gluck?"

"I don't like your tone, neighbor—I told you, no."

"What the hell are you carrying that blade for?"

"I'm thinking of becoming a barber."

"You could get into bad shit with that."

"I was born in bad shit. This is to cut my way out."

Guns, razors, psychedelic toads, murder . . . what a couple, Devore and Virginia. A pair of overheated youngsters, gifted with talent, cursed with demons, careening helter-skelter through the dark side of life. Bonnie and Clyde for the nineties. And who gets caught in the middle?

Ah, the Albie-ness of it all.

I retrieve my damp jacket from the heater, and, as Devore and I

leave the dark little lobby and step outside, we're greeted by the
ever-pounding rain and a ring of LAPD vehicles supporting a fear-
some display of firepower, aimed point blank at us.

I should have remembered from the Rodney King tape, these people are very sore losers when it comes to car chases.

Raindrops skip crazily off the gleaming head of Lieutenant Joseph
Danno as he stands beside one of the squad cars holding a microphone to his big, toothy mouth. "This is no game, boys. You're
either down on the ground or you're dead. It's your call to make—
but make it *now.*"

At this point I almost think twice about it, but the memory of
Sam, chestnut hair sprawled against the pillow, blue eyes locked to
mine in ecstasy, convinces me that of Danno's alternatives, I should
go with the first.

For the second time in three days, I'm facedown, handcuffed at
gunpoint and shoved into the caged end of a police car headed for
the Hollywood precinct.

As Chester A. Reilly used to say: *"What a revoltin' development
this is . . ."*

Whatever Danno has on me, he's keeping it to himself. He played
it closemouthed all the way downtown. Which, for a guy who equates
gloating with coming, had to be a painful triumph of willpower.
Devore and I were booked, fingerprinted, and photographed, then
told we could each make one phone call.

I couldn't decide who to call. Shrike? Sam? Boopsie? Figuring
that, of the three, the surest one to get ahold of was Shrike at the
office, I dialed *UP YOURS* and asked Rachel to put me through.

"Where are you, Marx? The cops were here looking for you."

"They found me. I just got booked."

"On what charge?"

"Danno won't say. I assume it's for Holman's murder. I haven't
been arraigned yet. I need a lawyer."

"I'll call Boopsie."

"And a bail bondsman."

"I'll look into it."

"Don't 'look into it.' Call someone."

"I will, I will."

"This isn't the sixties, Shrike. I'm too old for jail."

"Don't worry. I'm on the case."

"Hurry."

I hung up, hoping he'd be able to find Boopsie and that she'd be sober enough to spring into action. Then Devore and I were taken into a small room downstairs with a couple of cops. One was short and one was tall, and both were permanently sour.

The more sour of the two, the tall one, who apparently had never heard anyone speak in a normal voice, yelled everything at top volume. "STRIP DOWN TO YOUR BIRTHDAY SUIT! STAND SIDE BY SIDE! RUN YOUR FINGERS THROUGH YOUR HAIR! OPEN YOUR MOUTH AND STICK OUT YOUR TONGUE!"

The short cop checked out our mouths so thoroughly he must have thought we were warehousing assault rifles in there. God only knows what else he was looking for.

"LIFT UP YOUR DICK AND BALLS!"

"I only have two hands," Devore objected. "One of you guys wanna help?"

"SHUT UP!" screamed Sourface. "LIFT UP THAT DICK AND BALLS!"

Devore sang as he complied with the order, *"Tote dat dick, lift dem balls . . ."*

"SHUT UP!"

I gingerly lifted my genitals for the short cop to inspect underneath. What were they thinking? That I hid a hand grenade down there?

When that humiliation was over, Sourface yelled, "TURN AROUND, BEND OVER AND SPREAD YOUR CHEEKS!"

"I have diarrhea . . ." Devore warned.

"He didn't say that," I tried to say.

"SHUT UP!" Sourface screamed again. "DIGITAL EXAMINATION!" he told his partner.

"What's that?" I asked, horrified.

"Gotta check for drugs, keys, hacksaw blades," the short cop informed me, slipping on a rubber glove.

"Wait a minute. How could we . . ."

"No tellin' what you guys hide in them butt plugs."

"Butt plugs . . . ?"

"TURN AROUND, BEND OVER AND SPREAD 'EM!" Sour-face screamed furiously.

I've blanked out the memory of what happened next.

Satisfied we weren't concealing contraband, we were told to get dressed and taken upstairs.

When Devore was informed he'd be charged with, among other things, possession of *Bufo alvarius* (Colorado river toads), he started singing, *"This is the dawning of the Age of Alvarius . . ."* and was quickly silenced by a hard blow across the back with a towel-wrapped police baton. Then we were marched into a holding tank, where a half dozen other guys were milling around, waiting for arraignment.

Boopsie and Shrike still hadn't shown up, nor had a bail bonds-man. I was standing at the bars, peering down the corridor, as if the act of standing there looking for them would get them there faster. But instead, a fat-bellied biker was admitted, wearing a tank top, with death heads on his arms and "I HATE YOU" tattooed under the thick matted hair on his chest.

After the guards left, the biker stood at the bars, to my left, glaring in my direction. I ignored him. Then I felt something hard digging into me. I turned to look. He was pressing something against my rib cage.

"I have a message for you from Richard Sampson," he snarled in closed-lip prison talk.

Christ, I thought. The long arm of Gluck reaches everywhere. "Get away from me." I brushed his hand aside.

"Next time this will be a blade," he spat, showing me a small metal spoon. I wondered how he'd managed to get it past the digital examination.

"What is this? What does Sampson want?" I asked. "Do I look like I'm having a good time? Like I'm getting off on framing Gluck?"

"The message is, you have till tomorrow to straighten things out. After that, your ass won't be worth the paper to wipe it with."

Out of the corner of my eye I noticed Devore watching us.

"You'd better back off . . ." I cautioned the biker.

"Why? You got a machine gun?" His hand shot out and pushed me against the bars. "I could do you right here." The guy was amazingly strong.

He shouldn't have pushed me in front of Devore. In a nanosecond, my wild-eyed friend was all over him and the two huge animals went crashing down, then scrambled to their feet, thrashing about in a growling, snarling battle that gave every impression of ending in nothing short of death. Prisoners scurried out of the way as they careened from one end of the tank to the other, ripping, biting, tearing at one another.

A deafening alarm went off, instantly bringing a squad of prison guards on the run, descending on Devore and the biker with clubs, breaking up the fight and dragging them, kicking and cursing, out of the tank.

As he was being dragged off, Devore implored me to find Virginia and tell her he loved her. I promised I'd find her if it was the last thing I did—knowing that if I didn't, it would be. I felt bad for him. He was on my side, had jumped to my defense with the biker. I hoped he hadn't gotten himself in too much trouble. I yelled after him that I'd do what I could to get him out.

It was three or four hours later and still no one had shown up when I was taken out of the tank and brought over to the court, where I waited in line with a motley assortment of murderers, drug dealers, and child abusers—all innocent, of course—for arraignment.

When I finally stood before the judge, he perfunctorily told me my rights (not including the right not be judged in the press), then read the charges against me: "Conspiracy to commit murder; Resisting arrest."

"What does 'conspiracy' mean?" I asked.

"A person is guilty of conspiracy with another person or persons if he agrees with such other persons that they or one or more of them will commit the crime. Or if he agrees to aid such other person or persons in the planning or commission of such crime. Does that answer your question, Mr. Marx?"

"Yes, Your Honor."

"You have the constitutional right to a court appointed attorney if you are financially unable to retain private counsel. Bail is set at five hundred thousand dollars.''

"Five hundred thousand dollars? That's unreasonably high, Your Honor . . .''

"Considering that flight from prosecution constitutes consciousness of guilt in the state of California, you should get on your knees and thank me for setting any bail at all. Next case.''

And that was that. Half a million bucks. Which meant someone had to come up with fifty thousand or I would stay locked up with a bunch of maniacs, any one of which might be an assassin sent by Gluck's man, Richard Sampson. My nerves were getting ragged and my stomach burned like an acid sponge.

After being taken back to the holding tank to await assignment to a regular cell, I was allowed to make another call. I called the office again. According to Rachel, Shrike had reached Boopsie at her apartment, but her car was undrivable in the storm so he had to go out to the Valley to pick her up. Who knew how long that would take? I was getting beyond distraught. I was getting mad. Why was I stuck with a drunken, stumblebum lawyer? Why was Shrike playing fast and loose with my freedom? What evidence did Danno have that allowed him to obtain a warrant for my arrest on a murder charge?

It was all too much.

Then, once again, in my moment of darkness, my Sister of Mercy intervened.

I was taken to visitor's row where Sam was calmly waiting for me, separated by a scarred partition of prison Plexiglas. With limited time, she got straight to the point.

"I know everything . . . the motorcycle chase, the fight, your arraignment . . .''

"Your contacts are good.''

"Let's say they're well fed.''

"Can they eat into my bail? It's much too high.''

"Don't worry about the bail. It's being taken care of.''

"It is? By who?''

"It doesn't matter. What matters is digging our way out of this.''

I liked that she said "our," but I wanted to know where the money was coming from. "Fifty thousand matters. Who's putting it up?''

She hesitated, then said, "I am."

"You personally?"

"What difference does it make?"

"Is it you or *Real Life*?"

"*Real Life*? Carruthers wouldn't do that. It's me. I know you don't have it or you'd be out by now. Did you know Gluck was arrested, too?"

"No."

"He's out already."

"He's out. Or course. Equal justice for all—depending on how much money you have."

"Gluck does what he has to. So will you."

"The first thing I have to do is very clear, and until I do it, nothing else will make sense. I have to get into a room with the man who accused me."

"You can do that, but it won't help. Not anymore."

"What do you mean?"

"Gardner's dead."

"No. He died?" She nodded. "Great." Somewhere I'd held out the irrational hope that, even if I couldn't find Virginia, a face-to-face confrontation with Gardner would finally make him tell the truth and let me off the hook.

"Well, that's the end of that," I mumbled. "I'm on my own now."

"Not exactly." She tried not to look hurt.

"I'm sorry. Thank God for you." I placed my palm against the Plexiglas. She put hers up to mine. "Thanks for coming, Sam . . . Thanks for caring . . ."

"I'm compelled to fight injustice."

"You can find injustice anywhere."

"That's true . . ."

"You're not the type to hang out with broken-down old hippies."

"You're not a hippie."

"Thanks."

"And you're not broken down."

"I'm breaking."

"Don't give me that. I know your story, what you've been through

... The civil rights marches, the Vietnam War protests, the arrests, all the exposé's you've written. You haven't been broken by all that, you're stronger because of it. You've always stuck to your principles, you've offended people who needed offending—now one of them is striking back, that's all. We'll find out who it is. You'll be proved innocent . . .''

"Innocent. I have to stay positive. I'm not convicted of anything yet. Tell me, how did Gardner die? Was it the colon cancer?"

"That's the official story."

"Oy." Suddenly, my whole body tensed from a pain that shot through my stomach and ricocheted from interior wall to interior wall.

Alarmed, Sam asked, "What's the matter?"

"My cosmic link with Gardner's acting up . . ." I grimaced and bent over, trying to breathe deeply, to make the pain go away.

"Should I call somebody?"

"No . . ." I will not die of stomach cancer, I will not die of stomach cancer, I will not die of stomach cancer . . .

"I'm calling for a doctor . . ."

"Don't." I straightened up, despite the pain that kept biting into me. "Is it still raining out?"

"Yes," she answered, concern etched into her face.

"Is it supposed to keep up?"

"You know, the weatherman's never right . . ."

"What else do we know about Gardner? Anything?"

"I have someone checking his trail, looking for people who knew him . . . You're still in pain . . ."

"You said he was married . . ."

"His wife hasn't turned up yet. Albie . . ."

"I'm all right," I breathed, straightening up. "I'm all right."

She looked at me deeply, decided to half believe me, then asked, "What about the actress?"

"Virginia . . ."

"Did you come up with anything on her?"

"I was getting closer. How much longer will I be in here?"

"You'll be out soon, I hope. What's your lawyer's name?"

Hesitantly, I told her about Betty McDonald, making a point of

Shrike's unshakable faith in her legal talents. I neglected to mention the nickname, Boopsie.

Our time was up. Sam told me to hang in, the bail bondsman was working on it and they'd have me out as quickly as possible.

Neither of us counted on the "temporary mix-up" in the prison computer system that led to losing my location when the bondsman showed up with my bail. I was forced to spend the whole, horrible night in jail, cooped up in a tiny cell with a coked-out nut who called himself Johnny Angel and chattered nonstop about how he'd "whaled the piss out of two cops," then "blasted hair on the walls with a sawed-off."

A night with a sicko cop killer. A token of the esteem in which I was held by the LAPD.

Or, my friend Lieutenant Joseph Danno, giving me a taste of things to come.

DAY FOUR
WEDNESDAY, MARCH 18

I'm focusing in on two giant black holes, fathomless caves stretching into infinity . . .

. . . becoming clearer now, with tiny stalactites, almost like hairs, quivering microscopically . . .

. . . moving close, then away, then a voice, a woman's voice . . .

". . . Albie . . . Albie . . . can you hear me . . ."

I blink, clear my eyes . . . and realize . . . I'm lying down, on a couch, staring up into . . .

The perfect twin windtunnels of Bambi Friedman's Beverly Hills nose job.

What . . . how did . . . when did I . . . ?

It starts to come back, in dribbles . . .

The computer finally "located" me . . . I was let out of jail early this morning . . . I hadn't had a second of sleep . . . my eyes were burning . . . my mind crammed with Jonny Angel's revolting images of blood and guts spilled randomly, from one end of LA to the other, so vivid you could feel it . . . A night of gunpowder and meat . . .

I called Sam the minute I got out . . . thanked her, promised to repay the money.

I knew Gluck's soldiers would be out on the street looking for me. I needed something with which to defend myself. I remembered Bambi Friedman claimed to know something about the sovereign deal, something she implied was devastating . . . I called her at home.

She was nursing a terrible toothache, the root canal . . . her jaw was swollen, she didn't want to see me. I insisted . . . she tried to put me off . . . my head is clearing . . . I remember . . .

She was adamant about not wanting to be viewed in that condition. High vanity level. But not as high as my desperation level. I talked her into letting me come to her house. She gave me the address, in Franklin Canyon, off Mulholland Drive, on the other side of Coldwater where my son lives. Prime flood area.

Praying not to get stuck in a mudslide, I took the Jag out Sunset to Crescent, then headed up Coldwater Canyon to Mulholland. Even in the rain, I could see the once-spectacular view of the Valley from Mulholland Drive obscured by the pee-yellow smog . . .

And I remember wondering . . . if all the foul air I've taken in has something to do with the little white spot on my X ray, next to my ileocecal valve . . . maybe I can sue the city for medical costs . . .

Farfetched? Not in Los Angeles. Hordes of lawyers in this town would gleefully take a contingency run at a lucrative civil smog suit. And if one of them won, would that ever open the gates. I imagined billboards all over town urging:

LAWYER FEVER—CATCH IT!

It would be a battle but they'd get rid of the smog all right. It's never over till the contingency lawyer gets his cut.

Franklin Canyon, where Bambi Friedman lives, is a rustic, little-known ravine that dead-ends at a small, obscure reservoir in what is known as the Santa Monica mountains. Hippies like me discovered this pastoral paradise back in the sixties, when you could rent a big redwood country house with a pool and hot tub for four hundred a month.

In the eighties, property values skyrocketed and the hippies turned to yuppies, but now most of the houses sported realtor's FOR SALE signs. Last year was the first in the history where more people left

California than came into it. If the exodus continues, the place might become livable again.

Squinting at house numbers through the rainy sweep of my windshield wipers, I finally pulled up in front of a graceful, two-story house of redwood and glass, built for harmony with its natural environment, punctuated here and there by muted stained-glass windows, set like a jewel into the tree-studded hillside. A jewel that, in this downpour-that-never-ends, I could see breaking loose from its setting and clattering all the way down into the reservoir.

There were two cars in the driveway. A little red Miata convertible was parked behind a black Corvette. The Miata had one of those hip license plates that are supposed to make a statement about the owner. This statement wasn't the shy type. It read: *I D8 U.*

I parked behind the Miata, jumped out of my car and dashed through the rain like an open-field runner for the front door, weaving and hopping from flagstone to flagstone along a narrow walkway that bridged the mud. Unfortunately, a stretch of flagstone had been washed away and my left foot suddenly plunged into the ankle-deep muck. There was a wet sucking sound as I tried to yank it out, but my boot, which was half off my foot, was determined to remain mud-locked. I was getting soaking wet again, fighting to free my boot, when I heard a loud, dull cracking sound.

I glanced up to see, as if in slow motion, a gigantic, albino-barked eucalyptus tree, about fifty feet up the hill, starting to topple over— in my direction. Its roots were cracking as they broke and pulled out of the sodden ground. I assumed God was saying, "Your boot or your life," and, unlike Jack Benny, who hesitated between choosing his money or his life, I didn't have to think twice about it. I yanked my foot out of the boot and dove for safety. As the tree came crashing down I made a mental note to remember this moment the next time I start whining about a drought.

That was the last mental note I made before waking to the colossal nostrils of Bambi Friedman looming over me.

Now I clearly see her, clothes all splotched with mud, swollen dental jaw accentuated by the expression of deep concern plastered onto her plastically unlined face. My head is throbbing ferociously.

I feel like a giant blowfish. I reach up and wince as I finger the nasty bump under the cold compress lying across my forehead.

". . . Do you realize how hard you got hit?" she asks.

"You should see the tree . . ." I answer numbly.

"There's already been fourteen deaths from this storm."

"Give me a chance, it isn't over yet."

Behind her I glimpse a girl, young, blonde, cheerleader looks, splattered with mud like Bambi, watching me with the same distressed look. "Is that my nurse?" I ask.

Relieved I'm conscious, Bambi says, "This is Debra. She helped dig up your boot and drag you in here . . ."

"Thank you, Debra. I'll try to do the same for you someday . . ."

"I always assumed you had a hard head . . ." Bambi says.

"And now that you've seen it in action . . ."

"It's harder than eucalyptus, that's for sure."

"Well . . . I guess I can leave now," Debra says to Bambi.

"Thanks for the help, sweetie. Drive carefully, it's dangerous out there."

"In more ways than one," Debra laments.

"Just do what I told you. Don't take any crap."

"I won't."

"Get the cash first. I told him up front you won't take a check."

"Got it."

"And call when you're finished."

"I will."

"He's a son-of-a-bitch, but he's a steady client."

"Okay."

"And make him use protection. He'll try not to."

"What if he says he'll only do it his way?"

"Call me and put him on the phone. I can handle him."

"Okay," she sighs. She puts on her jacket and, as she walks out of the room, glances back at me and says, "Nice meeting you."

When she's gone, I look at Bambi. "Mind if I ask what business you and Debra are in?"

"Physical therapy." Said with a straight face.

"I see."

"And you're her . . . ?"

"Mother image."

"A little young for that, aren't you?"

"My plastic surgeon's good, but he can't turn the clock back. I'm old enough."

"Well, she looks like she could have a bright future."

"Only time will tell. But you're not here for physical therapy."

"That's right."

"That was a hell of a wedding Sunday, wasn't it?"

"Hell is the operative word," I point out. "And still is."

"I've been following the story . . ."

"I hope you've been entertained."

She winces and puts her hand to her jaw. "Can you believe these Beverly Hills dentists? Two thousand for a root canal."

"I've got a route canal of my own going. From the other end."

"Something you'd care to talk about?"

"Not really."

"I'm not squeamish."

"Are you a proctology buff?"

"Only on a client by client basis."

"Never mind. Look," I begin seriously, forcing myself to sit upright. "You said something to me at Holman's wedding . . . you know something that could wreck the Sovereign deal . . ."

"And a life or two . . ."

"Well, it's too late to wreck Holman's life . . ."

"I'll settle for someone else . . ."

"Who? Mitchell Gluck? Is it something about Gluck?"

"Mitchell Gluck is . . . How can I put this . . . a vicious little cocksucker."

"You don't have to beat around the bush with me."

"He was born without a soul. He's a spiritual leper."

"He's my co-defendant."

"Do you believe in reincarnation?"

"When it's applicable. Why?"

"To put it delicately . . . If bad karma were excrement, your co-defendant would come back as a porta-potty."

"Nice. If I weren't despondent already, I'd get really upset about that. As it is, I'm closer to the next life than I'd care to be. So. Tell me."

"On one condition: no one can ever find out it came from me."

"Why? If it's really juicy, you can make a bundle off it. Go on a talk show, a tabloid show, they'll pay you a fortune."

"I can't afford the publicity. Not in my line of work. Not with my client list."

"The physical therapy business is booming?"

"In Hollywood, always. The rich and famous are cheap, but they pay for their physical therapy—and their confidentiality. If I lost my clients a lot of young girls would be out on the street. You wouldn't want to be responsible for that, would you?"

"The problem is, if what you know bears on Holman's murder, it could be crucial to my case. How else would I be able to release the information?"

"That's not my problem. I'll accept your word as a journalist that you'll protect me as a source. But I won't say a thing without it."

"Well, I guess I'm better off having the information . . ."

"It's up to you."

"Okay . . . You have my word."

"I hope it's good. I came to you because I believe I can trust you. All right. Here's what I know . . . Years ago, when Holman and Gluck first got into show business, they were agents together at William Morris . . ."

"I read that in *Fortune*."

"Gluck was in the music department, Holman was in TV. Gluck hated Bert from day one, when they worked in the mail room together. He told everyone Bert was a greedy pig with delusions of grandeur. Which everyone knew applied to Gluck more than anyone else in the agency. Their feud was no secret.

"But, you know how it is, show business and politics, they make strange bedfellows. Bert and Gluck were jointly assigned to represent a major country-western star, someone who sold millions of records and had his own TV show. He's dead now, but for a year or two he was the biggest moneymaker in the agency. I don't want to tell you his name, but if you sit down with a short list of rhinestone cowboys who were big stars twenty years ago, you'll figure it out.

"Anyway, one night, three in the morning, Gluck gets a call. It's the cowboy. Panicked. There's a dead girl in his bed and he's freaking out. Wants Gluck to come to his house right away.

"You ask, why does he call Gluck? Because he knows there's nothing Gluck won't do when it comes to advancing his own career. Or, in this particular case, keeping it from sliding backward.

"Of course, being the nasty little prick he is, Gluck realizes that whatever's in store for him at the cowboy's won't be pretty. So he calls Bert, tells him the cowboy wants to meet with the two of them immediately, if they don't show up, the cowboy's leaving the agency.

"Bert has no idea what's going on, so he drops everything and drives up to the cowboy's house to meet Gluck. They find the cowboy in his boxer shorts and boots, stoned and scared out of his mind. There's a twenty-four-year-old girl in his bed. She's dead."

The name Jeannie Locke pops into my mind. The girl who knew Ozzie Baba twenty years ago. Could she be the girl in the cowboy's bed?

Bambi pauses to caress her jaw and stretch her neck. You think you know everything from the gossip rags and tabloid shows, but they never tell you the real stuff. In show business, power suppresses the real stuff.

"How did she die?" I ask, betting it had to be drugs.

"Drug overdose. She and the cowboy were doing poppers—amyl nitrate—come-bumpers, my girls call them, and her system overloaded. Heart stopped. Died.

"Gluck realizes, if the cops see this, the cowboy's career is over. Millions in commissions to William Morris, not to mention the damage to his career.

"Bert's enraged that Gluck got him there under false pretenses. He wants to call the police, regardless of the consequences. He doesn't want the bad karma.

"Gluck votes to save the cowboy's ass. He gives Bert the Golden Goose speech. The golden cowboy laid one bad egg, but Gluck's take is, the girl's dead already, what good will it serve to ruin three major careers over it?

"Eventually Gluck's perverted logic and the cowboy's pleading overrule Bert's conscience. He gives in. Gluck's plan is to drive the girl's car

David Debin

down to some dark street in Hollywood and leave it there, with her behind
the wheel. Nobody will ever know what happened . . ."

"Except Gluck, Holman, and the cowboy, who will have to live
with it the rest of their lives," I point out.

"The only one who had misgivings about that was Bert. But it's
off his conscience now, isn't it?"

"Who told you this story?" I ask.

"I protect my sources."

"How do you know it's true?"

"Irrefutable evidence exists."

"Do you know the name, Jeannie Locke?"

She looks at me, stunned. "Where did you hear that . . . ?"

"Do you know it?"

"That was the girl's name."

"Does the name Jack Schwarzberg mean anything to you?"

"Jack Schwarzberg? No. Who told you about Jeannie Locke?"

"I protect my sources. You're sure you never heard of Jack
Schwarzberg? How about Chief Ozuma Blackfoot?"

"Who are they?"

"They're Ozzie Baba's previous names."

"I never heard of either one."

"Someone suggested I ask Ozzie Baba about Jeannie Locke. Is
it possible he had something to do with Gluck and Holman? Or
the cowboy?"

"I told you what I know. I never heard Ozzie Baba connected
with the story."

"When did this all take place?"

"I'm not sure. 'Seventy-two, seventy-three, around there."

"I assume the cover-up worked out the way Gluck planned it."

"Everything always does, the little prick. Up until now, that is. I
doubt if he planned to get caught for Bert's murder."

"You think he hired Gardner?"

"Absolutely."

"You think he hired me, too?"

"I don't know."

"Come on."

"How would I know?"

"Because I'm telling you he didn't."

"All right," she yields. "Then think hard. Is there a reason for Gluck to want to get you?"

"Not that I know of."

"The man is clinically paranoid. He holds grudges. Secret grudges. Longtime grudges. And he always gets revenge. Are you sure you never did anything? Never wrote something to offend him?"

"It's possible. I've offended a lot of people. You think Gluck hired Gardner to kill Holman and frame me?"

"Maybe. And maybe it backfired. For some reason Gardner decided to pull Gluck down, too. Gardner's dead, we may never know . . ."

"But you don't sound convinced. Let me ask you something . . . If you think I'm involved with Gluck, why tell me all this?"

"Because, the way things stand now, whether you're involved or not, you have to make Gluck the bad guy in order to save your own ass. So you'll get the story out. Which is all I care about."

"You want me to accuse Gluck of assisting to cover up the possible homicide of a young girl twenty years ago?"

"Look, here's where I'm coming from . . . Gardner's confession put Gluck on the ropes for the first time in his life. I don't want him to get away. I want him nailed. Once and for all."

"Sounds like you and Gluck have an ugly past together."

"What motivates me is my business."

"You can prove the story is true."

"Absolutely."

"How?"

"Uh-uh-uh . . . I never play my hole card at the start of a game. The fact that you print it will make it true. If and when the time comes for proof, you can bet your life I will produce it."

By the time we ran my clothes through Bambi's washer and dryer, found my boots and scraped off the mud, she had me just about convinced that Gluck hired Gardner to kill Holman, then someone got to Gardner, convinced him to turn on Gluck and throw me to the wolves.

That someone is the key to the puzzle.

When I finally got Shrike on the phone, he told me Boopsie had communicated with the prosecutor's office and received some disturbing information. Gulping back my nausea, I asked where she was. He said she was asleep on his office couch, adding grumpily that I should get my ass over there, her snoring was interfering with business. I told him she was his choice, and he shot back if I didn't like her I could pay for my own lawyer.

I said I was on my way, then I called Sam at her show. Mr. Important said she hadn't gotten in yet, but she always kept in contact through her cellular phone. I told him to tell her I was on my way to *UP YOURS*, if she wanted to meet my attorney she should rendezvous with me there. He said he would give her the message.

The storm hadn't let up. If anything, it had grown more furious. Los Angeles was starting to look like news footage of Florida after Hurricane Andrew hit.

On the way to Hollywood I passed one horrible accident after another, caused by people who couldn't figure out how to drive in the rain and wind. The Jaws of Life were everywhere, cutting screaming, bloodied drivers out of their bent and twisted cars. The rain-whipped streets were flowing with blood and the weatherman said there was no end in sight.

At Fairfax and Sunset I saw one of those indispensably ubiquitous ATM cash machines, in a little bank vestibule, semiprotected from the elements. I was out of cash, so I stopped to refresh my pathetic bankroll. Amazing how fast five twenties goes, isn't it? But those machines keep coming up with new ones. Just stick in your card and take out the cash. Like the supply will never end.

I punched in my identification number, crossed my fingers and asked the God of Cash for a hundred bucks. Clank, clank, clank . . . BINGO. It spit that stack of twenties right out. Then my card. Then my receipt.

I glanced at the receipt to see if I had any balance left. I figured three, four hundred. The balance read, $50,367.23.

I looked again. $50,367.23.

I checked the account number on the receipt against my checkbook. Same account. The bank was telling me I had an extra fifty thousand dollars. It couldn't be.

Suddenly I broke out in a cold sweat. Fifty thousand. It was the amount Gardner said I was paid to supply the rifle. How did this happen? How did the money get into my account? Simple. Someone can't make a withdrawal from your account without forging your signature. But they can make a cash deposit without signing any name at all.

I was choking. The noose was tightening and I was helpless. I wanted to get my hands on whoever was doing this. Wring them out like they were wringing me. Then it occurred to me that I had to get rid of the fifty thousand before Danno found it. But if I withdrew it, it would still be on my bank record.

Fifty thousand bucks. That's a lot to bet on the justice system putting me away. Someone once said, "You can judge a man by his enemies." I must be a pretty formidable character ... I've got a bona-fide high roller on my ass. On the other hand, to someone like Mitchell P. Gluck, fifty thousand is chump change. A new dining-room set. A week in the south of France.

Maybe I could turn the tables on my unknown enemy and use his money to buy myself a great lawyer and save my skin. I could give Boopsie her stumbling papers and hire Arthur Gruntman. Tempting.

"Betty ... We're having a meeting ..." Boopsie is snoring away on Shrike's couch and he's trying to rouse her. "*Tempis fugit*, Betty ... You're losing money."

Sam looks at me in horror. "She's not your lawyer ... ?"

"She's prominent in the Valley," I tell her, hoping she doesn't make out the gloom in my voice.

"How did you get that bump on your head?" she asks.

"In jail," I lie. I'm not ready to tell her about Bambi Friedman, not yet.

Boopsie sputters, licks the spittle from her lips and opens two crimson eyes adrift in a blotchy sea of mascara.

"I'm thinking of letting her go," I tell Sam.

"Good thinking," she answers.

"Look, Betty ... Albie's here ... your client ..." Shrike's resorted to cooing.

"Got a beer?" Boopsie asks groggily.

"How about some coffee?" he counters.

"Beer."

"Get her a beer, please, Rachel," he says to the bemused receptionist. As Rachel goes for the brew he tells Sam, "After the first beer she's sharp as a tack. One of the great legal minds."

"Which one is Albie?" Boopsie asks, trying to focus in my direction.

Sam looks at me. "I don't believe this."

The fifty thousand is burning a hole in my pocket. "I have to let her go, Shrike," I announce. "This is my *life* she's playing with."

"Fine. You have the money to throw away, go get Gruntman, if that's who you want. I'm on record as saying he's not in the same league with Boopsie."

"Boopsie?" Sam asks.

"A childhood nickname," he explains, without really knowing.

"Unbelievable," she says again.

Rachel hurries back with an open Coors and hands it to Boopsie, who chug-a-lugs the entire bottle in one go.

"Ahhhhhh. . . ." she sighs. And belches loudly.

"I haven't seen anyone do that since I was seventeen," Shrike marvels.

"Hit me again," Boopsie says to Rachel, who looks to Shrike for permission, then hurries out for another brew.

"Where do I know you from?" Boopsie asks Sam, punctuating the question with another belch.

Fascinated, Sam forces herself to tear her eyes from Boopsie, and looks at me with a tentative half-smile. "This is a put-on, right?"

"No," I answer. Then, to Boopsie: "This is Samantha Shelton. From *Real Life*. The TV show."

"Who are *you*?" Boopsie asks me.

"Me? Who do you think I am? I'm Albie Marx."

Sam is looking at me like I should say something else, like, *you're fired.*

"Albie Marx . . ." Boopsie says, finally recognizing me. "You're in a shitload of trouble."

"Boopsie—*Betty*—Look . . . I appreciate anything and everything you've done for me so far. But, as of now, you're off the case."

I did it. God, that felt good.

"If I were you," Boopsie answers, her fog belched away in a gaseous hurricane of clarity, "I wouldn't be in so much of a hurry to spend that fifty thousand."

I literally do a double take. "How do you know about that?"

"I saw it on TV," she answers, pointing at Sam. "On her show. Gluck paid you fifty grand to supply the rifle that killed Bert Holman."

"That's not funny. How did you know I have the money?"

Sam looks at me. "You have fifty thousand dollars, Albie?" This, with both of us knowing she just lent me fifty to get out of jail.

"No. I mean, it's in my bank account but it was planted there . . ."

"Say it's a bank error in your favor," Shrike volunteers.

"The DA would love that," Boopsie chortles.

"How did you know about the money?" I ask her again.

"You may think I'm a clown," she responds. "Even I think I'm a clown. Sometimes. But I'm also the best goddamn criminal lawyer you ever got lucky enough to give your father's gold watch to. Which, by the way, I'm still willing to accept in lieu of a down payment. How do I know about the money? Try friends in high places. Friends you can't buy for five hundred an hour. Friends who hate five-hundred-an-hour lawyers."

Shrike was right. The beer cleared her head.

"You're saying you have a source in the LAPD?" Sam asks. "Someone leaking information?"

"Leaking? No. Leaking is when you talk to the press. This is business, the business of criminal law."

"It's a leak. And if it's leaking for you it will be leaking for others."

"You mean whatever this 'evidence' is, it could go public?" I ask, appalled. "If the media gets hold of anything remotely substantial they'll lynch me."

"Why would they lynch you?" Sam asks.

"Why? Tell her, Shrike."

"Everybody loves a lynching."

"That's not true," Sam objects.

"Everyone from the editor of *The New York Times* to a blue-collar family sitting around the TV at night. It's a diversion, a chance to forget your own problems and watch someone else get eaten alive. An electronic version of the Roman Coliseum. The media of today—and I don't exclude *UP YOURS*—is P. T. Barnum, selling tickets on a world-wide scale to watch the lions tear up the Christians.''

"There *are* honest journalists."

"I assume you're one of them," Boopsie says.

"Yes, I am."

"Then you won't use any of the information you're about to hear, correct?"

"Well . . . No, if you ask me not to, I won't. But somebody else will get it. With me, it will get a fair airing."

"I'm asking you not to," Boopsie pushes. "Is that agreed?"

"Yes. I will not personally use anything I hear in this room. Does that satisfy your requirement?"

"For the time being," Boopsie answers.

"How much *do* you charge?" Sam asks.

"Thirty-five," Boopsie answers.

"Thirty-five?" Sam repeats. "For how long?"

"An hour." Sam looks flabbergasted. "Too high? The fact is, people like Albie, the ones who really deserve it, wouldn't be able to afford justice if every good lawyer charged five hundred an hour. So I limit my material needs—primarily to liquids—and carry the banner of the oppressed into judicial battle.

"But that's enough of *my raison d'être*. Albie's the one we need to concentrate on. He's the one charged with Conspiracy to Murder."

"It's crazy! How can I conspire with people I don't even know?"

"The members of a conspiracy don't have to know each other, or even the part played by the others. As long as he knows the *purpose* of the conspiracy—which the State claims is the murder of Bert Holman."

"You mean somebody who commits a crime can involve anyone he wants? Just by saying they conspired with him?"

"Isn't the law a hoot?" Boopsie answers.

"If John Hinkley Jr., picked my name out of a telephone book and said I conspired to kill Reagan, they would have believed him?"

"I would have," Shrike volunteers.

"Just the fact of your name in newsprint requires you to prove your innocence," Boopsie laments. "Thanks to folks like Ms. Shelton here, that's the fishbowl we live in these days. Anyway, your preliminary hearing has been set for next week. The judge will determine whether they have sufficient evidence to support the charges against you. And let me tell you, according to what I've been told, the answer is an emphatic *yes.*"

"What evidence do they have?" I ask, unable to mask the depth of my dread.

"Let's start with the fifty thousand. Your friend, Lieutenant Danno, obtained a record of your account that shows you received the deposit Monday, the day after Holman's murder—the same day Gardner received his."

"Christ, if I were going to take money for something like that, I wouldn't go putting it into my bank account . . ."

"That's *your* story. Bottom line, the money's there and the police know about it. Which takes care of the *motivation* angle: you did it for the money. Danno also obtained your phone records. He doesn't like you, does he?"

"I think he confuses me with someone who raped his wife and tortured his kids."

"Right. Anyway, a call was placed from your telephone to Mitchell P. Gluck's private line less than two hours before Holman was shot. I assume you have a legitimate explanation for that."

"God. Carol . . . Virginia . . . the chauffeur . . . made a call from my house when she picked me up."

"Then we need her."

"She's disappeared. I'm trying to find her."

"I would suggest you accomplish that." She takes a long pull on the fresh Coors Rachel brought in. "What did she say to Gluck on the phone?"

"I . . . don't remember. I don't even know if she talked to him." (But I do remember I was too busy drooling over her uniform to listen to her conversation.) "She was wearing gloves. No prints on my phone."

"Well planned," says Boopsie.

Shrike pipes up. "So far his explanations are 'bank error' and 'the chauffeur did it.' Not exactly a juggernaut defense."

"But it's all circumstantial," Sam argues.

"Circumstantial evidence is good evidence. A lot of people on Death Row have been convicted by circumstantial evidence."

Sam is not overwhelmed. "They still haven't tied Albie to Gardner."

Boopsie answers, "I was getting to that."

"What else?" I moan.

"Danno searched Gardner's apartment. He found two used champagne glasses, one with Gardner's fingerprints. The prints on the other glass," she says ominously, looking at me, "belong to you-know-who."

They're all staring at me. Waiting for an explanation.

"We had a toast in the limo . . ." I explain weakly.

"You and Gardner?" Boopsie asks.

"No! Me and the chauffeur . . . Carol. Virginia."

"What were you toasting?" Sam asks. "Did you know her?"

"No. She was my driver."

"I don't toast with *my* drivers," Sam responds. "Did you maybe go a little beyond the passenger-driver relationship?" The edge in her voice is clear.

"We were waiting on line to pull up to the gate . . . We had some time. She poured us champagne. Of course, she was wearing gloves . . ."

"*Gloves!*" Shrike groans.

"I had no reason to believe she was anything but what she said she was."

"What did she say she was?" Sam challenges.

"A chauffeur. Sent by Bert Holman."

"The victim set you up to take the rap for his murder?" Boopsie asks incredulously.

"*That's* a unique defense," Shrike declares.

"That's not what I said. I doubt if Holman even knew about her. I checked. She wasn't sent by his office. It was a hoax. From beginning to end, a hoax. And I'm an idiot."

"I wouldn't go that far," Boopsie reassures me.

"I might," Shrike says.

"One thing's for sure," Boopsie concludes. "You've got to find the girl."

"I will." God willing. "The guy I was arrested with—Norman Devore . . . nobody stands a better chance of finding her than he does. We have to get him out."

Boopsie nods. I assume that means she's on the case.

"While Albie's doing that," Sam says, "I have people running down leads on Gardner. Looking for his wife . . . Any children . . . Tracking the check we gave him for the interview."

I turn to Shrike. "I need a researcher to do a Los Angeles *Times* and local periodical check, for the years 1970, '71, '72, maybe '73— find anything there is on a twenty-four-year-old girl found dead of a drug overdose in Hollywood. Jeannie Locke."

"Jeannie Locke? Isn't that the name you got from the Ozzie Baba tipster?" Shrike asks.

"The same."

"I'll follow up on discovery," Boopsie says. "I'll try to find out if there are more surprises and prepare for the preliminary hearing."

"What happens there?" I ask.

"Both sides go before the judge. We can challenge the prosecution's evidence and introduce our own. It's like a minitrial. That's where Perry Mason won all his cases."

"Perry Mason died," Shrike points out.

"Well, I'm still very much alive," Boopsie retorts.

"That remains to be seen," Sam whispers in my ear, clearly underwhelmed by my lawyer's newfound lucidity.

Every time Sam's beeper goes off it's bad news. We were in my office . . . making out like adolescents, after hashing out her questions about me and the chauffeur . . . when it beeped again. It was her producer, Harry Carruthers.

I stood and watched her face as she got on the line with him. She was listening and he was talking, and whatever he was saying brought dark clouds to her clear blue eyes. As it always does, the rosy glow of amour was rapidly turning gray under the grim paintbrush of reality.

When they were finished she set the phone down and looked at me. "I was right about the leak. The cops may not like five-hundred-dollar-an-hour lawyers but they never turn down cash. Carruthers knows everything. The money, the phone call, the champagne glass . . ."

"No."

"Yes. And . . ."

"And?"

"We're going on the air with it tonight."

" *'We're'* going on the air?"

"I am. *Real Life* is. *Real Life* is me. It's what I do. It's my job. My responsibility. This has nothing to do with what I heard in the room, with my agreement with Boopsie. This is Carruthers, on his own, with his own contacts. I'm not happy about it, but this is the way it is.

"In fact, if I didn't feel the way I do about you, Albie, I'd be thrilled to death. The biggest story in the news . . . breaking new evidence . . . dominating the ratings . . . It's what we dream about in my business. You'd feel the same way, wouldn't you? If you didn't know you and you were leading the pack with the story?"

" 'If I didn't know me.' Yeah. Sure, I'd feel the same way. A story's a story. Somebody's gotta break it. Might as well be someone I'm crazy about."

"We tape at three. Come on the show. Answer the charges. We'll up the offer. I'll get Carruthers to pay you thirty thousand."

"He paid Gardner three hundred thousand."

"But he knew Gardner would confess."

"You mean I'd make more money for being guilty?"

"Well, yes, if you put it that way . . . But you're not guilty."

"How much would you pay me to confess?" I couldn't help asking. "The same as Gardner?"

She stared at me a moment, like she wasn't sure where I was coming from, then answered, "I suppose so. Do you want to confess?"

"Do you think I should?"

"Why are you playing with me? I'm not your enemy."

"When you're in my position, it's tough to know who is and who isn't."

"Do you really mean that?"

"No, I don't mean that. Yes, I mean that, but not about you. What I mean is, I'm worried, really worried. The DA, the cops, the public . . . everyone has me guilty. I could be sent away, in jail forever. On top of that, I have less than twelve hours to confess and exonerate Mitchell P. Gluck or he'll send some maniac to execute me, guilty or not. And the one person I've come to count on and trust most in all this is going on television to show thirty million people evidence that I'm a murderer. Friends? Enemies? How am I supposed to know?"

"Will you come on the show?"

"Yes, I'll come on the show. If a friend can't help with your ratings, what kind of friend is he?"

"I really hope you don't think I'm in this with you for the ratings."

"Are you *not* in it for the ratings . . . ?"

I'm suddenly hit with a stab of pain in my stomach that knocks me down into my chair.

"Albie . . . !"

"No. I'm fine," I wheeze, trying to talk without breathing.

"What can I get you? Do you have pills?"

"In my jacket . . ."

She digs out the Zantac, grabs a cup of water from the hall cooler and watches me down two pills. When the sharpness subsides I force a smile and gasp, "It's just gas . . ."

"You looked like you might faint."

"I have an appointment at the hospital tomorrow morning." At her anxious expression, I explain, "It's just a proceedure, not an operation."

"It's the biopsy you told me about?"

"Right . . ."

"God, Albie . . ."

"No big deal," I lie. "They don't put you to sleep or anything."

"I want to come with you."

"That's okay, I'll make it all right."

"You shouldn't drive. I'll take you there and pick you up."

"No."

"Yes."

"You really want to?"

"Yes I do."

"Okay, then. Thanks."

She moves into my arms in one quick step. "You don't have to fight *me*, Albie. Save your strength for your real enemies."

"I'm sorry, baby. I do know a good thing when I see it, I just never learned how to keep it good. Maybe you can teach me."

"We can teach each other."

"Thank's for being in my corner."

"I have to go now."

"Typical woman."

"Don't forget—be at *Real Life* by three o'clock."

"I've been to hell and back by twelve. I'll be there."

With Shrike's researcher running down newspaper accounts of the Jeannie Locke story and Sam's people checking out Gardner's life and times, it was time to deal with Mitchell P. Gluck.

I called the number Sampson gave me in the limo.

Sampson himself picked up on the second ring. "Is that you, Marx?" he asked before I could say anything.

"You got a phone just for me. I'm flattered."

"I wouldn't waste time with jokes, my friend. You've got two hours and twenty-three minutes of life left."

"You got a watch, too. I'm doubly flattered."

"It's your life. What's your question?"

"The question is—why would I tell a stooge what the boss wants to hear himself? Know what I mean?"

A brief, burning silence. Then, "Mr. Gluck doesn't need to talk to you. He believes what I tell him."

"Then he's a bigger idiot than I thought. But, okay, it's just as well. Give Mr. Gluck this message. You got a pencil?"

"Yeah, I got a pencil," he growls.

"Okay. Tell Mr. Gluck this: the inconvenience he's suffering over the murder of Bert Holman is bat droppings compared to the mountain of shit that will come down when the world hears about Jeannie Locke."

He didn't say anything right away, so I assumed he was taking it down word for word.

"Sampson?"

"What . . . ?"

"You need me to spell any of that out for you?"

"If I decide to call you back, where will you be?" he asked brusquely.

I gave him the number of my private, unlisted office line. "I'll be here about five more minutes, then I've got meetings the rest of the day. Tell him it's now or never."

I hung up.

Less than two minutes later my phone rang. It was my turn to preempt the greeting. "Hello, Mitchell."

"What do you want?"

"Let's talk."

"Talk."

"Face-to-face."

"Is that necessary?"

"One thing you should understand: Everything I know about Jeannie Locke, Bert Holman, the cowboy, and you is on tape. There are several cassettes, sealed in envelopes, in the possession of close friends, to be opened if they don't hear from me in the very near future."

"Do you understand who you're fucking with?" he asks evenly. "You're so out of your league you can't even grasp the rules. You don't threaten me. You don't blackmail me. You don't affect my life. Those are the rules."

"Rule on this, Gluck—be at the Farmer's Daughter Bar and Grill, across from CBS on Fairfax, in thirty minutes. Or '*Jeannie Locke*' will be all over every cable station you own."

"Thirty minutes. That works for me."

"And keep in mind . . . killing me will cause you more problems than you'll ever be able to solve."

To play it safe, I told Shrike where I was going, then headed back into the storm for my high level meeting with the chairman of Gluck International.

The tide in Hollywood was rising to the level of a torrent, rushing along streets and flooding curb banks like a miniwhitewater river, sweeping along in its current various and sundry articles of Los Angeles existence ... mangled blue-blocker sunglasses, a sodden, stuffed O.J. doll, a red bucket seat from a small sports car, a thermal coffee cup from Dunkin' Donuts, a Nike high-top, a disembodied Elvis-style toupee. The Jag was a salvage boat plowing through the detritus of an extinct civilization, its tires submerged in water-logged artifacts ...

It all made me think of another of Shrike's favorite sayings, a twist on the old homily, "Nobody ever said it would be easy."

His version of the line goes, *"Nobody ever said it wouldn't be hopeless."* Vintage Shrike.

But I was feeling the awful truth of that viewpoint. I was Kurtz, in Conrad's *Heart of Darkness,* who spoke the final words, *"The horror! The horror!"* Kurtz's jungle had become my Los Angeles, his "heart of darkness" the primitive, subconscious heart of my sinking city.

1070 FM ALL-News Radio reports:

... Flood evacuations increase in Benedict, Coldwater, Laurel and Beverly Glen canyons ...

... Confessed murderer of game show king Bert Holman, James T. Gardner, dies in prison ...

... His alleged co-conspirator, underground journalist Albie Marx, freed on $500,000 bail ...

... Gluck International stock sinks to all-time low with the arrest of Mitchell P. Gluck for his alleged role in the conspiracy to murder Holman ...

... Holman Entertainment, under the leadership of Sheila Petersen Holman, announces an agreement with Southwest Telephone to bolster their joint offer for Sovereign Communications with additional Southwest stock ...

Sheila Petersen Holman. The dumb actress isn't so dumb after all. Moving right in to snatch Sovereign from the mortally wounded Gluck. That ought to make my meeting with Gluck a real pleasure. From what I know of the man, he'd rather eat live rats than lose.

Sheila's play will make him more determined to do what it takes to win. A fight to the death over a billion-dollar empire, and who's stuck in the crossfire? Albie Marx. A mosquito in dinosaurland, a guy so far down the scale from a billion he doesn't have the price of a sober attorney. But he's got moral fiber, friends, and a sensational woman beside him. And Boopsie. Don't forget Boopsie. It's never over till the drunk lawyer burps.

... In other news, Public Television's Mr. Rogers has been accused by hundreds of devoted young followers of performing oral sexual acts on them ... No charges have been filed as yet ...

I couldn't believe it. How could that stupid story get so far? Who was it, Goebbels, who said if you repeat the big lie often enough it becomes the truth? Or am I mengeling (pardon the pun) the quote?

Back to the news:

... The radical terrorist group AHA, Anti-Homogenization Army, struck again, using hundreds of pounds of explosives to destroy the twin Mulholland Towers, LA's largest transmitters of television signals ... damages, not including windows and structural stability to homes in the area, estimated at three to five million dollars ...

Stevie McDonald again. Dynamiting TV towers in the worst storm of the year. Takes more than bad weather to stop a man with a cause. If I weren't so sunk in my own morass, I'd find little Stevie, the last revolutionary. And when I found him, what? Would I stop him? Or join up with him? His father used to say it's a losing war, but if we don't wage it we're damned as they are. The zeal of the father, visited upon the son. Maybe that old ardor could reignite my sputtering spirit ...

Turning onto Fairfax, I glided past The Farmer's Daughter, a venerable old joint with a faded sign, a painting of a Daisy Mae farmgirl bending provocatively at the waist to serve perfect martinis to two happy salesmen. No chance Gluck would be comfortable in there.

I parked farther away than I had to, across from the famous Farmer's Market. Checking up and down the block for a tail, I took a palm-size can of Mace from my glove compartment, slipped it into my jean jacket pocket, then jumped out of the car and, hugging the storefronts for shelter, ran through the rain back to the bar.

I had picked The Farmer's Daughter on impulse. It was pretty much in the middle of Hollywood and had managed for years, with its cracked leather booths and forties decor, to remain just this side of seedy. It was still a neighborhood institution and even on a stormy Wednesday afternoon there were regulars inside, kibitzing with the beer-bellied bartender and the grizzled, beehive-haired waitress. I took a seat at the bar with a view of the front door and ordered my Cuervo and Corona.

Exactly thirty minutes from the time we hung up, Mitchell P. Gluck walked in—perfectly groomed and tanned, in spite of the pesky monsoon. He was wearing sharply pressed jeans and a precisely unwrinkled Ralph Lauren sport shirt. He adjusted his eyes to the change in light, recognized me and walked over. The bartender slipped a napkin in front of him and asked what he wanted to drink.

"Diet Coke," he answered.

The bartender filled his order and moved off down the bar. Without looking at me, Gluck said, "How much do you want?"

"You can't really think this is about money."

He turned and locked eyes. "Spare me the virtue. What's the magic number?

"Mitch . . . Mind if I call you Mitch?" I knew he hated it. "Mitch, believe it or not, you and I are on the same side. We're both looking for the person who got to Gardner. Isn't that right?"

"The only thing I'm looking for is the truth to be told in public."

"The truth about Bert Holman? Or the truth about Jeannie Locke?"

"The truth about anything. I haven't heard one thing in the last three days that passed for any semblance of it. I didn't know Gardner. I don't know you. I never heard of Jeannie Locke. I've had enough of this drama. I want to get on with my business."

"If you never heard of Jeannie Locke, why did you meet me here?"

"To pay a price and put this to bed."

"Your name, along with Bert Holman's, has come up in connection with her death. Along with a cowboy who you and Bert were agenting at the time. Did you ever represent a cowboy together?"

"We had Bobby Holiday. In the early days at William Morris."

"Did Bobby Holiday know a Jeannie Locke?" He put up his hand to stop me. "Did Holman know her?" I pressed.

"If you have a financial proposal, make it now," he stated flatly. "Otherwise, I'm out of here."

"All right. We'll put Jeannie Locke aside for a minute. Let's go to Holman. Square one: Gardner did not kill Bert Holman on his own. Can we agree to that?"

"I have no information, therefore no opinion."

"Then we agree. Square two: Gardner was hired by someone. If you agree to that, don't say anything." I took a sip of my Corona. His eyes remained focused on me. "I personally think it was you . . ."

He started to get up. I put my hand on his arm, which felt like a wire cable. ". . . But for the sake of discussion," I continued, "let's look at another possibility."

He looked at my hand like it was flaking with leprosy. I lifted it from his arm. "The bride. Sheila. Couldn't she have hired Gardner? She certainly had the most to gain. And it's obvious why she would frame you . . ."

"Are you speaking for someone else, Marx? Who's directing this grim little play?"

"Someone else?"

"If you and Gardner didn't come up with this on your own, put me in touch with whoever is running the show and I'll take it from there."

"I assume this is your way of ruling out the bride."

"I'm not ruling out anything. Give me a name. Give me a number. Give me something I can do something with."

"It looks like Sheila's going to get Sovereign. How does that make you feel?"

"I save my feelings for people, not business. I either do a deal or I don't. Then I move on."

"All she had to do was get Gardner to mention your name. If you had hired him to kill Bert, you spent money and got screwed. That ought to make you angry.''

Saying I rub Gluck the wrong way is like saying the Jews irked Hitler. He stood abruptly and, jabbing the air with his finger, unveiled the iceberg tip of his temper.

"You were at the wedding, Marx. Your fingerprints are on the rifle that killed Bert. They placed you with Gardner, they found the money. They're burying you in evidence.

"Against me, they have nothing. A confession from a terminally ill criminal. Alleged phone calls. A laughable motive. Would I kill Bert—or anyone else, for that matter—over a business deal? Other deals come along. Always do. Sovereign won't be the last studio to hit the sale block.''

"But it's one you want,'' I reminded him.

"What angers me most in all this is you,'' he went on. "You won't state what you want and you won't say who you're in bed with. Which does makes me angry. Very angry.

"What I want is for you stop playing games. Either you and Gardner killed Bert on your own or you were paid to kill him and drag me into it. It's time to tell the truth.''

"I will tell the truth, Mitch. In about an hour from now.''

"What does that mean?''

"I'm the featured attraction on *Real Life* tonight. And I'm not going in front of the world to confess something I didn't do. I have no intention of taking the rap for you or anyone else.''

He glared at me a moment, then abruptly stood and walked off. I watched as he left the bar, without so much as a backward glance. The bartender looked over at me and I asked for the bill.

One Diet Coke. At least Gluck was a cheap date. The fact was, he didn't believe me and I didn't believe him. Which, in this town, is a prerequisite for business partnerships and marriage.

The Farmer's Daughter was its own little world. There were no windows. You had to walk all the way to the front door to see outside. So I could have sat there and imagined it was a clear, sunny day with white cotton clouds, a fresh wisp of breeze and zero smog ... I could have imagined me and Sam in a red convertible, cruising up the Coast Highway with a picnic basket in the back and Jimmy

Buffet singing "Margaritaville" on the radio ... Or, the two of us in Hawaii ... wading out into the warm, crystal-blue ocean, arm in arm, the sun a loving spotlight for only us ...

Those were the kind of mental exercises I'd have to get very good at if Danno succeeded in his life's work: caging me up in a four-by-eight cell forever.

I paid the bar bill and went to the front door. Peering outside, the reality of the storm made me feel wet before I went into it. Pulling up my jacket collar, I stepped out the door. Standing just to my right, waiting impatiently under a windblown umbrella, was Ralph Sampson, Mitchell Gluck's Brooks Brothers hit man.

"Give you a ride to your car, Marx?"

His black Darth Vader limo was parked at the curb, its front bumper snagging tasty items from the curbside current: waterlogged take-out food boxes, a soggy flyer for a body-piercing salon, a distended condom ... That limo was the last place in the world I wanted to be alone with Ralph Sampson. Having experienced the .357 magnum he packed, my hand went into my jacket pocket and wrapped itself around my pathetic little cannister of Mace. Not exactly an even duel, but if he made a move, I was ready.

"Mr. Gluck wants to talk to you."

"We talked."

"No, you didn't."

"What is he, deaf?"

"Now that the preliminaries are over, he wants to get down to business."

"Preliminaries? What is it with you people? Can't you do anything like normal human beings?"

"We're getting wet standing here."

"I'll tell you what, Sampson ... I'll get into that car with Gluck, but not with you. You have to wait over there, in front of the Chinese restaurant, where I can watch you."

He swallowed an urge to grind me into the sidewalk, turned, and walked over to the limo, leaving me unprotected from the rain, which was blowing fiercely into my face. I ducked my head but kept my eyes on Sampson as the back window of the limo cracked open and he had a few words with the occupant. Then he walked back to me.

"Go on, get in there."

I answered by pointing at the run-down Chinese restaurant halfway down the block. He looked at me sadistically, then adjusted his eyeglasses and started away.

"The umbrella . . ." I said, hand out.

He stopped, swallowed hard and promised, "I'm going to make that bump on your head look like the only place you didn't get hit. Count on it." He handed over the umbrella and swaggered off. I don't think I made a friend for life.

Gluck was waiting in the backseat. The driver was the same guy who disconnected my starter wires downtown. I gestured to the raised glass partition and asked Gluck, "Where's the lock switch for this?"

"Don't be paranoid," he advised. "We're beyond violence."

"Maybe you and I are, but these two aren't. I want it locked from back here," I insisted, watching Sampson standing in the rain, eating Peking crow under the threadbare canopy of the Chinese restaurant.

Gluck made a show of pressing the lock button on the partition switch. "Okay, now?"

"Better," I answered, relaxing slightly.

"What do you know about Jeannie Locke?"

As briefly as possible, I repeated the story Bambi Friedman told me.

"That's a total lie," Gluck said when I finished. "Where did you hear it?"

"A source who claims to have irrefutable proof."

"Did you see the proof?"

"Not yet."

"There is no such proof. It never ceases to amaze me how evil people can be."

"I know, Mitch. It's like, here are you and I, clinging to our lifeboat of truth and integrity, surrounded on all sides by wicked, lying sharks . . ."

"Misplaced sarcasm aside, your metaphor is on the money. If you don't get with the program, you'll go down hard—and I don't want you taking me with you.

"You're a pawn in a plot to destroy me. The story you were told, which depicts me as the villian, not to mention an accomplice to a possible murder, is a deliberate part of the plan. By telling you that story, you were made to distrust me. The point is to split us up. To get you to work against me.

"Do you understand what I'm saying? Do you see the incredible lengths to which this person will go to hurt me? He's willing to destroy *you,* just to make sure he gets me."

"He?" I ask. "Who is 'he'?"

"Come on. We both know it's Jack Schwarzberg—Ozzie Baba to those who don't see through him."

Gluck is a megalomaniac, but he's not a dope. He didn't get where he is by being a patsy. He started out in the mailroom and made a billion dollars. If this is his real take on the case, I should at least listen with an open ear.

"You think Ozzie Baba's behind this?"

"Ozzie Baba, my ass. That is the biggest crock of shit ever swallowed by people who should know better. He's Jack Schwarzberg— a pimp. I met him at a Bel-Air party, twenty-five years ago. I was just starting out as an agent. Somehow, he convinced the people who were throwing the party that he had psychic powers. They thought if they directed enough money his way he'd transform them from ugly cows into beautiful angels.

"You remember those days. The Beatles with the Maharishi. Leary, and LSD. Every idiot wanted to be spiritual. Everyone wanted a guru, including a lot of young girls who came to Hollywood and found out they needed an identity to make an impression, something special, other than being just another good roll in the hay. They thought Schwarzberg would provide that identity. They went for it even more when he gave himself an Indian name and claimed to be channeling primitive Indian souls.

"Somewhere along the line, on the celebrity circuit, I introduced him to Bobby Holiday, who was a giant star at the time. Bobby saw through his *shtick* right away. He saw the guy was strictly in it for sexual favors. So Bobby, who was the horniest guy in the world, got Schwarzberg to provide female entertainment for him on off-nights, when Bobby felt like just staying home and doing take-out. Bobby sampled all the new spiritual stuff and Schwarzberg got to 'convert' all the groupies that trailed Bobby around. Bobby was so flush in those days, he bought Schwarzberg a place in the Hollywood Hills, to house his little tribe of Indian girls. They called it the Reservation. Schwarzberg had one wing to himself, where he did all his work on the so-called higher planes, channeling and soaking the Hollywood A-List of dollars they would have burned up on drugs anyway. The girls lived in the other wing, waited hand and foot on Schwarzberg ... *Chief Blackfoot*, or whatever-the-fuck he was calling himself. The girls were thrilled to meet and service a big star like Bobby Holiday who, I can tell you, had the libido and penis of a sperm whale ... to make up for the size of his talent, which was far less prodigious.

"One of the girls Schwarzberg brought up to Bobby's was named Jeannie Locke. The only reason I know is, the next day, Bert asked me to come into his office because Bobby was there. I went in and Bobby was broken down, in tears. Bert showed me a newspaper, opened to the page about this girl, Jeannie Locke, found dead in her car. Bobby had just poured his heart out to Bert, confessed that he and Schwarzberg were partying with her, doing alcohol and drugs—and she keeled over and died. They put her in her car, drove her down to Hollywood and left her there. Bobby said he was crying because he felt bad about the girl. The real reason was, he was afraid the cops would trace the girl to Schwarzberg, and Schwarzberg would lead them to him."

"As my publisher would say," I can't help but remark, " *'Beautiful people doing beautiful things.'* "

"Bobby asked me and Bert if he should give himself up. Having no firsthand knowledge of what actually transpired, I told him to follow his conscience. Bert advised him to keep quiet and wait, see if anything developed.

"Schwarzberg was eventually questioned and released, and the girl's death became history. Bobby never came forward and I never saw any reason why I should, either. The fact is, nobody but Schwarzberg and Bobby will ever know what happened that night."

"What became of Bobby?" I ask. "Where is he now?"

"He died. A stroke. He was a heroin addict, living somewhere off in Arizona, so brain-damaged he couldn't even recognize his own mother."

"Gee . . ." I said. "Thanks for unconfusing me." The conflicting histories were clanking around in my head.

"The point I'm making is this, Marx: it's clear Schwarzberg double-crossed you to make sure he got me. Given that, here's what I'm prepared to do: I'll get you Marvin Mendelson, the best criminal attorney in the world. Won't cost you a dime, I'll cover the whole thing."

"Marvin Mendelson? The lawyer who writes novels?"

"That's right. *The Big Retainer, Punitive Damage, Excessive Charges, Contingency Man . . .*"

"How do you remember all those?"

"I produced the movies. The point is, Mendelson has never had a client convicted of first-degree murder. He's the world's leading plea-bargainer. He'll get you a reduced charge . . . manslaughter, second degree . . . you'll be out in five years. Guaranteed. When you look at the alternative, it's a deal you can't turn down."

"And what do you want me to do for that? Lay it all at the feet of Ozzie Baba?"

"That's exactly what I'd like."

"How will that help you get Sovereign?"

"If you clear me now, I can steady my stock. When the police turn to Schwarzberg, I'll blast his relationship with Sheila Holman all over the networks. Southwest Telephone is so image conscious, they'll back off immediately. They want Sovereign, but they would never be in business with someone who the media suspected of murder. Without Southwest, the bottom drops out of Holman Entertainment's offer. And I win."

It appeared he was convinced I was in league with Ozzie. It would have been useless to try to change his mind, so I went in the other direction. "How do you know Mendelson can get me the reduced charge?"

"I'll put you together with him. He'll talk to you himself."

I had to think about that. It wasn't a deal I could turn away out of hand. If it came down to a plea bargain or life, I'd gratefully take five years. "Give me a day to think about it," I told him.

"What is there to think about? Every hour is precious."

"Twenty-four hours."

"Twelve."

"Twenty-four. That's what I need."

"Okay. But that's it. If you don't take the offer tomorrow, you're on your own."

Two different versions of the Jeannie Locke story. Bambi Friedman didn't mention Ozzie Baba, didn't know the name Jack Schwarzberg. Gluck put it square on Ozzie's shoulders. Who am I supposed to believe? Bambi? Gluck? Or the next person who comes along, with yet another version of the twenty-year-old incident.

Gluck's claim to innocence was convincing. Not that he's above foul play, but he's a lot more cunning than to resort to shooting his rival in broad daylight. And he could be right about Ozzie Baba. It would answer the right questions for me.

Q: Why kill Holman? A: To make Sheila Petersen, who appears unable to do anything without Ozzie, America's newest billionaire. Q: Why frame me? A: To keep me from digging up the truth about him and Jeannie Locke.

I needed to talk to the Happy One, and I needed to do it fast.

Normally, it's a fifteen-minute drive from Hollywood to Holman Entertainment in Century City. But it's been pouring without letup for nearly three days and the storm has knocked out half the traffic lights, littered the flooded streets with crashed and stalled vehicles and busted various sewer mains with the overload. On the radio, they're warning people who live in the neighborhood of sewage treatment plants that systems may overflow.

Close to an hour after leaving the Gluckster, I pull up at the gate of Holman Entertainment. The same guard with the black crepe armband is in the booth. I roll down my window and tell him I'm expected at *Real Life*.

By now my face has been all over TV and the newspapers and he greets me with a ferocious scowl. "You're gonna pay big-time for what you did to Mr. Holman," he seethes through the wall of rain between us.

"I didn't know you were the jury," I answer. "Lift up the fucking gate."

"You son-of-a-bitch! I'll watch you fry in the gas chamber!"

Another genius deciding my fate.

I float the Jag down to the *Real Life* studio, anchor it as close as I can to the stage door, and run inside. The first one to spot me is Mr. Important.

"You're barely on time," he says ugently.

"I had to wait for a drawbridge."

"Come on," he orders, missing the humor, and I follow as he quick-steps past the set where I'll soon sit with Sam, proclaiming my innocence, down a busy back corridor, to a large makeup room. Inside is a middle-aged blonde in a miniskirt, showing too much leg and much too much tummy, and a bony young man with long thin brown hair. They're sitting cross-legged, engrossed in conversation, smoking cigarettes and promulgating rumors.

"This is Albie Marx," Mr. Important announces. "Mimi is makeup, Mario is hair—they'll take care of you." He hurries off.

"Have a seat, hon," Mimi says, standing and patting a chair facing the mirror.

"Is it still raining?" Mario asks.

"You were just out there," she says to him.

"Well, it could have stopped."

"It hasn't," I told them. "And it won't. Maybe ever."

"Cheery today, aren't we? Come on now, hon, let's make that face beautiful." She pats the chair again.

"You're not going to wear those clothes are you?" Mario asks, wrinkling his nose.

"Why?"

"Well, for one, it looks like you slept in them."

"Now that you mention it," I recall, "I did." In jail.

"Yuk."

"You have something a little fresher?" I ask.

"Well, that's not Mission Impossible. What size are you? Large shirt? Thirty-six waist?"

"Thirty-four."

"Sure. I'll go dig something up." He stands and drops his cigarette in a styrofoam cup half full of coffee. "You want something to drink? Coffee? Juice?"

"That would be good. Orange juice and coffee. With fake sugar and real milk. Thanks."

"How about you, Mim?" he asks.

"I'm fine." As he's going out, she calls, "Make sure Sam knows he's here, will you, hon?"

I flop down in the chair and she drapes a plastic bib over my front. Frowning into the mirror, she asks, "How'd you get that nasty bump?"

"Chopped off a branch with my head."

"Ouch. Well, we'll cover that up."

She's dabbing away at me with her makeup sponge when Sam appears beside her in the mirror.

"Hi." She gives me a warm smile and touches my shoulder. Not exactly going out of her way to hide her feelings from Mimi.

"I got here on time," I point out.

"And won me five bucks. I bet Harry. He said you wouldn't even show."

"That guy's crazy about me, isn't he?"

"Well, one of us is."

I look at Mimi when Sam says this. Mimi just smiles and spreads pancake.

"We can say anything in front of Mimi. She's my surrogate sister."

"Anything?"

"Hey, I've heard it all, hon. Unless you got a brand-new way of doing it . . ."

"Are you going to cover his bump?" Sam asks.

"Would I let him go on the air, looking like Jake Lamotta?"

"How are you feeling?" Sam asks me.

"Better. Now that you're here."

"What a sweetie," says Mimi.

"He is."

"Wait till you get to know me . . ."

"You're not what you appear to be?" Sam asks.

"Nothing is what it appears to be . . ."

"Ooooh, *deep*," Mimi kibitzes.

"Eric found something very interesting today."

"Eric?"

"My assistant. The fellow you call Mr. Important. He came up with something on Gardner."

"Should I know what it is before our interview?"

"It wouldn't hurt."

Eric appears at the door carrying a small combination TV/VCR. "In here?"

"Yes," Sam answers. "Set it up on the counter." As he puts up the TV and plugs it in, she explains, "Eric found this in the Holman Entertainment library. It was taped less than a year ago. Is it cued up, Eric?"

"Affirmative."

"Okay then."

He hits the play button. I've only seen the show a couple of times, but it's enough to tell me I'm watching an excerpt from *The Shame Game*.

Bob Lange, the compassionate host, is saying, ". . . And now it's time to share firsthand some of the horrible things that can happen to ordinary people like you and me. Let's begin with James T. Gardner. Hi, James, welcome to the show."

Gardner is forty pounds heavier and has more hair, but his eyes are still planted sorrowfully in the deep black bags, his mouth has the set of permanent pain and he's standing hunched over, like God came up and yanked the spine out of him. He nods grimly in response to Lange's greeting.

Lange asks, "Are you ready to play *The Shame Game*?"

Gardner nods again.

They cut to a wide shot of Lange, Gardner, and the other two contestants, a man and a woman. The man is smiling dazedly at Lange, as if he's surprised and happy to find himself on the show. The woman looks like she's been worked over by a heavyweight boxer. Lange says to Gardner, "Your category is CANCER, James. This is your opportunity to convince our home audience that fate has abused you worse than Mel and Felicia here. Are you ready?"

"I'm ready, Bob . . ."

"Okay, then. Tell us about it."

"Well, Bob . . ." Gardner sighs, "the real-estate agent never mentioned anything about the power company's right-of-way . . ."

As Gardner relates his tale in an emotion-laden voice, we're treated to a filmed "Dramatic Re-creation" of his story, just like the shows that reenact crimes. Watching the drama unfold with actors, we hear Gardner's voice narrating the events.

His story is basically that he spent all his savings on a house for his family, without being told that the power company had a right of way to erect a high-voltage electrical tower fifteen feet from his front yard. The grid went up after they moved in. Over the years, aside from the constant low hum, they never thought much about it. Until both of his children were diagnosed with leukemia. A number of experts came forward and attributed the kids' illness to EMF, the electromagnetic force emanating from the high power lines. As the kids got sicker, Gardner and his wife became more distraught. They tried to get the power company to move the tower but company officials claimed it was cost prohibitive because it would affect the whole grid. Gardner couldn't afford to get a lawyer, but one finally stepped forward, willing to take the case on contingency, on the basis that if the power company finally did move the tower, it would be an admission of guilt and the Gardners could sue for the kids' leukemia. All this time, the kids were getting sicker and sicker. Eventually, the lawyer told Gardner it was a losing battle and dropped the case. Gardner suspected something amiss when the lawyer subsequently went to work for the power company. Meanwhile, the medical bills for the kids had eaten away everything Gardner owned. He was barely able to make his house payments. Without the house, the family would be homeless. When his ten-year-old daughter succumbed to the disease, Gardner put the house up for sale. But, because of the electric grid, nobody bought it. Nobody even looked inside it. Both Gardner and his wife were suffering terribly through all this, Gardner contracting stomach ulcers and his wife going through a series of nervous disorders. When their twelve-year-old boy finally died, Mrs. Gardner snapped. She climbed the tower with a wire clipper to cut the wires. Cutting through the main line, she got a jolt that blew her off the tower. When she landed she suffered near-fatal internal injuries. She was taken to the hospital, spent sixteen hours in surgery, came out pinned together and was placed on a battery of life-support machines. For cutting the main power line, which led to an eight-hour blackout all along the grid, the police charged Mrs. Gardner with malicious mischief. The power company's lawyers, led by Gardner's ex-attorney, placed a lien for two hundred fifty thousand dollars on his house, the cost of shutting down the substation and repairing the damage. Gardner's neighbors and other consumers in the area who were affected by the power loss became so angry, they threw stones through Gardner's windows and left signs in his yard, "Keep Your Hands Off Our Power Lines." The hospital demanded that Gardner pay for his wife's life support. He had no insurance, so they were threatening to discharge her. As a result of all that had happened—his children dead of leukemia, his wife on costly life-support systems in the shadow of the hospital's threat to pull the plug—Gardner's ulcers developed into full-blown colon cancer and he was given less than a year to live. The diagnosis was confirmed for the *The Shame Game* by its staff medical specialist, Dr. Alan Rissman.

The filmed reenactment of Gardner's ordeal is so melodramatically done that, when I look in the mirror at Sam, Mimi, and Mario, standing behind me watching the show, their eyes are filled with tears. As a matter of fact, I realize, so are my own. It was been a gut-wrenching thing to watch. When they cut back to Gardner himself, fighting to keep from coming apart on camera, Mario starts sobbing. Even Eric, Mr. Important, with his precise, businesslike front, ducks his head to conceal his emotion. Sam is involuntarily squeezing my shoulder. I reach up and hold her hand tightly as we all watch Bob Lange, who literally has to blow his nose into a handkerchief, tell Gardner, "That was a wonderful story, James, and I'm sure everyone in the audience . . . well, I know their hearts go out to you. We have to take a break now for some important messages, then we'll come back with our current champion, Felicia Meezner, whose terrifying tales of life with a homicidal husband have already earned her a new Ford minivan and a kitchen ensemble by Maytag. Don't go away . . ."

*   *   *

Eric switches off the monitor. The subdued silence is broken by Sam. "Compelling, isn't it?"

"Just awful . . ." Mario sighs.

"We're cutting this into tonight's show. It will run just before your segment."

A production assistant appears at the door to announce, "Five minutes, please. Five minutes to tape."

Mimi takes the plastic bib off me. Mario, still sniffling, steps in to work on my hair.

"What do you think?" Sam asks me.

"What do I think? The son-of-a-bitch framed me and I'm sitting here crying for him. I'm a bigger idiot than the people who watch that show."

"It explains why he needed money."

"Does anyone know what hospital his wife is in?" I ask Eric.

"No. Someone is looking up the info sheets—the forms the contestants fill out when they apply for the show. That might tell us."

"I didn't know Al Rissman was *The Shame Game* doctor," I mention to Sam.

"He was Bert's personal physician. Bert put him on the payroll."

"There," declares Mario, with a little half-hearted flick of his styling comb. "That's as good as it's gonna' get. I put clean clothes in the dressing room next door . . ."

"Thanks."

"Oh!" he exclaims hoarsely. "That poor family! Excuse me . . ." He runs out of the room.

"He's very sensitive," Mimi explains. "That show always makes him sick to his stomach."

"That show is seen by more people than any other television show in the world," Sam points out.

"It's a brilliant concept," Eric declares.

"Nobody ever accused Bert of not being brilliant," Sam agrees.

"You know what I love about it?" Mimi says. "It's got everything—the poignancy of Oprah, the raciness of Geraldo, good-looking actors from the soaps—and somebody wins a prize for all they've been through!"

"It's sick," I tell her.

"Tell you what, hon . . . I wouldn't mind winning a prize for some of the shit I've taken . . ."

"Well, James T. Gardner didn't win anything," Sam muses. "He was dying anyway, so killing Bert was no big deal."

"And he made a bundle for it," I conclude.

"But he would only have made fifty thousand. We paid him an obscene amount to confess on the show . . ."

"Everyone knows how the media works these days. He probably killed Bert knowing someone like you would come along."

"Do you think we encouraged him to commit murder?"

"Not you, not specifically, no—"

"You two better discuss this after the taping," Mimi interrupts. "Seeing a crew sit and wait is like watching money burn."

"Right, Mim. I'll meet you on stage," Sam says to me, moving up and kissing me lightly on the lips. Before she can step away, I put my arm around her and make the kiss last.

"Oooh!" Mimi gasps dramatically. "Be still my heart!"

We're in Sam's Blazer. Before we left the studio there was an announcement that mudslides had closed the Pacific Coast Highway. There was no way Sam could get home, so we're navigating the streaming streets of Hollywood in the fading light, in four-wheel drive with me at the helm, our course set for my house in Los Feliz.

Between mesmerizing sweeps of the windshield wipers, we're silently watching the mayhem unfold: shallow-rooted trees that have toppled onto cars, houses, blocked roadways . . . black plastic garbage bags the sanitation department couldn't collect, floating along in curbside currents . . . spare tires from marooned vehicles bobbing around in the swirling eddies of sewer mouths . . .

And yet the traffic keeps moving, like it always does, in spite of earthquakes, fires and everything else God dishes out to our tiny piece of the earth. Proving that nothing can bring this city to its knees. Could be, that's why I'm so fascinated by it. Maybe I identify with it. Maybe I'd like to believe that like LA, I'll still be standing after all the elements God sent to test me have petered out and slithered away in defeat.

Earlier, Sam and I had a disagreement over something that happened on her show.

They began by running the full-length version of Gardner's heart-rending appearance on the *The Shame Game*.

Then Sam introduced me. They projected photographs of me back in the sixties as a civil rights demonstrator . . . leading the famous KILL NIXON rally . . . touring with Janis Joplin . . .

Question by question, Sam elicited the story of my involvement in the murder, during which they interjected clips of my arrest at Bert Holman's, leaving the Hollywood precinct, my release from LA County Jail . . .

Sam asked, and I explained, how I came to be standing with Gardner, holding the rifle that killed Holman when the security guards converged on us. I told about Virginia and even held up the *Player's Guide* photo of her and appealed to the audience to call in if anyone knew her whereabouts.

Sam also brought up, graphically demonstrated on a screen behind us, each specific piece of evidence Carruthers had dug up from his contacts in the prosecutor's office: the phone call, the fingerprints, the money . . .

Even though I had a legitimate answer for every question, at one point, to my complete horror I realized that, to a typical viewer, every answer sounded like a lie, every explanation an invention. Simply the act of defending myself became damning in itself . . . a result, I guessed, of conditioned responses built up over years of watching shows like *60 Minutes,* where someone responding to the aspersions of Mike Wallace or Morley Safer appears guilty, by the fact of *having* to respond.

It was a terrifying understanding, because, as I sat there under the glaring lights, proclaiming my innocence to the world, I knew that no matter how the whole thing turns out, I'll always be guilty to some people, tainted to others and remembered by all as the guy who was accused of Bert Holman's murder . . .

As if that weren't enough, Sam shocked me at one point by asking, "You told me you met another woman at the wedding, a Bambi Friedman . . . and that she claimed to have information about your co-defendant, Mitchell P. Gluck of Gluck International. Has she told you anything that would lead you to believe that Mitchell P. Gluck was indeed involved?"

For a very long second, I was stunned speechless. I remembered telling her about Bambi the other night at her house, when I was drunk and spewing my guts out. But I hadn't mentioned her again. Bambi was someone I wanted to keep to myself, a piece of the puzzle no one else had access to—not to mention the fact that I had sworn to protect her identity. Suddenly, Sam had blurted her name on national TV.

I forced myself not to glower at her on camera. "To tell you the truth, I haven't seen or heard from her since the wedding."

She went blithely on. "Have you tried to contact her?"

I couldn't believe she was pursuing it. "I haven't had enough time to feed my animals, never mind date new women," I answered. "But thanks for the interest. If we ever get together, I'll let you know how it turns out."

At the end of the show, the lights dimmed and the director announced from the control booth, "That's it, folks, it's a wrap. Good show. Thank you."

I was straining to confront Sam, to make her tell me why she brought up Bambi Friedman, but I had to sit and wait for a sound man to remove the little microphone they had clipped to my shirt. The waiting wound me up even more.

Finally, when we were alone, I said, "That was a low blow. I suppose you have an impeccable reason for doing it."

"You sound angry."

"I sound *angry*? I think I sound bewildered. But if 'angry' works for you, it works for me, too."

"You don't have to be sarcastic."

"And you don't have to be Lois Lane."

"Excuse me?"

"Anything for a scoop? Does that ring a bell?"

"Calm down, you're stressed out . . ."

"Don't patronize me. Why did you blindside me with Bambi Friedman?"

"You didn't tell me not to mention her."

"You couldn't resist going for the bombshell."

"I was doing my job, which is to get at the truth."

"Don't use that word. Not in connection with what you do."

"You don't think we're all after the same thing? You're going to sit there and tell me *UP YOURS* is the only bastion of truth and integrity in the world?"

"Don't turn it around . . ."

"Then don't preach to me. I'm getting tired of all the critics badmouthing TV and tabloid news and this and that and everything but what they do. 'Exploitation.' 'Sensationalism.' 'Pandering to the lowest common denominator.' You're telling me people get the truth from *The New York Times*? That Peter Jennings has some monopoly on integrity? That college media professors refused to watch the Gulf War and the Lorena Bobbit penis trial on principle? There's no entertainment in news? People aren't fascinated by tragedy? If that's true, then *Oedipus* and *King Lear* would have closed out of town."

"You're comparing your show to *Oedipus* and *King Lear*?"

"For today's audience, yes. I know, you think that makes me an intellectual midget. Where do I get off thinking *Real Life* can do something to make people understand the world and feel compassion? You know what the answer is? *Real Life* tells people what they want to know about the news and, believe it or not, it makes them feel something about it."

"*The Shame Game* makes them feel, too. But it's demented."

"*The Shame Game* is today. *Real Life* is today. I didn't create the present, but I'm living in it. And making what I think is a contribution. If you want to call it 'entertainment,' I accept that. But don't call it dishonest and don't call it pandering. Unless you think those words describe me, too."

"That sort of limits my options . . ."

"If you want, I'll apologize for bringing up Bambi Friedman. But I don't think I did something wrong."

That's where we were when we heard the news about the Pacific Coast Highway closing. The elements had conspired to keep us together for the night, and neither of us could hide the fact that we were happy about the prospect. I was so happy that my indignation quickly melted into a mealy-mouthed state of warm anticipation. What we suddenly wanted more than anything else was to be alone with each other and make wild, wonderful, passionate love. That's the beauty of men and women—when it comes right down to it, nobody ever really thinks with their brain.

Now we're close to my house and feeling the excitement in the warm pressure of each other's hand.

When I finally turn onto Valley Oak Drive and head for my driveway, two things make an immediate impression. One, Norman Devore's mansion is lit up, as if every light bulb in the place is burning.

"That's Devore's house," I indicate to Sam. "He must have gotten out of the can." The other thing that attracts my attention is that there are lights on in my house, too. There's also a black BMW parked in my carport.

"It's my son's car," I tell her as I pull the Blazer up, switch off the wipers, turn out the headlights and kill the ignition.

"Did you know he was here?"

"I didn't know he knew where 'here' is. He hasn't been here since he became Jonathan Grant."

"Who was he before?"

"Freedom Marx."

"*Freedom Marx* ... I like that. Jonathan Grant ... that's sort of obnoxious."

"Do me a favor ... he likes to be called Jonathan. Play along. It'll make life easier."

"If he's your son I'll like him, whatever his name is."

I have my doubts about that. On the other hand, maybe she will like him. They're probably more like each other than they are like me. After all, she's closer to his age than mine.

We're about to make a run for the house when she notices a five-foot-high pyramid in the corner of the carport.

"What is that?"

"That? Avocado pits."

"Pits ... ?"

"Don't ask. Which reminds me, where are my animals? Jed! Tank! Come on! Come on, guys! Daddy's home!" No response. Only the incessant tapping and hissing of the rain.

She follows me as I dash to the front door. It's opened by Freedom, just as I reach for the handle.

"My house collapsed," he announces, harassed and disheveled in his rumpled business suit and tie. "It's a pile of of mud and sticks. With all my stuff in it."

"No . . ." is all I can muster up.

"It's gone."

"Completely?"

"Everything."

"That's horrible . . . Thank God you weren't in it. You weren't in it, were you?"

"I was at my office. The emergency force called to tell me."

"As long as you're physically okay . . . I know it's a terrible blow, but everything else can be replaced . . ."

"Just don't say 'I told you so.' "

"I didn't"

"You will."

"Will what?"

"Say that buying a house on stilts is like bending over in the YMCA." To Sam he says, "Excuse the metaphor, it's his, not mine."

"I'm sorry. This is Samantha Shelton . . ."

"I know, Dad. I had a television." By way of introduction he tells her, "I'm Jonathan Grant."

I still can't get used to that name.

"I'm sorry about your house . . ." she says.

"Mine's not the only one that went. It's just the only one I care about."

"Jonathan belongs to the Church of Personal Happiness."

"The Happiness Foundation," he corrects.

"He's an Ozzie Baba-head."

"I can't do anything about other people's houses," he states with a convert's conviction. "And even if I could, it's not my job to make them happy. If I concentrate on my own house, resurrect my own life, it will make me happy and set an example for others . . ."

". . . which in turn will make them happy," I conclude.

"That's the way it works, Dad, believe it or not. It wouldn't make you happy for me to sit around here and cry about my house, would it?"

"No, I guess not . . ."

"Anyway, it was impossible to get a hotel room, so I figured I'd spend the night. If you don't mind."

"Of course I don't mind. You can stay here as long as you like." There goes my night of passion.

"Do you have flood insurance?" Sam asks.

"Flood, but not mud. I may not be insured."

"How can there be mud without flood?" I ask.

"You can't buy mud without buying flood. If you want mud, you have to take flood. They don't tell people that. We get flood and we think we have mud. But we don't. We have *bupkis*. It's another rip-off. I'll deal with it tomorrow."

"We should turn on the news," Sam says. "See what's going on out there . . ."

"There's no reception here," Freedom tells us. "Stevie blew up the Mulholland transmitting towers."

"Stevie . . . ?" Sam asks.

"An old hippie term," I explain quickly. "A word we used in the sixties for violent radicals. Like they called the North Vietnamese 'Charlie.' As in, Stevie just held up the Bank Of America." I don't want her to think she has an inside track on the AHA story. We have enough trouble staying on the same page of the Albie Marx story.

She volunteers, "I know who 'Stevie' is. It's a group called the Anti-Homogenization Army. They blew up the Sovereign satellite on Monday. And the Mulholland Towers are owned by Gluck International. Interesting coincidence. I'd give anything to get an interview with the AHA . . ."

"Anyway, there's no reception in whole areas of the city," Freedom says, agilely moving off the Stevie angle.

"Do you have a radio?" Sam, the news junkie, inquires.

"In the bedroom."

"Mind if I . . . ?"

"Go ahead," I tell her, and point the direction. She makes a beeline for the radio.

"Some woman named Boopsie called," Freedom says. "Sounded drunk out of her mind. Said to tell you 'Devore was bailed out last night and she's trying to find out who put up the bond.' I guess you know what that means . . ."

"It's good news. Thanks."

"So . . . I guess I'll just sleep on the couch. I'm beat."

"The house is yours. Do whatever you want. Stay as long as you like."

"Thanks." Hearing Sam turn on the radio in the bedroom, he whispers, "You're going out with Samantha Shelton?"

"I was on her show tonight . . ."

"God, that's right! I missed it. How'd it go? Was she rough on you?"

"Only once. But we settled that."

"So? Are you two . . . ?"

"Are we what?"

"You know . . ."

"I don't know. Maybe. We'll see."

"She's a knockout."

"I'm afraid so."

"By the way, there was a giant dog under the carport when I got here."

"That's Jed. Where is he?"

"He's okay. He went with the cat."

"Where did they go?"

"They were chasing something up the hill. I think it was a skunk."

"A skunk! Great. That'll be a pleasure."

"Don't worry. The dog didn't look like he could catch anything faster than a three-legged turtle . . ."

I give him sheets, towels, pillows, and blankets, then pop into the bedroom, where Sam is lying comfortably on the bed, her boots off, engrossed in 1070 FM All-News Radio.

"They just said my ex-husband Michael formed an investment group . . . and made an offer for Sovereign."

"Michael Whitehead? He's going after Sovereign?"

"It's on the news. I just put in a call to him."

"You're fast."

"Lois Lane."

"I apologized for that . . ."

"No, I like it. It means you're Superman."

"With you, I am."

So Michael Whitehead wants to steal Sovereign from Gluck and Holman. Will the sharks never stop biting?

"You never told me ... how long have you and Whitehead been divorced?"

"A little over a year."

"How long were you married?"

"Four years."

"Any children?"

"Not that I know of."

"Are you surprised by his move?"

"He made BMA the biggest agency in the world. Power intoxicates. I knew he couldn't stop there."

"Be interesting to see what Gluck and Sheila Holman do about it. I'm going to take a quick run up to Devore's. Check if he's home."

"Mind if I wait here? This is the first moment I've had to relax all day."

"No, that's fine."

"Albie ... Where is Freedom's mother?"

"Susan? In Arizona. On flying saucer patrol."

"What's that?"

"She's with the Van Heisel Group. They communicate with aliens called 'Old Ones.' "

"Really ... ?"

" 'Really' is a big word. Let's not get carried away ..."

"Everything's possible."

"Each to his or her own, right? She believes in aliens."

"Hey, there are college professors who believe in aliens. That doesn't make someone crazy."

"But it can make them disconnected. Anyway, let's not talk about ex's. When I come back from Devore's, Freedom will be asleep ..."

"And I'll be awake. Waiting."

I sit on the bed and kiss her. "Dear God, thank You for delivering this parcel," I whisper. She's the best-smelling thing on the planet.

Outside, the wind has picked up and the rain is slanting down in furious sheets. An umbrella would be useless. I tuck in my chin and start the long drudge up the mud driveway to the brightly lit Steinberg mansion, hoping Devore is in there and not too frogged out.

As I approach, the sound of Elvis's voice mingles with the uproar of the storm, and as I get closer I make out the words, "... *down at the end of lonely street, it's Heartbreak Hotel* ..."

Devore knows how to carry a torch. Can't blame him. Virginia's a hell of a girl. If you like that type. I wish I'd never seen her, that's for sure.

"*... Although it's always crowded, You still can find some room* ..."

Half-expecting Devore to appear in a window with a spotlight and shotgun, I run the last twenty feet to the front door, which turns out to be cracked the slightest bit open. I carefully let myself in. I don't want to take him by surprise and become an accidental shooting victim.

Like last time, the stereo is turned up to Mach III. Elvis is battering the beams and joists with the unmitigated brute force of heartache and pain.

"*... YOU MAKE ME SO LONELY BABY, YOU MAKE ME SO LONELY BABY, YOU MAKE ME SO LONELY I COULD DIE* ..."

"Norman!" I shout. "Norman!"

Nothing. Just Elvis. I move into the vast living room. The old house has sprung more leaks than a drive-by victim. Everywhere are pots and glasses, cups and vessels of all kinds, overflowing onto the floor. Devore's stereo is sitting next to a musty, decaying armchair that's probably a hundred years old. A glance at the CD player tells me the "Heartbreak Hotel" cut is on REPEAT, which means it will play forever until someone shuts it off. Which I do.

The silence is startling. Agony to serenity is a long road to travel in a nanosecond. I can still hear the rain and wind out there, but except for the drip, drip, drip of the leaks, everything inside is suddenly still.

"Norman! It's me! Albie! Are you here?"

No answer. Maybe he's in the study, working on his computer.

Suddenly there's a sound, a frenzied scraping on the floor, coming from the study. I stiffen and clutch the can of Mace in my jacket pocket. Then it hits me. The disgusting stench of . . .

Skunk.

. . . as Jed and Tank barrel out of the study and run straight at me . . . with Hi, Dad! in their eyes and the worst stink this side of the Ganges on their fur. I step backward.

"NO! NO JUMPING! NO! NO RUBBING! OUTSIDE! NO!"

Too late. They're all over me. It's horrible, a disaster. I make them back off, then chase them through the living room, out the front door and slam it after them.

The odor sticks. I'm rancid. All three of us will have to take tomato juice baths. The night I was going to Paradise.

Does the name *Job* mean anything here?

"Norman! Damn it! Norman! I'm leaving!" No answer. I'm not about to go through the entire house. Before I leave I'll just take a look in the study.

Getting close to the door, the reek of skunk is overwhelming. The reflection of a steady, clinical gray light from Norman's computer screen is shimmering in the surface of a saucepot sitting on the floor, running over with water from one of the leaks.

I feel something in my stomach that I think I've been denying since I found the front door open. Something bad has happened here.

Something very bad.

I take two very slow steps to the threshold of the room. I look inside.

Devore is sitting in his swivel chair, head back, shirt torn open, pants pulled down to his thighs. One of his hands covers his butchered groin. Three big, black-and-blue holes are torn into his chest.

Virginia is sitting—actually, propped up—against the wall at Norman's feet. She has the face of an angel and a bullet hole in the forehead.

On the floor in front of her is the pearl-handled razor Norman had used to threaten Frederick, the director.

Beside Devore's razor is Virginia's tongue, cleanly sliced off like a cut of sushi.

Stuffed into her slack-jawed mouth are Norman's severed genitals.

As mesmerized as I am repulsed, I take an involuntary step forward . . . and notice Devore's other hand, resting on his desk.

He's clutching a blood-soaked copy of a hardcover book that was popular many years ago . . . the book that made me famous . . .

Roger Wellington Rat.

DAY FIVE
THURSDAY, MARCH 16

———◦——

I'm lying here staring up at the ceiling, catatonic. Before this I stood under the shower for forty-five minutes without moving. My eyes are burning, but I can't relieve them, can't let them close. Every time I do, the hideous tableau of Norman and Virginia appears, a surreal sculpture lit by a stroke of psychic lightning. It has eliminated any possibility of sleep.

Here Lies Albie Marx, Casualty Of Terminal Insomnia.

My night in a cell with the deranged cop killer Jonny Angel was a walk in the park compared to last night.

At first I was paralyzed, standing in Norman's study, eyes locked on the mutilated bodies of Norman Devore and Virginia Hurley. Then alternatives began to flash on and off in my consciousness like seedy neon signs. They all led straight to hell. Cover the bodies? Hide the book? Call the police? Leave the country?

Finally, a fully formed thought began to stir: Turn your fear and impotence into anger and action. Anger and action are all that exist between you and destruction. Survive. Your goal is survival.

When the storm outside subsides, the city will still be standing. Next month the floods will be forgotten with the sunny blue skies washed clear by the rain. Next year this nightmare will be a memory, a frightful dream that came and went like a passing siren in the night. If you can turn your fear to anger, your impotence to action.

I realized I couldn't just leave the house as if I'd never been there. Mudprints of my feet were all over the floor. My fingerprints were on the front door, on the CD player, and who knows what else. Nothing would be worse than to leave, then have the police place me at the scene of the crime.

But the finger of innuendo pointed at me, the killer had seen to that. With everyone in a frenzy over my role in the Holman murder, the fact that *Roger Wellington Rat* was found in the hand of a murdered man would tip the media scales and dispel whatever presumption of my innocence remained in the public mind.

I thought of removing the book from Norman's hand but that would upset evidence that could be meaningful. Not even the cops wanted the murderer caught more than I did.

The first thing to do was to call my lawyer. *Real Life* paid me thirty grand for my appearance, which I could use to hire Arthur Gruntman. But I owed fifty to Sam for advancing my bail. It had to be Boopsie. If ever there was a "clutch," we had come to it.

My thoughts spinning crazily in my head, I backed out of the study, cutting the visual cord to the hypnotic scene. In my shirt pocket was a slip of paper with Boopsie's number. There was a phone on the floor in the living room. If the rising water level hadn't rendered the instrument inoperative, I would use it to call her.

The phone was functioning. Boopsie picked up on the seventh ring, all thick-tongued and gravely. "What . . . ?"

Turn fear into anger, impotence to action. "This is Albie. Wake your ass up and get something to write on."

"Who is this . . . ?"

"This is your last wake-up call, Betty. Deliver now or be a piece of shit drunk the rest of your life. You up to it?"

"Albie . . . ?"

"You don't get it together now, you never will. You'll be a cripple for life. You'll be the living dead. And nothing you tell yourself in your drunkenest dreams will convince you otherwise. You ready for that? You think alcohol can blot that out?"

"No . . ."

"I have money to call another lawyer. Someone who gives a shit about themself so they can give a shit about me. I'm fried. I don't have the energy to resuscitate your self-respect. I barely have the energy to make this speech. Am I getting through?"

"Yes . . ."

"Do you think you can bear to stop killing yourself?"

"Killing myself . . . ?"

"Yes! While you violate your trust as a lawyer and take innocent people with you! The current's too strong for me, Betty. I can't hang on to you and save myself, too. You're going under."

"I don't want to go under."

"Get a pencil and paper."

"Okay . . ."

"Now."

"I have it. I'm ready."

"Then take down this address: 3745 Valley Oak Drive. That's where I live in Los Feliz. You got it?"

"Got it."

"I just found the bodies of Norman Devore and Virginia, the missing chauffeur. They've been slaughtered. I have to call the police, but I wanted to call you first."

"You did the right thing. Okay . . . I'll grab a taxi and be there in . . . it's still raining, isn't it? . . . let's say forty-five minutes to an hour, maybe longer if the canyons are all closed. But an hour more or less won't make any difference. Just don't do anything. Wait for me."

"I shouldn't call the police?"

"Wait in your house. I'm coming. Don't worry. However bad it is, we'll handle it."

"It doesn't get any worse than this."

"We're up to it. Wait. And breathe deeply. I'm on my way."

I went down to my house. Freedom was fast asleep on the couch. I quietly moved past him, but the stink of skunk was too strong. He opened his eyes and sprang up.

"What the hell's that smell?"

"The dog caught the skunk. Go back to sleep."

"That's rank."

"I'm going to take a shower."

"Please." He pulled the covers over his head.

In my bedroom, Sam was still on my bed, reading a copy of *UP YOURS*. "That smell! Is that you?"

"Norman's been murdered. Virginia's been murdered. It's a slaughterhouse up there."

"My God."

"We're dealing with a maniac. The sickest motherfucker in the world."

"What's that smell?"

"Skunk."

"It's awful. What happened up there?"

"I found them in the study. It's horrible."

"I want to go up," she says, swinging her legs over the side of the bed and reaching for her boots. "I want to see."

"Boopsie's coming. I have to wait here . . ."

"How were they killed?"

"Looks like they were shot. But they've been mutilated. You don't want to go there."

"Are you kidding? We're the first to see it? I have to go."

"Why?"

"Because I'm a journalist. And this is the biggest story I've ever had . . ." She stops pulling on her boots. "You think someone's still there?"

"I don't know. I didn't see anyone. But I didn't look."

"I'm going up anyway . . ." she says, building her courage.

"The blood's all coagulated; whoever did it could be long gone. What are you going to do up there? We have to wait for Boopsie before we call the police."

"I won't call the police. I'll just run up and take a few pictures . . ."

"Pictures! Are you nuts?"

"I have a camera in my glove compartment. These could be the most valuable shots in the world. Why would you object? The police will take pictures. And they'll be hell to get your hands on, if you want them. This way you'll have your own. For your own defense, if necessary."

"My defense. Christ, this is nuts. Okay. But don't touch anything. Don't disturb anything. Just take them and get out."

"When will she be here?"

"In about an hour."

"You should take a shower. And get rid of these putrid clothes. I'll take some quick shots and come right back down."

She left and I took off my clothes and threw them out the back door, into the rain. Then I scrubbed my skin raw in the shower and doused myself with after shave.

By the time Boopsie arrived I was climbing the walls. Freedom was awake, I'd told him about it, and Sam had returned, ashen-faced, from her photo op. The lightning-lit freeze-frame of Norman and Virginia had already begun to flicker on and off nonstop in my mind.

I took Boopsie up to the mansion and forced myself to wait in the living room while she surveyed the scene.

"Rough stuff," she said, coming out of the study. Then, with a reassuring clinical equanimity, "They've been dead a while. How long ago did you find them?"

"Just before I called you. About an hour."

"Can you account for your whereabouts all day?"

"I got out of jail around seven A.M. Went to Bambi Friedman's in Franklin Canyon ... left there about ten-thirty, eleven ... Met with you, Shrike, and Sam at *UP YOURS* ... Left to meet Gluck at The Farmer's Daughter in Hollywood, that was around one ... Taped Sam's show at three, came home. Except for getting from one place to the next, which took forever in the damn rain, I was always with someone."

"You met Gluck at The Farmer's Daughter. What is that, a restaurant?"

"A bar and grill."

"Were there other people present?"

"Bartender, waitress, customers."

"And Bambi Friedman? She's a friend?"

"That's another story, one I still have to tell you. But the answer is no, I just met her at Holman's wedding."

"Was there anyone else at her house with you? Someone to confirm your being there?"

"Actually there was. A girl named Debra."

"Know her name?"

"No. Her license plate is *I D8 U.*"

"Not the shy type."

"No. Maybe we should run the license."

"I will. You went straight from Bambi's to *UP YOURS?*"

"Yes."

"Umm. The book the dead man's holding . . . you wrote it?"

"Yes."

"It's hard to believe you'd deliberately leave a calling card like that. I don't see a judge buying it as probable cause to issue a warrant."

"I don't get it. Who the hell could be so mad at me, to do something like this?"

"Don't feel left out, but the anger here wasn't directed at you. The book could be an afterthought."

"Now they're both dead. Gardener and Virginia. There's no one to back up my story about the Holman killing."

"This race is a long way from over. Let's not jump to any conclusions."

"What do we do now?"

She unties the plaid bow reining in her wild red hair, runs her fingers through the thick mop, pulls it together again, reties the bow. "You and Lieutenant Danno have had personal problems, haven't you . . . ?"

"We go back to the sixties. He hates me."

"Put in a call to the Hollywood precinct. Tell them it's urgent you speak to him in person. He'll be home in bed. Make them put you through."

"Why?"

"It doesn't matter, do it."

"He'll crucify me."

"No he won't."

"We don't want to wake this guy up, he's surly to bed and surly to rise . . ."

"Call him."

With all the confidence of a girl who's been told her date won't come in her mouth, I followed Boopsie's instructions. Getting the desk jockeys to put me through to Danno's home was an exercise in dealing with officious cretins that transcended even the post office, but I finally got him on the line. He told me to stay put and not to touch anything. Surprise.

We didn't have very long to wait. In less than fifteen minutes, half the cops in Los Angeles were swarming around the property.

Danno wanted to know why I called Boopsie before I called him. I explained that I felt he had something personal against me and I wanted my lawyer to be there. He said he had nothing personal against me. He just hated me on general principles.

The fact that Norman Devore was with me when Danno arrested us less than two days ago was not lost on him. When I identified Virginia as Carol, the missing chauffeur, his eyes narrowed and his lips tightened. He looked like James Cagney about to deliver the famous line, *"You dirty rat!"*

"This has gotten as far as it's gonna go, Marx. You have a very serious problem and it's getting worse by the minute. If you think that reporting this crime diverts attention from you as a suspect, you're sorely mistaken. If you think that planting that stupid fucking book makes it look like you couldn't have possibly been that clumsy, you're mistaking the mentality of this country. People today are not the sheep that you led around by the nose in the sixties. People are smart, they've seen all the shit they're ever gonna have to know on TV. They've seen everyone take the fall. Presidents, movie stars, they've seen what garbage people can be. They have no illusions about innocence. All I have to do is tell the press out there that you're our suspect and no matter what happens after that, for the rest of your life people will look at you like an individual capable of murder and mutilation. Try walking into one of your liberal fund-raisers with that floating over your head. You want to talk about uncomfortable?

"Here's the way I see it: If the world found out how much money you really got paid for whacking Bert Holman, they'd have no trouble believing you'd kill two innocent kids to keep from parting with it.

"And guess what? I'm gonna see to it the world finds out. I'm gonna make sure every man, woman, and goofball within a hundred miles of a television gets to hear how much cash it takes to shoot, kill, and mutilate three human beings."

"That's exactly why we called you first, Lieutenant," Boopsie pipes up. "Because if anyone can get totally unsubstantiated and irresponsible evidence straight to the hands of the media, it's you. By the time you're finished blabbing every piece of innuendo and misinformation to the press, there won't be an icicle's chance in hell for my client to get a fair trial in this or any other city. He'll walk without ever seeing a jury. Try explaining that to your chief and the district attorney."

"Anything that came to the press through me was verified five hundred times before they got it."

"Oh? What is this unspecified amount of money you allege my client got paid?"

"Come on, lady, this little piss-ant got paid close to half a million bucks. Let's quit jerkin' each other off."

"Who do you think you're talking to, you bald buffoon? Hold on to your balls because I'm going to tell you something that's going to make you think they took a hike: I have recorded proof of you tipping a KTLA news stringer that my client had previous knowledge of James T. Gardner—in a telephone call made before the official announcement that champagne glasses with his fingerprints were found in Gardner's apartment. *Before* the official announcement. Next?"

"For a lawyer who's supposed to be a lady, you've got all the moves of a wrestler."

"For an officer who's sworn to protect and serve, you've got all the restraint of a fascist."

"I know your story: wake up with gin, spend the day with gin, try to keep from falling over before sundown. We know about you, lady."

"Good. That makes us even. I love an even fight. I'm so tired of defeating pygmies. Finally, an intelligent giant to lock horns with. I'm reinvigorated. I'm revitalized. And I owe it all to you."

"Look, I've got a mess to clean up in there . . ."

"Are you planning to detain my client?"

"That's not all I'd like to do to him."

"Are you going to detain him?"

"Maybe yes, maybe no. Maybe he'll say something that changes my whole opinion of him . . ."

"Are you placing him under arrest?"

"I don't know! When I'm finished interviewing him I'll tell you! Okay? Now, how about shutting up and letting me ask him the questions?"

Danno proceeded to go at me for half an hour. Pending autopsy, the coroner on the scene gave him an estimated time of death of somewhere between 12:00 A.M. and 12:00 P.M. At least I had an alibi. I was either in jail or at Bambi Friedman's.

At various times during the interrogation, Danno accused me of lying about my whereabouts, disturbing evidence at the crime scene, and interfering with an investigation by not calling the police immediately.

Then he intimated that the bump on my head was a result of a struggle with Norman Devore, who was a much larger man than me.

I told him I got it from being hit by a tree limb falling in Bambi Friedman's front yard. I suggested that a trace of my blood, if the rain hadn't washed it away, might still be on the limb. He didn't look very convinced.

In fact, he had every intention of putting me back in the slammer. If Boopsie weren't there, he almost certainly would have. But she sat beside me through the entire interview. When he finished, she stood up and made the statement that if he arrested me we would file a false imprisonment action that would impact on his entire case, including the Holman conspiracy charge.

He challenged her grounds and she told him that all it took was for him to have any knowledge of information "that could induce a reasonable doubt in his accusation," such as my being in his jail or with Bambi Friedman at the time of the double murder. Or the lack of any singular clue giving him probable cause to believe I was the perpetrator. She made an additional argument: that his personal history with me over the years, all the spurious arrests with never a conviction, would mitigate in my favor in a judge's eyes.

Danno took Bambi Friedman's phone number and said if she

didn't confirm my alibi, he would inform the press I was the leading suspect in his investigation. But he didn't arrest me. Boopsie had prevented that. For the first time since Sunday, when the security guards jumped me at Holman's wedding, I felt protected.

I had to hand it to Shrike. Betty McDonald had come through in the clutch. We were still losing the fight, getting killed on the score-card, but it felt pretty decent to finally come out of a round unbloodied.

"Where did he get that stuff about how much I got paid?" I asked.

"I have no idea, but I guarantee I'll find out. How do you feel?"

"For the first time since this started, I'd have to say . . . decent."

The decent feeling turned to shit the minute we walked out the front door of the mansion.

It was like walking onto the field of a stadium during a night game in the middle of a typhoon. The entire rain-whipped hill was lit up to a dreamlike daylight by an army of police, press, TV, and film crews. LAPD and media helicopters circled like dragonflies, beaming their searchlights all over the gothic old mansion and its soaking, muck-covered grounds.

The police had attempted to rope off the immediate area to search for clues, but in the tumult of weather and people, no order could be maintained. Reporters mixed with police mixed with TV crews mixed with neighborhood rubberneckers . . . all played out in the glaring artificial light. It was like watching chaos under a microscope, watching the human race flop around, fully clothed and equipped, comically trying to emerge from the primal ooze.

Boopsie and I were surrounded immediately. Somehow they'd got-ten behind us, so we couldn't retreat into the house even if we'd wanted to, which we didn't. It was pouring, yet there we were, blinded by the glare, eyes averted, trying to keep our balance in the deepening mud, surrounded by screaming media maniacs bombarding us with questions, accusations, suppositions, false quotes, misinfor-mation, idiotic opinions, and every type of personal libel that sprang to their degenerate minds.

We kept moving forward. Boopsie nearly slipped, which they would have loved, but I grabbed her arm and supported her the rest of the way down the hill to my house. Which looked like a stagecoach surrounded by a tribe of hostile Indians. They had even set up tents on the street to supplement the endless rows of idling news vans curling all the way up and down the hill. The Waco Circus had come to Los Feliz.

"We're gonna run for it," I whispered in Boopsie's ear, then tightened my grip on her arm and led her into a trot in the direction of my back door.

To my complete lack of surprise, the fat TV reporter, a grade A pain in the ass from day one, stumbled out of the shadows and into the gleaming rain, dead square in our way. He had apparently tripped on something, and when he looked up and saw us coming at him, he beamed with delight.

"GET THAT CAMERA HERE!" he screamed at his cameraman, who was trying to keep from slipping in the mud. The large video camera on his shoulder was connected to a long, thick electric cable which I assumed trailed back to a mobile news van.

The cameraman tugged on the cable to get some slack, and I saw a wire pull loose from the back of it and begin to spark. The fat reporter was standing up to his ankles in a pool of water that had gathered where the ground was more rock than soil, screaming at the cameraman to get over there.

I tried to warn them, but it was too late. The fat guy took a step toward us as the cameraman followed him, stepping into the pool of water.

That was all it took. The shock stood the cameraman stiff as a flagpole, then he toppled over backward with the weight of the camera. He looked dead.

The fat reporter, unaware the cameraman had been electrocuted, shouted crazily at him to get up and follow as he wildly careened after Boopsie and me in the driving rain.

I'm still lying here, unmoving. The sun is shining. It doesn't matter. All I can see is Norman hacked up, and the blood-caked root where his genitals had been.

And Virginia, a frozen dead mannequin, Norman's penis and testicles hanging hideously from her mouth.

I called Bambi the second I got into my house. There was no

answer, only her machine. Her message said she was out of town for a long weekend, but was in touch with her machine and would return all calls. I hung up. I didn't want to leave a message. If he got hold of it, Danno would probably find a way to use it against me.

Boopsie sat up all night with Sam, Freedom, and me. At one point the rain stopped. People didn't believe it, then they started cheering. As Norman and Virginia's bodies were carried out and loaded into police ambulances, the press corps was cheering the end of the rain.

They quieted down when an ambulance came for the cameraman. The loss of one of their own sobered them up. They eventually receded with the police, leaving only a handful of subordinate watchdogs behind.

When the blue-black sky began pulsing with the light of dawn, Boopsie finished her last beer and wearily climbed into the cab I had called for her. Freedom sank back into the couch, faded out, and Sam and I finally climbed into bed. We were too drained, physically and emotionally, to give lovemaking the respect and focus it deserved, so we just cuddled up like two spoons. Sam went right off to sleep.

But I keep seeing Norman and Virginia. Every time I close my eyes.

So I stare at the ceiling and listen to the soft, soothing sound of Sam breathing deeply beside me. The hours go by and I listen to Freedom get up, use the bathroom, get dressed, leave the house, start his car and drive off. I listen to dark voices telling me there is no hope of escape from a dungeon of false information, no release from a prison of gossip and rumor. I hear Sartre blurt his stark realization, "Hell is other people!" And I hear the distant voice of an old comrade-in-arms, who once told me the reason we've all been put on earth is, "To keep each other busy until the sun burns out."

Sam wakes from a deep sleep with a sudden start, bolts upright. She looks over at me wide-eyed, lets out a plaintive exclamation and buries her head in my chest.

"Bad dreams . . . ?"

"Horrible. Just hold me. Hold me tight."

I wrap my arms around her. She's shaking. "What kind of monster is this ... what kind of person could do that to people?'' she whispers.

"I don't know. It's outside my sphere of comprehension."

"He's got to be caught. God knows who's next. It could be you or me ..." She hugs me so tightly her strength surprises me.

I hold her protectively. "You're safe if you stay alert. If you don't let yourself get trapped with the wrong person in the wrong place. Like Norman and Virginia. Someone they trusted ... maybe it's someone we know—or think we know. You have to stay alert."

"You're right. Alert—that's the word." She puts her lips to my ears, murmurs softly, "Alert ..." Then moves her lips down and kisses my neck, giving me chills, alerting me to incredible possibilities. I breathe her in ... I get high on her smell ...

Suddenly, the image of her and Michael Whitehead together appears center stage in my mind. What is their relationship? She called him last night, after the announcement of his offer to purchase Sovereign. What did they say to each other? What tone of voice did they use?

"What are you thinking about, Albie?"

"How good you feel ..." His clothes are still in her house. Do they still see each other? Do they sleep together?

"I can hear the gears turning ..."

"No gears are turning ..." She called him to get the story. With her it's always the story.

"Where are you, Albie?"

"Here ..." Like bringing up Bambi Friedman on *Real Life*. If I had told the Jeannie Locke story it would have finished off Gluck. Sovereign would be Whitehead's in a cakewalk.

"I don't feel like you're here."

"I am." Then she went up to the mansion. To take pictures. Pictures of Norman and Virginia.

"Please tell me what you're thinking."

"I'm thinking I'm intoxicated by you ..." Pictures. Is there nothing she won't do for a story?

"Albie ..."

I told her I hadn't seen Bambi, but last night I told Danno I was at Bambi's house at the time of the murder. Wait till she hears about that.

She takes my head in her hands and looks me in the eye. "What's going on in there?"

"I'm wondering if you always had that sexy little gap in your front teeth."

"You think it's sexy . . . ?"

"Did you ever think of getting braces?"

"My parents wanted me to, but I wouldn't."

"Why not?"

"I don't know . . . I wasn't interested in being pretty. I was more into music and writing . . . riding horses . . . baseball . . ."

"You played baseball?"

"We had a great team. We were girls, but we were good. We never lost. Well, once. And I hated it."

"Winning's the ultimate turn-on for you, isn't it?"

"It's one of them. Would you like me if I were a loser?"

"I thought it's how you play the game that counts."

"You can play fair and still win."

"What position did you play?"

"Catcher." She jumps out from under the covers and sets up on her knees on the bed with one hand out, as if she's holding a catcher's mitt. I never went for catchers before, but I've never seen one naked like this . . .

"Put it over the plate!" she barks, pounding her "mitt" with her other fist. "Put it right in there!" Boy, do I want to put it in there.

"See?" she says. "I didn't care about boys. Being good-looking caused more problems than it solved."

"You didn't want to be pretty?"

"Not especially."

"You must be a big disappointment to yourself."

"Did you always have that sexy little cleft in your chin?"

"Ever since I was old enough to run into things."

"You love to live dangerously, don't you?"

"I don't think so."

"But you always have."

"I guess so. Except for Jewish holidays."

"Very funny. You should take better care of yourself . . . How is your stomach? Aren't I supposed to take you to the hospital this morning?"

"My biopsy at Cedars. I forgot about it."

"Do you still want to go?"

"No . . ."

She sits up indignantly. "You'd take a chance on being sick now that I've found you? Forget it. You're going."

"Right. I'm going. I want that biopsy. I *want* that scope down my throat."

"You bet you do. Come here . . ." she purrs, pulling me to her, "Let's warm up that throat with something a little more enjoyable . . ."

She presses her open mouth against mine and we sink down into the bed . . .

When Sam and I leave the house, the media leeches attack us.

"Did you two meet on *Real Life*?"

"Did you know each other before Bert Holman's murder?"

"Samantha, do you feel your relationship with Albie is a conflict of interest as a journalist?"

"Albie, was the murdered girl your accomplice in the Holman killing?"

"Was it a love triangle? Did you and Norman fight over Virginia?"

"What's your alibi for the time of the murder?"

"Are you two getting married?"

They're scum. It's hard to get past them when they're all over you, but Sam and I manage to make it into the Blazer without punching anybody.

"How does it feel, being on the receiving end of this shit?" I ask as we pull out of the driveway with reporters and cameramen running along beside us.

"I can handle it. I was a receiver in baseball, remember?"

"They'll make a big deal out of the conflict of interest angle."

"Let them. It'll only boost the ratings."

Always thinking of ratings. She's not easily rattled. Definitely a catcher's mentality.

"Look at this day," she says, guiding the Blazer down the hill toward Hollywood. "It's magnificent. This city is a paradise after it rains."

She pushes a button and opens the sunroof. She's right. The sunshine feels so good you can almost smell it. The smog is gone, the sky is blue, the air vibrantly fresh. The palpable gloom that was the storm has vaporized, turned into molecules of memory and dispersed into the ether.

Now all the gloom's in my head.

When she pulls up in front of the north tower of Cedars Hospital, she puts the Blazer in park and turns to face me.

"You need me to pick you up, don't you?"

"No. You have enough to do today. I'll get a cab."

"Don't worry about this test. It's going to turn out fine."

"Do I look worried?"

"You look scared to death."

"I am."

"Don't be."

She leans over and kisses me. It's not enough. I take her in my arms and we kiss like it's the last good-bye. People on the sidewalk are stopping to look at us.

"They're watching us," I whisper into her delicious hair.

"If they can't take the heat let 'em get off the sidewalk."

As she drives off it occurs to me that I wanted to say I love you. It also occurs to me that it's foolish and immature to say I love you when you've known someone three days.

I take the elevator to the fourth floor and find the office of Dr. Paul Pierson, stand-up comedian and gastrointestinal genius. I'm right on time for my consultation.

As Al Rissman told me, Pierson's a laugh track in hospital scrubs. He has an encyclopedic knowledge of low physical humor, acts out the jokes with oversize gestures and low-brow eyebrow action, and chortles unabashedly at his own punchlines. In alarm I picture him doing a pratfall as he's shoving his scope down my throat.

As he's doing his *shtick,* I notice he looks even more suntanned and pampered than the standard Beverly Hills doctor.

When I comment on this, he explains, "My wife and I took a two-week vacation in Bora Bora. In fact, we just got back late last night."

"Bora Bora? What is it like there?" Maybe Sam and I will go, when this is behind us.

"The one thing they got right is the name. The biggest activity was sitting and looking at each other. Eight hundred a day to sleep on a mat and eat tasteless food. I get that for free at my mother-in-law's."

"It wasn't beautiful?"

"Yes, it was," he answers, serious now. "I did need to get away. I have a lot of famous patients. They can be very demanding."

Like the rest of the professionals in this town, Pierson is obviously a celebrity hound.

"My nurse told me she saw you outside with Samantha Shelton," he says, in the familiar tone affected by people who fancy themselves show business insiders. A big producer once told me, "Everyone has two businesses—his own and show business."

"She's a friend," I tell him.

"Her boss is a patient of mine. Bert Holman."

"*Was* a patient."

"What do you mean?"

"You don't know?"

"Know what? I've been in a grass hut for two weeks."

"No TV in Bora Bora?"

"Are you kidding? For excitement we watched barnacles fuck."

"Bert Holman's dead."

"Oh." He lets out a breath and says softly, without surprise, "So it happened." He shakes his head. "I liked Bert . . ."

"What do you mean, 'it happened'?" I ask, noticing I'm sitting on the edge of my chair.

"Well . . . he's gone?"

"Yes."

"Then, I suppose I can tell you. Bert had a malignancy of the duodenum."

"Intestinal cancer?"

He nods. "By the time we found it, it had spread to his colon.

Which is why we like to see patients like you quickly. So we can diagnose and prevent things from happening.''

"Bert Holman was dying?''

"It's too bad. He was very nice to me and my wife. Invited us to his wedding. But we had our vacation . . .''

"Who else knew about it?''

"Besides your doctor, Al Rissman—who also referred Bert to me—I don't know. I was told not to say anything.''

"But he still got married . . .''

"I wondered about that.''

No wonder Holman looked so terrible at the wedding. He was on his way out.

"How long did he have? I mean . . . how long did he have to live?''

"Bert was farther gone than anyone knew. He didn't want people to know about it . . . I guess it had to do with the big Sovereign studio deal.''

Incredible. Gardner, a dying man, kills Holman, a dying man. A whole new dimension to this thing. My mind is whirling with implications.

"Bert Holman didn't die of cancer, Dr. Pierson. He was murdered at his wedding.''

"Murdered? No. You've got to be kidding . . .''

"He was shot by a man named James T. Gardner. You don't know that name, do you?''

"James T. Gardner? No. I don't know him. You're telling me he shot Bert Holman? At his own wedding?''

I quickly go over the whole thing for Pierson, highlighting my innocence and the frame-up. He grunts and moans in empathy for my plight, then remarks that none of this stress is good for my system. I tell him about the increased stomach pain I've had lately. He says we'll find out what's going on, and reassures me the endoscopy is nothing to be frightened about. Then he sends me off with his nurse, who takes me up to the floor where the procedure will be performed.

When we get into the room, which is crammed with all kinds of video screens and high-tech equipment, she has me change into a hospital gown, then tells me to lie on the table and hold my breath while she sprays my throat with a local anesthetic. Then she sticks a bowl under my chin.

"Just let the saliva drain out the side of your mouth," she says. Albie Quasimodo.

She sticks an IV in my arm, starts a Valium drip. By the time Pierson comes in, I'm zoned out enough to let him do anything.

Sticking his finger into my mouth he guides the tip of the long black snakelike instrument to the back of my throat. I feel like I'm going to gag when he says, "I'll do the gags around here." I assume it's a standard line.

It's hard to relax with a Roto-Rooter down your throat, but the muscle tension in my esophagus eases enough for Pierson to push the scope in, sending it all the way down my esophagus, then into my stomach and my small intestine. He peers into his end and makes a bunch of clinical observations to the nurse.

When it's all over and I'm lying outside in the recovery area, Pierson comes over and puts his hand on my arm.

"I took a tissue specimen and some cells. There's no need to be concerned until we get the results."

"How long will it take?"

"We'll know in three days."

"What exactly will we know?"

"Basically, if we need to go in there or not."

"Go in?"

"It could be nothing, an abscess . . ."

"Is that the same thing you told Bert Holman?"

"Just try to relax."

"That's what I'll do. Relax."

"You may be burping for a while."

"Attractive."

"And you'll have a sore throat for three or four days. My nurse will give you some lozenges and you can gargle with saltwater if it gets too uncomfortable. Do you have a ride home?"

"I'll call a cab."

He gives me another reassuring pat on the arm and leaves. When my head clears a little, I get up and walk down the hall to a phone booth where I call Shrike at the office.

"Christ, Marx! Where the fuck have you been?"

"I just had my biopsy at Cedars."

"I've been calling you every ten minutes."

"I turned my phone off. It was ringing off the hook with media jerks."

"Are you forgetting? That's us? We're the media."

"I'm seriously thinking of retiring."

"From what? You haven't given me anything in a week."

"That's nice."

"I'm not nice. I'm a business."

"And I'm a victim of the business. Let's not argue. Did you get any information on Jeannie Locke for me?"

"That's what I wanted to tell you. By the way, your friend Lieutenant Danno just left here an hour ago. He had a warrant to search your office."

"Am I supposed to be surprised?"

"Stoic to the end. Great act, Marx."

A thunderous belch escapes from my mouth without warning.

"What the hell was that?" Shrike asks, stupefied.

"I burped. What did you find on Jeannie Locke?"

"You ought to have that looked at."

"I just did."

"You're not gonna go and die on me, are you?"

"It was a burp."

"Spooky. Anyway, we got the old *LA Times* pages. There wasn't much, a couple of boxes in the back. April 23, 1972. Jeannie Locke was found dead in her car on a residential street in Hollywood. Overdosed on drugs. No criminal investigation."

"That much I know. Did they mention Jack Schwarzberg?"

"Yeah. She was living at his house in the Hollywood Hills at the time. He was calling himself Chief Blackfoot and the house was The Reservation. Can you believe him? Once an asshole, always an asshole."

"Did the police question him?"

"Yep. He said he was home at the estimated time of her death.

Two other girls who lived at the Reservation backed him up. The police had no reason to suspect him of anything.''

"Nobody else was questioned?"

"Just the girls she lived with. Claimed they didn't know where she went when she left that night."

"That's all?"

"No. Jeannie Locke was survived by a daughter. No name given."

"Who was the father?"

"That took some digging. Good thing we have friends in the media. We got access to ancient file boxes at the *Times*. Found the original unedited story that was filed. The father was John Locke, US Infantry, killed in Vietnam. The daughter would be around twenty-six, twenty-seven now."

First thing that pops into my head—could Sam be the daughter?

"What happened to her?" I ask, not wanting to hear the answer.

"She wasn't living with the mother when she died. The daughter was being raised by the grandparents."

"Mr. and Mrs. Locke?"

"No. The mother's parents—Mr. and Mrs. Petersen."

"Petersen. Don't tell me ..."

"You got it, Sherlock."

"... the little girl's name was Sheila."

"Bull's-eye. Mrs. Bert Holman."

The person who answered Sheila Holman's phone, a housekeeper type, informed me that Mrs. Holman could be reached at the offices of Holman Entertainment.

I was headed there anyway, to pick up my car, which I'd left in the parking lot outside the *Real Life* studio. I called a cab and went down to the hospital entrance to wait for it.

Sheila Petersen Holman is Jeannie Locke's daughter. I wonder if Bert Holman knew that. I wonder if Sheila knows Bert was dying. Everyone has their secrets. Sheila, Ozzie, Bambi, Gluck ... Everyone but me.

The security guard at the entrance to Holman Entertainment tried to kill me with a look when my cab pulled up to the gate.

"Tell Mrs. Holman I'm here to see her," I ordered.

He sniggered. "Fat chance." Picking up his phone, he dialed and said, "Albie Marx is here. Says he wants to see Mrs. Holman."

There was a prolonged wait, during which he glared at me the whole time. When he got his answer, his expression switched from hate to disgust. Shaking his head, he raised the gate and, without a word, turned his back.

I paid the cabdriver and walked into the lobby of the executive office building. My old friend, Stu White, was at his post behind the reception counter.

"Hello, Stu. I'm here to see—"

"I know what you're here for. Come with me."

"You're taking me up?"

"Don't ask questions."

I shrugged and followed as he walked past the elevators and opened the door to a small storage room. "In here," he said bluntly.

"I don't think so . . ."

"Hey, you can walk out now. No skin off my nose."

"What's in there?"

"You wanna see the boss, do as you're told. Otherwise, beat it."

I peered into the room. Nobody was inside. I walked in and Stu followed me.

"Turn around, hands up against the wall."

"What is this?"

"I gotta pat you down."

I put my hands to the wall and he gave me a detailed and thorough frisking.

"Easy there, Stu, this is only our second date." Fortunately, I'd left my mace in the glove compartment of the Jag.

"Okay, I'm finished," Stu said, and led me out of the room, over to the elevators. "Twenty-first floor. Someone will be waiting for you."

"Thanks," I said, but his eyes were blank. Nice to be popular with the help.

The elevator went up to twenty-one and, as promised, there was another security guard waiting for me when the doors opened. The decor and furnishings up there were all high-ticket. Deep, rich maroon carpeting, soft Tiffany lamp lighting, beige linen wallpaper, polished French and English antiques, Currier & Ives originals on the walls . . .

"This way, Mr. Marx," the guard said. Things were improving. A little respect.

He took me to a genteel lady secretary, mid-fifties, sitting at an old French desk outside the closed door of an office that appeared to occupy half the side of the twenty-first floor. She looked so perfect in that spot I thought the building had been built around her.

"Mr. Marx, I presume."

"Yes."

"I'll tell Mrs. Holman you're here."

She got up and strode erectly into the office, closing the door behind her. After a minute she opened the door. "Mrs. Holman will see you now."

I walked past her into the office. As she closed the door behind me, Sheila Petersen Holman rose from a comfortable armchair to greet me. She was all in black and totally stunning.

"I was going to call you," she said. "You beat me to it."

"It wasn't even a toll call."

"Thank you for coming."

"Thank you for seeing me."

"Have a seat."

"Thank you. I'm sorry about your husband."

"Thank you."

"You should have had more time to enjoy each other."

She acknowledged with her eyes.

I sat in the armchair opposite her. Between us was a coffee table with a silver pot of coffee, a silver basket of pastry, and service for two. "Coffee?" she asked. "Pastry?"

"Yes, thank you."

She poured us each a cup. "Would you like to do the sugar and cream yourself . . . ?"

"Thank you." I put some sugar and cream in my coffee, picked out a doughnut and held the basket out to her.

"I'm just having coffee, thank you."

"I'm breaking my fast with this," I told her.

"You were fasting?"

"Twelve hours. For a test. At Cedars Hospital."

"I hope you're all right . . ."

"I'm fine, thank you. My doctor knew your husband. Paul Pierson. Upper gastro man."

"Oh, yes. We invited them to the wedding. They were on vacation."

"I also have the same general physician, Al Rissman."

"I know Dr. Rissman quite well."

There was a short reflective silence as we both sipped our coffee.

"Lovely office," I remarked.

"Thank you. Bert was generous. He gave me an unlimited budget."

"You've been here a while?"

"Yes."

"It's very nice."

"Thank you."

We sip some more coffee.

"Mrs. Holman . . ."

"Please. Sheila."

"Sheila . . . why are we sitting like this, thanking each other around the block, when we both know perfectly well that somebody's trying to play somebody for a sucker?"

"Because, Mr. Marx . . ."

"Albie."

"Because, Albie, we're both compassionate human beings who understand that no matter how we suffer personally, everyone has burdens of their own."

"You're right. This is the way civilized people should act. I wish more people were as civilized as we are."

"You can civilize people. That doesn't make them happy."

"I didn't say they had to be happy."

"Ozzie Baba says, 'There is nothing more beautiful than the reflection of a happy person.' "

"How is Chief Blackfoot? He loved Bert like a brother, didn't he?"

"Please. We can communicate without sarcasm."

"Did you know Bert was dying?"

"Of course."

"Did Ozzie?"

"You'll have to ask him."

"I'd love to. If he'd stop ducking me."

"Did you know James T. Gardner was dying?"

"I didn't know James T. Gardner."

"Yes, that's right. You met at my wedding."

"I didn't meet him. I tried to stop him from killing your husband. You'd think someone would give me credit for that."

"If it's true, I'm sure someone will."

"You don't feel it's true?"

"I don't know. Hopefully, the whole truth will come out in court."

"You're sure you want the whole truth? If you'll pardon the expression, I know where some of the bodies are buried."

"That's not amusing."

"I'm sorry, but as Ozzie would say, it's not my job to amuse you. I'm trying to solve a life-or-death puzzle. Let's start with the first piece. Ozzie must have told you I brought up the subject of Jeannie Locke." She nodded. "Since then, I've learned a lot more."

"What have you learned?"

"I'll tell you if you tell me."

"Tell you what?"

"What really happened to her."

"All I know is she was once a girlfriend of Ozzie's, when he first became enlightened. He speaks about her occasionally."

"Let's stop fucking around, Sheila. He knows you're her daughter, doesn't he?"

She looked at me thoughtfully. It's hard to tell if the question took her by surprise, but she was definitely thinking about her answer. "Yes. Ozzie knows she was my mother."

"Bert knew, too?"

"Bert knew."

"He wasn't concerned you might be out for revenge?"

"Revenge for what?"

"For his part in your mother's death."

"I don't know what you think you know, but let me set you straight. Bert Holman was a terrific man. He was caring, honest, and principled. It took him a long time to learn how to make himself happy, but he never gave up. A lot of people today are happy because of it.

"When I was a baby my father was killed in Vietnam. My mother was pregnant and didn't want to have an abortion. But she was young. She hadn't done anything with her life and there was a lot she wanted. She loved to sing, and she was good. She'd always wanted to go to Los Angeles, become a singer, get a record deal . . .

"Her parents knew how much she wanted a career in show business. They volunteered to take care of me while she spent a year in Los Angeles, trying to make it. Every other weekend she'd come back up to San Francisco and spend it with me. I wasn't abandoned. We loved each other.

"Los Angeles is a city of sharks. She was fortunate enough to meet Ozzie, who was a channel for the descended soul of an ancient Indian chief, Ozuma Blackfoot. My mother was living in a run-down apartment, working as a waitress. He offered her a room in his house. There were three or four other girls living there, all at the hospitality of Ozzie, who never asked for anything in repayment.

"During that time she met an agent at William Morris. His name was Mitchell Gluck. He was a typical Hollywood sleaze, he wanted to get her in bed and, because she didn't give in to him, he tried even harder. He told her he would help her career.

"She asked Ozzie what to do and he told her if Gluck was serious about helping her career he should show some proof of it. She told that to Gluck. He said he would introduce her to his client, the country western singer Bobby Holiday, who was a big star on TV at the time. Gluck told her he'd get Bobby to put her on his show.

"There was another agent at William Morris, whom Ozzie had met. His name was Bert Holman. He co-represented Bobby Holiday with Mitchell Gluck. When Bert heard that Gluck was making promises to my mother, he told Ozzie that Gluck was full of baloney, that everything he said was to get into her pants.

"One night she was home with Ozzie and some other girls. She got a phone call from Gluck. He told her he was with Bobby Holiday and Bobby wanted to meet her right away. They were at Bobby's house, waiting for her.

"She told Ozzie she was going. He wanted to go along but she didn't want to offend Gluck. When she didn't come home hours later, Ozzie called Bert Holman to tell him what was happening.

"Bert didn't like it. He promised to check it out. He called back and said he'd talked to Gluck and Bobby but they hadn't seen her. They told him they hadn't called her, either.

"The next morning she was found in her car, dead of a drug overdose. My mother had never taken drugs.

"Ozzie was devastated. Bert came to the house and consoled him. They told the police that she'd received a call from Holiday and Gluck, went off and never came back.

"When the police went to Holiday and Gluck, they told them they'd never seen my mother that night. No one could prove otherwise. The police weren't inclined to push a case against a big star, especially when nobody could prove he had called the victim. Bobby Holiday and Ozzie both lived in the Hollywood Hills, so the area codes were the same. But there was no record to prove whether or not the call had been made.

"The police labeled her death an accidental overdose and that was where they left it. Ozzie and Bert always believed she was with Gluck and Holiday when she died. That's why Bert hated Gluck to his dying day. Because of my mother."

She averted her eyes. It was clear she was getting teary.

She took a sharp breath, got up, took a tissue from her desk, dabbed at her eyes and sat back down.

The Jeannie Locke story, version number three. Implicates Gluck and Holiday, makes Ozzie and Bert heroes.

"I assume you married Bert out of gratitude."

"I won't even respond to that."

"I apologize."

"Now it's your turn to tell me something."

"Anything you want to know."

"What would it take to make you happy?"

"I thought only I can make myself happy."

"You can make yourself happy by telling me what it would take to make you happy."

"I would like to clear my name and go on with my life. That would make me happy."

"If I could clear your name, would you go on with your life and stay out of mine?"

"Are you saying you can do that?"

"I'm asking what it would take to make you happy. Would you be happy if you could go on with your life and forget you ever heard of me, Bert, Ozzie, or my mother?"

"How could you clear my name?"

"I didn't say I could. I said *if* I could."

"What about Norman Devore and Virginia Hurley? You could take care of that, too?"

"If I could clear your name ... totally—would you be happy enough to go away?"

First Gluck offered to pay for the services of Mendelson, the famous plea-bargain attorney. Now Sheila offers to get me off on all charges. The offers were improving. Maybe the next would be freedom *and* money.

But I couldn't wait for the next. I needed to get out now. I was thinking, take the deal. If Sheila clears you and you walk away, what have you lost? You escaped with your hide and washed your hands of a mess.

In other words: Make yourself happy.

Then there was that demon voice, the one that's hounded me all my life, the one that whines in my ear, "WHAT ABOUT THE TRUTH?"

Who cares about the goddamned truth? I want my life back. I don't need to be the only guy on Death Row with integrity. I need to be the only guy in my shoes who isn't headed for Death Row.

As the war between survival and principle raged on in the battlefield of my mind, Sheila asked, "Well, Mr. Marx? What do you say?"

"I have one problem with your offer ..."

"I suppose you want money, too."

"Well ... no, I don't think so. My problem is, what if Gardner didn't conspire with Mitchell Gluck to kill Bert? What if Gardner conspired with someone else? I'd basically be letting a murderer go free by backing away, wouldn't I?"

"I don't see what choice *you* have in the matter."

"I hate to see the bad guy win."

"Mr. Marx . . ."

"Albie."

". . . You're making me feel like I'm wasting my time."

"I'm sorry, Sheila. Would you prefer we went back to thanking the shit out of each other . . . ?"

She was about to tee off on me when her phone rang. She snapped it up. "I told you to hold my calls!"

Her secretary must have had a great reason for interrupting, because Sheila barked, "All right! Put him on."

She raised a finger and looked at me to indicate she'd be done in a minute. "Hello, Walter. Yes I am, I'm furious. Well, you've stabbed me in the back, haven't you? That's the way I see it. Don't talk lawyer talk, I'm not a lawyer . . ."

I would have loved to know who Walter was. The only possibility I could think of was Walter Armstrong, Bert Holman's lawyer.

". . . We all have to do what we have to do," she went on. "Oh, really? Then we'll be speaking through other people. Yes. No. Hold on."

She put Walter on hold and turned to me. "I have to take this. Do you accept my offer?"

"I have to think about it . . ."

"Your alternatives are freedom or captivity. What is there to think about?"

"It's not as easy as that . . ."

"I think we've finished here," she said, standing suddenly.

I stood, too. I was going to ask if I could take some Danish with me when a huge, grotesque belch sprang from the depths of my stomach.

"I hope that was out of necessity, not showmanship," she complained.

I tried to explain, "That was from my cancer test . . ."

But she'd had it. "Please. I'd like you to leave."

"I couldn't control that." She was not convinced. It was time to say good-bye. "Well, thanks for your time," I said, getting out of my chair. "Can I take two of these . . . ?"

"Take them all! Just get out!"

I grabbed a couple of Danish, thanked her again and left.

Just outside her door, as it closed behind me, I "accidentally" dropped the pastries. Bending down and fumbling to pick them up, I listened to her voice inside.

". . . You're leaving us for Whitehead? Fuck you! Fuck Whitehead! You two pricks and an army of lawyers won't get Sovereign . . ."

I got the pastries together, smiled at Sheila's impassive secretary and followed the security guard back to the elevator. So Armstrong was leaving Holman to join up with Whitehead. Things looked bad for good old Sheila.

On the way down, I took stock of our meeting. All she really told me was that she knew Bert was dying and Bert knew she was Jeannie Locke's daughter. Along with another version of the Jeannie Locke story. How was I to know if one word of it was true? One thing I'll say for her: the rap about being a dumb actress was way off base. The girl had a brain and knew what to do with it.

Crossing the Holman lot, from the executive building to the *Real Life* studio, I had to walk around a huge puddle. It reminded me of the one Norman Devore and I hydroplaned through on his Harley-Davidson, running from Danno's patrol cars. Poor Norman. What was his crime? Loving Virginia too much? Is that why they were killed? Was it a love triangle?

I walked past *The Shame Game* studio. There were three huge tour buses parked outside. An excited audience of hefty tourists in bright, synthetic outfits was all abuzz, waiting to be admitted to their seats for the show. Very soon, some poor son-of-a-bitch's pain and torment would entertain these vampires, give them something to crow about to the folks back home. The way my life was going, I could be a contestant on the show. As long as I was going to suffer, I might as well get a dishwasher for it. The one I had now left streaks on my fake silver flatware.

It was almost two o'clock when I walked into the *Real Life* studio. An hour from taping. I asked for Sam and was told she was in her office.

She didn't look happy to see me. The first words out of her mouth were, "You made me look like a fool."

"What do you mean?"

"You lied to me on the show last night. Either that or you lied to the police."

"About Bambi Friedman?"

"Did you go to her house yesterday? Yes or no?"

"What is this? A cross-examination?"

"Yes or no?"

"Yes."

"Did you see her? Did you speak to her?"

"Yes."

"How could you lie to me? Do you know what that does? It destroys my credibility. This whole show is about credibility."

"This is a TV show, not a court of law. Its purpose is to keep people locked in while you sell products."

"It's a place people expect to get the truth."

"You're telling me everything you put on this show is the truth?"

"To the best of my knowledge, yes."

"If you really wanted to get the truth, why didn't you ask in advance if I was willing to talk about Bambi Friedman? Why did you spring it on me like some rabid DA?"

"We went through this last night. You never told me not to ask about her. Then you went and told the police you were at her house."

"Are you upset that I have an alibi for Norman and Virginia's murders?"

"That's a terrible thing to say."

"That's the impression you're giving."

"I'm wondering who will believe you anymore. You either lied to the police or to millions of people."

"It's not my responsibility to tell millions of people a damn thing!"

"Why do you think we paid you thirty thousand dollars? To tell lies?"

"No, to buy yourself ratings. This is entertainment, Sam. People watch it to be entertained, not to hear facts."

"You don't think the truth is entertaining? Do you set out to bore your readers?"

"I write it the way I see it. If people want to read it, fine. If not, fine."

"I doubt if your boss agrees with that."

"I'm not my boss."

"Why were you afraid to tell me you were with Bambi Friedman? Is there something between you two?"

"I don't believe you're asking that."

"Do you have a relationship with her?"

"No. Of course not."

"Did you have one with Virginia?"

We were sliding off the deep end. Luckily, someone knocked on her office door. "Sam?"

Looking at me unhappily, she said, "Yes, Harry?"

The door cracked open. It was Carruthers, her producer, in his disheveled shirt and tie. "Oops. Am I interrupting?"

"Yes," I said, "you are."

"Got the overnights," he said to Sam, ignoring my ill will. "We went through the roof. Great show. You, too, Marx. I know if Bert were alive he'd be excited about the ratings, we're breaking one record after another, the biggest show ever in our time slot. I want you to know, Marx, I have no hard feelings toward you. I'm grateful you agreed to come on the show. Sam, we're meeting in the conference room in five minutes."

"I'll be there."

"Thanks again, Marx. You're always welcome on *Real Life.*"

He closed the door and was gone.

"Well?" I said. "I think you owe me an apology."

"For what?"

" *'The biggest show ever'?*"

" *'In our time slot.'* "

"What's with you? Is it ever enough?"

"Not so far."

"What, did your parents punish you for getting a red ribbon instead of a blue one when you rode your horse?"

"I don't have time for psychoanalysis right now, Albie."

"Carruthers isn't holding the Bambi thing against me. Why should you?"

"Carruthers will say anything for ratings."

"And you won't?"

"I have a meeting."

"In five minutes."

"I have to prepare."

Another knock. "Sam?"

"Yes, Eric?"

"Harry wants you to make sure the photos are camera ready before the meeting."

"Okay."

"Thanks." He's gone, too.

"What photos?" I ask.

"We're using parts of the pictures."

"What pictures?"

"The ones I took last night."

"You're not using those."

"Yes, I am."

"You promised you wouldn't."

"That was when I thought you told the truth about Bambi."

"You're going to put those pictures on TV?"

"Only parts of them. No nudity. Almost no gore."

"Almost no gore?"

"As little as possible."

"Why are you doing this?"

"Because people want to see it."

"Since when is it your job to make them happy?" Did I say that?

"That's what I get paid for. It isn't my job to make *you* happy."

"It's not my job to make you happy, either." This was degenerating beyond reasonability.

"Albie, I tape in forty-five minutes and I have a million things to do."

"Where does that leave us?"

"You can tell me what happened with Bambi Friedman. If it bears on Bert's murder, come back on the show and tell your story."

"But you're still using the pictures?"

"Yes."

"This will make me look bad with the police."

"They won't know where we got them."

"You once accused me of thinking you were the type to do any-thing for your career, anything to get ahead . . ."

"You still think that?"

"What else can I think?"

She went over and opened the door for me. "Excuse me. I have a meeting."

"Do you mind if I make a call?"

"Be my guest," she answered, and walked out of the office.

What is it with women? Just when you think you know one, the roof caves in. I suppose I should look at my own culpability. I haven't seen anything to make me believe she's not concerned with the truth. And I did lie to her on her show. That was a slap in the face.

I guess I felt I wanted something of my own, some little piece of information I didn't have to share with millions of cretins watching the show out of morbid fascination. A man assassinated at his wed-ding, his head blown to pieces in front of his bride . . . the grisliness of it was irresistible.

Now, with the public appetite whetted to all-out, no-holds-barred bloodlust, the mutilation killings of Norman and Virginia were just what Dr. Neilsen, the ratings specialist, ordered. Murder, mayhem, and mutilation, a certain ticket to carry Sam to the top of the charts.

I had to admit, unsavory and sickening as it was, there was some-thing insanely reasonable and pragmatic about her approach. I couldn't legitimately call her hypocritical. Yesterday she said to me, "I didn't create the present, but I'm living in it." Was it her fault she hadn't experienced a time of greater thoughts and aspirations, like we did in the sixties? Was it her fault that life today has been poisoned by the explosion of cable TV and media overkill? As much as I despised the idea of her using those pictures, I felt that she didn't know any better. Maybe she never would.

But, my floundering romance aside, I had to move into action and take care of Albie Marx. First on my list was Bambi. I had to be assured she would corroborate my alibi for double murder. She also claimed to have "indisputable proof" that her version of the Jeannie

Locke story was the real thing. She gave me the *tell* part of the story. Now it was time to *show*.

Bambi still had the same message on her machine. She'd gone off for the weekend but was in touch with her machine and would return all calls. Again, I didn't want to leave a message for the cops to pick up. It was Thursday afternoon. Her long weekend could prove too long for me.

Heading out of the studio, there was nobody on the *Real Life* set except Eric, Mr. Important, who was fussing with the teleprompter.

"Did you pull the info sheet on Gardner?" I asked.

"I went through half the storage boxes down in the basement."

"Did you find it?"

"Of course. I gave it to Sam this morning."

"Excellent work."

"Did you hear about the ratings? We're number one in our time slot this week. Can you believe that?"

"Great news. I'm really excited for you guys."

"Well, you were part of the team. Last night's overnights were the highest so far."

I encouraged him to "keep up the good work" and headed back to Sam's office. I figured she was so preoccupied when we had our disagreement that she'd forgotten to tell me about Eric finding Gardner's info sheet.

When I got to her office there was no one at her secretary's desk and the door was open. I guessed everyone was in a meeting or running around getting the show ready, so I walked into the office. There was a mass of material on Sam's desk and I shifted through it. Sure enough, near the top of the pile, I found a *Shame Game* info sheet with the name James T. Gardner at the top. There were three zeroxed copies attached to it, so I stuck one in my pocket and left a little Post-it note on the original, telling Sam that I'd taken one of the copies. When I walked back out, I didn't see Sam or Eric, so I headed out of the studio.

Outside, I looked over the sheet. It was a printed form, which Gardner had filled out in a bland, unimpressive handwriting. There were the standard questions: name, address, telephone number, date of birth, Social Security number . . .

He listed his address on a street in Pasadena with an apartment number. Under Occupation he'd answered "Firefighter. (Currently unemployed)." The question asking for his spouse's name was answered by "Eunice." Next to the inquiry regarding children he had written, "Deceased."

On that word the ink had been smudged by something wet. Perhaps a tear.

The next question was an essay type: Briefly Tell Your Story. Gardner had written his account, basically the same story he told on the show.

After that he was asked to answer: In Your Opinion, What is the Most Heartbreaking Part of Your Story? Here he had made a reference to the deceased children. There was another ink smudge.

Then came a part of the form entitled: Things I Would Like To Win. There were a wide variety of prizes listed, and Gardner had checked the boxes next to things he wanted.

Following the prize list was a question asking the prospective contestant to list his or her pet projects and hobbies. I assumed it had to do with deciding on prizes. Gardner had written in, "Hunting rifles. Repair them and fire them. Target shooting."

If he was so familiar with rifles, why would he need an ex-hippie like me, who knows nothing about them at all, to provide one? I knew what Danno's answer would be: Gardner needed me to smuggle the murder weapon onto the grounds.

The final question was: Is There Anything About Your Statement You Wish To Remain Totally Confidential and Private? Here, Gardner had scribbled, "I do not want to upset my wife because of appearance on show. I do not wish her to be bothered. I do not wish anybody to know she is in hospital under assumed name. (St. Vincent under Mrs. June Stockwell but please do not say this on show. Thank you.)"

I knew St. Vincent's Hospital in Pasadena. As far as I was aware, Gardner's wife had not yet been located. If she had been, the press would have been all over her. Maybe this was my chance to come up with something on my own. Before *Real Life* got around to taking it public.

St. Vincent's was a long way past Bambi Friedman's house in

Franklin Canyon. I needed to see Bambi, but this information on Gardner's wife had to be acted on immediately. I decided to drive to Pasadena first, then try to reach Bambi again.

When people tell you the world's most unreliable car is a Jaguar, don't believe them. It's in the top three. But my little '67 sedan never lets me down. It started right up after sitting all night in water up to its wheel wells.

Even the Hollywood Freeway was a thing of beauty this day after the rains. Clean and fresh was the air, the mountains, the sky, with sunshine sparkling in everything that came into contact with the eye. With my windows and sunroof open, the ride out to Pasadena was the ultimate "breath of fresh air," a chance to clear my head of the thick, incomprehensible web of odd bits of information, half-truths and suspicions that were fogging it up.

My mistake was to turn on the radio. 1070 FM All-News Radio would always be there to muddle things up:

... A representative of the LAPD told members of the press that the mutilated bodies of a man and a woman, discovered last night in a mansion adjoining the Hollywood property of journalist Albie Marx, might be linked to the murder of game show king Bert Holman ...

... An independent poll conducted by *USA Today* concluded that 89% of Jewish Americans think Marx is innocent of conspiracy in Holman's murder ... 83% of non-Jewish Americans say Marx is guilty ...

Jewish Americans? Non-Jewish Americans? What kind of poll is that? I guess it proves how vitally concerned people are with the Truth. As opposed to being influenced by bigotry, misplaced hero worship and sheer, unadulterated, good old American ignorance.

I could just see it. I go to trial. The judge is a woman, Park Avenue Irish. The jury is four born-again Christians, two African Americans, a Mexican-African Native American, a Jew For Jesus, a German American, two Fruits of Islam, and one Italian lawyer who lost his job in a Jewish law firm to a partner's son.

To the shock and outrage of the Jewish community, I get convicted. The Jews riot. Beverly Hills explodes in violence. Jews throwing Molotov *dradles*, beating gentiles over the head with rolled-up torahs, breaking into Italian leather boutiques, looting delis, circumsizing Negroes . . . The police use excessive force to stop the rioters . . . Rabbis and Bnai Brith leaders cry "racial discrimination" and demand equal justice . . .

Back to 1070 FM All-News radio:

. . . Attorney Marvin Mendelson, speaking for Gluck International CEO Mitchell P. Gluck, filed suit against the City of Los Angeles for false arrest, claiming damages of over $1,000,000,000. Mendelson stated the figure one billion is the amount his client could potentially lose as a result of negative publicity generated by Gluck's arrest for his alleged role in the murder of Bert Holman. Gluck International stock has sunk to a new low . . .

Mendelson! The lawyer Gluck promised to get to represent me in a plea-bargain, the guy who wrote the hit book, *Excessive Charges*. Suing the city for a cool billion. Brilliant. If Gluck is innocent, he wins the false arrest suit and comes out richer than he went in. If he's guilty, he won't need the money anyway. A no-lose legal maneuver.

Hey . . . it's never over till the Jewish lawyer sues.

. . . The Sovereign Communications Board of Directors will go into emergency session tomorrow morning, and are expected to approve the last-minute offer of BMA president Michael Whitehead . . . Whitehead's group stepped into the picture when Gluck International and Holman Entertainment experienced difficulties over Holman's murder and Gluck's alleged involvement . . .

And Sheila's lawyer, Walter Armstrong, just defected to Whitehead. How big are Whitehead's aspirations? If he takes over Sovereign, can a weakened Gluck International be a target, too? And if he got Gluck, would Holman Entertainment, with the inexperienced Sheila Petersen Holman at the helm, fold easily into his hands? And if Sam's ex-husband, Michael Whitehead, ruled the world-wide entertainment industry, would the fiercely ambitious and competitive Samantha Shelton become more than just the host of a tabloid TV show?

... Caught in a firestorm of accusations and threatened lawsuits over sexual abuse charges, television's Mr. Rogers today attempted to take his life with a massive overdose of St. Joseph's aspirin ...

My God. That's my fault. I made that up. I have to call somebody. I have to tell the truth. Who would believe me? Me, an alleged murderer? Would anyone? Not a chance. Poor Mr. Rogers is on his own.

... At approximately 3:25 A.M. this morning, residents of Studio City were awakened by a loud explosion from the CBS Television studio complex ... Firefighters arrived to find one building destroyed by the blast. The building housed film stages and production offices for *Inside Copy*, the popular television current events show ... Damage was estimated at three to four million ... A call placed to Studio City police claimed responsibility for the blast on behalf of the Anti-Homogenization Army ...

Good old Stevie. I'm starting to root for him. I'm going to make a wish list of targets, just in case we run into each other.

The last item on the news is a sound byte with a well-known California psychic who had predicted a massive earthquake for this very date. He insists that although his timetable may be off by a day or two, we should be grateful for this coming wake-up call from Mother Nature and the benefits it will shower upon us—the much-needed economic stimulus for rebuilding the city, the spiritual stimulus to thank God for what we already have, and the psychological stimulus to get everything we don't have before the clock runs out.

Shades of Ozzie Baba.

St. Vincent's was one of those very old hospitals on the border of a neighborhood that's been in a gradual decline for as long as most people who live there can remember, a bit like the old industrial towns of the Northeast.

Unlike the hospital I went to this morning, Cedars, which is constantly being donated new wings and towers with names like Spielberg Annex and Streisand Clinic, St. Vincent's has fought to maintain its basic functions while preserving its image as a decent hospital to go to if you have to go to a hospital. It isn't an institution that can afford to keep people indefinitely on life support without getting reimbursed for it. It was the kind of place that would send a letter very politely explaining they would have to pull the plug if you didn't pay the electric bill.

I asked at the information desk for Mrs. Jane Stockwell and was directed to the Intensive Care Unit. The nurse up there had a badge that identified her as "Karen Guy—Duty Nurse." She was reading a mystery novel when I walked up to her counter. I hoped it was evidence she didn't watch the tube. If she was a TV addict, I'd be dead in the water.

"Hello."

"Yes?"

"I'm Arthur Stockwell. I'm Jane Stockwell's brother-in-law."

"Really!"

"Yes."

"Well, how about that! I didn't know Mr. Stockwell had a brother. He's the only one who ever comes to see her. Jane, that is."

"I'm in town from Minnesota. This is the first chance I've had to visit Los Angeles since my brother moved Jane here to St. Vincent's."

"Well, I'm sure she'll be glad to see you. Not that you'd be able to tell. She isn't what we call alert. Your brother must have told you that."

"Yes, he's told me. I thought perhaps that seeing me might cheer her up."

"Well, isn't that thoughtful of you? It's a shame something so awful happened to such a nice family."

"She sustained quite a shock and fall."

"She certainly did. How is Mr. Stockwell? It's been a while since we've seen him. Poor man. How is he getting along?"

"He's still under the weather. I'm doing some things for him while I'm in town. Taking care of business and such."

"How nice, to have a brother who can do that. Well, what are we standing here blabbing for? You're here to see Jane, not me. Come along this way."

She led me to a room that had more wires, tubes, gauges, and contraptions than I'd ever seen before. At the end of all these wires and tubes lay a woman who looked like Phyllis Diller with a lobotomy.

She was somewhere off in Galaxy 26, eyes fixed on something nobody else could see, but which obviously was very clear to her. She looked like a cheapie low-budget movie version of a dead woman come to life. And someone, maybe Nurse Guy, had been kind (or funny) enough to put rouge and lipstick on her.

With Nurse Guy at my side I stood there and babbled to "Jane" like an old family friend, even though the nurse and I both knew I was pissing in the wind. The woman was in that space occupied only by very high Buddhist priests and cabbages.

After five intolerable minutes I gestured to Nurse Guy that I'd had enough. She smiled brightly at old comatose Jane, puffed up her pillow and led me out of the room.

"She looks wonderful. You're doing a heck of a job."

"All the nurses love Jane. She's a lovely spirit."

"Yes. She's very ... serene. Tell me, where is your billing office?"

"First floor. Room 1300."

"Could you do me a favor? Call and tell them I'm on my way down. I'd like to go over some records."

"Of course."

She got on the phone and told the billing office that Mr. Stockwell's brother was coming down and that I was a very nice man whom they would enjoy meeting. I thanked her and took the elevator to the first floor.

Mrs. Sheets, the hospital bookkeeper, welcomed me so cordially I thought she mistook me for someone else.

"I'm so pleased to meet you," she gushed. "Your sister-in-law is one of our favorite patients."

"Jane Stockwell?"

"She's a wonderful spirit."

"Thank you. My brother asked me to pick up a copy of his statement. He's under the weather."

"I have it right here." She handed me the hospital statement.

I looked it over. The patient was given as Jane Stockwell, the "responsible party" as her spouse, James Stockwell. The hospital was unaware that James Stockwell was James T. Gardner.

As of March 8, eleven days ago, there had been an outstanding balance of forty-three thousand dollars. That was about as far as a hospital like St. Vincent's would go without giving old Jane the boot.

Then, on March 9, a personal check was received for fifty thousand dollars. That was a week before Bert Holman's wedding. A week later, March 16, another check was received, this one for the staggering sum of four hundred fifty thousand dollars.

"Is this figure correct?" I asked, indicating the four hundred fifty thousand dollars on the statement.

"Yes," Mrs. Sheets answered reverentially. "We received that check by overnight mail Tuesday morning. Mr. Stockwell himself called to make sure it had arrived."

"So you now have five hundred thousand?"

"We are very appreciative. To be candid, the second check was the largest single payment we've ever received."

"I'm sure you'll earn it."

"It will guarantee Mrs. Stockwell superb care for nine more months."

"Nine months? That's all?"

"Would you like me to explain the billing?"

"If you would. Briefly."

"Intensive Care Unit base charge is fifteen hundred dollars per day. Extra supplies—that's tube changes for ventilator, IV, nasogastric, dressing changes, IV dressings, skin protectors—come to about a hundred dollars per day. The air bed is eighty dollars per day. You've got X rays, CAT scans, other diagnostics ... charged as needed. Physicians' fees, general maintenance, and specialists run about a hundred dollars per day. That comes to approximately eighteen hundred dollars per day. Which comes to fifty thousand dollars per month. It adds up, doesn't it?''

"Yes, it does.''

"I know it sounds like a lot of money . . . but how can one put a price tag on human life?''

"One can't. Unless one were forced to maintain it without being reimbursed.''

"A hospital is a business, Mr. Stockwell, just like any other. The only difference is, we call our customers patients.''

"I understand. Well, thank you very much, Mrs. Sheets. I'll be sure to tell my brother how helpful you've been.''

"You're quite welcome. And give him our regards. He's a very nice man. A lovely spirit.''

Out in the lobby I thought, who is she kidding? *How can one put a price tag on human life?* When the money ran out they'd rip those tubes out of Mrs. Gardner so fast Nurse Guy wouldn't have time to tie on incontinence diapers.

I knew that Gardner got paid three hundred thousand dollars to appear on *Real Life.* That meant he got another two hundred thousand for killing Holman and framing me. He got the first payment of fifty thousand a week before the murder, which he paid to St. Vincent's, and then the rest, which he also promptly turned over to the hospital.

Last night Danno accused me of being paid half a million for my share. Maybe he knows about Gardner's payment to the hospital and figures I got the same amount.

The big question is, how was the transfer of monies accomplished? I assume Gardner gave the hospital a personal check on the account of "James Stockwell" for the first fifty thousand. The bookkeeper, Mrs. Sheets, told me the big check for $450,000 was delivered Tuesday morning. That would be following Gardner's appearance on *Real Life.* And Gardner called to make sure it had arrived. If it hadn't, he would have turned around and changed his story.

Three hundred thousand of the four fifty came from appearing on the show. The other hundred and fifty thousand must have been from the person who hired Gardner. Payment for confessing to the crime and involving me and Gluck.

Which pretty much ruled out Gluck as a suspect. If he had hired

Gardner, then Gardner double-crossed him by implicating him in the televised confession, Gluck wouldn't have paid him a cent. Like me, Gluck is an innocent victim. Maybe I should sue the city, too. My stock hasn't exactly soared since my arrest.

One thing I have to admit: much as I hate Gardner for framing me and putting me through all this, I can't help but feel touched that he did it all for nine more months of life for his wife, Eunice. You can bet that a year from now—barring her winning the lottery— Eunice will be up in that great vegetable garden in the sky.

From a pay phone in the hospital lobby I called Bambi. Again, her machine answered. Out of town for the weekend. Again, I left no message.

I called Boopsie. For the first time, the voice that answered her phone was sober and alert. I quickly filled her in on what I'd learned—that Sheila Petersen Holman was the daughter of Jeannie Locke. I described my meeting with Sheila and her claim that she could exonerate me if I agreed to walk away. I told her about Sam showing the death photos on *Real Life*, and about Eunice Gardner and the half million dollars.

"You've had a busy day."

"And it's only four o'clock. Anything new on your end?"

"Had my hair and nails done."

"I can breathe easy now."

"The coroner narrowed the time of Devore and Hurley's death to between six A.M. and noon yesterday."

"I was either in jail, in my car, or at Bambi Friedman's."

"Have you reached her yet?"

"No."

"Danno obtained a search warrant for your office and house."

"Shrike told me they came to the office."

"Are we in for any surprises? In either place?"

"Not unless someone planted something."

"Given what's already happened, I wouldn't call that a surprise. Is there anything in either place that you know of?"

"No."

"I wish you could get a hold of this Bambi Friedman."

"Did you run her friend's license plate? The I D8 U?"

"I did. The car is a red Miata?"

"Right."

"It's registered to Debra Van Horn, 2676 Dorland Avenue, Los Angeles. I looked for her in the phone book—there's no listing."

"2676 Dorland."

"What are you going to do?"

"Find her. I want to cement my alibi. I want it written in stone."

I promised to stay in touch. I figured the phone call cost Shrike around twelve bucks, a third of Boopsie's hourly fee.

By the time I found Debra's street it was getting to be five o'clock. I was already thinking of the evening ahead. Would I speak to Sam? Would we spend the night together? Was she still ticked off? Was I? Was this what they mean by not mixing business with pleasure?

I was relieved to see the red Miata convertible in the narrow driveway of a sweet little bungalow-style house, vintage LA, circa 1940. I parked on the street, went to the front door and rang the bell. After a minute it was opened by Debra, who looked at me in sharp surprise and told me to get inside quickly.

"What are you doing here? I didn't make a date with you," she said, closing the door behind us.

"Where's Bambi?"

"Out of town."

"Where?"

"Look," she said, folding her arms and starting to pace back and forth. "I don't want any trouble. Whatever you all are doing, leave me out of it."

"What's the matter?"

"You're mixed up in these murders. Think I want a part of that? No, I don't think so. I think I don't want to know anything you know. Don't talk to me. Go away. You didn't come here. I never saw you."

She was picking up the pace of her pacing. "Hey, slow down. I'm an innocent man. It's a frame. It's a big frame."

"I don't want to hear anymore."

"You have to. You're my alibi."

"Oh, no . . ." she moaned, throwing her head back.

"Nobody's going to know what you do for a living."

"Stop talking."

"I was with you—you and Bambi—when those kids were killed."

"I didn't hear that."

"What is it in this town? You didn't hear that, Marty Wilde didn't say that . . ."

"Who's Marty Wilde?"

"He's in sort of the same business you are . . ."

"I suppose you're going to tell me he's an agent."

"How did you know?"

"Think I haven't heard that joke before? Give me a break."

"Debra . . . I need you to help me."

"What about me? What about *me*?"

I felt like slapping her, the same as I feel like slapping my son when he spouts that self-centered Ozzie shit.

"Doesn't anybody give a shit about anyone but themselves anymore?" I nigh-well pleaded.

"IT'S NOT MY JOB TO MAKE YOU HAPPY!"

Oh, no. Another Baba-head. Exactly what I deserve.

"Debra, I do not want to discuss the meaning of Happiness. I want you to come with me right now, to the police . . ."

"The *police*? Are you out of your fucking mind? They don't know I exist, and I'm not about to tell them."

"Debra, you are not doing something so illegal it can endanger your freedom. You're a physical therapist. That's what you tell them."

"Oh, they're going to believe that, right?"

"What are they going to do? Make you demonstrate? Even if they know you turn a few tricks, they don't give a shit. We're talking about three murders here, not some misdemenor for hooking."

"I don't appreciate that kind of talk."

"I didn't kill anybody and I need you to prove it."

"How do I know that?"

"Because I'm telling you."

"Why should I believe you?"

"Because you know I didn't do it."

"How?"

"I was with you when it happened. I was unconscious. You and

Bambi dragged me into the house. Was I in any condition to commit murders?''

"Look, I don't know anything. Bambi got out of town because they threatened her. I don't want the same thing happening to me.''

"Who threatened her?''

"I don't know. Some guy called and threatened her and she got out of town.''

"Till when?''

"Till this blows over.''

"This?"

"These murders. Come on, Alvie . . .''

"Albie.''

". . . leave me alone. I can't afford to fuck with the police. I have businesses. Your stuff has nothing to do with my stuff.''

"Sorry, Debra, but it does.''

"SHIT!''

Then her telephone rang, not a beep-style ring, but a ringing ring.

"DOUBLE SHIT!'' she yelled.

"Answer it.''

"No way.''

"Maybe it's Bambi.''

"It's not Bambi.''

"How do you know?''

"She wouldn't call me on that line. It's my 900 number.''

"Maybe she's calling on that number to play it safe.''

"Sure. That number's anything but safe.''

"What is it for?''

"It's private.''

"Then answer it.''

"Not with you here.''

"What is it?''

"You really want to know?''

"Yes.''

"Okay. It's for phone sex. Now you know my day job. Okay? Happy?''

"What do I care?''

"I know how people judge.''

"What are you so sensitive about? Answer the damn phone."

"Okay. I'll answer it. But don't forget you asked me to."

She went over and flopped down on the sofa. As I sat opposite, wondering what in the world she was going to do, she picked up the phone, which was sitting amidst a pile of magazines on the coffee table, and started a large digital stopwatch beside it.

Her voice was suddenly velvety soft. "Hello . . . ? Who? Oh, Marcus! You're calling again. I'm so happy. Oh, yes, I am. Sweetie, it's my job to make you happy. What? You're getting tired of making yourself happy? Oh, baby, I know what you mean. Yes, I do. I'm getting a callous on my finger. I can't keep my hands off my sweet, hot little twenty-one-year-old pussy."

Oh, my God. A sex call.

"Sweetie, you want me to get down to my bra and panties? My panties are getting soaked just talking to you. Okay, hold on a second . . ."

She looked at the stopwatch and started leafing through a copy of *People* magazine. Every few seconds she glanced at the timer and gave out a little squeal, just to keep Marcus hooked. I was beginning to perspire.

After a minute or so she breathed into the mouthpiece, ". . . There. That's so much better. Yes. Can you see how wet I am? Yes, I want you to lick my panties . . . Yes, right where it's sweaty and juicy . . . Ummmmmm. Yes . . . You want them off? Yes, I'll hurry . . ."

I could see what was coming and didn't want any more of it. I gave her a signal to hurry the fuck up and went into the kitchen.

In the refrigerator I found a bottle of Corona and gratefully drained it. There was a copy of *Black's Law Dictionary* and a yellow legal pad on the kitchen table. I was thumbing through the book and opening another beer when Debra suddenly started screaming.

"OH, GOD! OH, GOD! OH, NO! OH MY GOD!"

I dropped the beer and ran into the living room. Debra was still on the phone, hyperventilating and shouting, "NO! I MEAN, YES! OH, GOD! YES DEEPER! FASTER! MARCUS! GOD! YES!"

She suddenly sat up straight and looked at the phone in dismay. "WHAT? You did? So fast? You couldn't hold off? Gosh, Marcus

... Of course I felt it. I felt it! Yes. All the way to my ... to the bridge of my nose. I felt it, damn it.''

She looked up at me and rolled her eyes. She was obviously not a fan of quick ejaculations, not when she was getting paid by the minute.

She looked down at her stopwatch and said, "That was eight minutes. Well, seven minutes and forty-eight seconds is eight minutes to me, Marcus ... Thank you. That's ... let's see, what's eight times $3.95? Let's call it thirty-two even. Thirty-two even. *Yes*, I have your Visa number. What? No tip? Just kidding, sweetie. Thirty-two even. I know, you always check your statement. You trust me. Good. Will you call again, soon? Great. I gotta run. Talk to you soon. Bye.'' She put the phone back on its hook.

"Hung like a chipmunk, poor guy."

"That was some show you put on."

"You think so?"

"I'm impressed."

"I take pride in what I do."

"Marcus got his money's worth."

"Oh, Marcus. He calls three times a day."

"You make a hundred a day just off him?"

"He's not even my best customer."

"What do you do with all the money?"

"Save it."

"For what?"

"Law school. I'm taking my prelaw degree at UCLA. I'm going to be a famous criminal attorney."

"Perfect."

"Now you understand why I don't want the police to know me. I can't have anything on my record."

"And you understand why I desperately need you to corroborate my alibi for the time of the murders."

"How about this: let's you and I go to Bambi's. Maybe she's home but she's not taking calls. She could be screening them on her machine. If she's there, forget about me. If not, I'll go to the police with you. What do you say?"

"It's a deal."

As we got up to leave, her phone rang again.

"Don't answer that," I told her.

"What if it's Bambi?"

"You said she wouldn't call on that line."

"But what if she does?"

"All right. But if it's not her, get rid of them."

She picked up the phone, once again the sultry-voice vixen.

"Hello? Marla? Oh, hi, baby. Oh, you're such a nut. Yes, sweetie, I'd love to eat your hot dripping wet pussy . . . Oh yes, I want you to come in my face . . . Don't say that, you're making me crazy . . . Sweetie, I have to do some little-girl things, can you call me back in a couple of hours? Yes, I *do* want you to sit on my face. I *love* when you let your bladder go. Two hours. I promise. What? Your tongue? How far up would you *like* to stick it?"

The sun has descended, streaking the sky bright red and orange, a stain of incomparable violence and beauty. The evening star is as bright as the moon and Franklin Canyon has been born again in God's magnificence, baptized by the holy rains.

Pulling up to Bambi's house, Debra is behind me in her Miata, its gleaming red finish ablaze with the sunset's reflection. We took our own cars, optimistically anticipating Bambi would be home, but the first sign doesn't look promising. There's no car in the driveway. The eucalyptus tree that crashed down on me in the storm yesterday morning is still on the front lawn where it fell.

We go to the front door and ring the bell. No response. We ring again, several times. Nothing.

"Just my luck," Debra grumbles.

"Let's hope something hasn't happened to her." I try the door. It's locked.

"Her Corvette's gone. She's not here."

"Unless she's inside and can't get to the door."

"Well, you find out. I'm not going in there."

"How the hell do I get in?"

"With this." She reaches behind a terra-cotta pot overflowing with flowers and comes up with a key. I put it in the lock and turn it. It works.

"Okay. I'll go in and look around. You wait here."

"Just hurry up. I'm losing money standing around."

"How'd you get to be such a sweet kid?"

"You try being a kid in this world."

"I see your point," I say, and walk into the house, leaving Debra standing beside the open door.

I walk through the rooms on the first floor, look into the closets, check the utility room—no Bambi. There are three bedrooms upstairs. One is obviously Bambi's and has its own bathroom. I glance into the bathroom and see, stuck to the mirror over the sink with one of those little suction cups, a bright pink affirmation card that reads in big letters:

"IT'S NOT MY JOB TO MAKE YOU HAPPY!"

Not Bambi, too. Another Ozzie Baba zombie. This is reaching the level of a cult. I mean, it already is a cult, but it's getting way out of hand. Everybody's spouting that cold-blooded slogan. Everybody's screaming "Me First!" Everybody's acting like the pursuit of happiness is a blitzkreig instead of a blessing.

I go back down to the front door where Debra is waiting impatiently. "Nobody's here."

"Shit."

"I'm going to call somebody. You want to come in?"

"No."

"All right, I'll be right back." I go to the phone that's on a stand off the living room, beside Bambi's answering machine, then dial the Hollywood precinct and ask for Danno. I'm told he's not available. I try his home number. Not even a machine. I wanted to bring Debra directly to him. I don't want to deal with middlemen at this stage of the game.

I'm trying to decide what to do when the phone rings. After three rings the machine picks up. I turn up the volume control to hear, in case the caller leaves a message.

A man's voice, familiar but I can't quite place it.

"Bambi, it's me. Where are you? Things are moving very quickly. We should talk. Call me at the Foundation after Happiness Hour."

The Foundation? That's got to be Ozzie.

I snatch up the phone. "This is Albie Marx, Jack . . ." Too late. He's gone. I hang up. Then remember to wipe my fingerprints off the phone. And off the volume knob on the answering machine. I track back to the front door where Debra looks like she's mad enough to take a shit.

"What the hell's going on? I'm not standing here all night! Let's get the damn thing over with!"

"Debra, I need to ask you a favor."

"All right! I'm coming with you! Okay? Let's go."

"I need a couple of hours."

"For what?"

"I have to see somebody. Someone very important. Will you go home, lock your door and wait for me?"

"I'll go home and lock my door. I have other things to do besides wait for you."

"Good. Take some phone calls, read a law book, calm yourself down. I'll be there in two hours, three at the most."

"Bye." She turns abruptly and walks to her car. I close the door, lock it, wipe all my prints off everything and replace the key in the pot.

The Happiness Foundation. This is going to be a giant pain in the ass. Jack Schwarzberg alias Chief Ozuma Blackfoot alias Ozzie Baba. We know how hard he's going to try to make me happy.

The Happiness Foundation is located in a refurbished art deco movie theater on Third Street in Santa Monica. The marquis overhangs the sidewalk bearing the announcement:

HAPPINESS FOUNDATION
OZZIE BABA
HAPPINESS HOUR LECTURE EVERY NIGHT EXCEPT SUN-
DAY, 7 P.M.
TONIGHT: CHANNEL SURFING TO HAPPINESS: TUNE IN
AND TURN ON

It's already past seven-thirty by the time I find a parking spot and get to the theater. A sign in front of the box office says, "Ozzie Baba's Happiness Hour Lecture, $20 Per Person Tax Deductable Donation."

The girl in the ticket booth smiles condescendingly when I slip my Writer's Guild card under the window and ask for a discount. "Sorry, sir. This is a charitable organization. No discounts."

"All right. One for tonight's lecture."

"Tonight's lecture is in progress."

"So?"

"No admittance after the lecture begins."

"Look, this is an emergency. I am miserable. I'm so unhappy I can't eat. I'm getting unhappy enough to do some serious body piercing. You have to let me in."

"We do have a special rate ticket for late admittance."

"Great. Give me one of those."

"That will be a forty-dollar donation, please."

"Forty dollars? That's twice as much!"

"It's twice as deductible. Would you like one?"

"Do I have any choice? Give me a forty-dollar ticket. You take checks?"

"With driver's license."

Since I don't have forty in cash I write her a check. She checks the picture and signature on my license, stamps the back of my check and gives me a ticket along with a standard IRS short form for declaring charitable donations.

"For your records," she says. "Thank you."

There's a well-muscled All-American young man standing at the entrance, wearing jeans, an open-collared sport shirt, and a blue sport jacket with a big red-and-white button pinned to the lapel which tells all and sundry:

"IT MAKES ME HAPPY TO SERVE YOU"

He smiles with a hundred gleaming white teeth and takes my ticket. Then he softly directs me to the auditorium door, which is just beyond a large, colorful sale display of Ozzie's latest hit book, *Take Back Your Power: Twelve Inspirational Portraits of People*

Who Overcame Compulsive Compassion Syndrome To Achieve Complete Happiness.

The theater is packed. On the stage, sitting in a tall director's chair, parked directly in front of a microphone, is Ozzie Baba. His manner and tone are completely conversational, the opposite of what you'd expect when you hear the word "lecture."

"... so I just said, Mom, this conversation is interfering with *Seinfeld* ..."

His audience ripples with laughter.

"Yes, she's my mother ... but some things are sacred."

A huge laugh from the audience, filled to the brim and overflowing with obsequiousness.

I take a seat against the back wall, one of the few empty ones left. Everyone looks relaxed and casual, their attention glued to the lovable little guru.

He's so small that his feet are barely touching the footrest of the director's chair. He's wearing white jeans, tan sandals, and a bright orange Hawaiian shirt with blue, white-bearded Santas frozen in various stages of high dives: flips, swans, triple butterflies, inverted twists. If you stare at them too long from a distance they'll make you dizzy.

"... But seriously, people, the point of the story is, there are those out there who pass judgment with their noses in the air: 'Don't do this, you shouldn't do that, this is bad for you, that's not good for you.' They'll tell you TV kills brain cells, gives you cancer, makes you lazy ... and, you know, I applaud them. It's not their job to tell you what you want to hear. It's their job to tell you what they think, because thinking makes them happy.

"But it's not your job to listen. It's not your job to live up to someone else's opinion of good and bad, right and wrong. Your job is to live your own life. To make yourself happy. And let's face it ... TV makes us happy. It entertains us. It informs us. It keeps us company. It makes us feel good. It links us together, and what could be better than that?

"The intellectuals will give you one reason after another why TV is bad for you, why TV destroys the fiber of society ... but have you ever met a happy intellectual?"

The audience applauds crisply. They like that one. Even from my seat all the way in back I see Ozzie's mesmerizing eyes twinkle darkly. They're a deep polished black, a black so intense the pupils seem light by comparison. If he were to get some serious airtime, those eyes could take Ozzie a long way in a world hypnotized by TV. With the right format and exposure, he could connect with millions of people as they stare into the tube, helplessly open to suggestion.

He goes on in the same vein for the rest of his talk, amusing his listeners with more intimate anecdotes about his personal life and then closes with the famous quote from *My Dinner With O.J.*, by Robert Shapiro: "The medium *is* the message, so have fun with it."

With the lecture over, a swarm of people move to the foot of the stage, lining up for Ozzie to sign their copies of his book. He's sitting on the lip of the stage, legs dangling down, simultaneously signing books and whispering observations into the ear of an eager young female assistant.

I don't have a book, but I get on line.

When I get to him he reaches out for my book without glancing at me. "We have to talk, Jack," I say firmly.

He turns and recognizes me immediately.

"Hello, Albie," he says congenially, his deep black eyes quietly scanning the theater for a security guard.

"It's too late for security, Jack. If I go down, I'm taking you with me."

"This is not the place to discuss this . . ."

"I was at Bambi's when you called. She left town. She's scared shitless. What happened to Norman and Virginia wasn't pretty."

"All right," he says in a crisp, businesslike tone. He motions me to come up the steps onto the stage. Then he turns to his adoring assistant and I hear him whisper, "Tell these people I got a call from Kevin Costner on location, I had to take it, I'll sign their books next time."

"Okay."

"And tell them I said, 'if they don't like it it's not my fault.'"

"It's not your job to make them happy."

"Exactly."

He picks himself up from the lip of the stage and heads for the wings. I get to the top of the steps and follow him off-stage. He doesn't turn to look at me as I fall in and walk along, a couple of feet behind him. Looking down on his little round head as we go, I realize how cute he is. A shade over five feet tall, with an adorable little bald spot surrounded by a shoulder-length fall of fine flaxen hair so bouyant it bounces as he walks. It's funny. He thinks he's Caesar but he's really Paul Williams.

He comes to a door. He opens it, exposing a corridor with offices on either side and cubicles for secretaries. Most of the workers have gone for the day but those who are left are working at faxes, modems, computers, TV screens—the place is well-equipped to communicate. Apparently, The Happiness Foundation is gearing up to reach out beyond the borders of upscale Los Angeles. Ozzie obviously has plans to expand his parish. By continents.

I follow him as he goose-steps along the corridor, acknowledging the admiring glances of his devotees with a Pope-like benevolence. He stops at a door marked MEN.

"I've gotta take a leak," he says, and I follow him inside.

I'm thinking he'll go to the low urinal, but he passes it up and stands in front of a standard one. This ought to be interesting.

"Well, you finally got your interview . . ." he says with his back to me. He's doing his best not to stand on tiptoes and thinks I can't tell. "What would you like to know?"

"What do you usually get asked?"

" 'When were you first touched by spirits?' That's a standard opener . . ."

"When were you first touched by spirits?"

"Nineteen fifty-three, in Brooklyn. I was fifteen. For no reason at all I climbed onto the roof of an Oldsmobile and assumed the full lotus position."

"The stuff of which legends are made . . ."

We wait in silence for the sound of the tinkle. When it finally starts, he says, "Lord, that's good. Is this one of the greatest feelings in life or what?"

"Look, Jack . . ." I like calling him Jack, spitting out the name. "I've got an offer on the table from Mitchell P. Gluck. Gluck hires

Marvin Mendelson for my defense, I cop a plea, take five years, do a year and a half and I'm out."

"And what's your end?" he asks. "Exonerate Gluck?"

"That's half of it. The other half is to bury you. Say it was you who hired Gardner and me to kill Bert so Sheila would get his estate. You'd have a hell of a time digging your way out of that."

"I disagree, but that's irrelevant. The fact is, Sheila and I offered to take you out of Bert's murder completely, no bullshit, no jail time. You have to agree, that beats Gluck's deal."

"I don't agree with anything you agree with."

"Don't be so negative. We both agree it's good to be happy, don't we?" He finishes up, shakes and zips, goes to the sink, washes his hands, fluffs up his hair in the mirror. "You should be thankful you're not going bald, like me." As satisfied as possible with his reflection, he's back on his horse. "Let's go to my office."

I follow him out of the men's room and down the hall. He opens a door and lets us into a small, cozy office, a well-preserved nook of the original art deco building.

He walks behind a small desk, opens the top drawer, and withdraws a manila envelope which he places on top of the desk in front of me. Then he goes to the door and locks it from the inside. "Take a look," he says.

I open the envelope and remove a document. It says, LAST WILL AND TESTAMENT: BERTRAM ALAN HOLMAN.

"All you have to read is the cover letter," Ozzie says, sliding into his comfortable old desk chair.

From a letter-size envelope I extract a handwritten letter on Bert Holman's private stationery.

February 10, 1995

To Whom It May Concern:

This has been, for me, an agonizing decision. Not the act of which I will speak but the one of confirming it before God and the world on paper, in my own handwriting.

As can be attested by Dr. Alan Rissman, Dr. Paul Pierson, and certain others with whom they have consulted, I am now suffering from inoperable colon cancer. I am a terminal patient. I have

been given two, perhaps three months to live. This diagnosis has been verified by the leading cancer specialists in the field. I have no doubt of its veracity.

I know that I am going to die soon. There are things I want to accomplish before I go. There are wrongs in my past I want to make right. I do these things because it makes me happy to do them, and my goal is to die happy.

Therefore, I am taking the following actions for the following reasons:

1. I am marrying Sheila Petersen because I love her.

2. I am instructing my attorney, Walter Armstrong, to change my will in order to make my fiancée, Sheila Petersen, my sole and complete heir.

3. I have entered into an agreement with James T. Gardner. This agreement requires Mr. Gardner to assist in my suicide. The method he has agreed to use in fulfilling this obligation is gunshot. Because I do not wish to waste away from cancer, Mr. Gardner has agreed to fulfill his obligation within one month of the date of this letter, but in no event before Sheila Petersen and I are legally pronounced man and wife. I have requested that Mr. Gardner use his own discretion so that I do not know when the end is coming. In this way I will live every day as if it were my last.

4. In exchange for his services, I have agreed to provide Mr. Gardner with $350,000, paid in the following manner:

A. A $50,000 advance payment one week prior to my wedding.

B. A guarantee of $300,000 to appear on Holman Entertainment's nationally syndicated television show, *Real Life*, on which he will falsely confess to killing me of his own accord.

For many reasons, both obvious and otherwise, it is my hope that this letter never be exposed to public light. However, as we all know, there exists a principle which states, if something can go wrong it will go wrong. I do not anticipate anything in this agreement to go wrong. In the event something does, however, this letter is to be used to clear up any and all misunderstandings.

The letter is signed, *Bertram A. Holman.* Below his signature is the signature of his witness, *Walter Armstrong, Esq.*

"If this is the real thing . . ."

"Absolutely real," Ozzie asserts.

". . . then somebody got to Gardner after he made the deal with Holman and paid him another hundred fifty thousand to frame me and Gluck . . ."

"Now you're showing some brain power."

". . . And that person got Virginia Hurley to play along . . . Maybe he had something on her . . ."

"It's within the realm of possibility."

". . . Then he got scared I would find her and convince her to turn him in . . ."

"You're on a roll."

". . . Maybe he was in love with her . . . and hated Norman because she loved Norman. So he killed them both . . ."

"I'm surprised—I never thought you could impress me."

". . . He planted my book in Norman's hand to make it look like I did it . . ."

"You're nearly at the finish line."

"Who is he?"

"What makes you so sure it's a he? It could be a they, couldn't it?"

"It could be you and Sheila."

"Why would we do such a thing? Bert was dying. Sheila was going to get his whole estate anyway."

"But you still needed to tie Gluck up. To win the fight for Sovereign."

"Maybe. But why would we do such an awful thing to you?"

"To stop me from digging into the Jeannie Locke story?"

"Jeannie was Sheila's mother. It would be painful to Sheila and her grandparents, but we're not afraid of the story coming out."

"I don't know if I believe that. But, okay, let's say you and Sheila had nothing to do with Gardner. Who got to him?"

"Who, besides Sheila and I, knew about his deal with Bert?"

"Walter Armstrong. Bert's lawyer."

"If I knew you were this brilliant, I'd have granted the interview long ago."

"Armstrong paid Gardner to incriminate Gluck?"

"Now you're being stupid again. You're so uneven."

"You know, I'd really like to bust you in the mouth, Jack. Just to see you cry."

"What company did Armstrong just leave Holman Entertainment for?"

"BMA?"

"And who runs BMA?"

"Michael Whitehead."

"Thank you."

"Michael Whitehead payed Gardner to incriminate me and Gluck?"

"Yes. Whitehead planned it from the beginning. Armstrong is his buddy. Armstrong told him about Bert's private deal with Gardner. Whitehead knew Gardner was going to kill Bert."

"Did he know how Gardner was going to do it?"

"Nobody knew Gardner had such a flair for the dramatic. But it didn't hurt Whitehead. All he had to do was get Gardner to implicate Gluck in his confession. He got rid of Holman Entertainment and Gluck International in one fell swoop. Now he's stepping in to take Sovereign."

"It was all planned?"

"You don't put an investment group like that together overnight. He assembled his investors weeks in advance, just waiting to move. Gardner implicated Gluck on Tuesday. Thursday morning, Whitehead steps in."

"All right ... I can see in principle why Whitehead would go after Gluck—but why *me*?"

"That takes us all the way back to Jeannie. Whitehead doesn't want you digging into that."

"Why?"

"Think. He's an agent. Before he formed BMA, where did he work? Where did he get his start?"

"How the hell do I know?"

"What if I told you it was the William Morris Agency? What if

I told you Whitehead started his career as Mitchell P. Gluck's assistant?''

Here it comes. Another version of the Jeannie Locke story. "Sheila told me her mother was with Gluck and Holiday when she died.''

"Sheila told you the truth.''

"So how does Whitehead figure in?''

"You can't see Bobby Holiday or Mitchell Gluck driving a dead girl into Hollywood and ditching the body, can you? Gluck made his assistant do it. Michael Whitehead. That's why Gluck can't attack Whitehead now. Neither one of them wants to answer questions about Jeannie's death.''

Ozzie sits back and looks at me smugly. I hate to admit it, but everything he's said has made sense. Whitehead was Norman's agent. He could have been in love with Virginia. He could have promised to make her a star if she played her role well. He could have done every single thing Ozzie just said he did. I just didn't want to know the answer to the next question. But I had to ask it.

"Whitehead is a he. Who is the other person? Who is your *they*?''

"I wish I could tell you it's Armstrong. But I don't think Armstrong knows about Norman and Virginia. He's nervous enough about being a party to Bert's suicide.''

"Are you sitting there telling me this other person is someone I know?''

"Unfortunately, I am.''

"Are you implying it's Sam? Samantha Shelton?''

"You've been had, Albie—up, down and sideways.''

I called Sam's beeper and reached her at the *Real Life* production office. She and Carruthers were working late, probably into the wee hours, pulling together pieces for tomorrow's show. I told her we needed to talk as soon as possible and she said she'd call me at home the minute they were finished.

It's nine-thirty and I'm headed to Debra's house. I'm in a terrible mood, despite the fact that I'm no longer a framed man. With Debra to back up my alibi, I'm off the hook for Norman and Virginia's murders. And Sheila Holman's offer this morning turned out to be legitimate. Bert's last letter will lift me out of the morass of the

Holman murder. Coupled with Gardner's hospital statement showing he paid St. Vincent's a hundred and fifty thousand more than he got from Bert, I have a very strong case for being wrongfully implicated by an unknown third party.

Unknown. Or is it?

Michael Whitehead makes perfect sense. His friendship with Armstrong, the fact that Armstrong defected from Holman Entertainment to Whitehead's camp, the new investment group manufactured overnight to take over Sovereign, the fact that Whitehead was Norman's agent and most likely knew Virginia, that Whitehead was Gluck's assistant and could have been involved in Jeannie Locke's death . . . The building blocks to support Ozzie's accusation fit powerfully together.

But why did Ozzie include Sam? What is her relationship with her ex-husband? They were on friendly enough terms for her to call and talk to him from my house last night. I didn't hear the conversation because I was at Norman's. She said she called him when she heard the news on the radio of his bid for Sovereign. But what if that was a lie? What if she realized, after calling him, that the toll call would be logged on my bill? That I would know it was her who called his number. What if she didn't call about something she heard on the radio? What if they were talking about something else? Like what I was doing? The horrific discovery I was about to make in the Steinberg mansion . . .

I can't think about it. I don't want to think about it. I don't want to believe I can be so far off when it comes to judging a person. Especially Sam. She has done nothing that I out and out know of to hurt me.

Except maybe broadcast the photos of Norman and Virginia on *Real Life*. But that was to get ratings, not to hurt me.

To get ratings. Is that what it's all about for her? Or could it be more? Could she be out to run Holman Entertainment? She doesn't think much of Sheila Holman, she's made that more than clear. What if she's working with Whitehead to pave the way for a takeover of Holman after he swallows up Sovereign?

Enough. Anything is possible. "What if" is a dangerous game. It leads to too many possibilities, most of them no more than fantasy and suspicion.

But I can't stop my mind. What was it Bert Holman said in his letter . . . ? ''There are wrongs in my past I want to make right . . .'' So he marries Sheila and turns over his entire estate to her? Billions of dollars, to a girl he hasn't known that long or that well? Could it be that he was carrying some incredible burden of guilt, something having to do with her mother, Jeannie Locke?

I'm relieved to see Debra's red Miata with the I D8 U license plate in the driveway when I pull up to her little house. I park the Jag on the street and I'm heading for her front door when I notice her roll-down garage door is open almost a third of the way. Wondering why she parks on the driveway and not in her garage, I walk over to take a look.

Peering inside, my eyes are greeted with the sight of a black Corvette, one that looks the same as the black Corvette that was parked in Bambi Friedman's driveway two days ago in the rain. The license plate reads, *Great D8*. It's got to be Bambi's.

She's here, at Debra's. What's going on? I thought she was out of town. That was the message on her machine. And Debra told me that.

Wake up, asshole! Debra told you that? Since when is Debra anybody's definition of honesty? Maybe Bambi never left town. Maybe she's been here all the time.

Bambi has a lot to answer for. She started this whole round of Jeannie Locke stories. She approached me at Holman's wedding with a secret that could sink the whole Sovereign deal. What's her stake in this?

I don't want to knock on Debra's door and give them time to get organized, so I walk around the back, quickly and lightly. Don't want any neighbors to report a stalker.

There's a light over the back door as I turn the corner of the house. The door is off the kitchen, leading out to a little porch which is up a short flight of steps from the backyard. I quickly step back into the dark bushes.

Standing out on the porch, leaning over the wooden railing, smoking a cigarette and looking very hassled, is Bambi Friedman.

She's smoking with her right hand and clicking the long fingernails of her left hand nervously. I'm wondering what I should do when Debra wanders over and sticks her head out the door. She's holding a phone, talking into the receiver which she's holding in place with her head and neck, and smoking a cigarette.

I move closer and because the night is clear and still, I can hear every word they say. Debra is talking into the phone.

"... Sorry, but I have to keep a friend of mine company. No, it's not that I don't want to tie you up and put a leash on you. I want to do that. I just can't do it now. I have a friend who needs my attention. Yes, it's a *live* friend. What do you think I'm running here? What's that supposed to mean?"

She listens, stomps out her cigarette, takes the receiver in her hand and holds the mouthpiece against her hip so the person on the other end can't hear. She leans over and says to Bambi, "What the hell is a 'necrophiliac'?"

"Get rid of him," Bambi says with a dismissive gesture.

Debra goes back to the person on the other end of the line. "Buddy. If you ever say that to me again, we're over. I will not take your calls. I will not tell you every little single terrible horrible twisted fucking thing I'm going to do to you! I'll make you figure it out for yourself. How would you like that?" Apparently, she gets the answer she wanted. "Okay, then. Don't say things like that to me. Yes, you can call me. Later. I can't talk now. No, I have a friend—"

"Get rid of the idiot!" Bambi barks in exasperation.

Debra grunts into the phone, "I gotta go! Call me!" and hangs up. "Jesus Christ Almighty, some of these creeps are unbelievable."

"What am I going to do?" Bambi asks, half to herself. "I can't go home, the police are looking for me because Albie Marx gave them my name for an alibi and some bastard is likely to show up in the middle of the night with a gun or a razor blade ..."

"Well, that's just great! A guy's gonna slit your throat, so you come to *my* house? What did I do to deserve this?"

"Well, what do you want me to do? Where should I go?"

"You have parents? A sister? Childhood friends who you're always spending so much time with? You have somebody else but me?''

''You are an ungrateful little wretch. I do everything for you and you act like you don't want to know me!''

''Well, those maniacs are your customers, not mine. They're too weird for me.''

''Oh, really. There's something that's too weird for you?''

''Yeah.''

''What could that be?''

''I'm not a goddamned necrophiliac.''

''You're right. You're not even a necrophiliac's dummy.''

''What is that supposed to mean?''

''Try it this way: you can lead a whore to culture but you can't make her think.''

''Will you stop it? Please! You always have to prove how smart you are.''

''You're smart, too. When you use your brain.''

''Well, I'm going to be a lawyer—what else do you want from me?''

''Nothing. I'm sorry. I feel like total shit. This is worse than running out of money.''

''Getting your throat slit is *not* worse than running out of money.'' Debra's trying to lighten the tension with a joke. I think.

Bambi concedes a little laugh.

Debra says, ''I'm sorry I acted like that. I love you.''

''Sure. You love me like you love your next blowjob.''

''I'm sorry, Bambi. I apologize, Bambi. I won't do it again, ever ever ever, Bambi . . .''

''Don't make fun of me.''

''Don't get hysterical on me.''

''Okay.''

''Say you're sorry.''

''I'm sorry.''

''I'm sorry, too.''

They move into each other's arms, Bambi still holding her cigarette and Debra still holding her phone. At first they just embrace gently but then they slowly start to kiss and move up against each other seductively. These women are in love.

I step out of the bushes into the light, looking up at the girls on the porch. "You ladies are going to the police with me if I have to tie you up like a couple of prize hogs."

"Oh, Christ. Not you," Bambi moans.

"Yes, me," I answer, taking the steps two at a time. "Both of you get inside and turn off the lights. You're a target for any sicko who wants to nail you."

"Are you referring to yourself?" Debra asks in a huff as I try to move her along.

"Get inside!"

I physically push and shove them both into the kitchen, close the door and turn off outside the porch light.

"Where's the switch for the kitchen lights?" I ask Debra.

"Over there on the wall," she says, beginning to get worried.

I move quickly to the switch and kill the lights. Now we can't be seen from outside.

"Is someone out there?" Bambi whispers.

"I don't know if anyone's there or not, but I'm not taking any chances. You have to be crazy, standing out in the open like that."

"What's the difference? I'm fucked any way you look at it."

"That's a great attitude."

"When someone tells me I'm going to end up with a bullet between my eyes and someone's severed cock in my mouth, I tend to let it drag me down a little. I can't help it, I'm the moody type."

"Who said that? Who threatened you?"

"A guy. On the phone."

"Did you recognize his voice?"

"If I recognized his voice I wouldn't say 'a guy,' would I? I'd say his name. He sounded like one of those whistleblowers who go on TV and don't want to be recognized. Like they're talking underwater."

"You have no idea who he could be?"

"I have opinions."

"Why did he threaten you? What else did he say?"

"Oh, God . . . You know, Albie, it's nothing personal but I wish I'd never met you."

"The feeling is mutual, believe me, but I didn't start this. Why were you threatened?"

"For telling you about Jeannie. For opening my big stupid mouth when I should have known better."

"How did you know about Jeannie?"

"She was my friend."

"You knew her?"

"We both came to LA around the same time. We lived at the Reservation together."

"You lived at the Reservation? You told me you didn't know Jack Schwarzberg."

"I lied. I didn't want to drag Ozzie into it. I just wanted that bastard, Mitchell Gluck, to get what he deserved. Here he is, Mr. Success, Mr. Billionaire, taking over every company in show business, making and breaking careers like a king. Then he has to go for the same company Bert wanted? The hell with him. It was time to get even."

"Even?"

"For helping Bobby Holiday get away with what he did to Jeannie. Like I told you."

"You also told me you had irrefutable proof your story is true."

"I do. I have Bert Holman telling it himself, on tape."

"That's not proof. That's Bert Holman's version."

"Well, it's good enough for me."

"Let's backtrack here . . . You were threatened because you told me the story?"

"Yes."

"How many people could have known you spoke to me? Who did you tell about it?"

"Nobody. That's why I'm so pissed off at you. You swore you'd protect my identity."

"I did . . ."

"I hope you write better than you keep secrets. You did tell someone."

"Just my lawyer. And . . ."

"And Samantha Shelton."

"And . . . Samantha Shelton."

"And Samantha Shelton goes on TV and blabs to the whole world . . . 'What about this Bambi Friedman woman?' I nearly choked to death when I heard that."

She's absolutely right. If I hadn't told Sam, if Sam hadn't asked me about Bambi on *Real Life*, nobody would have known. Sam swore she brought it up because I didn't specifically ask her not to. That's getting harder to buy. Everything keeps pointing at Sam and Whitehead. With each layer that gets peeled away, Ozzie is looking more like the person with the right angle. I wish it weren't true. I want to be in love with Sam.

"Did you know Mitchell Gluck back then, too?" I ask Bambi.

"Yes."

"Who was his assistant at William Morris?" Maybe Ozzie was lying about that.

"Michael Whitehead."

There it is. The odds are building. "Could Michael Whitehead have helped Gluck dispose of Jeannie Locke's body?"

"I don't know, I wasn't there. I guess he could have."

There's nothing else Bambi can tell me.

"I've got to go. I want you both to stay in this house and keep all the doors locked. Don't go out and don't answer the phone."

"What about my customers?" Debra squeals.

"Let them use their imaginations."

"Then what would they need *me* for? I have to pay for law school, buster!"

The drive to Holman Entertainment went by so fast I can hardly remember it. My mind was an absolute blur. All I could think of, over and over, were the bright little trail markers Sam had left, all along the way, that I ignored, one after the other, until Ozzie made me open my eyes and look.

It's almost midnight when I get to Holman Entertainment, and the guard booth at the front gate is lit up inside. The night-shift man is sitting back in the booth with his feet up on the counter, talking and laughing on the telephone.

I park the Jag on the street and walk toward the booth, keeping myself in the shadow of the executive building. At the booth, I check the preoccupied guard, then scoot past the gate and find another safe shadow.

I walk past *The Shame Game* building and keep going toward the *Real Life* studio. As usual, the backstage door is unlocked, and I open it quietly and let myself inside. The place is very dark. The only light is a worklight over the stage. The place is deserted.

I walk past the set and toward the production offices. It's all dark except for bright fluorescent lights coming from the conference room at the end of the hall.

From my vantage point I see two people in the conference room, heatedly arguing. The two people are Sam and Carruthers. She's got her back to me and he's standing in front of a breakfront filled with video equipment.

I move forward, keeping close to the wall, to see how far I can get before they spot me. They're so involved in their confrontation, whatever it is, that neither of them notices me. A few steps more and I'm close enough to hear what they're saying.

Carruthers is defending himself. "I've always done what I thought best at the time . . ."

"You're too sneaky, Harry. I can't trust you."

"I've always acted in the best interests of you and the show . . ."

"Forget it. You're history. I wish I didn't have to get rid of you myself, but there's nobody left with the balls to do it."

"You can't do this, Sam . . . you'll never forgive yourself . . ."

"Are you out of your mind? I can't forgive myself for letting you go on this long. I'm sorry, Harry, but it's over."

Harry steps back as she reaches down to pick up something on the table in front of her. I can't see what it is because her back is to me, but if it's a gun I'm going to be a witness to a murder. I have to make my move.

"STOP! DON'T! DON'T DO IT, SAM! DON'T SHOOT!" I yell, charging with all my force into the room.

They both turn to look at me. They're stunned.

"What the hell are you doing, Marx?" Carruthers demands.

"Saving your piece of shit life, Harry. Put that down, Sam," I say, as she turns to face me head on.

She's holding the remote control for the VCR.

"Are you totally out of your mind?" she asks in amazement.

"I thought . . ."

"This guy has serious mental problems," Harry says.

"You said you were going to get rid of him," I stammer.

"You bet your ass I am. He's fired. Finished. Off this show."

"You're firing him . . . ?"

"Men are such half-wits sometimes. You think I don't have the power to fire him? Tell him, Harry."

"Sam, this is between you and me. Make him wait outside."

"This involves him, too," she answers. "Now that you're here, look at this," she says to me, aiming the remote at the console and pressing a button. The screen blips on; she presses it again and a tape begins to roll.

It's a tape of news footage. Some kind of event with limousines lined up outside . . . Wait, it's Bert Holman's mansion. It's his wedding!

Now the tape stops and another version of the same image begins, digitalized to focus in on one particular area of the tape, one of the limos waiting in line.

Another version, tighter this time, looking closely at the window of the limo.

Another version, even tighter, looking inside the limo. The images of two people can be vaguely made out.

A final, digitalized super-duper closeup of the two people. Me and Virginia, toasting with champagne glasses, so clear you can see her gloves.

I'm in shock.

"Harry's had this since Monday," she tells me. "He could have cleared you anytime since then."

"You lousy son-of-a-bitch . . ."

"I just saw it tonight," she goes on. "Now that Virginia's dead he figures it's time to bring it out . . . 'New Evidence' . . . 'Never Seen Before' . . . 'Only on *Real Life*' . . . 'Tomorrow Night' . . . 'The

Ultimate in Investigative TV' ... 'Dead Girl and Sixties Radical Photographed Together' ...''

"That's enough," I tell her. "I get the picture."

"Last night we got the best rating of any show this year!" Harry screams. "And it's going higher when we get the numbers tomorrow! We're as hot as *The Shame Game*! We're Number One! *We're Number One!*"

"I don't care!" she shouts back.

"You do! You love it!"

"You used me, Harry, and I don't like it!"

"If Bert were alive he'd have approved."

"You don't know anything about Bert ..."

"I knew him better than anybody in the world, including that idiotic guru!"

"You think because you knew him the longest you knew him the best? If you knew him so well, why did you never advance in this company? Why are you still producing this stupid show? Why isn't it you running the company, instead of a blond bimbo whose IQ isn't equal to the combined ages of your two kids?"

"She's a lot smarter than she looks. And she's his widow. What am I supposed to do?"

"She's Ozzie Baba's puppet."

"How do you know that?"

"I have eyes, ears and a brain."

"Fuck you, Sam. Bert asked me, many times, what I wanted to do in this company. It was my choice. I wanted to stay with this show you call 'stupid.' I happen to love this show. What is that, something you look down on? At least I'm not a hypocrite with my puss out in front of the camera."

"Bert told me he kept you on out of mercy."

"Bert never did a thing in this business without consulting me."

She laughs out loud at this one.

"It's true! From his first day as an agent at William Morris I was the one guy he trusted."

"You were with Bert at William Morris?" I ask, surprised.

"I was his first assistant."

"Not only was he Bert's assistant," Sam says, "but I just found out he's covering up something he and Bert did years ago that could have wrecked Bert's career from the very start.''

"That's outrageous!'' he yells.

"Michael Whitehead just told me, Harry. Michael worked for Gluck and he knew you both. He told me what you and Bert did. How you saved Bobby Holiday's ass and your own careers by dumping that poor girl's body. You might as well face it, it's coming out.''

"I have nothing to hide.''

"What about this?'' she asks, looking him in the eye as she hands me a little pink slip with a telephone message. "This is from the night of Bert's murder. Harry's voice mail transcribed by his secretary.''

I read it. It's from James T. Gardner. It says: "First half of mission accomplished. Your move.''

Finally, it all makes sense. Harry Carruthers. The guy who never liked me. Who acted like Bert's faithful dog, who said I wasn't fit to shine Bert's shoes. Who made Sam go on the air with the police evidence against me. Who probably convinced her to use the photos of Norman and Virginia to get even higher numbers. The guy who's been using this whole sordid affair to pump up his ratings and make himself a hero.

"It was you who got to Gardner.''

"What of it?''

"It's been you all the time ...''

"I did nothing illegal.''

"You payed off Gardner to incriminate me. You got Virginia to take a part in it ...''

"Gardner called me to set up an interview ...''

"... You wanted to stop me from digging into the Jeannie Locke story ...''

"You're having a psychedelic flashback, Marx.''

"You bailed Norman out to attract Virginia and killed them both ...''

"Sam ... are you seriously spending time with this mental patient?''

"He's making sense to me, Harry. Somebody killed those kids.''

"You think it was me?'' he sneers. "I'll let you in on a secret,

Samantha: I think it was you. You and your mentor, the fabulous Michael Whitehead."

"Grasping at straws," she says contemptuously.

"Really? Let's see you deny that Whitehead is trying to get this company for you to run."

"Let's see you come up with an alibi for eleven A.M. yesterday morning."

"I have nothing to prove to you."

"I know you weren't here."

"How do you know? You weren't here, either."

"Eric told me."

"I was in my studio at home, working on the limo blowup."

"The kids were in school, your wife was out and there was no one else in the house, right?"

"You're taking your job too seriously, Sam. You're not a DA," he snaps.

"Ask him if anyone was home," she says to me.

"Is there anyone to confirm your alibi?" I ask.

"What about hers? Where was she?"

"Where were you?" I ask Sam.

"You're asking me for an alibi?" she says, eyes wide.

"Of course not. I'm trying to figure this fucking thing out . . ."

"What difference does it make where I was?"

"You see?" Harry says. "She's so guilty she can't even lie about it."

"Shut up, you son-of-a-bitch, or I'll rip your tongue out," I growl, taking a step toward him. "I don't care where you were," I tell Sam. "Forget it. My head is exploding with lies. Forget I asked."

"Yesterday morning," she explains anyway, "because of the storm, the coast Highway was a parking lot. I called the office to say I'd be late and Eric told me you wanted to rendezvous at your office, at *UP YOURS*. So I took Malibu Canyon to the 101 and went straight to your office. Don't you remember me being there?"

"Where was Whitehead?" Carruthers persists.

"I told you to shut up, Harry. You can do all your talking to the police from now on." I reach for the telephone on the conference table.

"This is a frame-up!" Carruthers shouts. "You two are in it together with Whitehead!"

"You're a murderer, Harry," Sam says. "The worst kind—you did it for ratings."

"Lies!" Carruthers screams.

"You're a sad case, Harry," I say as I pick up the phone with the intention of dialing 911.

Suddenly, Carruthers lurches from where he's standing to the near wall where the light switches for the room are mounted. He hits the switches, plunging the room into darkness before I can dial the police.

My first thought is to protect Sam. I grab her and pull her down beneath the table with me. The room is black. We listen for a sound. There is none. "He may have a gun ..." I whisper in her ear.

I want to go after Carruthers, but I don't want to leave Sam alone. I'm wondering what to do when he suddenly solves my problem by bolting out the door of the room, silhouetted by the dim office light of the corridor, and takes off at full speed.

"Turn the lights on and call the police!" I tell Sam. I get up and take off for the door, which I can see in the darkness because of the hallway light beyond.

I'm almost to the door when I get hit with bolt of pain that fires through my entire body and explodes in my brain.

"OH!" I go down like a sack of bricks.

"Albie!" Sam cries, alarmed. "Albie! What happened?"

"I banged my shin on the fucking cabinet!"

"Carruthers is getting away!"

"Shit! Okay. Turn all the lights on. He knows this place better than I do."

"Okay! Go get him!"

"I'm going! Call the police!"

"I will after I turn on the lights."

"Good."

"He's going to get out of the building."

"Okay, I'm going." I tell myself there's no pain in my shin bone and take off again after the fleeing killer.

Up ahead, I see him turn left at the end of the corridor. Good thing for me I'm a runner and he looks like he's in pathetic condition.

I pick up speed. The corner he turned leads to the stage. Once he's out in the open I'll run him down and beat the living shit out of him—just for fun.

What's with Sam? I wish she would turn on the lights already. Why is she waiting? I have to see the guy to catch him.

I turn the corner and, careful not to run into anything in the dark again, slow down as I reach the stage. She still hasn't turned on the lights.

I hear a sort of muffled clanging sound to my left, from the long counter where Sam and I sat during our interview. I whirl in that direction, but it's too dark to see anything except for the silhouette of a display of some kind on the counter.

I listen closely, holding my breath, but he's not breathing either. If only Sam . . .

Suddenly, the lights come on. All at once. Bright as day. I'm looking at the counter. A display has been set up for a camera beside it to shoot a closeup, but the object which was its centerpiece is missing. I realize that the clanging sound I just heard was Carruthers removing the object. A sign next to the bare exhibit reads:

MACHETE SIMILAR TO THAT WHICH SEVERED NORMAN DE-VORE'S GENITALS

So, the machete mentioned on the sign is what's missing from the display . . .

SWOOSH!

The sound of the machete cutting through the air . . . I spin around to see Carruthers bury the blade of the machete into the top of a wooden prop stand. He's three feet away as he pulls the blade out and raises it menacingly.

"Don't make me do it! Don't make me use this!" he snarls in my face.

"The police are coming, Harry . . . Don't make it worse for yourself."

"Worse? What's worse than getting framed for murder?"

"What's worse than getting framed for murder?"

"Yes! What?"

"There must be something . . ."

"Nothing is worse, and you know it! You and Sam will lie to the world that I killed those kids and everyone will believe you!"

"Not if you're found innocent in a court of law."

"A court of law? The only court of law is *Real Life*! Nobody knows better than me how it works. I designed it. You think this show was Bert's idea? It was mine! I created the show! I produced the show! I don't own the show! But you can't have everything, can you? You want to create, to be an innovater, you have to take a backseat to money. I didn't care. I still don't. I created a whole new idea. I created a way to hook people with *real life stories*. We tell them anything we want and for all anyone knows or cares, it could be the truth! That's the key! They think they're getting the truth! Nobody's ever done that before! Nobody's ever made money by telling the truth!"

"You don't tell the truth!"

"But they think we do and that makes them happy!"

"It's not your job to make them happy!" I didn't say that.

"I'm walking out of here, Marx . . ."

"No, you're not."

"Don't fuck with me."

"You want to put that machete down?"

"Forget it."

"You narcissistic, despotic megalomaniac. You would eat shit on a stick if you saw your own reflection in it. Don't tell me what you gave to the world. You're a lowlife. A drug dealer. You gave them a drug. You hooked them, all right. They can't get enough of your endless exhibition of the worst humanity has to offer. You turned them into the perfect lynch mob—hypnotized and programmed by an insatiable lust for more graphic, more bloody, more cynical sensationalism. *Fire, ready, aim!* That's your motto. Execute anyone you can use to sell toothpaste, cars, deodorant . . . You created the monster, Harry, and I hope it tears you limb from limb . . ."

"You bastard . . . !"

Before he can swing the machete again, I lunge for him, grabbing the arm with the blade as he fights me off. We stumble backward, up against the show's logo. The logo goes over and we crash down on top of it, fighting for control of the machete as we roll around on the huge, colorful letters that spell *Real Life*.

We're battling for the machete when a voice from behind us yells loudly, "THAT'S ENOUGH, GENTLEMEN!"

The machete skids out of Carruthers's hand and onto the floor as our heads swivel in unision toward the sound of the voice. My first thought is, the police have arrived.

It's not the police.

It's the Wizard of Happiness.

Ozzie Baba.

Standing beside him is Sam, her hands cuffed behind her back.

Ozzie is wearing gloves and holding a gun half the size of his arm, a .357 magnum with a silencer. The barrel is pressed against Sam's head.

"This looks like a lover's triangle to me," Ozzie says, as if he were an author working up his next potboiler. "A-type producer Harry Carruthers and Samantha Shelton, his beautiful star, in long-time secret sexual tryst . . . Enter Albie Marx, fading sixties romantic and suspected slasher . . . Shelton, needing more meaning in her existence than she gets from *Real Life*, falls for the old radical. She tells the jealous Carruthers it's over . . . They argue . . . He takes to the air with a barrage of evidence and innuendo meant to destroy his rival for the beautiful Shelton. The rival, Marx, shows up. He wants revenge. He finds Shelton alone with Carruthers. Shelton tells Carruthers it's over between them. Carruthers flips out. He has a gun. He pulls it and fires, hitting Marx three times in the chest and Shelton in the face . . . then he turns the gun on himself and pulls the trigger, blowing his brains all over yesterday's ratings sheet . . ."

"What the fuck is this?" I ask, as Carruthers and I get to our feet.

"Fantasy time. Time to do what makes me happy. Time to say good-bye."

He cocks the hammer of the gun pointed at Sam's head.

"Wait!" I yell, "You can't do that! You don't want to . . ."

"If you're trying to stall for the police, forget it. She didn't get the chance to call them."

"You can't just kill us. Not without telling us why . . ."

"Ignorance is bliss, Albie. You'll thank me for letting you die happy."

"You at least have to tell us what really happened to Jeannie Locke," I stall, gauging if there's any way I can get to the machete.

"Don't even think about it," he says, reading my mind. "This is real life, not some cheap mystery novel where the bad guy spills his guts long enough for the good guy to get the drop on him. You want to know all the whys and wherefores, read the sequel in your next life."

He looks at Sam, ready to pull the trigger.

At that moment we hear a low, eerie rattling sound, which quickly grows louder. Each one of us involuntarily glances toward the source of the sound.

It's coming from the machete, which is still lying on the floor a few feet away, but it's . . . it's actually moving . . . on its own . . . rattling against the floor, as if being jostled by an unseen hand . . .

Then we hear what can only be described as a Rumble from Hell.

Then, a giant hand—it *feels* like a giant hand—reaches down, grabs me around the chest, lifts me into the air and body-slams me to the floor with such force that it knocks the wind out of me.

Then all hell breaks loose.

It's . . .

an . . .

EARTHQUAKE!

And you ask why I love this town? Because I finally have it trained.

Nobody really knows how long thirty seconds can be until they've spent them in an earthquake.

The floor beneath us comes alive with malevolence, the building rolls and then bounces, sending stage lights from the grid crashing down, exploding around us like angry glass bombs.

Cameras and sets topple over, monitors rattle on their mounts, everything quivers and shakes like it's about to come down.

Ozzie gets thrown to the floor and his gun squirts out of his hand. It skitters across the stage, along with the machete, various pieces of sound equipment and boxes sprawling their stage props.

My first thought is, *the psychic predicted this on the radio*, fol-lowed by, *it's the final nightmare: twenty bucks for a pint of milk.*

Then I go for Ozzie. Defying the rolling floor, he's slipping and sliding and scrambling to get to his feet.

I make a wild lunge for him.

The power goes out.

We're plunged into darkness, but my lunge is true and I tackle the felonious monk at the knees. His legs are small but powerful and he kicks furiously. But the building is still rolling and I have the advantage in leverage, lying on the floor with my arms around his legs.

"Sam!" I call out. "Are you all right?"

"I'm scared to death!"

"Find a doorway and get under it! This can't go on much longer!"

I turn out to be right. After what feels like three lifetimes, the building stops moving as suddenly as it began. All is quiet, except for the last few objects that fall or settle themselves into their final positions.

Ozzie has stopped struggling. If he were to get free, where would he go? It's pitch black and he's less familiar with this place than I am.

"Sam? Where are you?"

"Here . . . Oh, God . . . that was so . . . *exciting!*"

"I told you I'd make the earth move for you, didn't I?"

She laughs. "I like it when you get rough."

Suddenly, the entire studio lights up. Carruthers steps out from behind a panel. "Remote control for the emergency generators," he explains. "Installed at my request."

"No one ever said you were stupid, Harry," Sam says. "Just a pain in the ass. Untie me."

Carruthers unties Sam's hands and they come to where Ozzie and I are lying on the floor, his legs in my viselike grasp. The Happy One has become the Brooding One.

"How's the little turd? All in one piece?" Carruthers asks.

"How are you, Ozzie?" I ask, but His Happiness won't deign to answer.

"What do we do now?" Sam ponders.

"His Happiness was just about to explain a few things he thought we were dying to know. Is that right, Jack?"

"I have nothing to say," Ozzie states flatly.

"You have plenty to say," Carruthers barks.

Ozzie's response is steadfast silence.

"Give me a hand, will you, Harry? Grab his arms."

Harry sits on the floor and wraps his arms around Ozzie's upper torso. With me holding his legs and Carruthers on his arms, the little martinet is pinned immobile.

"He's not going anywhere now, Sam. Feel like plucking a few cranial hairs?"

She looks at me questioningly.

"Ozzie's so proud of these long, golden locks—what there are of them, anyway—maybe if we start separating him from what he has left, he'll see the light and reconsider his decision. How does that sound, Jack?"

Ozzie can't completely hide the look of panic, but he remains adamantly silent.

"Sam? Will you do the honors?"

She sits down beside Ozzie's head, running her fingers through his hair. "So beautiful . . . be a shame to lose it . . ."

"Pull one out," Carruthers grumbles impatiently.

Sam latches on to one of Ozzie's fine silken hairs, wraps it several times around her forefinger, then yanks hard.

Ozzie yelps and his body springs into motion. He's not going anywhere because Carruthers and I are a human straightjacket.

"Who paid Gardner the extra hundred and fifty thousand?" I ask.

The Sultan of Silence refuses to answer. Sam begins to wrap another hair around her finger. "There are enough of these to last all night . . ." she muses.

"Who paid Gardner the extra hundred and fifty?" I ask again.

"Me," Ozzie answers sullenly, resigned to losing the game of Truth or Baldness.

"Explain," I order.

"I knew Bert was dying of cancer. He came to me. To tell me. He was resigned to dying, but he wasn't happy. He didn't want to die unhappy. I asked him what would make him happy and he said setting things straight. We both knew what he meant. He was the one who dumped Jeannie Locke's body with Bobby Holiday. They had a three-way sex scene and she overdosed on cocaine and amyl nitrate."

"What about Gluck?" I asked. "Where was he?"

"Gluck was never there. He found out about it the next day when Bert told him she'd been with Bobby."

"What was your part in it? And don't lie, you little bastard."

"I had no part. I knew she was with Bert and Bobby, but I never told anyone. I lied by ommission."

"So you're saying Bert wanted to make amends for what he did to Jeannie Locke? He wanted to make it up before he died?"

"Yes."

"And he came to you?"

"He believed in Happiness. He thought I could help. He confided in me. I knew Sheila was Jeannie's daughter. She had come straight to me when she got off the plane from San Francisco. I introduced them and told Bert who she was. I told him he would die happy if he married her and left all his worldly goods and holdings to her. That would make up for her mother's death. He agreed. He did it. He died happy."

"How nice for him," Sam says. "And for Sheila, too. What does she *think* happened to her mother?"

"She thinks Gluck and Whitehead killed Jeannie. She would never have married Bert if she knew he was involved."

"Where did Bambi get her version of the story?" I ask.

"From Bert. He used to . . . visit her. He told her that Gluck and Bobby Holiday did it. He even put it on tape at one of their physical therapy sessions."

"Physical therapy?" Sam asks.

"A euphemism for expensive ejaculation," I explain, then turn to Ozzie. "Who called me about the story? In the beginning. Before the wedding."

"Probably Gluck," he answers. "He wanted to smear Bert, but it had to be anonymous. Then, when you told Bert you wanted to ask me about Jeannie Locke, we realized something had to be done. We told Bambi to approach you at the wedding and get our version of the story to you. Which she finally did—when it was too late.''

"Why did you threaten her?''

"She blew the whole thing by telling the story after the fact. I had to get her out of the picture.''

"So you knew about Bert's deal with Gardner . . .''

'I saw Bert's letter with his will.''

"And you got in touch with Gardner to decide the exact moment to kill Bert . . .''

"That's also when I decided to set you up, to get you off our backs while we were fighting for Sovereign. And to keep you from digging up Jeannie's story.''

"Why did Michael Whitehead tell me it was Bert and Harry who killed Jeannie?'' Sam asks.

"You were married to the guy. You ought to be able to figure it out.''

"I'll figure it out while I'm pulling clumps—''

"No! Michael Whitehead is working for Gluck! It's Gluck's money behind Whitehead's bid! Gluck figures he'll eventually be cleared. And when he is, he'll come out from behind the scenes and announce he's the controlling shareholder in Sovereign, BMA, and his own company—which will make it the biggest communications and media conglomerate in the world. With Mitchell P. Gluck at the helm.''

"And what happens to this company?'' Carruthers asks. "Holman Entertainment?''

"It folds right in. Sheila made a deal with Gluck tonight. We're all working for him now.''

"My God,'' Carruthers winces.

"What about Virginia?'' Sam asks. "How did you get her to set Albie up?''

"She was a Happiness Foundation girl. She just followed instructions. She was supposed to go away, lay low until after your trial, then come back. She was well paid for it. But she screwed up, too. You can't trust the help.''

"I'm glad you're getting your sense of humor back. It'll make it less painful to tell us why you killed Virginia and Norman," I tell him.

"I didn't kill them!"

"Sam?"

She yanks one, then two, then three hairs in succession, each followed by a scream of pain and useless twisting and straining.

"Why did you kill those kids?" I demand.

"I had to! When Norman got arrested, Virginia panicked! She came back to town and bailed him out with the money I paid her. She told him what she did to you. He called and told me to get over to his house right away, I had explaining to do. The only thing I explained to that son-of-a-bitch was good-bye."

"You had to kill Virginia, too?" Sam asks. "Wasn't one enough?"

"She was the only one left who could turn things around. I had to get rid of her. It was necessary."

"And the mutilation?" Harry asks.

"That was for fun," Ozzie admits.

"You subhuman pig," Carruthers growls.

"I thought putting your book in Devore's hand was a nice touch ..." Ozzie says, to me, fishing for a compliment.

"Any more questions?" I ask, restraining myself from wringing his neck.

"Yes," Sam says. "I have one more. What was in this for you? What did you do it all for?"

"I was going to get my own cable station. The Happiness Network. My motives were pure. I did what I did to make myself happy. Think of all the unhappy people out there, waiting for someone to come along and change their lives. I was going to be the one to tell them the truth. I was going to tell them nobody can do it for them. That they have to do it for themselves. I was going to tell them straight out I was only in it for the money and the girls, to make myself happy. That whatever they need for their own happiness had nothing to do with me. I was going to give them the truth for the first time in their lives. If you're miserable and depressed, nobody's going to come along and turn it around for you. You have to do it yourself."

"Harry!" Sam says suddenly. "I just got an incredible idea!"

"What?"

"How many people would give anything to see Ozzie confess to killing Norman and Virginia, *live*, on TV?"

"Millions."

"How about satellite, with a world-wide simulcast?"

"Tens of millions."

"What if we showed a dramatic re-creation of the crime? Starring Ozzie himself?"

"Fifty million, maybe."

"And the photographs? All the gore in full color?"

"We can't do that. No network or cable would go for it."

"What about pay-per-view? What if Ozzie told the story on world-wide pay-per-view? With a dramatic re-creation and the actual bloody photographs with severed genitals, the whole works . . . How many people would pay to see that?"

"World-wide? Seventy-five, maybe a hundred million."

"At how much per home?"

"Make it cheap. Cheaper than a movie. Ten bucks."

"That's how much altogether? Seven hundred fifty million?"

"Your math is right."

"What do you think? How many people watched the O. J. confession?"

"Sixty-five million, world-wide, at twenty bucks a pop. And that was *after* the trial."

"How much did they make?"

"Gross? Over a billion. Shapiro's take alone was two hundred million."

"What do you say, Ozzie?" Sam asks the little guru. "That's big money. It buys a lot of lawyering. A lot of appeals. A comfortable life in prison."

"How much would my end be?" Ozzie asks.

I can't believe I'm sitting here, listening to this insanity.

"You'd clear a hundred million," Sam assures him.

"Think of the conjugal visits that can buy," Carruthers adds. "You're going to the can anyway. Might as well make it a trip to remember."

I can't take it anymore. "Hold it!" I order. "Stop! I will not be a party to this."

"What's wrong with it?" Sam asks. "People would love to see this."

"That's exactly what's wrong with it. And after this, what will they want to see next? Real death? Has watching people die on CNN become boring already? We need some murders, some good American murders. Pretty soon you'll have people sending in home video snuff tapes for money. Worse, for prizes. *Best Murder by Strangulation. Funniest Mutilation. Most Gory Disemboweling.* And what does that lead to? People calling ahead, getting live news crews to come out and watch them slit their kids' throats. *Murder Live At Five.* All because people want to see it. That's the world we're giving our children. Morbid, exploitive, voyeuristic and violent. You two can be the Barnum and Bailey of Death if you want. I don't want anything to do with it. I'm out of this. You can have your circus, but I'm not one of the clowns."

My tirade keeps Sam and Carruthers quiet for a while, but I see by their knowing exchange of glances that they won't be able to resist. They'll do it. And so will Ozzie.

But I absolutely refuse to watch it.

ONE MONTH LATER

"...Since the Los Angeles earthquake of March 17, which measured 7.2 on the Richter scale of ground motion, killed 124 people and caused an estimated 50 billion dollars in damage, the Phoenix Chamber of Commerce has been receiving 100 more calls per day from Southern Californians wanting relocation information. The Las Vegas Chamber reports double the number of such requests from Californians since March ..."

Freedom and I are sitting on my couch, watching another earthquake program on the news. When it's over, we're going to watch the Ozzie Baba Special on pay-per-view, which Freedom insisted I sign up for.

He's still living with me. His house had been situated on top of one of the main sewer lines, running from the Valley through the canyons to Santa Monica and to an outlet two and a half miles off the coast, where the sewage is supposedly carried away by ocean currents.

The epicenter of the earthquake was almost directly under his property. The land split open and the sewer line broke, spewing millions of gallons of sewage over Coldwater Canyon.

The water department said it would take from three to six weeks to fix the break, during which time the "effluent" would continue to flow out of the ground. Unable to divert the waste, the city has now been pumping 170 million gallons of clean water a day from another treatment plant through the ruptured pipe to make sure the entire canyon doesn't become permanently contaminated.

At the point where Freedom's house once stood, an amazing "plume of effluent" from the ruptured pipe now rises a majestic hundred feet into the air, attracting photographers, tourists, filmmakers, news teams . . . everyone with a lens.

Without the official hyperbole, what these legions of *noodniks* are watching, photographing and marveling over is, technically, a man-made artesian hydrostasis of untreated human materials—known to the layman as a good old-fashioned gusher of shit.

But my son is resourceful. At this moment he has a team of writers relentlessly pounding away to develop the story as a movie for Disney with the working title, *Honey, I Flushed The Toilet*.

As for me, the Steinberg mansion up the road collapsed but my little house remained miraculously undamaged by the quake. On the other hand, the earthquake shook so many avocados off the trees that it cost five hundred dollars to have the vet pump Jed's stomach.

So many thousands of people have been displaced by the two natural disasters that Freedom has no other choice but to stay with me until things get less frantic.

So here we are, about to spend an evening with Samantha Shelton and Ozzie Baba on pay-per-view.

When the show begins, Sam and Ozzie are sitting in a comfortable study, facing each other in padded armchairs.

"How did you let her get away, Dad?" Freedom moans as the camera gives us a closeup of Sam. "She was crazy about you."

"That's not quite what happened. A woman like that you don't *let* do anything. She does whatever she wants. I'm too narrowminded for that kind of relationship."

"Narrowminded? You took acid in the sixties. You led demonstrations, you were arrested, you made speeches, you preached love and understanding . . ."

"I still believe in all that. But love and understanding together can be a volatile combination. You can love somebody, madly, wildly, insatiably, as in not being able to stand being more than a fingertip away from this person, ever.

"At the same time you can understand that this person is so different from you that you'll eventually have to question some of your own basic values, just to find a common ground.

"And if this person has a cause, one she's passionate about, it better not be the opposite of yours or you'll wind up trying to make yourself happy by compromising your conscience.

"Therein lies the difficulty. You mistake *happy* for *expedient*. You want what you want when you want it because that's what we're told America is about. And the assumption is that if you *get* something you *want* you will therefore be *happy*.

"It doesn't work that way. You need to have a rapport with a woman deeper than physical and emotional fascination. I'm not saying she has to be someone who thinks exactly like you. If you hate Jews you don't have to marry a Nazi. If you feel compassion for animals you don't have to marry an animal rights activist.

"But if you believe that people are inherently capable of making the right choices, the good choices, of being generous, compassionate, with a modicum of dignity, then you won't find a common ground with someone who believes exactly the opposite—that people want to see and experience the worst of humanity, that their fascination with gore and murder is a part of their makeup that needs to be and *should* be satisfied. You start making adjustments to that kind of thinking and you not only lower your own spiritual vibration, but you encourage everyone else to join in. I have too much hope for this world, in spite of all the shit I've seen, to give in to that.

"Sorry about the speech. You asked a simple question. 'Why did I let her get away.' The answer is . . . the *truth* is, I'm a little too old at this stage to become a lion tamer. Even though it sounds exciting."

In spite of all I said previously, I have to admit *The Ozzie Baba Special* is entertaining to watch. In dramatizing Ozzie's story, they ingeniously made a ninety-minute movie faster than they turned out the David Koresh and O. J. Simpson stories and, because they had so much money guaranteed from the pay-per-view, were able to pay big stars outrageous money to appear in the mini-pic.

Mel Gibson played the part of me. Sam was played by Michele Pfeiffer. Danny DeVito was Ozzie. For Sheila they somehow got Madonna. Freedom was John Cusack. John Heard played Carruthers, Michael Madsen was Norman Devore and Uma Thurman made a perfect Virginia.

As Bambi Friedman they introduced Heidi Fleiss in her first movie role and as Debra they cast Rosie Perez. Another great move was getting Courtney Love and Garth Brooks for Jeannie Locke and Bobby Holiday in the flashbacks.

In some wonderful cameos, Mickey Rourke did a perfect Shrike, Shirley MacLaine hammed up Boopsie, Danno was played to a T by Bert Reynolds without his wig, Rush Limbaugh was side-splitting as the fat reporter, and Howard Stern played with himself, as usual.

The amazingly tight little movie was produced and directed by Steven Spielberg, for ten percent of the gross up to a billion and twenty percent thereafter, with a fifty-fifty split on all merchandising and recordings, and a sixty-forty split in his favor for all toys and things that can be considered toys or intellectually understood to be toys, etc.

I can't watch the mutilation scene. When they get to that part I excuse myself and take a hike to the kitchen, leaving Freedom glued to the screen.

It's a shame, I think, pouring myself a shot of Cuervo and opening a bottle of Corona. The world is becoming more primitive every day. Primitive people with computers and rockets and invisible jet bombers are still primitive people. They're just highly technicalized. But they haven't grown up intellectually and emotionally yet. They still haven't awakened to the fact that their higher selves are more powerful than their lower selves.

Too bad people feel that way. In the sixties we tried not to.

After the movie, Sam and Ozzie engage in a discussion about the concept of mixing murder with mirth, then Sam leaves Ozzie alone on stage, takes a roving mike and goes out into a studio audience to solicit additional comments and questions.

A large, red-faced woman in a dark business suit raises her hand.
"Yes. Over here," Sam says, putting the microphone to the woman's mouth. "What would you like to ask Ozzie?"

The woman stands, looks at him and asks, "How hard was it to sever Norman Devore's genitals? He was a large man, wasn't he?"

Sam looks at the stage. "Can you answer that for us, Ozzie?"

"Well, sure. You know I used a razor, which wasn't as sharp as I thought it was. I actually decided to cut out Virginia's tongue before I sliced off Norman's genitals, just so I'd have enough room in her mouth for the whole package. That was interesting. She was dead, and it wasn't all that easy to get a good grip on her tongue to pull it out so I could saw it off. I actually had to pry her jaw open— I never knew someone's jaw could freeze closed when they die— and pull her tongue out with a pliers, which I happened to have with me. Then I sort of sawed through the tongue with a back-and-forth motion ... The blade wasn't sharp enough to slice through it like sushi ..."

"I need another beer," I tell Freedom, jumping off the couch and starting for the kitchen before I threw up.

"No, wait!" he says, grabbing my arm. "Wait a second." He's peering intently at the TV screen.

"What? I'm not going to sit here and listen to—"

"LOOK!" he shouts, jumping to his feet. "Sitting on the aisle, right next to where Sam is standing!"

"What? Who? Look at what?"

"That's *Stevie McDonald!*"

"Are you serious?"

He goes to the TV and lays his finger on the face of a young man wearing an overcoat, sitting beside Sam on the aisle. He has his hand raised to ask a question.

"It's Stevie McDonald, I swear to God!" Freedom howls.

"Well, what is he doing there ... ?"

We look at each other. *UH-OH.*

"Okay, let's see ..." Sam says. "This young man here ..."

She's looking at Stevie. He stands up and she puts the microphone in front of him.

"What's your question for Ozzie?" she asks.

"I have a comment, not a question," Stevie says.

"Well, what's your comment?"

"My comment is, get a life."

"Excuse me . . . ?"

"This is the most sickening, despicable display of humanity I've ever seen!" He suddenly whirls around to address the rest of the audience with wild, piercing eyes.

"You immerse yourselves in other people's tragedies, instead of living your own lives! You follow the sleepwalking herd and your individual souls go to sleep! Well, I'm here to say, IT'S OVER, BABY!"

I know what he's going to do. I shout at the screen, *"NO! DON'T DO IT, STEVIE!"* I'm shouting at an inanimate object.

Stevie's voice is rising. "DOWN WITH HOMOGENIZATION! LONG LIVE INDIVIDUAL THOUGHT! LONG LIVE SPIRITUAL AWARENESS! LONG LIVE THE SIXTIES! LONG LIVE ABBIE HOFFMAN!"

With that he throws open his coat to reveal that he's wired from the waist up with giant fat sticks of dynamite.

I rush to the TV screen, put my hands over Stevie's chest and scream, *"NO!*

The look of shock on Sam's face is indescribable. She knows now who Stevie is, and what he is about to do.

"SAM!" I shout. "RUN!"

The director of the show, caught up in the drama, switches from a TWO-SHOT of Stevie and Sam to a CLOSEUP of Sam to a CLOSEUP of Ozzie to a WIDE SHOT of Carruthers charging up the aisle to the rescue of a CLOSEUP of Stevie . . .

"RUN, SAM!" I shout at the lifeless screen.

Stevie *detonates.* In CLOSEUP.

There is a horrific BLAST and a huge fireball.

The screen goes blank.

Freedom and I are staring at the empty screen, our mouths hanging open in shock.

Stevie McDonald blew up the studio. With Carruthers and Ozzie. And Sam.

"My God . . . Oh, my God . . ."

Freedom mutters, "That was the most incredible thing I've ever seen . . ."

"Excuse me a minute . . ." I struggle to my feet. My heart is pounding, I feel sick to my stomach.

"Where are you going?"

"Nowhere. Outside."

Stepping outside I'm engulfed by a dizzying wave of nausea. Why did it come to this? Why are we trained to believe that violence is the answer to everything? That killing a problem is the fail-proof way to solve it?

To think of Sam . . . annihilated in that inferno . . . gone forever . . . is paralyzing. For better or worse, she was a vibrant life force, passionate about her beliefs, her dreams, her desires, her aspirations. Now she's nothing. A hole in the lives of people who knew her, of people who watched her show. A gaping emptiness in my life.

There was no thought of continuing our romance, but there promised to be a connection that would endure on other levels, in areas of our lives where we could help each other. I guess the word is friendship. I lost an ex-lover, yes, but far more heartbreakingly, I lost a friend.

Concerned, Freedom follows as I start walking around to the rear of the house. There are some shovels and a pickaxe leaning against the wall, from the time a few months ago when I decided to start a garden. I lift up the pickaxe.

"What are you going to do?" he asks.

"Make myself happy." I march back into the house, with Freedom following on my heels.

"Don't do anything crazy, Dad, you'll regret it . . ."

The TV screen isn't blank anymore.

The fat reporter is standing on the street, in front of the burning, demolished studio. Fire engines, police vehicles, ambulances are swarming like locusts as he looks somberly into the camera.

". . . all we know at this point is that at least five hundred people are dead or buried in the wreckage of this devastated television studio in the heart of Hollywood . . ."

I go to the TV with the pickaxe.

"What are you going to do, Dad?" Freedom pleads.

"It's not my job to listen to their lies, it's not my job to buy their products, it's not my job to see their horrors, it's not my job to watch their tragedies, it's not my job to be seduced by their twisted views of humanity . . ."

"Dad . . ."

The fat reporter is holding up to the camera a photograph of Mr. Rogers, swinging by a knotted sheet from the light fixture of a hospital room. ". . . as rescue workers here at Pay-Per-View studios search through the wreckage, we've just received this photo by fax . . . We were the first to break the story of Mr. Rogers and now we're the first to bring you these actual suicide photos . . ."

I raise the pickaxe and with one violent swing send it crashing into the face of the fat reporter. The screen explodes in an eruption of sparks and glass.

Silence.

I killed the TV.

Freedom and I are standing there, transfixed by the dying tube, when the phone rings.

"If it's Danno," I tell him, "say I did it. I killed the TV. He can come and take me away."

"Calm down, Dad. You can't get arrested for breaking a television."

"I don't care. Let him come. I'm free. The chains are broken."

"Do you want me to answer it?" he asks.

"Nothing can hurt me. It's dead. I declare this a television-free house."

Shaking his head in consternation, he picks up the ringing phone. "Hello? Hello? Shit. You better do it," he says, holding it out to me.

I take the phone. "Yes?"

A prerecorded voice is saying, ". . . and thank you for letting Cedars take care of your hospital needs. If you are using a touch-tone phone, please press ONE now."

I press one.

"Welcome to the Cedars Biopsy Hot Line. For the results of your . . . (computerized voice) *second* . . . biopsy, please press ONE now."

I press one again.

"Your ... (computerized voice) *second* ... biopsy results are ... (computerized voice) *inconclusive*. Your general health is ... (computerized voice) *at risk*. Please make a new appointment at your earliest convenience. If you have any additional questions, press ONE now."

I press one again.

"Thank you for pressing ONE now."

I don't know what I'm supposed to do. I press one again.

"If you are using a touch-tone phone, please press ONE now."

Oh, my God. It dawns on me. Finally. Sartre was wrong. Hell isn't just other people. It's other people *with modern technology*.

Hell is humans with cave-dwelling mentalities wielding the means to control lives and minds.

Hell is knowing all this and trying to do something about it.

Hell is having a conscience.

EPILOGUE

Remember the story about the guy who went looking for the meaning of life? He found this old man on top of a mountain in Tibet. The old man told him, "Life, my son, is like a pickle." And the guy said to the old man, "That's it? That's all? Life is like a pickle?" And the old man blinked a couple of times and asked, "Life is *not* like a pickle?"

At first it sounds like the old man doesn't really know the meaning of life. Is life like a pickle or not? The story appears to be a joke.

But if we interpret it in a Zen context, we see that it's not a joke. Zen, it is said, teaches nothing. It merely enables us to wake up and become aware. It does not teach, it points.

And that is what the story does. It points.

So where does it point? That's not a Zen question. But we'll try to answer it.

Besides being described in the dictionary as "an article of food (as a cucumber) that has been preserved in brine or in vinegar," a pickle is also described as "an unpleasant or difficult situation or condition." A bind, a box, a corner, a difficulty, a dilemma, a fix, an impasse, a jam, a mess, a pinch, a plight, a quandary, a scrape, a spot, a trap . . .

So life is like a difficult situation. What else is new?

269

What's new is the spin you put on the word "difficult." A situation that is difficult can also be exciting, challenging, rewarding and enlightening. As they say at Gold's Gym, "No pain, no gain."

In baseball, pickle is the term used when a runner is caught in a rundown between two bases.

Here you have two opposite poles, the two fielders, and you are the runner between them. You are in the process of becoming safe or out. At any moment you may be tagged out or you may slide safely into a base.

You don't have time to think about what being out will mean, or what being safe will mean. You're so completely occupied with eluding the tag that the rundown itself becomes, for you, the embodiment of the entire game.

Another way of putting it is, you are living 100 percent in the present. You are in the process. You know the future holds a win or a loss for you. Your past is also a record of wins and losses. But the *present* is the excitement of *not* knowing what will happen or how it will make you feel about what happened before.

The *excitement* is in living the moment.

So, when you go out there to play the great game of life, remember the old man on the mountain. Remember what he said.

"Life, my son (or my daughter), is like a pickle."

Batter up!

. . . and just in case, in spite of all you know, you still get discouraged . . .

Don't ever forget . . .

IT'S NEVER OVER AS LONG AS THERE'S ONE LAWYER LEFT STANDING.

                                        I didn't say that.